# KIM & KIM
# LOVE IS A BATTLEFIELD

writer
agdalene Visaggio

pencils & inks
Eva Cabrera

colorist
Claudia Aguirre

letterer
Zakk Saam

editor
Katy Rex

Linguist
Kirsten Thompson

cover art
ess Fowler & Matt Wilson

this edition, additional design
Phil Smith

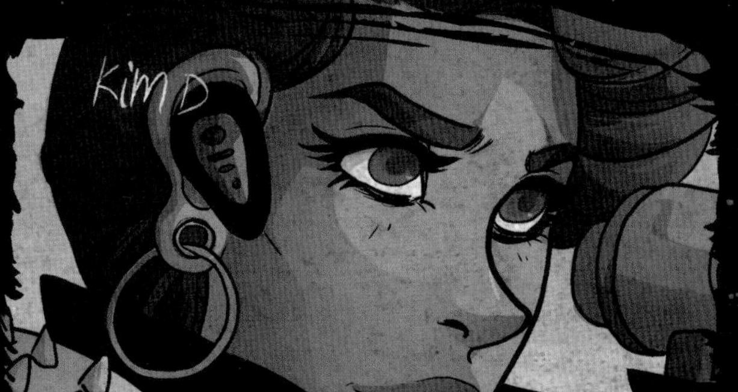
KIM D

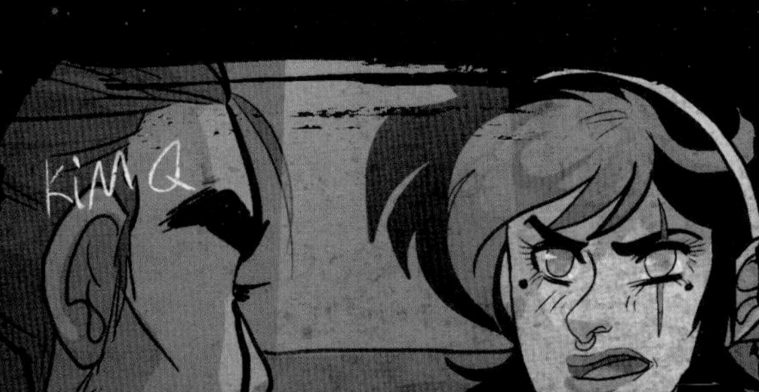
KIM Q

BY
SAGGIO

SPECIAL THANKS TO:
Ryan Cady & Tini Howard

MASK

PUBLISHED BY BLACK MASK STUDIOS LLC
MATT PIZZOLO | BRETT GUREWITZ | STEVE NILES

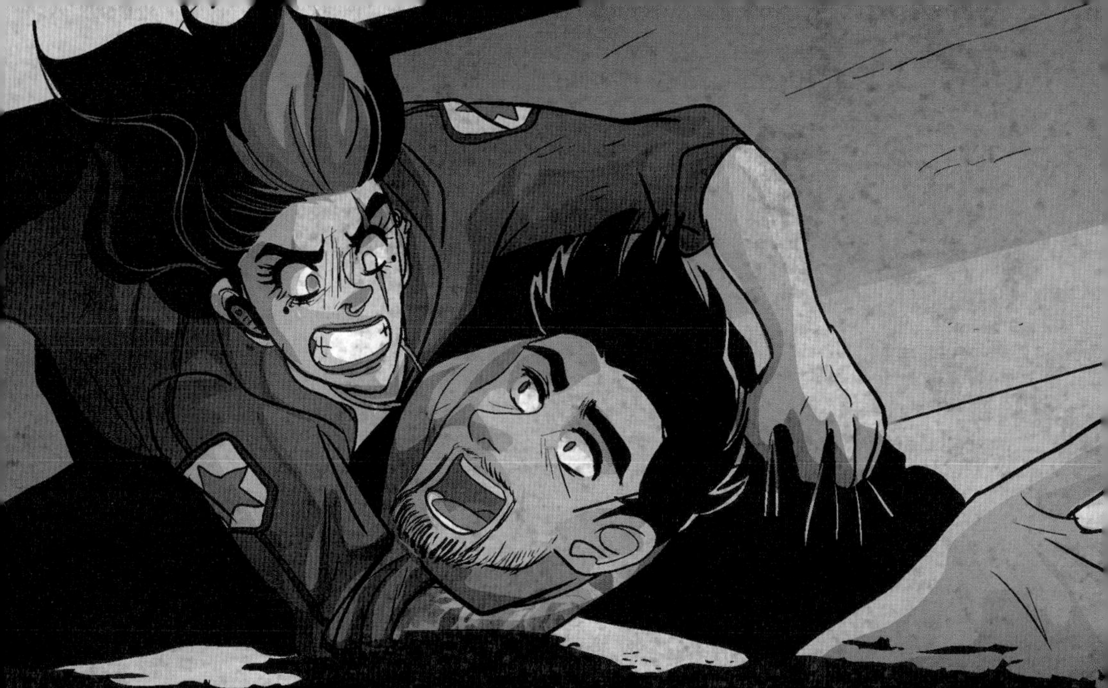

# 1

## "EXES AND WOES"

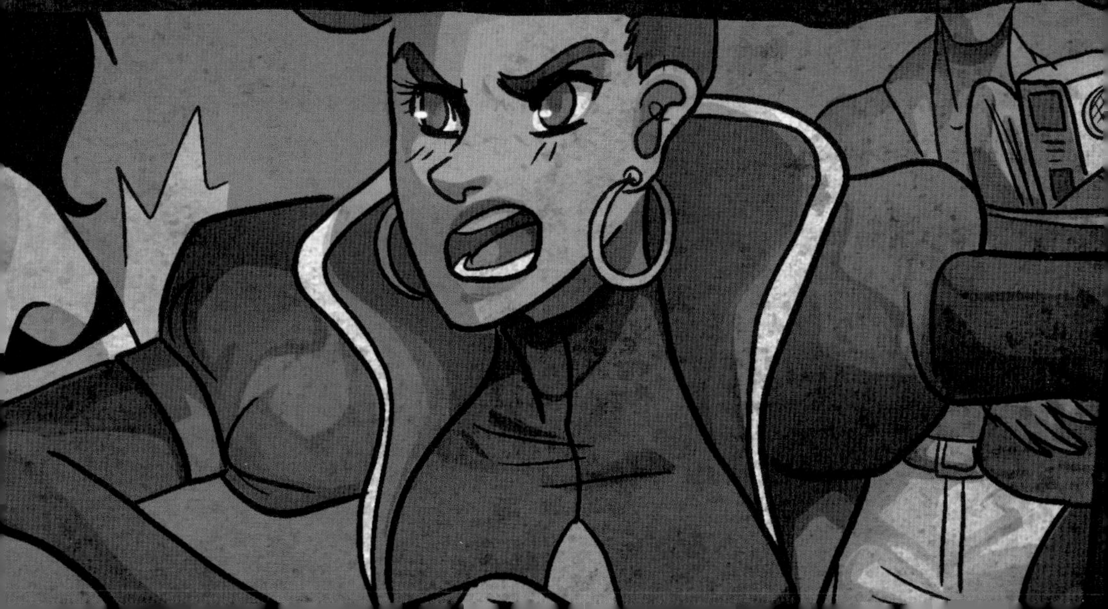

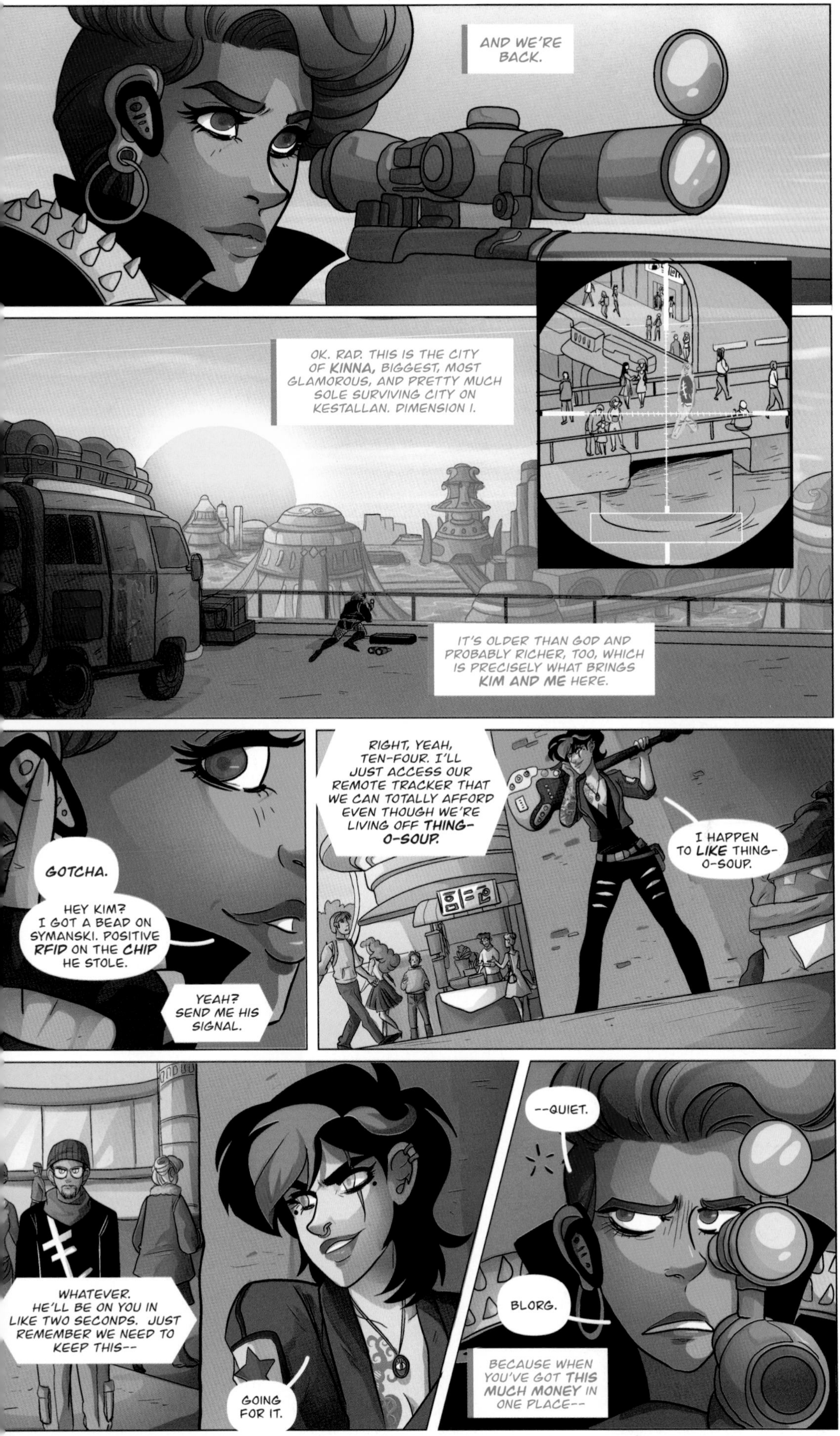
AND WE'RE BACK.
OK. RAD. THIS IS THE CITY OF KINNA, BIGGEST, MOST GLAMOROUS, AND PRETTY MUCH SOLE SURVIVING CITY ON KESTALLAN. DIMENSION I.
IT'S OLDER THAN GOD AND PROBABLY RICHER, TOO, WHICH IS PRECISELY WHAT BRINGS KIM AND ME HERE.
GOTCHA.
HEY KIM? I GOT A BEAD ON SYMANSKI. POSITIVE RFID ON THE CHIP HE STOLE.
YEAH? SEND ME HIS SIGNAL.
RIGHT, YEAH, TEN-FOUR. I'LL JUST ACCESS OUR REMOTE TRACKER THAT WE CAN TOTALLY AFFORD EVEN THOUGH WE'RE LIVING OFF THING-O-SOUP.
I HAPPEN TO LIKE THING-O-SOUP.
WHATEVER. HE'LL BE ON YOU IN LIKE TWO SECONDS. JUST REMEMBER WE NEED TO KEEP THIS--
GOING FOR IT.
--QUIET.
BLORG.
BECAUSE WHEN YOU'VE GOT THIS MUCH MONEY IN ONE PLACE--

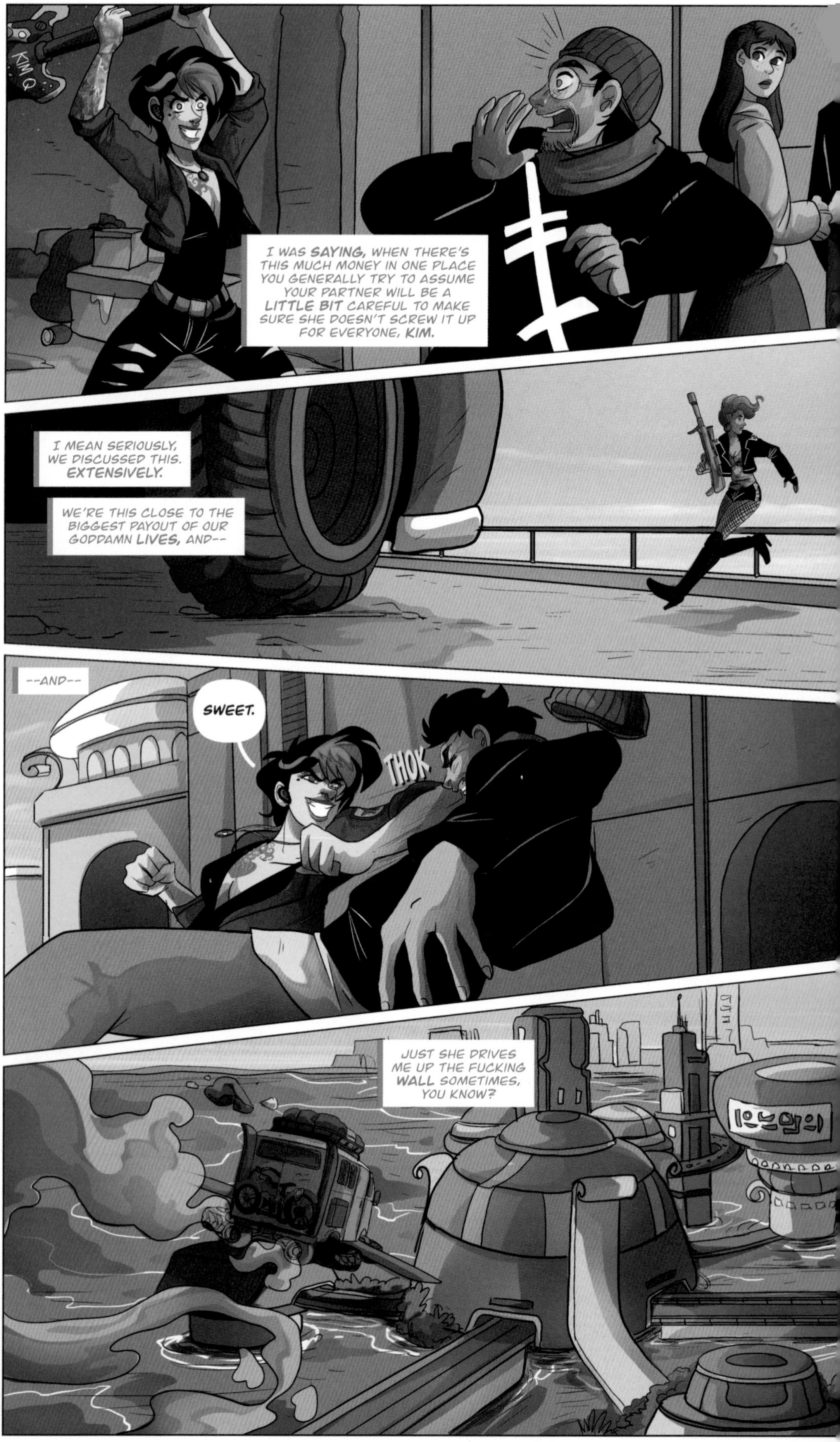

KIM Q
I WAS SAYING, WHEN THERE'S THIS MUCH MONEY IN ONE PLACE YOU GENERALLY TRY TO ASSUME YOUR PARTNER WILL BE A LITTLE BIT CAREFUL TO MAKE SURE SHE DOESN'T SCREW IT UP FOR EVERYONE, KIM.
I MEAN SERIOUSLY, WE DISCUSSED THIS. EXTENSIVELY.
WE'RE THIS CLOSE TO THE BIGGEST PAYOUT OF OUR GODDAMN LIVES, AND--
--AND--
SWEET.
THOK
JUST SHE DRIVES ME UP THE FUCKING WALL SOMETIMES, YOU KNOW?

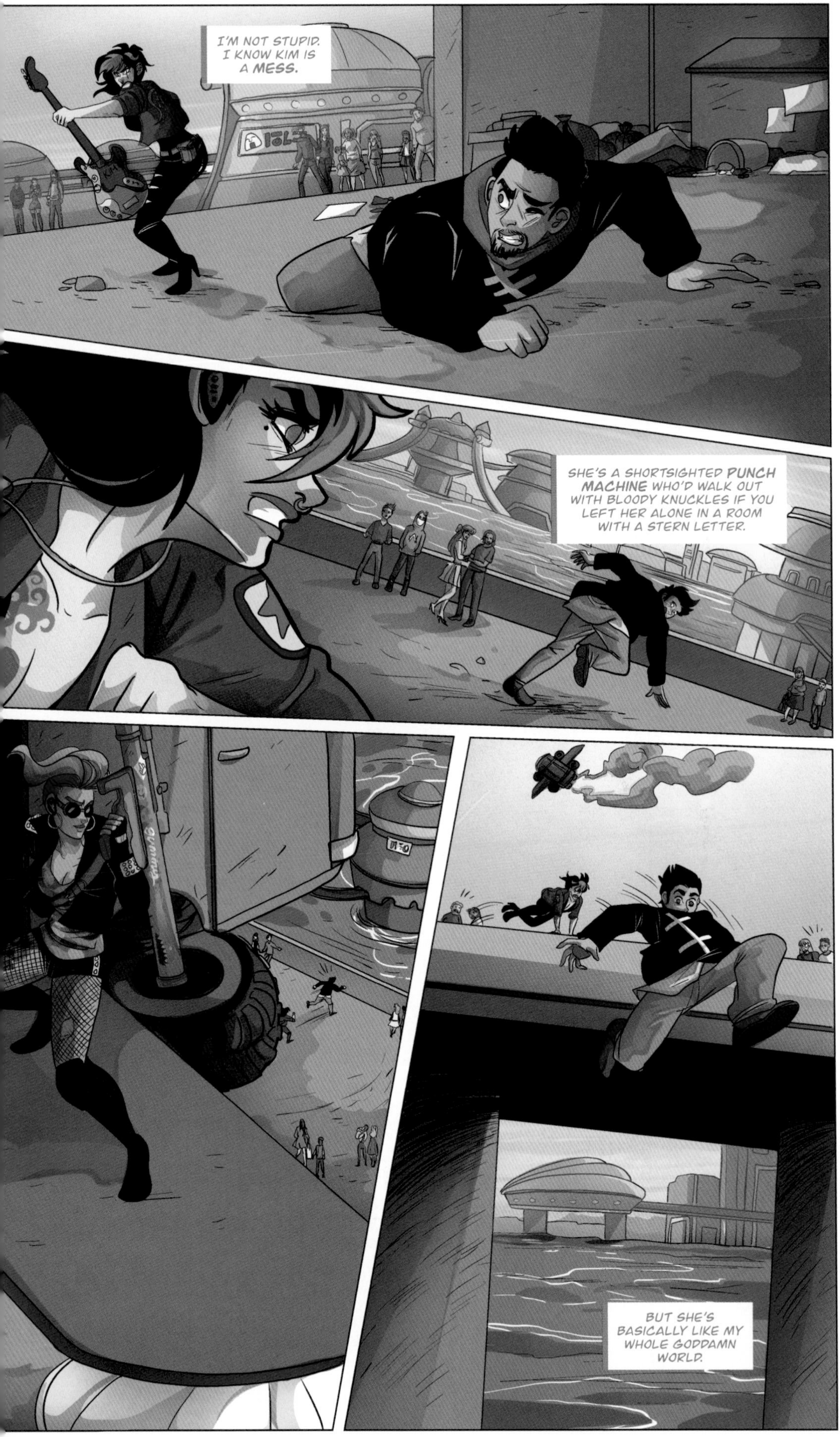
I'M NOT STUPID. I KNOW KIM IS A MESS.
SHE'S A SHORTSIGHTED PUNCH MACHINE WHO'D WALK OUT WITH BLOODY KNUCKLES IF YOU LEFT HER ALONE IN A ROOM WITH A STERN LETTER.
BUT SHE'S BASICALLY LIKE MY WHOLE GODDAMN WORLD.

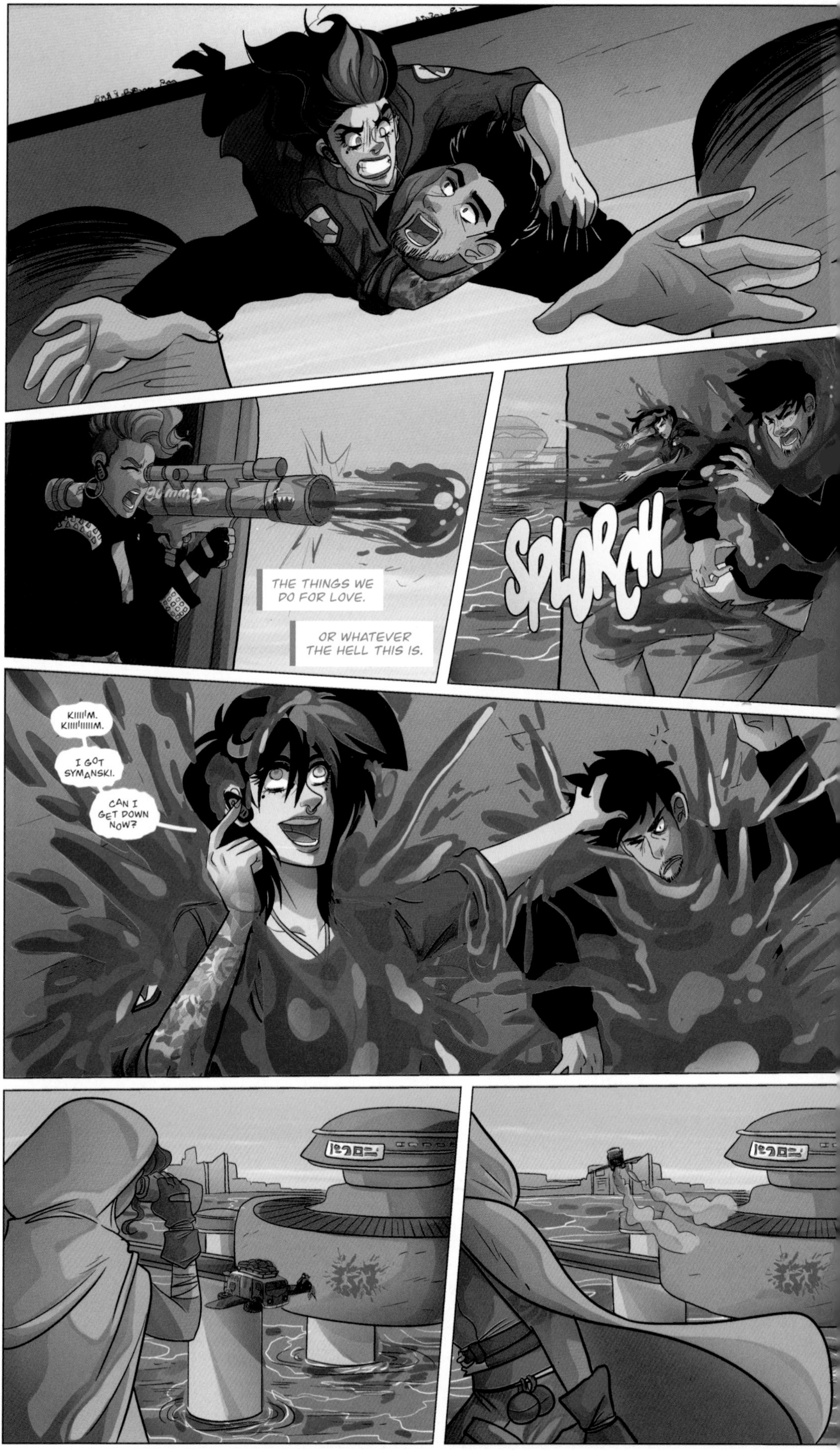
THE THINGS WE DO FOR LOVE.
OR WHATEVER THE HELL THIS IS.
SPLORCH
KIIII'M. KIIIIIIIIIM.
I GOT SYMANSKI.
CAN I GET DOWN NOW?

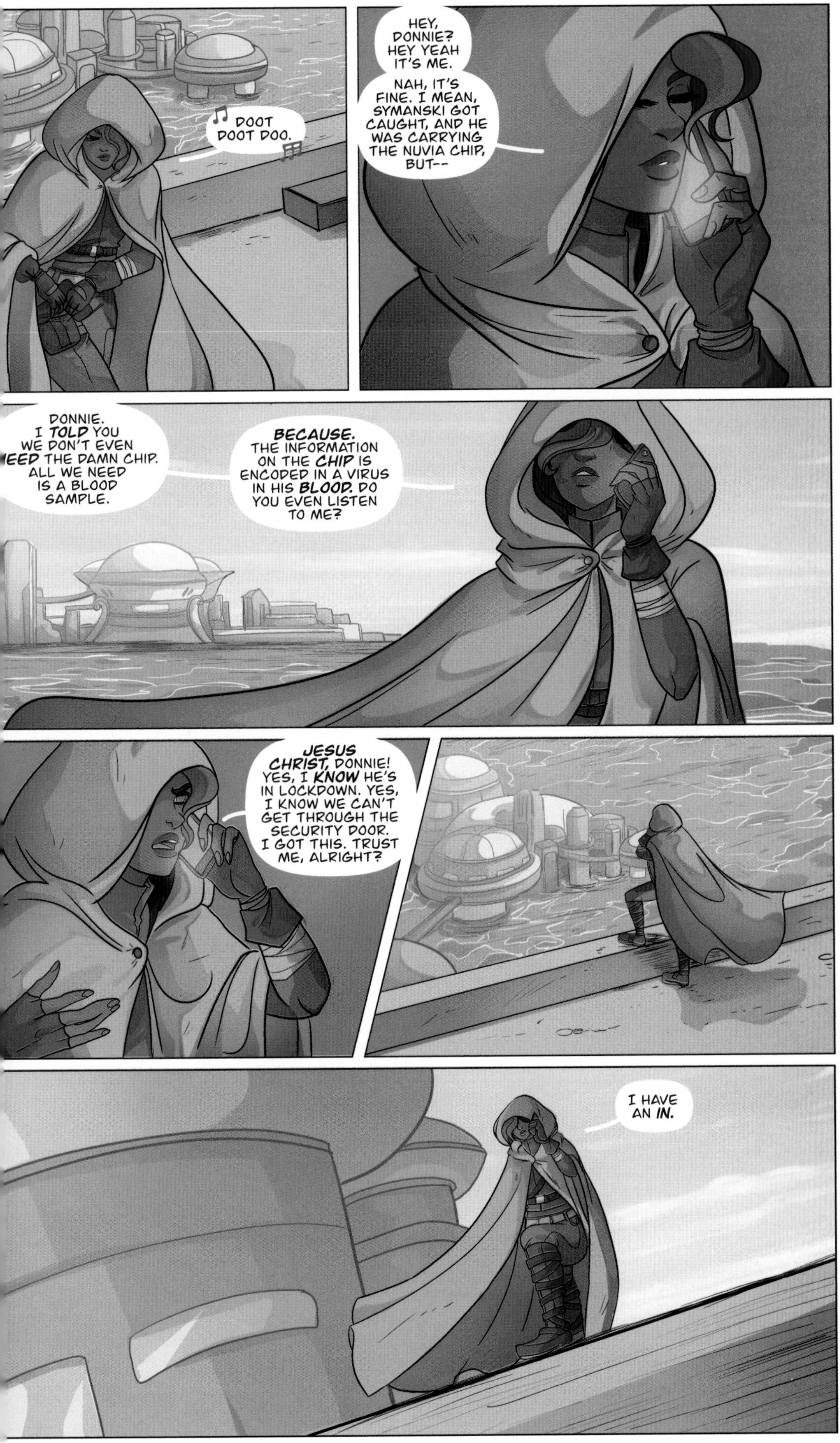
DOOT DOOT DOO.
HEY, DONNIE? HEY YEAH IT'S ME.
NAH, IT'S FINE. I MEAN, SYMANSKI GOT CAUGHT, AND HE WAS CARRYING THE NUVIA CHIP, BUT--
DONNIE. I **TOLD** YOU WE DON'T EVEN NEED THE DAMN CHIP. ALL WE NEED IS A BLOOD SAMPLE.
**BECAUSE.** THE INFORMATION ON THE **CHIP** IS ENCODED IN A VIRUS IN HIS **BLOOD.** DO YOU EVEN LISTEN TO ME?
**JESUS CHRIST,** DONNIE! YES, I **KNOW** HE'S IN LOCKDOWN. YES, I KNOW WE CAN'T GET THROUGH THE SECURITY DOOR. I GOT THIS. TRUST ME, ALRIGHT?
I HAVE AN **IN.**

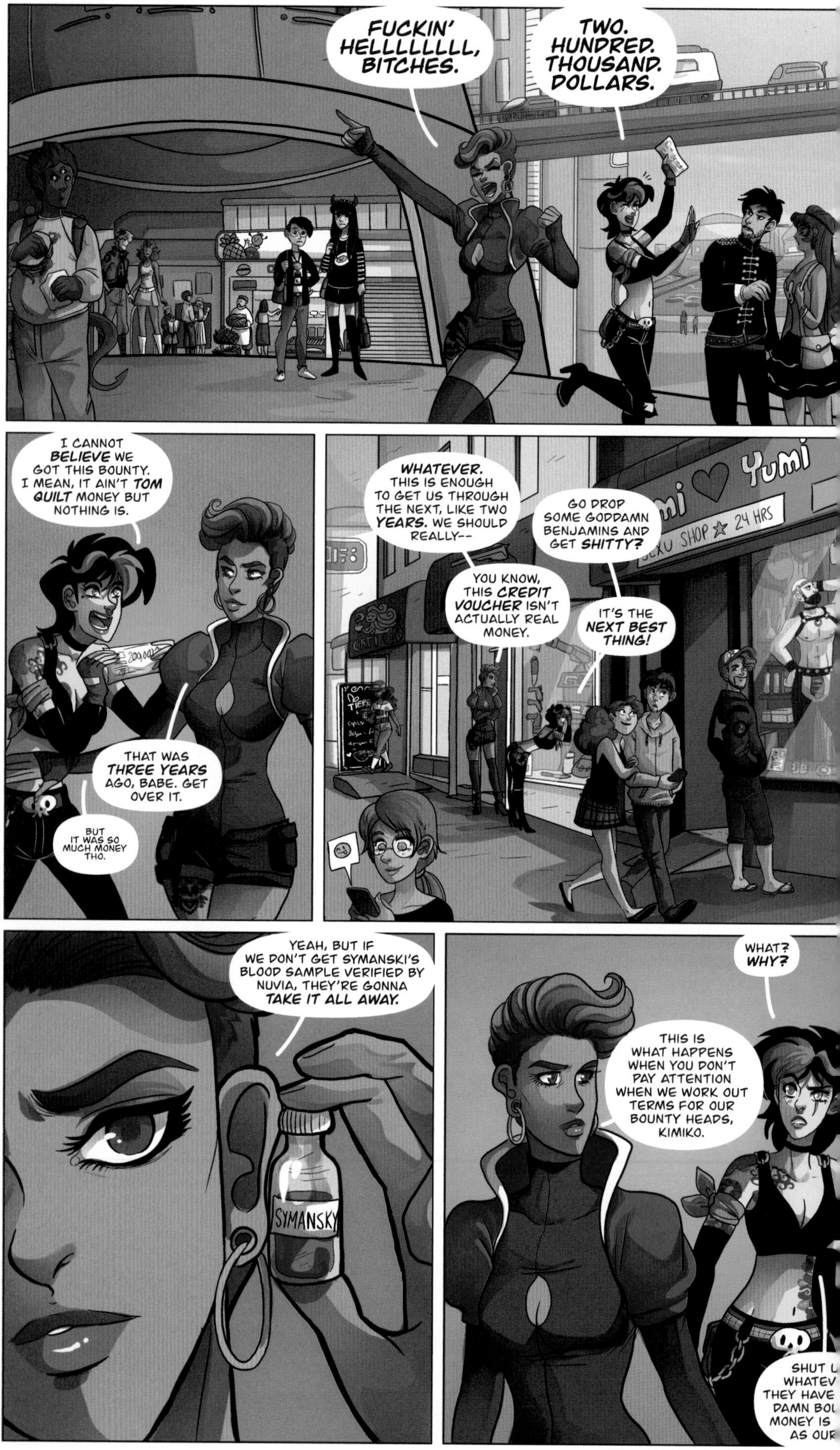
FUCKIN' HELLLLLLLL, BITCHES.
TWO. HUNDRED. THOUSAND. DOLLARS.
I CANNOT BELIEVE WE GOT THIS BOUNTY. I MEAN, IT AIN'T TOM QUILT MONEY BUT NOTHING IS.
THAT WAS THREE YEARS AGO, BABE. GET OVER IT.
BUT IT WAS SO MUCH MONEY THO.
WHATEVER. THIS IS ENOUGH TO GET US THROUGH THE NEXT, LIKE TWO YEARS. WE SHOULD REALLY--
GO DROP SOME GODDAMN BENJAMINS AND GET SHITTY?
YOU KNOW, THIS CREDIT VOUCHER ISN'T ACTUALLY REAL MONEY.
IT'S THE NEXT BEST THING!
YEAH, BUT IF WE DON'T GET SYMANSKI'S BLOOD SAMPLE VERIFIED BY NUVIA, THEY'RE GONNA TAKE IT ALL AWAY.
SYMANSKY
WHAT? WHY?
THIS IS WHAT HAPPENS WHEN YOU DON'T PAY ATTENTION WHEN WE WORK OUT TERMS FOR OUR BOUNTY HEADS, KIMIKO.
SHUT U
WHATEV
THEY HAVE
DAMN BO
MONEY IS
AS OUR

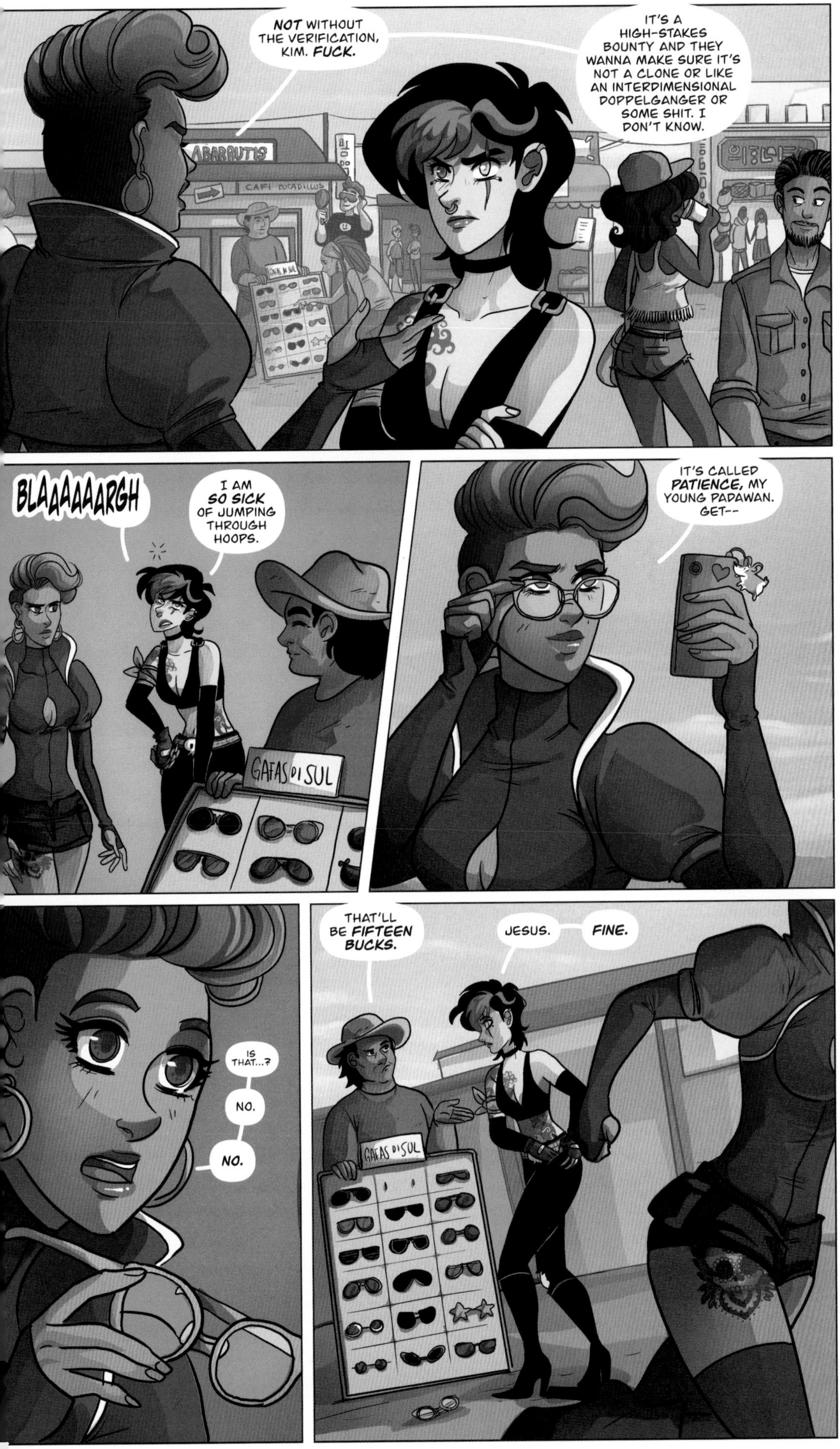
NOT WITHOUT THE VERIFICATION, KIM. FUCK.
IT'S A HIGH-STAKES BOUNTY AND THEY WANNA MAKE SURE IT'S NOT A CLONE OR LIKE AN INTERDIMENSIONAL DOPPELGANGER OR SOME SHIT. I DON'T KNOW.
BLAAAAAARGH
I AM SO SICK OF JUMPING THROUGH HOOPS.
GAFAS DI SUL
IT'S CALLED PATIENCE, MY YOUNG PADAWAN. GET--
IS THAT...?
NO.
NO.
THAT'LL BE FIFTEEN BUCKS.
JESUS.
FINE.
GAFAS DI SUL

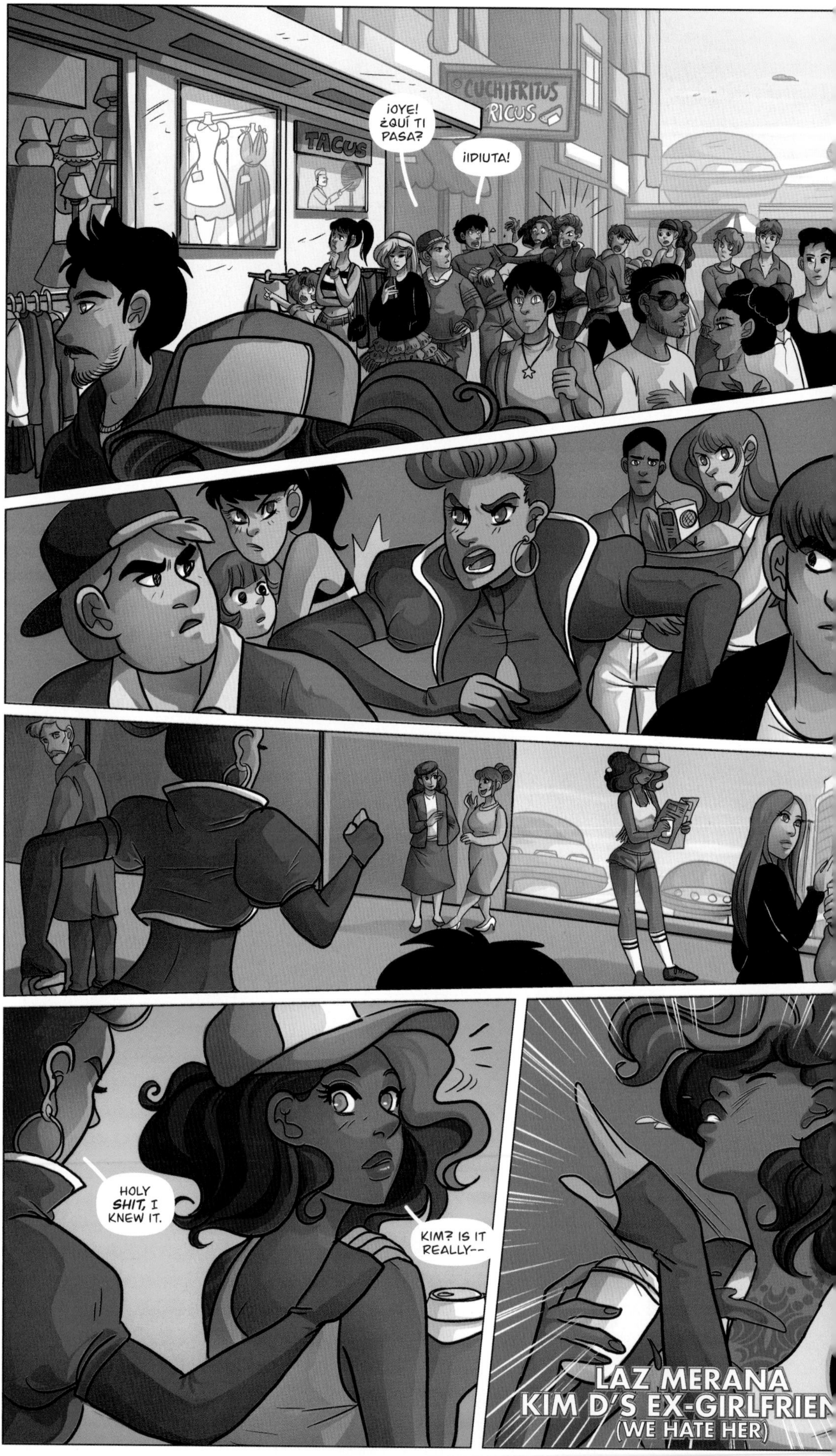
CUCHIFRITUS
RICUS
TACUS
¡OYE! ¿QUÍ TI PASA?
¡IDIUTA!
HOLY SHIT, I KNEW IT.
KIM? IS IT REALLY--
LAZ MERANA
KIM D'S EX-GIRLFRIEN
(WE HATE HER)

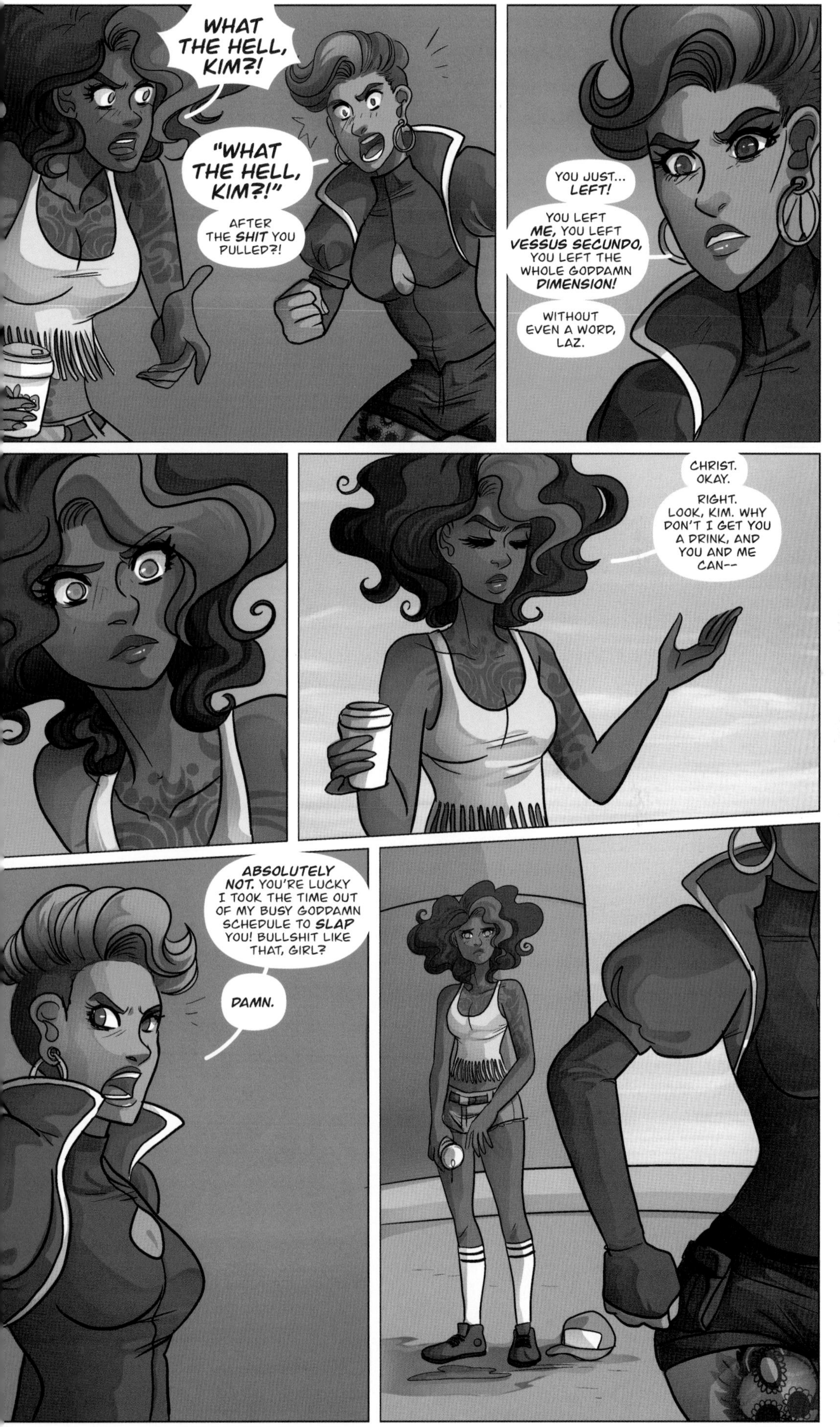
WHAT THE HELL, KIM?!
"WHAT THE HELL, KIM?!"
AFTER THE SHIT YOU PULLED?!
YOU JUST... LEFT!
YOU LEFT ME, YOU LEFT VESSUS SECUNDO, YOU LEFT THE WHOLE GODDAMN DIMENSION!
WITHOUT EVEN A WORD, LAZ.
CHRIST. OKAY.
RIGHT. LOOK, KIM. WHY DON'T I GET YOU A DRINK, AND YOU AND ME CAN--
ABSOLUTELY NOT. YOU'RE LUCKY I TOOK THE TIME OUT OF MY BUSY GODDAMN SCHEDULE TO SLAP YOU! BULLSHIT LIKE THAT, GIRL?
DAMN.

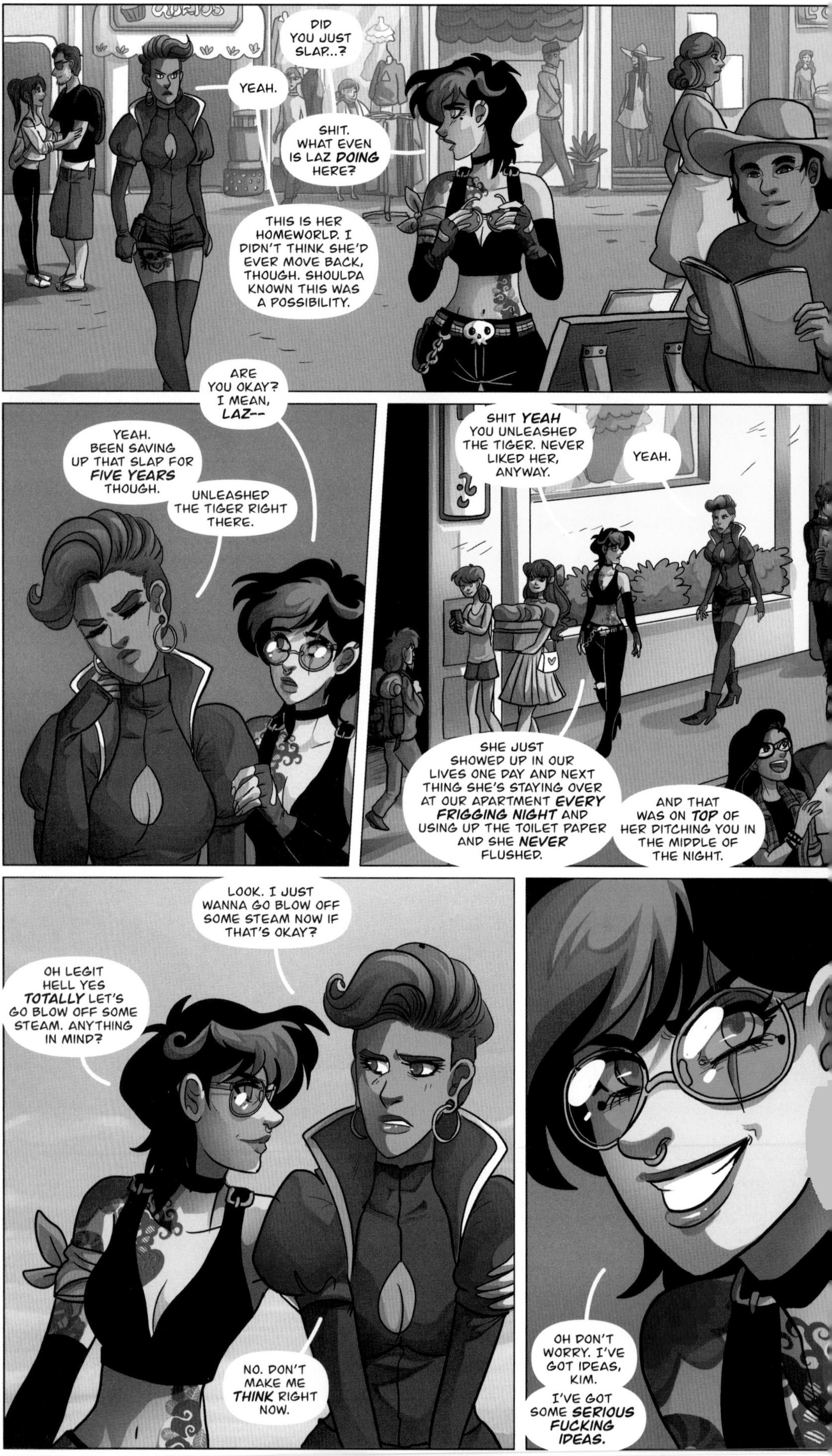

DID YOU JUST SLAP...?
YEAH.
SHIT. WHAT EVEN IS LAZ DOING HERE?
THIS IS HER HOMEWORLD. I DIDN'T THINK SHE'D EVER MOVE BACK, THOUGH. SHOULDA KNOWN THIS WAS A POSSIBILITY.
ARE YOU OKAY? I MEAN, LAZ--
YEAH. BEEN SAVING UP THAT SLAP FOR FIVE YEARS THOUGH.
UNLEASHED THE TIGER RIGHT THERE.
SHIT YEAH YOU UNLEASHED THE TIGER. NEVER LIKED HER, ANYWAY.
YEAH.
SHE JUST SHOWED UP IN OUR LIVES ONE DAY AND NEXT THING SHE'S STAYING OVER AT OUR APARTMENT EVERY FRIGGING NIGHT AND USING UP THE TOILET PAPER AND SHE NEVER FLUSHED.
AND THAT WAS ON TOP OF HER DITCHING YOU IN THE MIDDLE OF THE NIGHT.
LOOK. I JUST WANNA GO BLOW OFF SOME STEAM NOW IF THAT'S OKAY?
OH LEGIT HELL YES TOTALLY LET'S GO BLOW OFF SOME STEAM. ANYTHING IN MIND?
NO. DON'T MAKE ME THINK RIGHT NOW.
OH DON'T WORRY. I'VE GOT IDEAS, KIM.
I'VE GOT SOME SERIOUS FUCKING IDEAS.

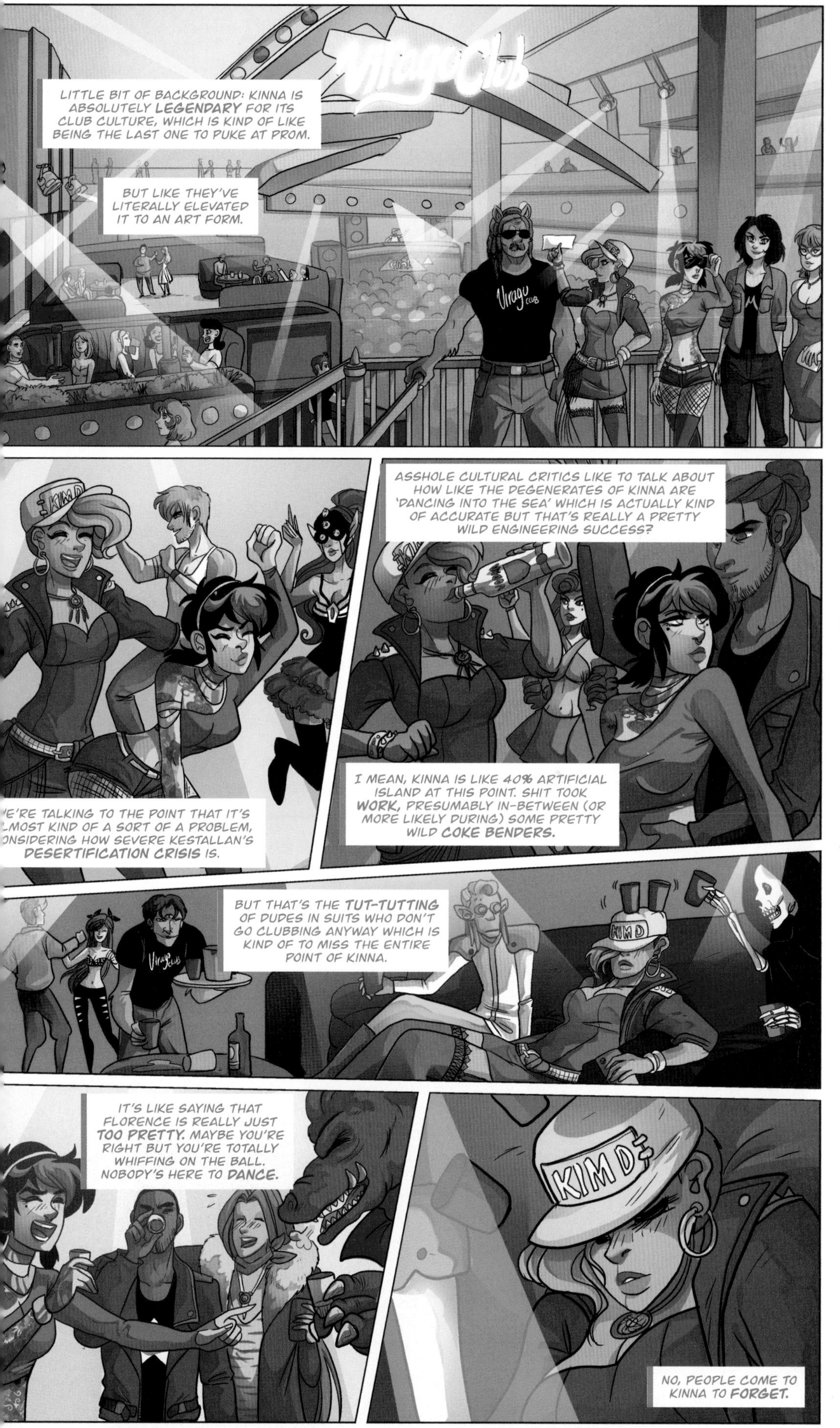

LITTLE BIT OF BACKGROUND: KINNA IS ABSOLUTELY **LEGENDARY** FOR ITS CLUB CULTURE, WHICH IS KIND OF LIKE BEING THE LAST ONE TO PUKE AT PROM.
BUT LIKE THEY'VE LITERALLY ELEVATED IT TO AN ART FORM.
Virago Club
Virago CLUB
WE'RE TALKING TO THE POINT THAT IT'S ALMOST KIND OF A SORT OF A PROBLEM, CONSIDERING HOW SEVERE KESTALLAN'S **DESERTIFICATION CRISIS** IS.
ASSHOLE CULTURAL CRITICS LIKE TO TALK ABOUT HOW LIKE THE DEGENERATES OF KINNA ARE 'DANCING INTO THE SEA' WHICH IS ACTUALLY KIND OF ACCURATE BUT THAT'S REALLY A PRETTY WILD ENGINEERING SUCCESS?
I MEAN, KINNA IS LIKE 40% ARTIFICIAL ISLAND AT THIS POINT. SHIT TOOK **WORK,** PRESUMABLY IN-BETWEEN (OR MORE LIKELY DURING) SOME PRETTY WILD **COKE BENDERS.**
BUT THAT'S THE **TUT-TUTTING** OF DUDES IN SUITS WHO DON'T GO CLUBBING ANYWAY WHICH IS KIND OF TO MISS THE ENTIRE POINT OF KINNA.
Virago CLUB
KIM D
IT'S LIKE SAYING THAT FLORENCE IS REALLY JUST **TOO PRETTY.** MAYBE YOU'RE RIGHT BUT YOU'RE TOTALLY WHIFFING ON THE BALL. NOBODY'S HERE TO **DANCE.**
KIM D
NO, PEOPLE COME TO KINNA TO **FORGET.**

SHOVE THIS UP FURIOUS' GODDAMN ASS!

WHAT?

I SAID, SHOVE THIS UP FURIOUS' GODDAMN ASS.

DUDE, THAT'S MY BOSS.

UM SAAR THAT'S MY DAD WHICH MAKE EVEN *MORE WEIRD* DISGUSTING.

I EARNED THIS ON MY *OWN* BUT WITH KIM SO FURIOUS CAN GO EAT A DICK.

A *BAG* OF 'EM.

DIDN'T EVEN NEED TO CALL ME IN FOR SUPPORT FOR ONCE.

WHAT ARE YOU EVEN *DOING* ON KESTALLAN?

CAN'T A GUY GO ON VACATION?

COINCIDENTA ON THE SAME P I'M WORKING ON *THING BR*

NOT EVERYTHING REVOLVES AROUND YOU, KIM.

GOD, FINE.

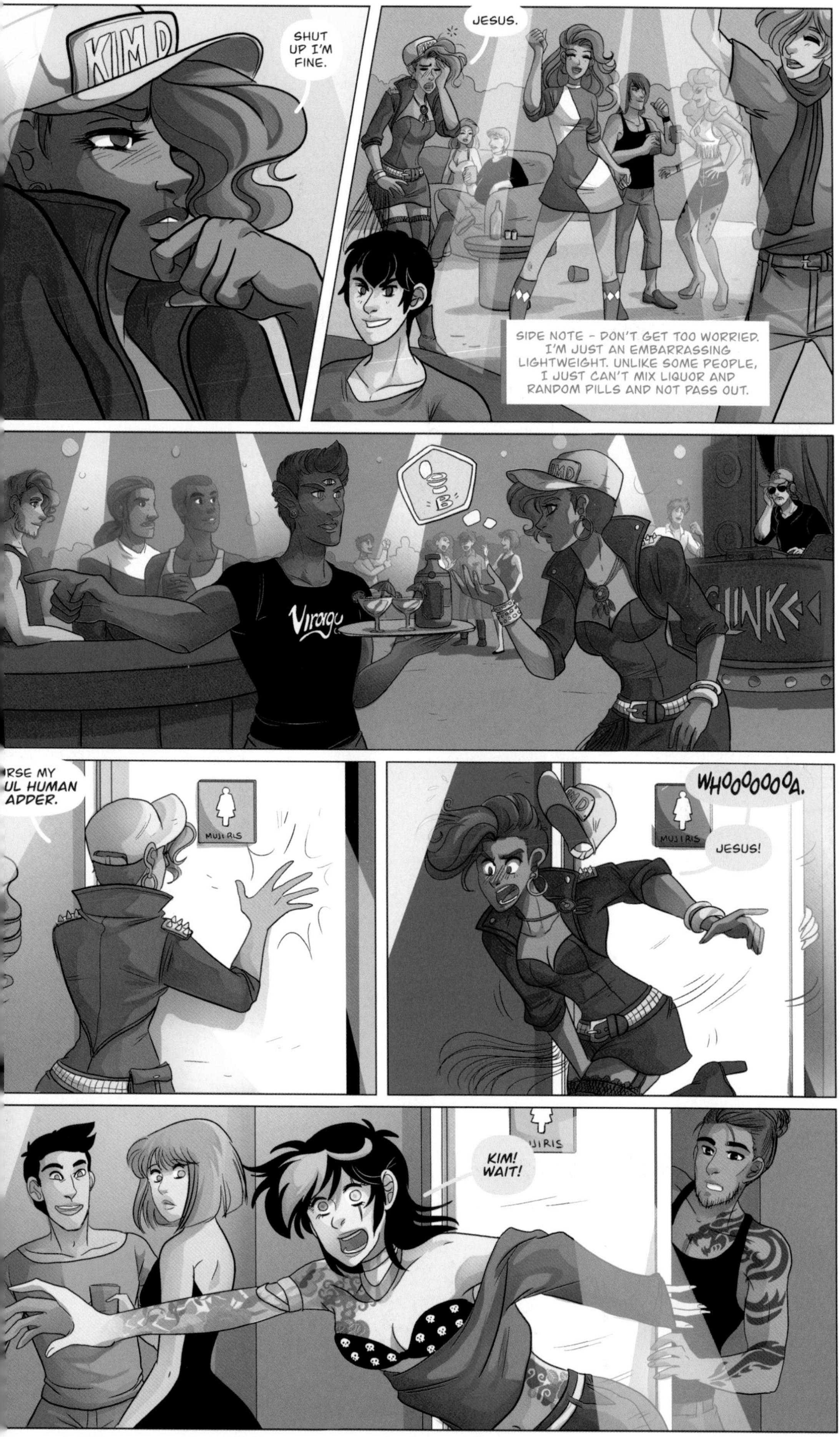
SHUT UP I'M FINE.
JESUS.
SIDE NOTE - DON'T GET TOO WORRIED. I'M JUST AN EMBARRASSING LIGHTWEIGHT. UNLIKE SOME PEOPLE, I JUST CAN'T MIX LIQUOR AND RANDOM PILLS AND NOT PASS OUT.
Virago
RSE MY UL HUMAN ADDER.
MUJIRIS
MUJIRIS
WHOOOOOOA.
JESUS!
MUJIRIS
KIM! WAIT!

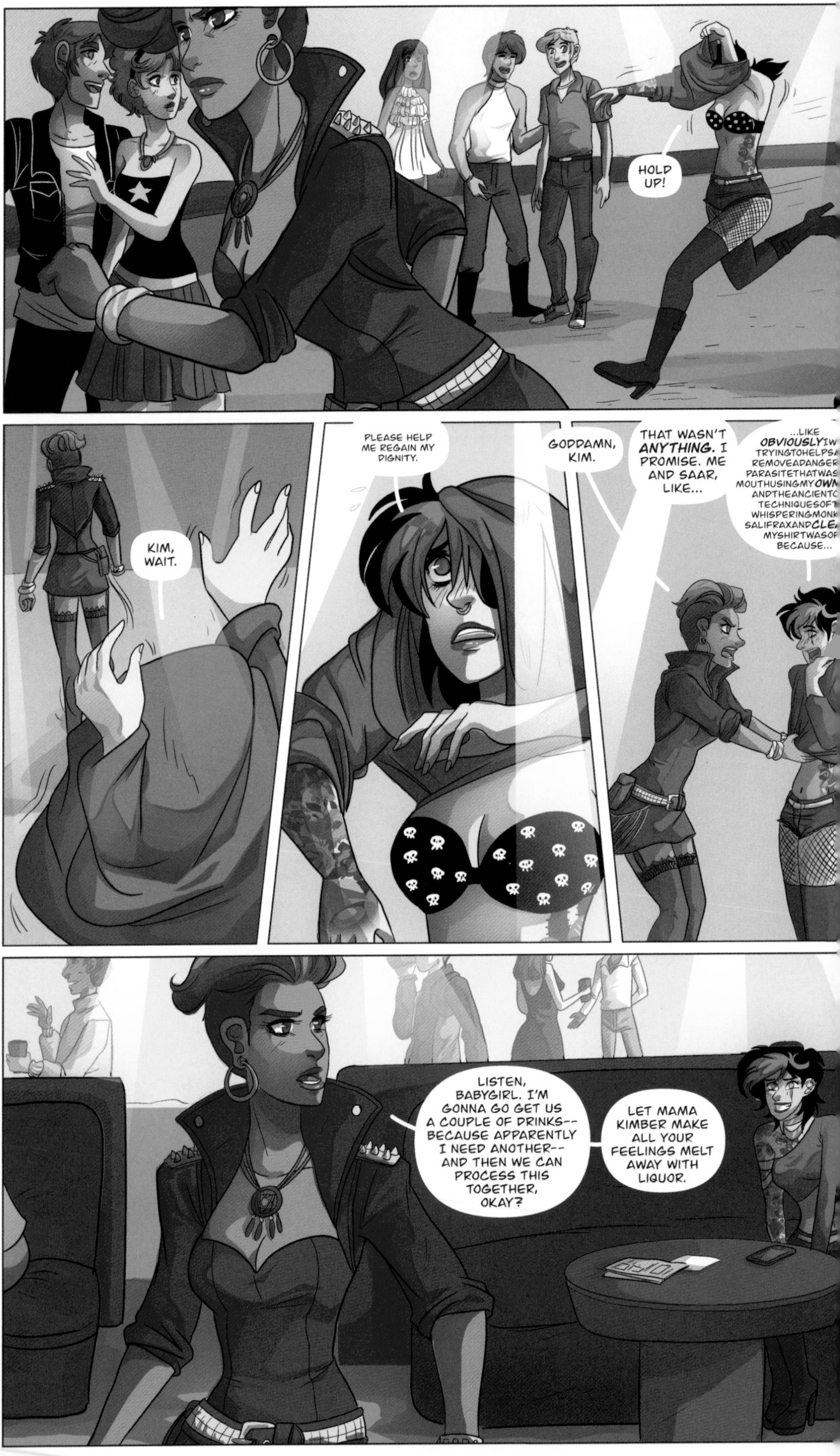
HOLD UP!
KIM, WAIT.
PLEASE HELP ME REGAIN MY DIGNITY.
GODDAMN, KIM.
THAT WASN'T **ANYTHING.** I PROMISE. ME AND SAAR, LIKE...
...LIKE **OBVIOUSLY**IW TRYINGTOHELPSA REMOVEADANGER PARASITETHATWAS MOUTHUSINGMY**OWN** ANDTHEANCIENTC TECHNIQUESOFT WHISPERINGMONK SALIFRAXAND**CLE** MYSHIRTWASOF BECAUSE...
LISTEN, BABYGIRL. I'M GONNA GO GET US A COUPLE OF DRINKS-- BECAUSE APPARENTLY I NEED ANOTHER-- AND THEN WE CAN PROCESS THIS TOGETHER, OKAY?
LET MAMA KIMBER MAKE ALL YOUR FEELINGS MELT AWAY WITH LIQUOR.

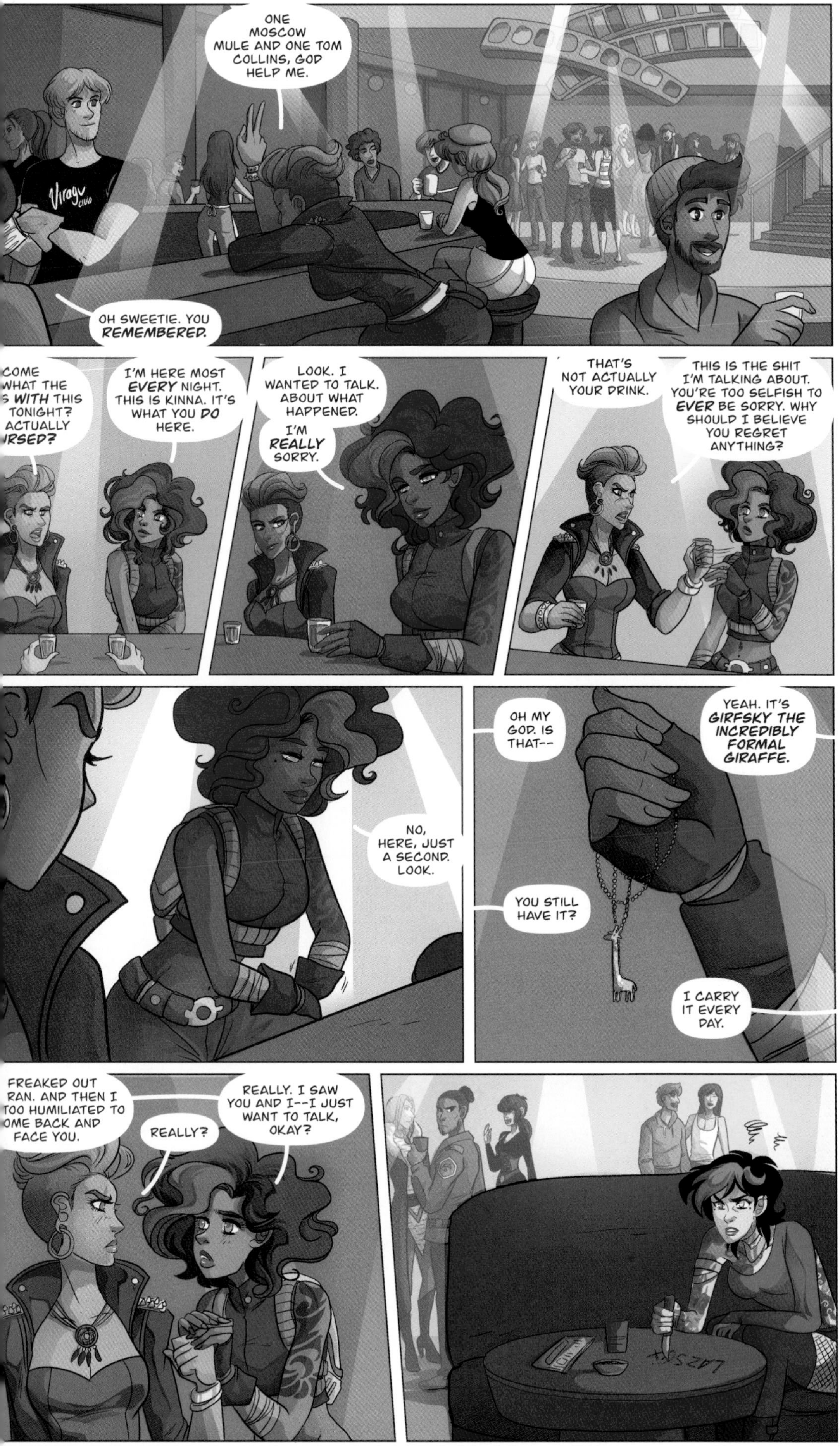

ONE MOSCOW MULE AND ONE TOM COLLINS, GOD HELP ME.
Virago club
OH SWEETIE. YOU REMEMBERED.
COME WHAT THE S WITH THIS TONIGHT? ACTUALLY RSED?
I'M HERE MOST EVERY NIGHT. THIS IS KINNA. IT'S WHAT YOU DO HERE.
LOOK. I WANTED TO TALK. ABOUT WHAT HAPPENED.
I'M REALLY SORRY.
THAT'S NOT ACTUALLY YOUR DRINK.
THIS IS THE SHIT I'M TALKING ABOUT. YOU'RE TOO SELFISH TO EVER BE SORRY. WHY SHOULD I BELIEVE YOU REGRET ANYTHING?
NO, HERE, JUST A SECOND. LOOK.
OH MY GOD. IS THAT--
YEAH. IT'S GIRFSKY THE INCREDIBLY FORMAL GIRAFFE.
YOU STILL HAVE IT?
I CARRY IT EVERY DAY.
FREAKED OUT RAN. AND THEN I TOO HUMILIATED TO OME BACK AND FACE YOU.
REALLY?
REALLY. I SAW YOU AND I--I JUST WANT TO TALK, OKAY?

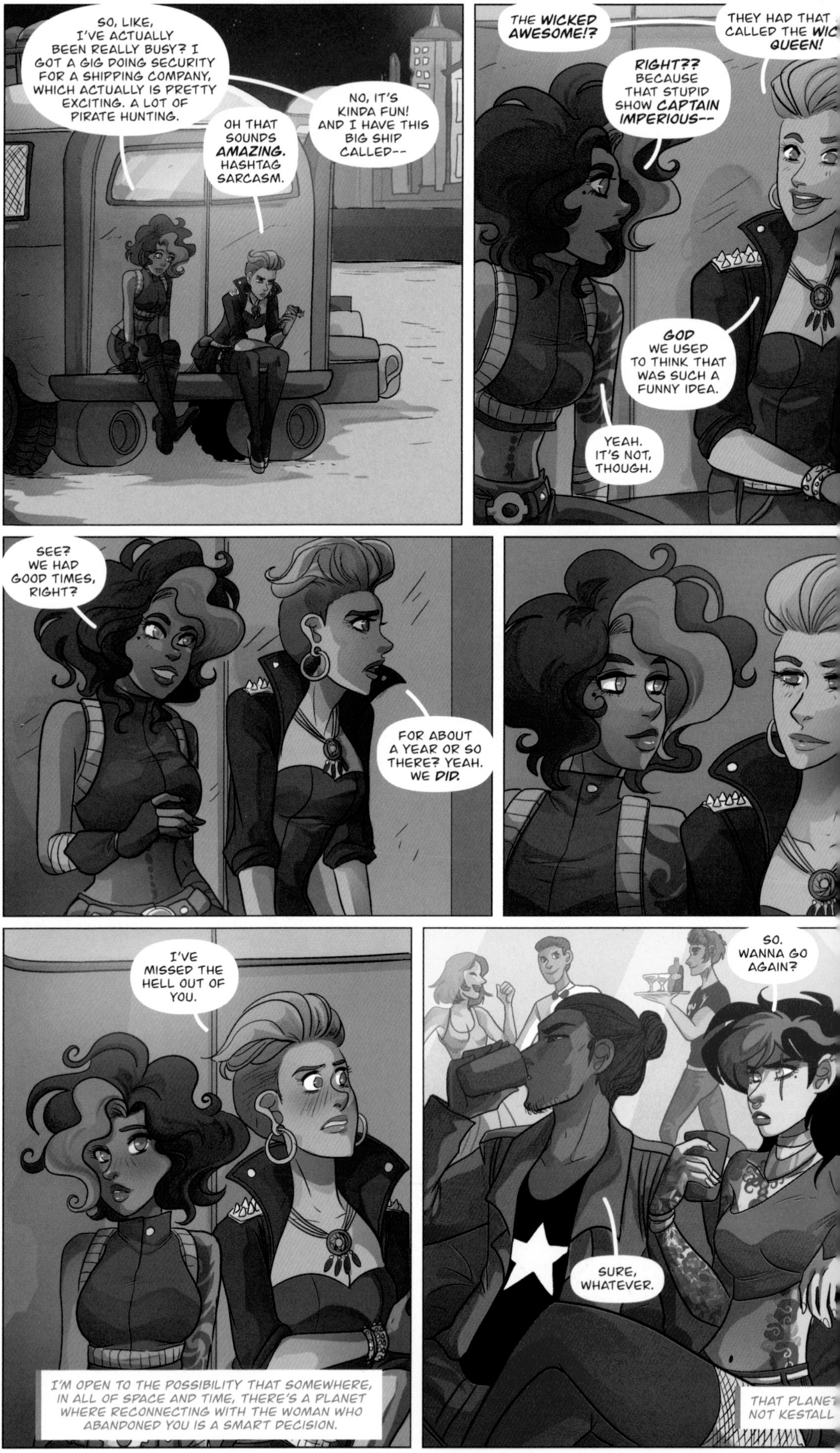
SO, LIKE, I'VE ACTUALLY BEEN REALLY BUSY? I GOT A GIG DOING SECURITY FOR A SHIPPING COMPANY, WHICH ACTUALLY IS PRETTY EXCITING. A LOT OF PIRATE HUNTING.
OH THAT SOUNDS **AMAZING.** HASHTAG SARCASM.
NO, IT'S KINDA FUN! AND I HAVE THIS BIG SHIP CALLED--
THE **WICKED AWESOME!?**
THEY HAD THAT CALLED THE **WIC QUEEN!**
**RIGHT??** BECAUSE THAT STUPID SHOW **CAPTAIN IMPERIOUS--**
**GOD** WE USED TO THINK THAT WAS SUCH A FUNNY IDEA.
YEAH. IT'S NOT, THOUGH.
SEE? WE HAD GOOD TIMES, RIGHT?
FOR ABOUT A YEAR OR SO THERE? YEAH. WE **DID.**
I'VE MISSED THE HELL OUT OF YOU.
*I'M OPEN TO THE POSSIBILITY THAT SOMEWHERE, IN ALL OF SPACE AND TIME, THERE'S A PLANET WHERE RECONNECTING WITH THE WOMAN WHO ABANDONED YOU IS A SMART DECISION.*
SO. WANNA GO AGAIN?
SURE, WHATEVER.
*THAT PLANE NOT KESTALL*

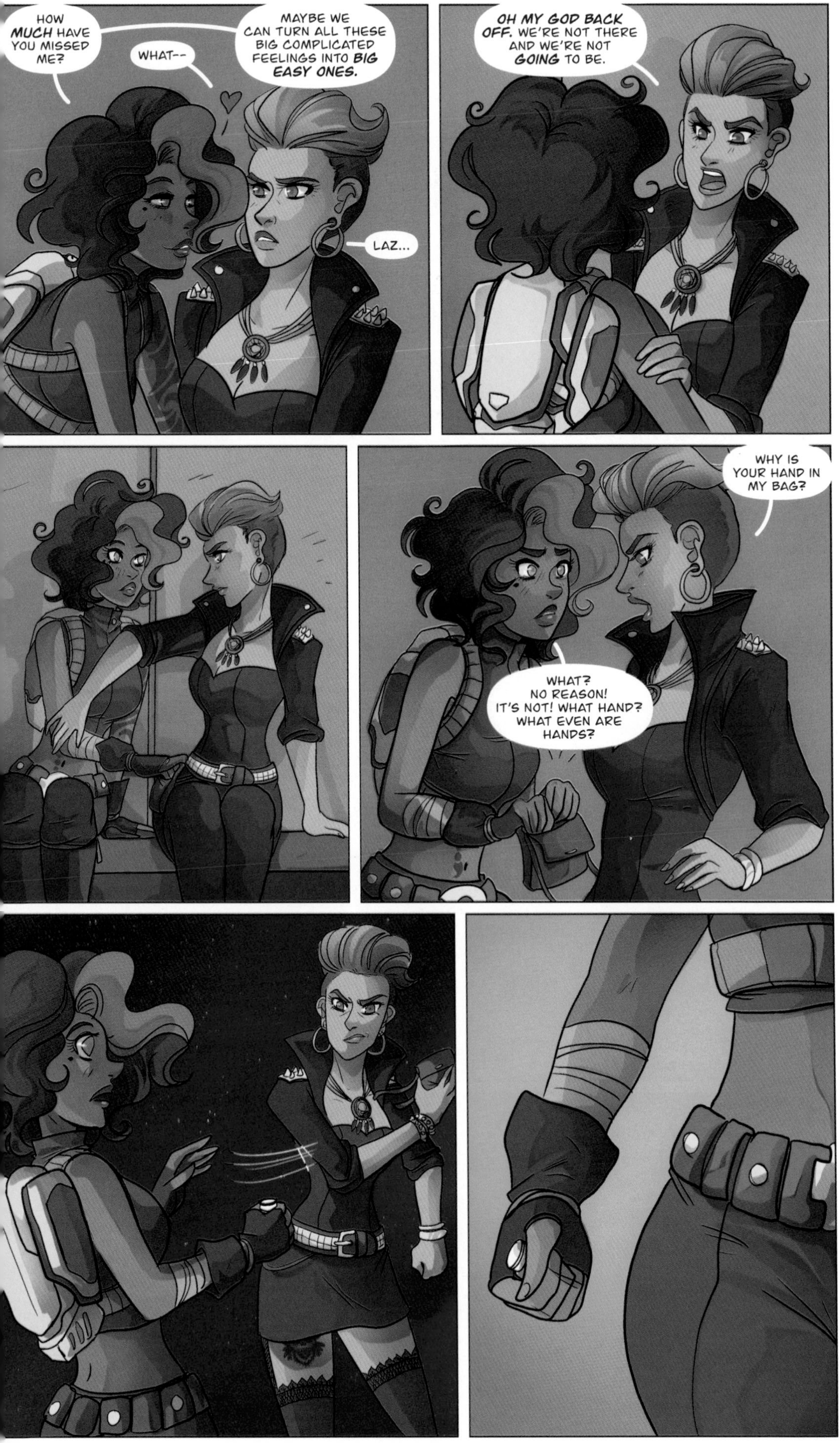
HOW MUCH HAVE YOU MISSED ME?
WHAT--
MAYBE WE CAN TURN ALL THESE BIG COMPLICATED FEELINGS INTO BIG EASY ONES.
LAZ...
OH MY GOD BACK OFF. WE'RE NOT THERE AND WE'RE NOT GOING TO BE.
WHY IS YOUR HAND IN MY BAG?
WHAT? NO REASON! IT'S NOT! WHAT HAND? WHAT EVEN ARE HANDS?

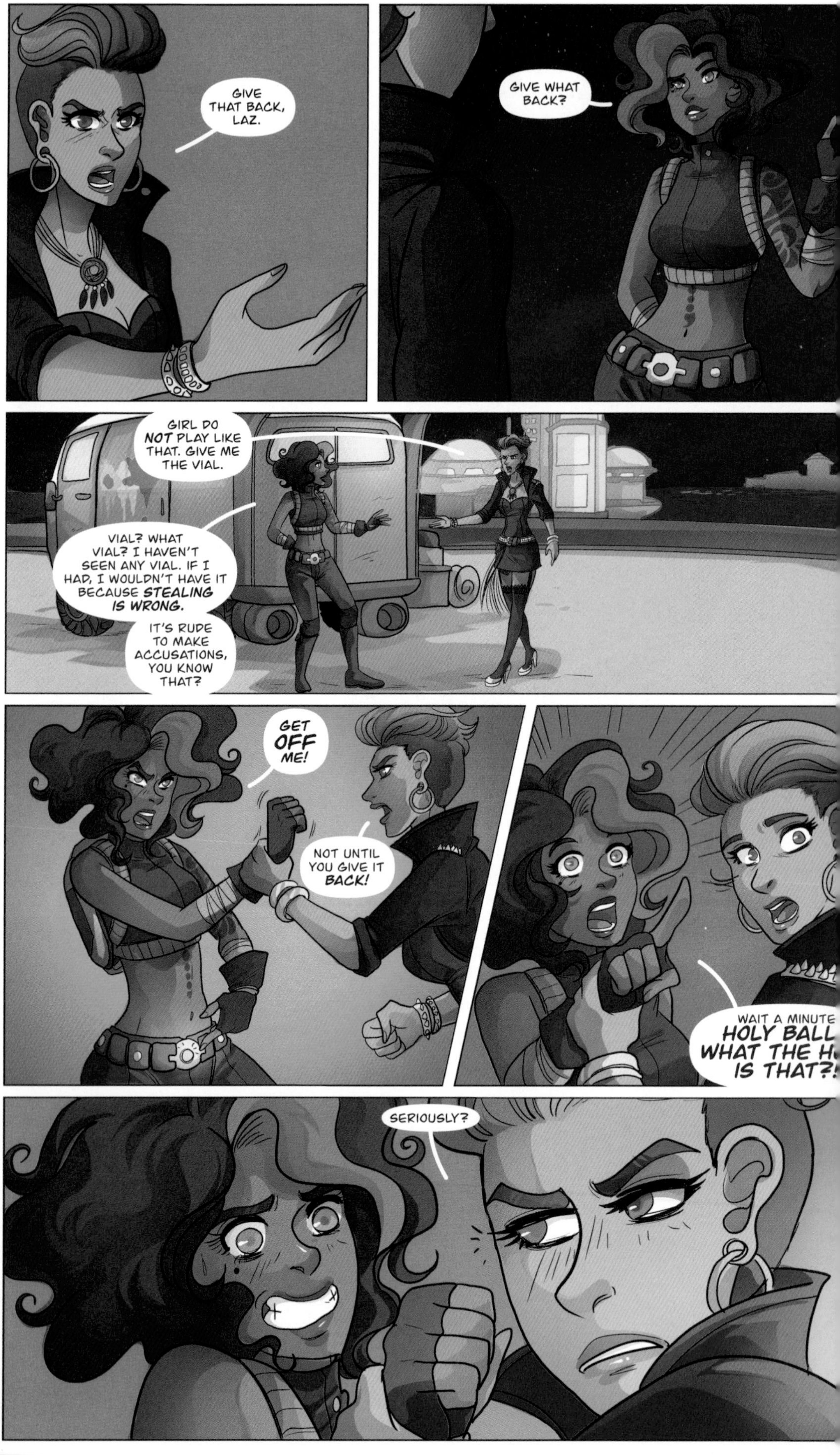
GIVE THAT BACK, LAZ.
GIVE WHAT BACK?
GIRL DO **NOT** PLAY LIKE THAT. GIVE ME THE VIAL.
VIAL? WHAT VIAL? I HAVEN'T SEEN ANY VIAL. IF I HAD, I WOULDN'T HAVE IT BECAUSE **STEALING IS WRONG.**
IT'S RUDE TO MAKE ACCUSATIONS, YOU KNOW THAT?
GET **OFF** ME!
NOT UNTIL YOU GIVE IT **BACK!**
WAIT A MINUTE
**HOLY BALL**
**WHAT THE H**
**IS THAT?!**
SERIOUSLY?

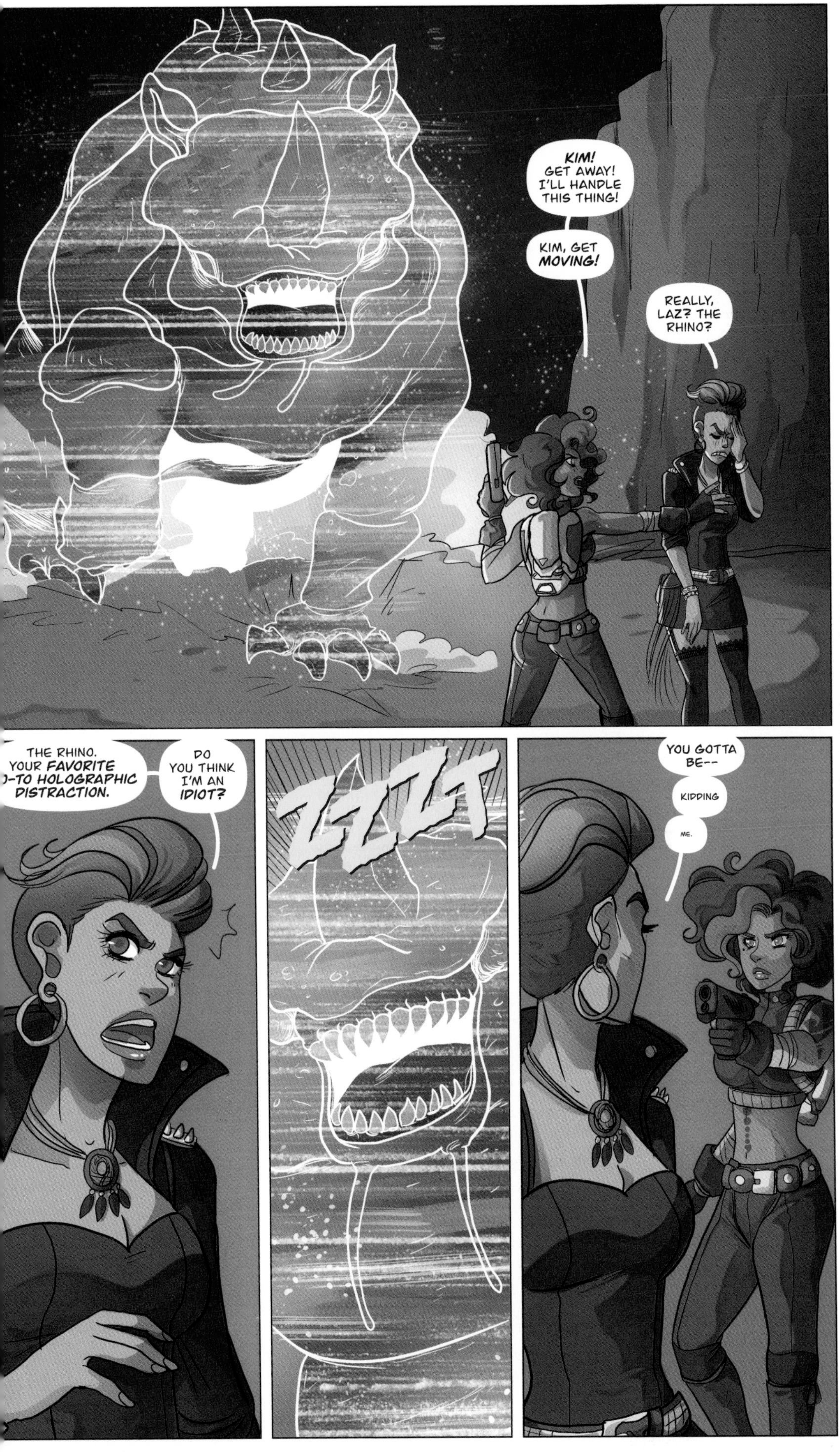
KIM! GET AWAY! I'LL HANDLE THIS THING!
KIM, GET MOVING!
REALLY, LAZ? THE RHINO?
THE RHINO. YOUR FAVORITE -TO HOLOGRAPHIC DISTRACTION.
DO YOU THINK I'M AN IDIOT?
ZZZT
YOU GOTTA BE--
KIDDING
ME.

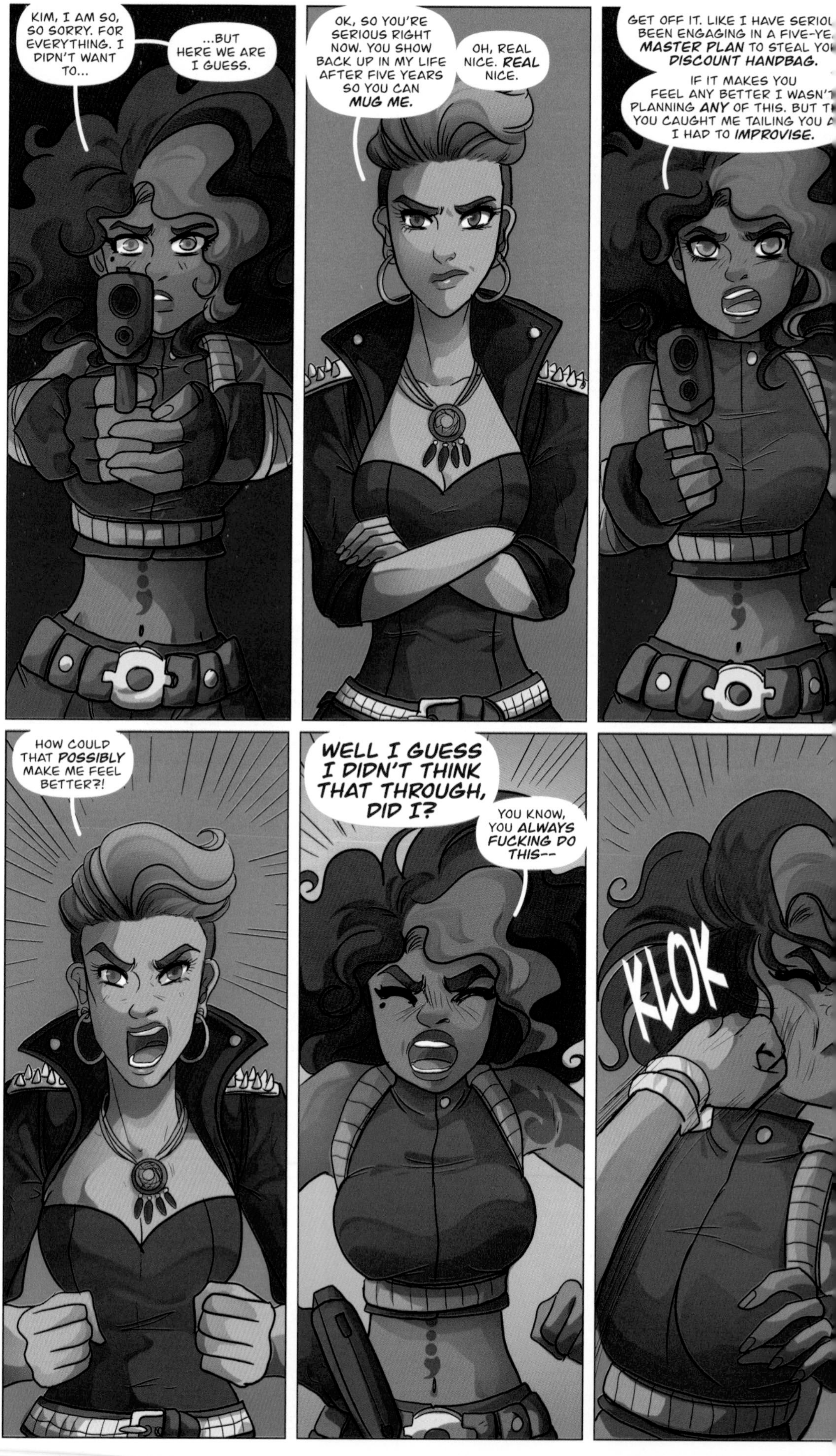
KIM, I AM SO, SO SORRY. FOR EVERYTHING. I DIDN'T WANT TO...
...BUT HERE WE ARE I GUESS.
OK, SO YOU'RE SERIOUS RIGHT NOW. YOU SHOW BACK UP IN MY LIFE AFTER FIVE YEARS SO YOU CAN MUG ME.
OH, REAL NICE. REAL NICE.
GET OFF IT. LIKE I HAVE SERIOU BEEN ENGAGING IN A FIVE-YE MASTER PLAN TO STEAL YO DISCOUNT HANDBAG.
IF IT MAKES YOU FEEL ANY BETTER I WASN'T PLANNING ANY OF THIS. BUT T YOU CAUGHT ME TAILING YOU A I HAD TO IMPROVISE.
HOW COULD THAT POSSIBLY MAKE ME FEEL BETTER?!
WELL I GUESS I DIDN'T THINK THAT THROUGH, DID I?
YOU KNOW, YOU ALWAYS FUCKING DO THIS--
KLOK

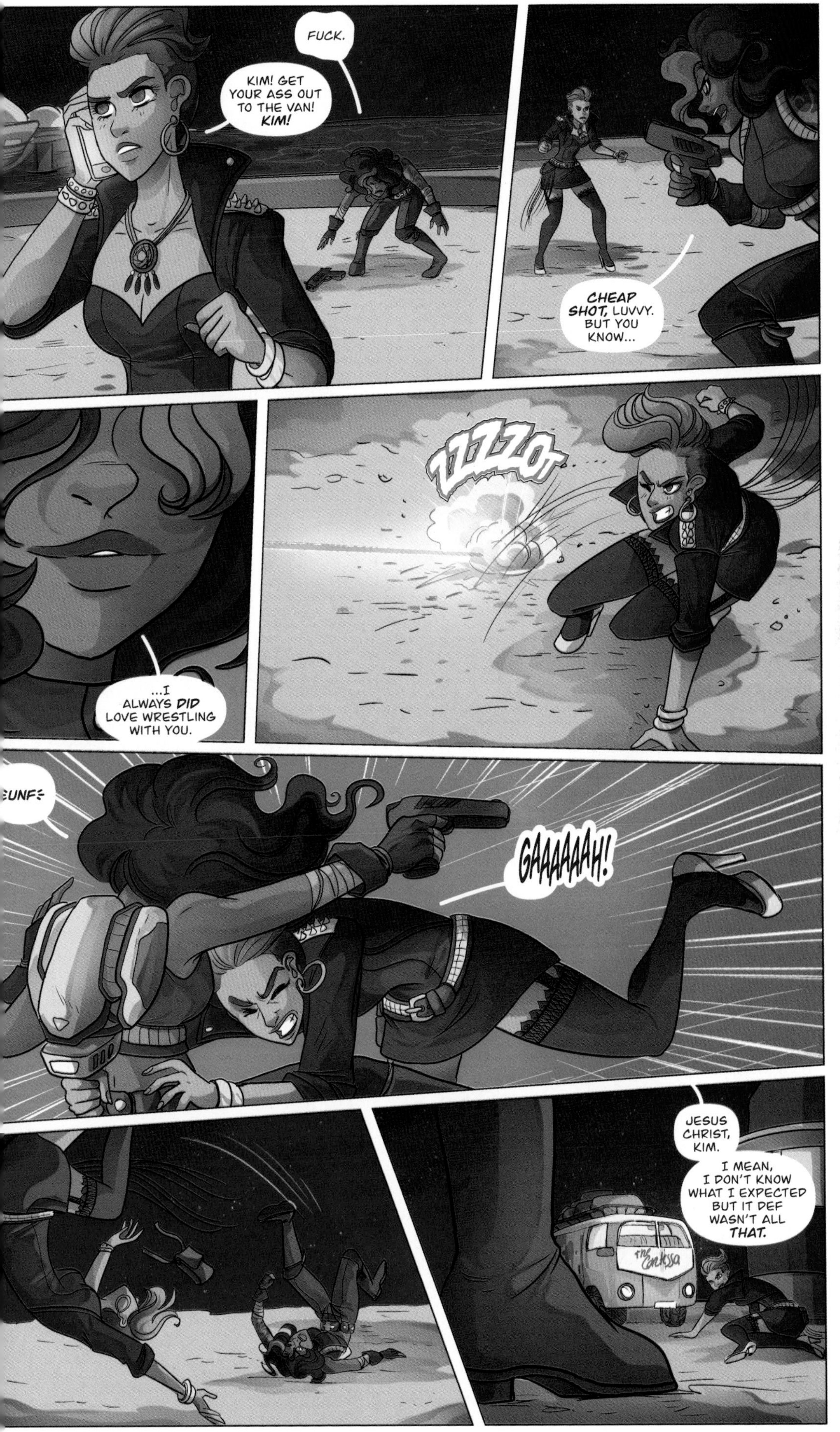

KIM! GET YOUR ASS OUT TO THE VAN! KIM!
FUCK.
CHEAP SHOT, LUVVY. BUT YOU KNOW...
...I ALWAYS DID LOVE WRESTLING WITH YOU.
ZZZZOT
UNF
GAAAAAAH!
JESUS CHRIST, KIM.
I MEAN, I DON'T KNOW WHAT I EXPECTED BUT IT DEF WASN'T ALL THAT.

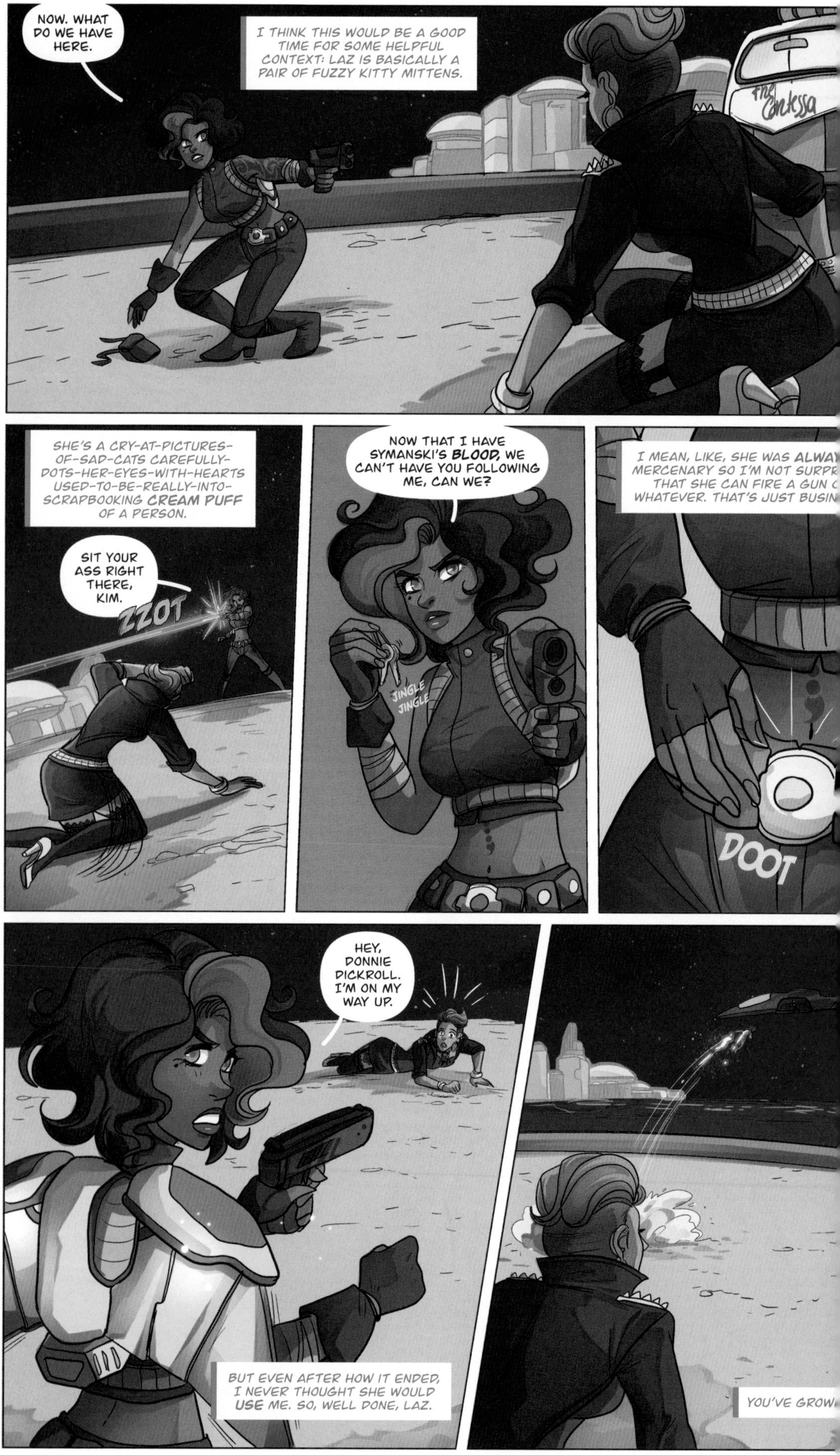
NOW. WHAT DO WE HAVE HERE.
I THINK THIS WOULD BE A GOOD TIME FOR SOME HELPFUL CONTEXT: LAZ IS BASICALLY A PAIR OF FUZZY KITTY MITTENS.
The Contessa
SHE'S A CRY-AT-PICTURES-OF-SAD-CATS CAREFULLY-DOTS-HER-EYES-WITH-HEARTS USED-TO-BE-REALLY-INTO-SCRAPBOOKING **CREAM PUFF** OF A PERSON.
SIT YOUR ASS RIGHT THERE, KIM.
ZZOT
NOW THAT I HAVE SYMANSKI'S **BLOOD,** WE CAN'T HAVE YOU FOLLOWING ME, CAN WE?
JINGLE JINGLE
I MEAN, LIKE, SHE WAS **ALWAY** MERCENARY SO I'M NOT SURPR THAT SHE CAN FIRE A GUN O WHATEVER. THAT'S JUST BUSIN
DOOT
HEY, DONNIE DICKROLL. I'M ON MY WAY UP.
BUT EVEN AFTER HOW IT ENDED, I NEVER THOUGHT SHE WOULD **USE** ME. SO, WELL DONE, LAZ.
YOU'VE GROW

SHIT! KIM! ARE YOU OKAY?

WHAT THE SHIT **HAPPENED?**

**LAZ** HAPPENED.

OH **FANTASTIC.** MISS ON'T-EVER-FLUSH-THE-GODDAMN-TOILET-AND-O-ALSO-LEFT-YOU-WITH-OUT-A-WORD IS BACK IN OUR LIVES.

RAD.

I WAS SO **STUPID,** LISTENING TO HER. LETTING HER IN JUST SO SHE COULD HURT ME AGAIN.

HEY, SO, YOU KNOW IT'S NOT YOUR FAULT IF SHE'S AWFUL, RIGHT?

AND SHE IS AWFUL, WHICH IS 100% ON HER.

SHE'S THE **LITERAL WORST HUMAN EVER.**

YOU DON'T NEED HER, AND SHE DOESN'T HAVE THE RIGHT TO USE--

SHE TOOK EVERYTHING.

WHAT EVERY-THING?

**EVERYTHING** EVERYTHING. THE VIAL OF SYMANSKI'S BLOOD. THE VOUCHER. BASICALLY EVERY DOLLAR TO OUR NAME.

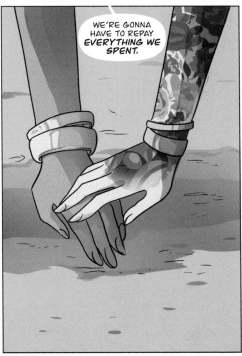

WE'RE GONNA HAVE TO REPAY **EVERYTHING WE SPENT.**

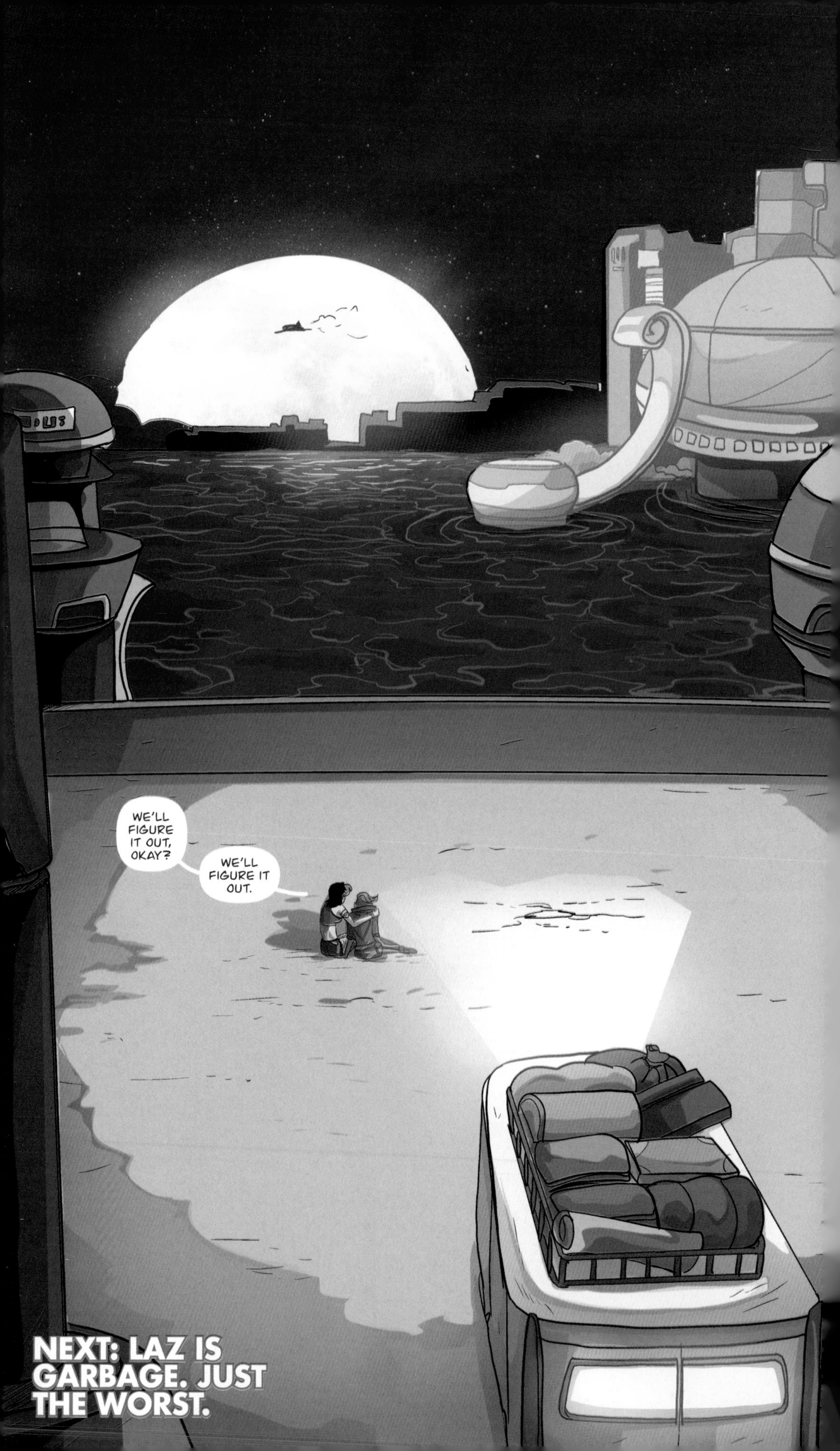
WE'LL FIGURE IT OUT, OKAY?
WE'LL FIGURE IT OUT.
NEXT: LAZ IS GARBAGE. JUST THE WORST.

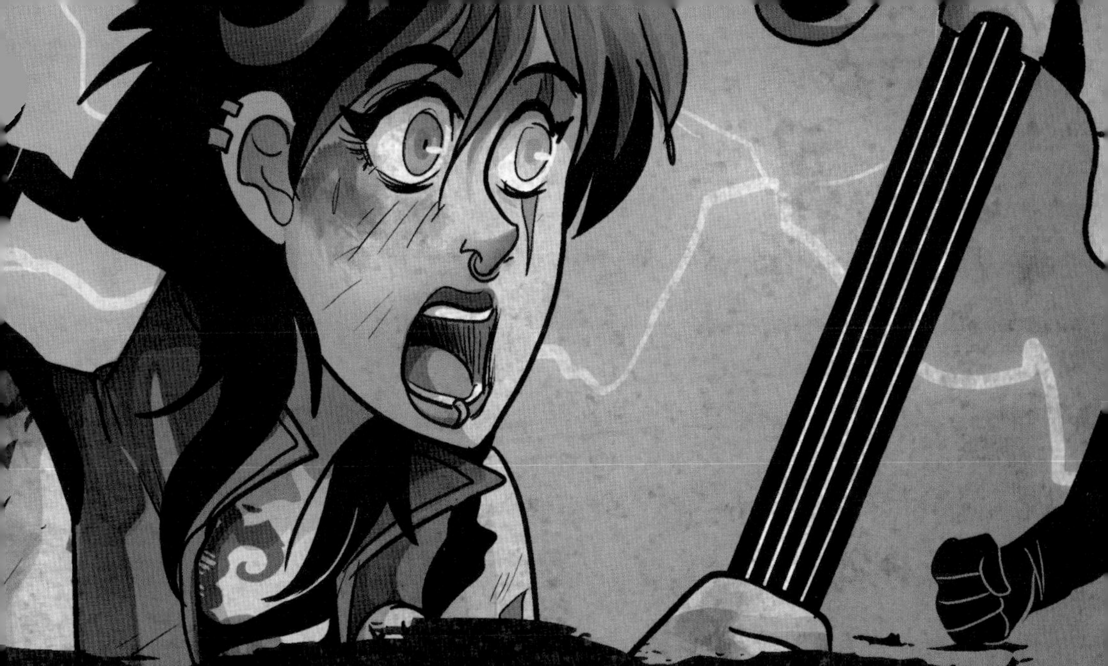

# 2

## "WE HATE HER"

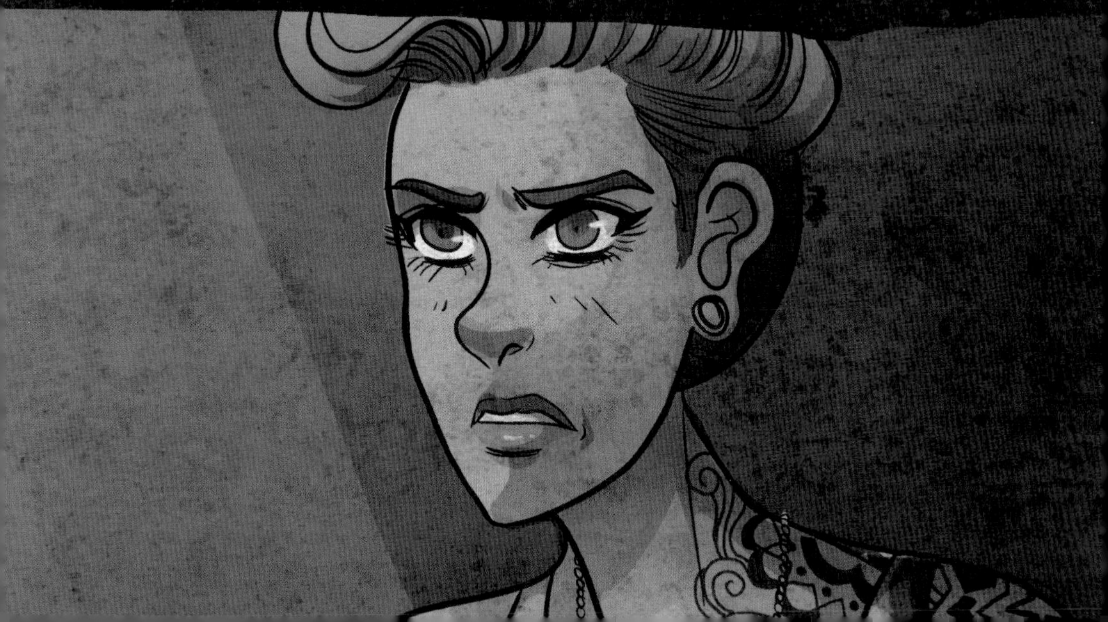

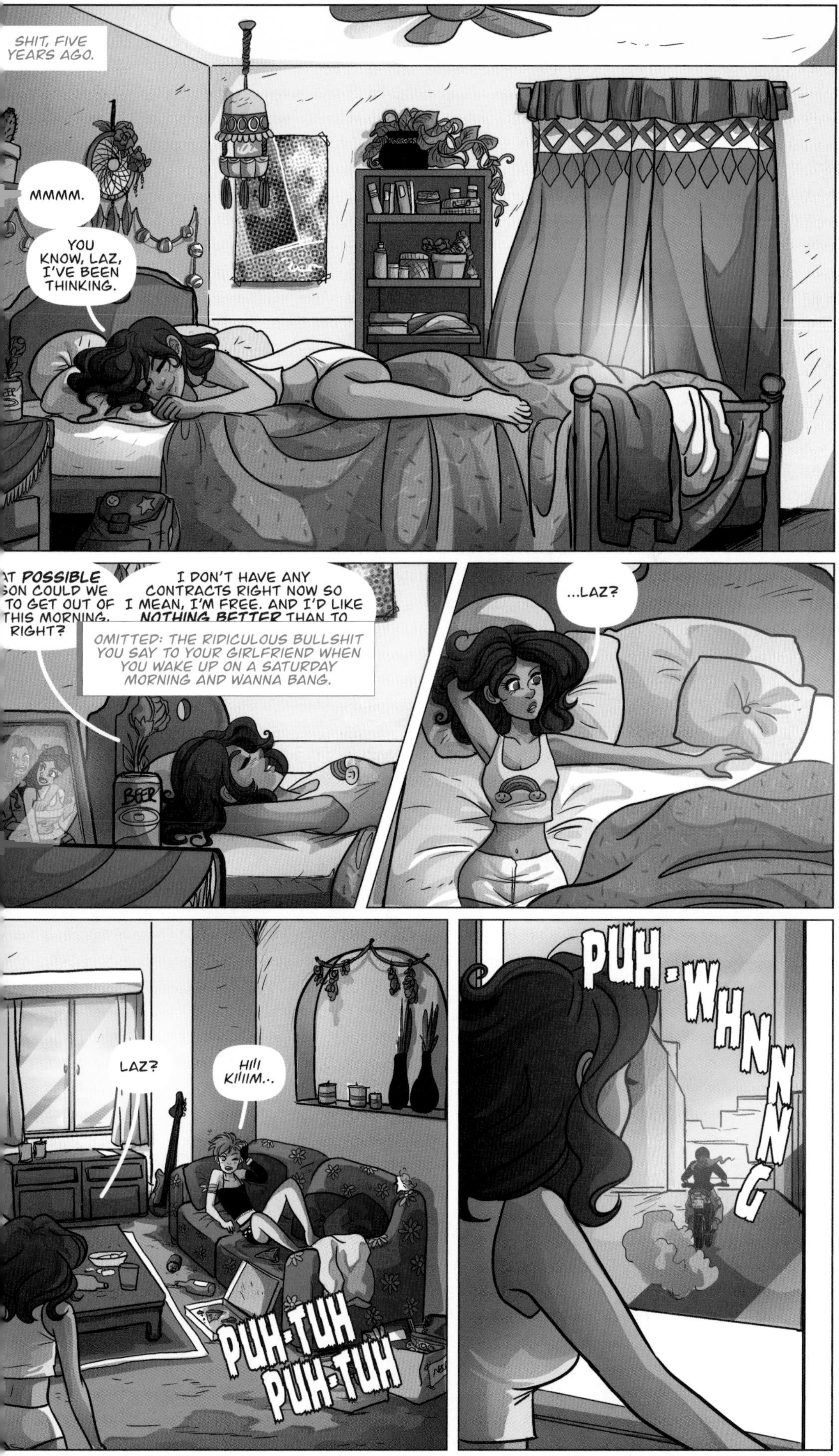
SHIT, FIVE YEARS AGO.
MMMM.
YOU KNOW, LAZ, I'VE BEEN THINKING.
AT POSSIBLE SON COULD WE TO GET OUT OF THIS MORNING, RIGHT?
I DON'T HAVE ANY CONTRACTS RIGHT NOW SO I MEAN, I'M FREE. AND I'D LIKE NOTHING BETTER THAN TO
OMITTED: THE RIDICULOUS BULLSHIT YOU SAY TO YOUR GIRLFRIEND WHEN YOU WAKE UP ON A SATURDAY MORNING AND WANNA BANG.
...LAZ?
LAZ?
HI!! KI!!IM...
PUH-TUH PUH-TUH
PUH-WHNNNNG

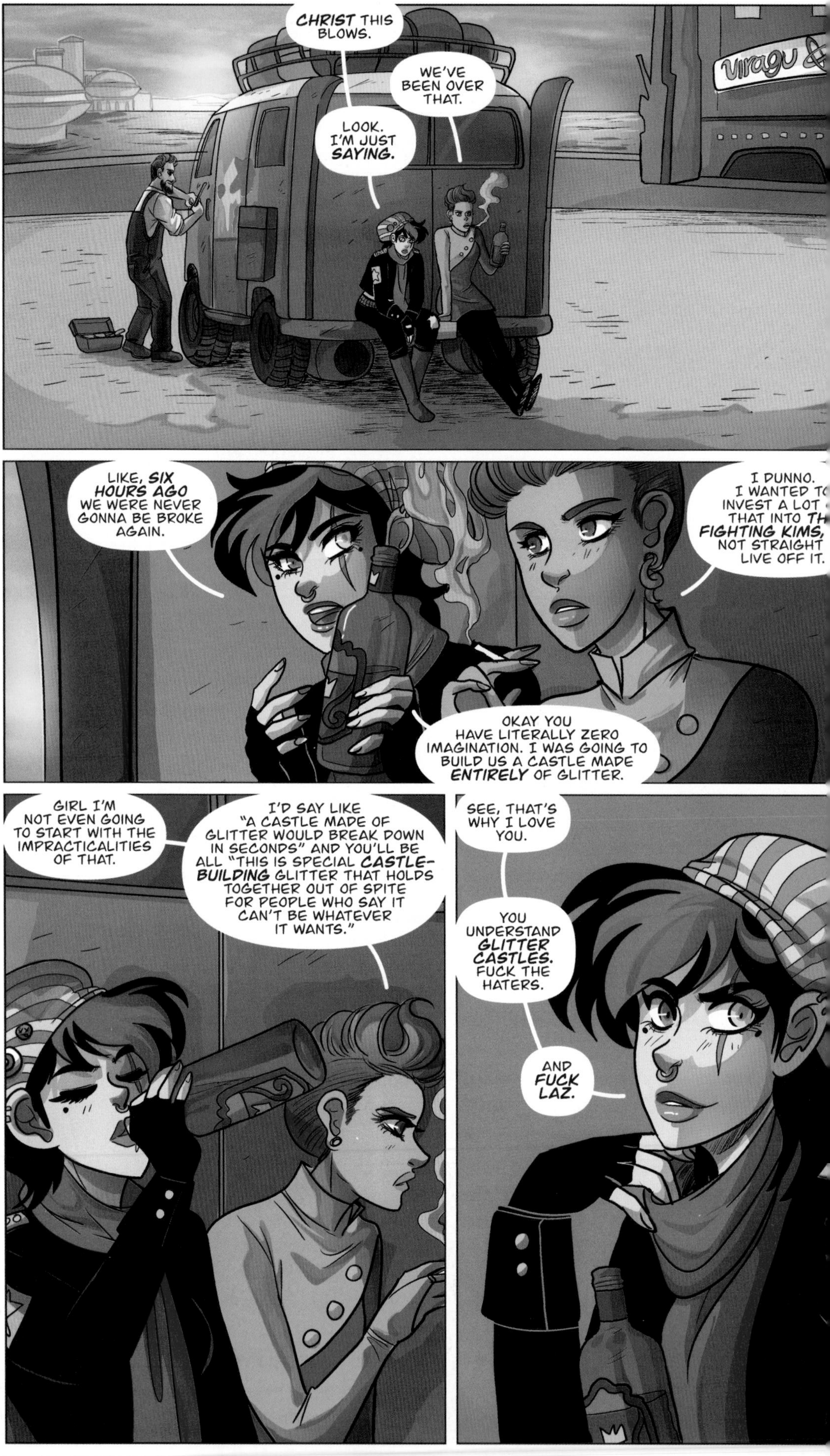
CHRIST THIS BLOWS.
LOOK. I'M JUST SAYING.
WE'VE BEEN OVER THAT.
Viragu
LIKE, SIX HOURS AGO WE WERE NEVER GONNA BE BROKE AGAIN.
I DUNNO. I WANTED T INVEST A LOT THAT INTO TH FIGHTING KIMS, NOT STRAIGHT LIVE OFF IT.
OKAY YOU HAVE LITERALLY ZERO IMAGINATION. I WAS GOING TO BUILD US A CASTLE MADE ENTIRELY OF GLITTER.
GIRL I'M NOT EVEN GOING TO START WITH THE IMPRACTICALITIES OF THAT.
I'D SAY LIKE "A CASTLE MADE OF GLITTER WOULD BREAK DOWN IN SECONDS" AND YOU'LL BE ALL "THIS IS SPECIAL CASTLE-BUILDING GLITTER THAT HOLDS TOGETHER OUT OF SPITE FOR PEOPLE WHO SAY IT CAN'T BE WHATEVER IT WANTS."
SEE, THAT'S WHY I LOVE YOU.
YOU UNDERSTAND GLITTER CASTLES. FUCK THE HATERS.
AND FUCK LAZ.

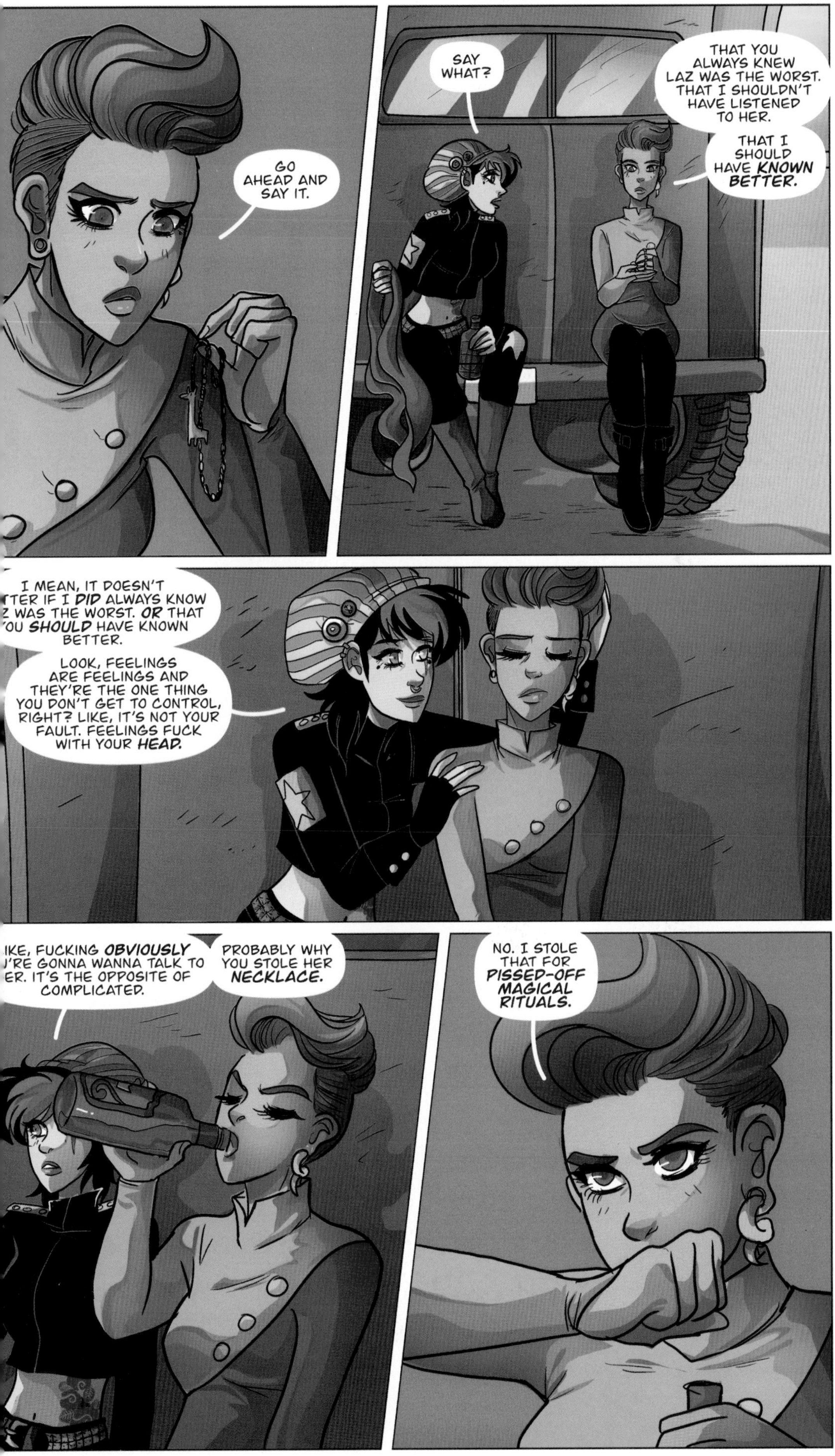
GO AHEAD AND SAY IT.
SAY WHAT?
THAT YOU ALWAYS KNEW LAZ WAS THE WORST. THAT I SHOULDN'T HAVE LISTENED TO HER.
THAT I SHOULD HAVE **KNOWN BETTER.**
I MEAN, IT DOESN'T TTER IF I ***DID*** ALWAYS KNOW Z WAS THE WORST. ***OR*** THAT OU ***SHOULD*** HAVE KNOWN BETTER.
LOOK, FEELINGS ARE FEELINGS AND THEY'RE THE ONE THING YOU DON'T GET TO CONTROL, RIGHT? LIKE, IT'S NOT YOUR FAULT. FEELINGS FUCK WITH YOUR ***HEAD.***
IKE, FUCKING ***OBVIOUSLY*** I'RE GONNA WANNA TALK TO ER. IT'S THE OPPOSITE OF COMPLICATED.
PROBABLY WHY YOU STOLE HER ***NECKLACE.***
NO. I STOLE THAT FOR ***PISSED-OFF MAGICAL RITUALS.***

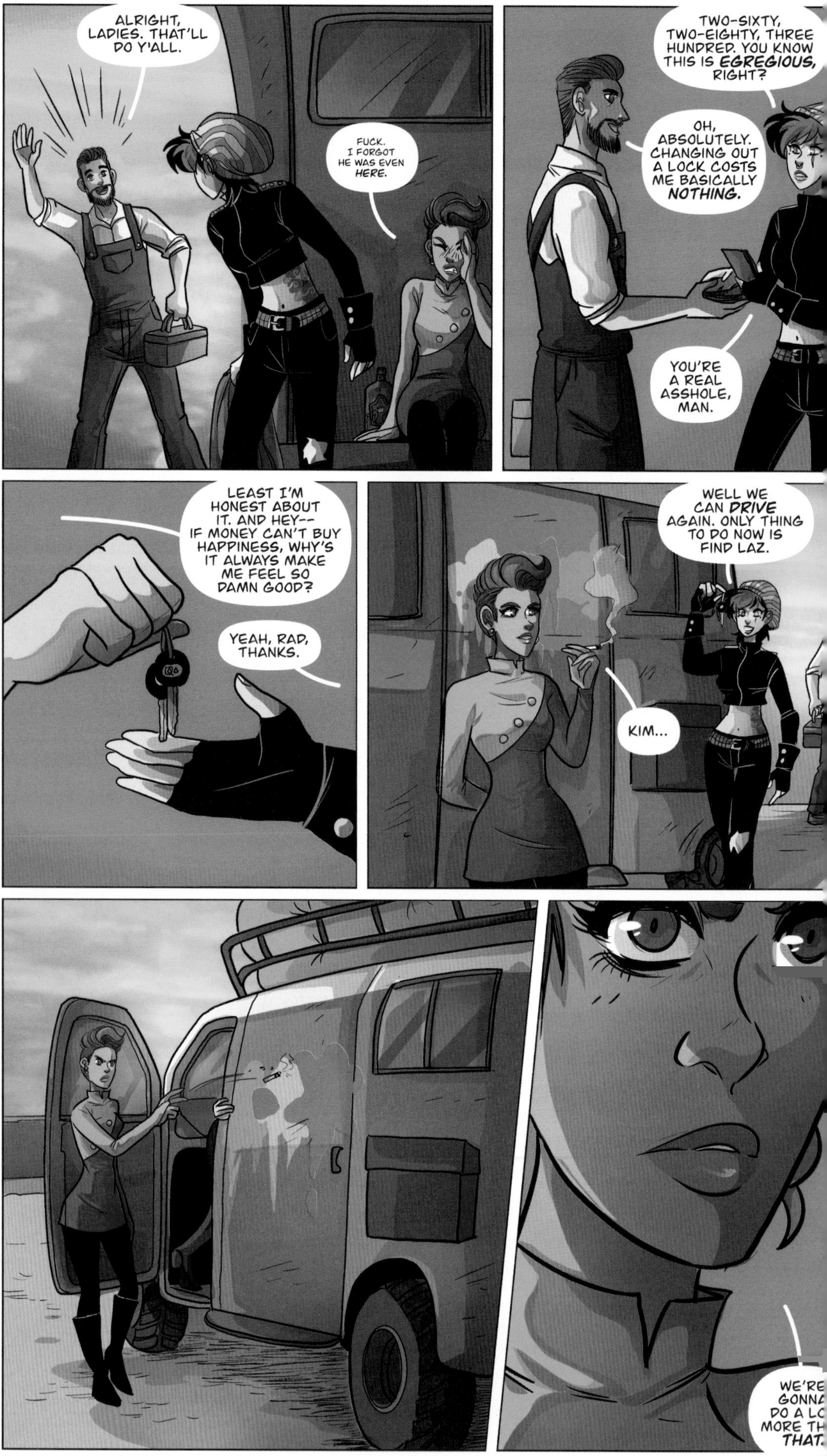
ALRIGHT, LADIES. THAT'LL DO Y'ALL.
FUCK. I FORGOT HE WAS EVEN HERE.
TWO-SIXTY, TWO-EIGHTY, THREE HUNDRED. YOU KNOW THIS IS EGREGIOUS, RIGHT?
OH, ABSOLUTELY. CHANGING OUT A LOCK COSTS ME BASICALLY NOTHING.
YOU'RE A REAL ASSHOLE, MAN.
LEAST I'M HONEST ABOUT IT. AND HEY-- IF MONEY CAN'T BUY HAPPINESS, WHY'S IT ALWAYS MAKE ME FEEL SO DAMN GOOD?
YEAH, RAD, THANKS.
WELL WE CAN DRIVE AGAIN. ONLY THING TO DO NOW IS FIND LAZ.
KIM...
WE'RE GONNA DO A LO MORE TH THAT.

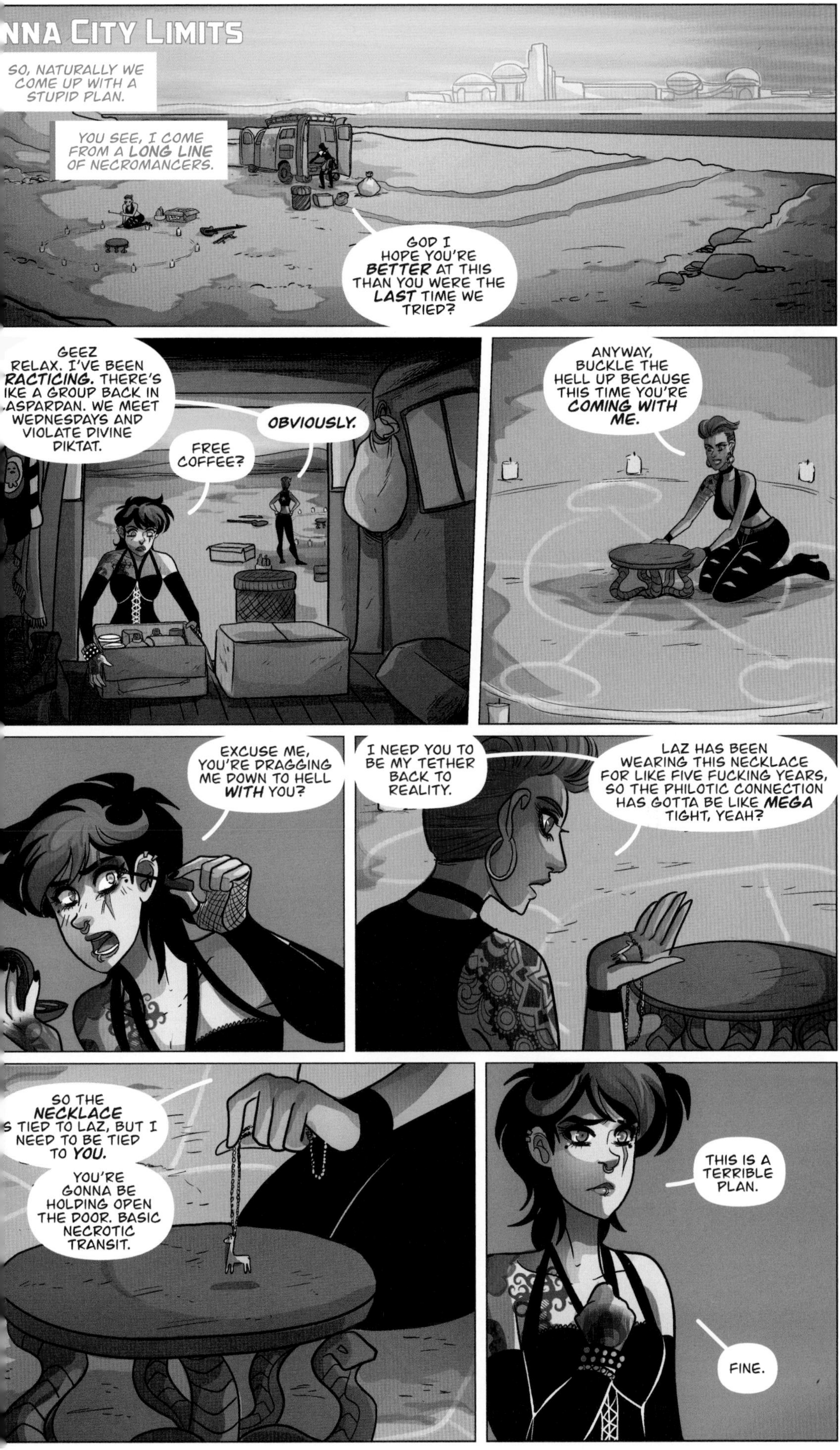

NNA CITY LIMITS
SO, NATURALLY WE COME UP WITH A STUPID PLAN.
YOU SEE, I COME FROM A LONG LINE OF NECROMANCERS.
GOD I HOPE YOU'RE BETTER AT THIS THAN YOU WERE THE LAST TIME WE TRIED?
GEEZ RELAX. I'VE BEEN RACTICING. THERE'S IKE A GROUP BACK IN ASPARDAN. WE MEET WEDNESDAYS AND VIOLATE DIVINE DIKTAT.
FREE COFFEE?
OBVIOUSLY.
ANYWAY, BUCKLE THE HELL UP BECAUSE THIS TIME YOU'RE COMING WITH ME.
EXCUSE ME, YOU'RE DRAGGING ME DOWN TO HELL WITH YOU?
I NEED YOU TO BE MY TETHER BACK TO REALITY.
LAZ HAS BEEN WEARING THIS NECKLACE FOR LIKE FIVE FUCKING YEARS, SO THE PHILOTIC CONNECTION HAS GOTTA BE LIKE MEGA TIGHT, YEAH?
SO THE NECKLACE S TIED TO LAZ, BUT I NEED TO BE TIED TO YOU.
YOU'RE GONNA BE HOLDING OPEN THE DOOR. BASIC NECROTIC TRANSIT.
THIS IS A TERRIBLE PLAN.
FINE.

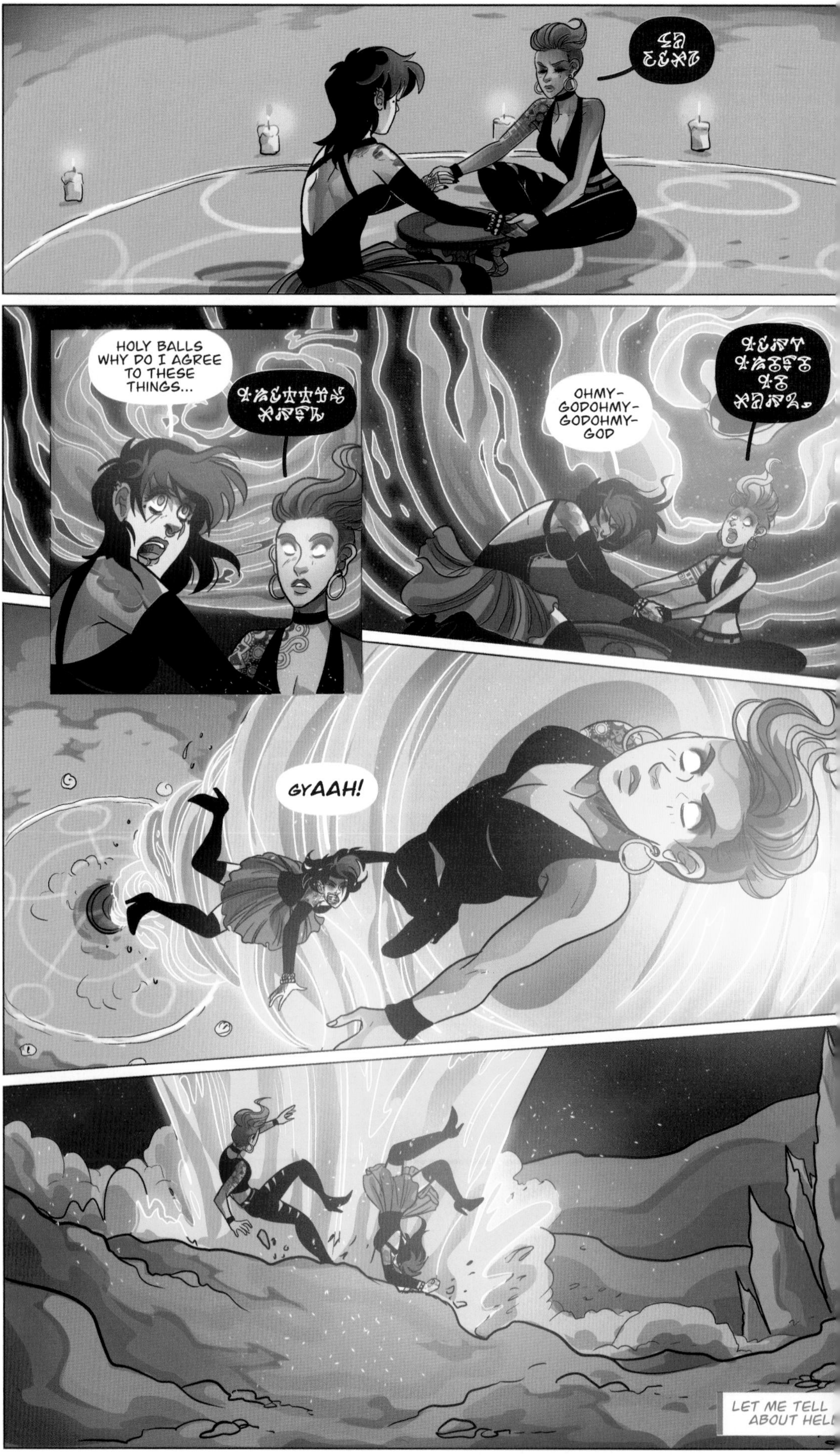
HOLY BALLS WHY DO I AGREE TO THESE THINGS...
OHMY-GODOHMY-GODOHMY-GOD
GYAAH!
LET ME TELL
ABOUT HEL

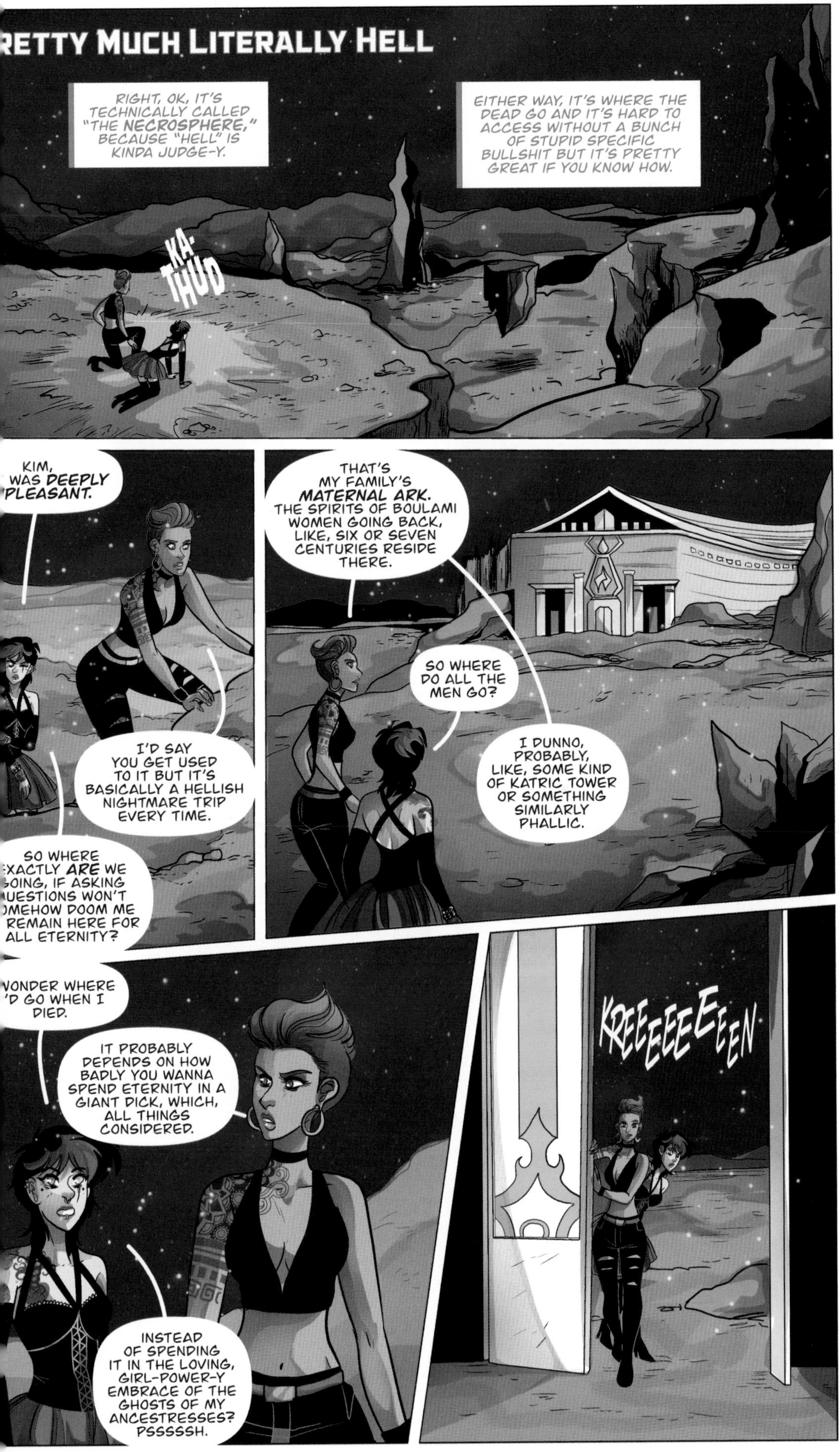
RETTY MUCH LITERALLY HELL
RIGHT, OK, IT'S TECHNICALLY CALLED "THE NECROSPHERE," BECAUSE "HELL" IS KINDA JUDGE-Y.
EITHER WAY, IT'S WHERE THE DEAD GO AND IT'S HARD TO ACCESS WITHOUT A BUNCH OF STUPID SPECIFIC BULLSHIT BUT IT'S PRETTY GREAT IF YOU KNOW HOW.
KA-THUD
KIM, WAS DEEPLY PLEASANT.
I'D SAY YOU GET USED TO IT BUT IT'S BASICALLY A HELLISH NIGHTMARE TRIP EVERY TIME.
SO WHERE EXACTLY ARE WE GOING, IF ASKING UESTIONS WON'T OMEHOW DOOM ME REMAIN HERE FOR ALL ETERNITY?
THAT'S MY FAMILY'S MATERNAL ARK. THE SPIRITS OF BOULAMI WOMEN GOING BACK, LIKE, SIX OR SEVEN CENTURIES RESIDE THERE.
SO WHERE DO ALL THE MEN GO?
I DUNNO, PROBABLY, LIKE, SOME KIND OF KATRIC TOWER OR SOMETHING SIMILARLY PHALLIC.
WONDER WHERE 'D GO WHEN I DIED.
IT PROBABLY DEPENDS ON HOW BADLY YOU WANNA SPEND ETERNITY IN A GIANT DICK, WHICH, ALL THINGS CONSIDERED.
INSTEAD OF SPENDING IT IN THE LOVING, GIRL-POWER-Y EMBRACE OF THE GHOSTS OF MY ANCESTRESSES? PSSSSSH.
KREEEEEEEEN

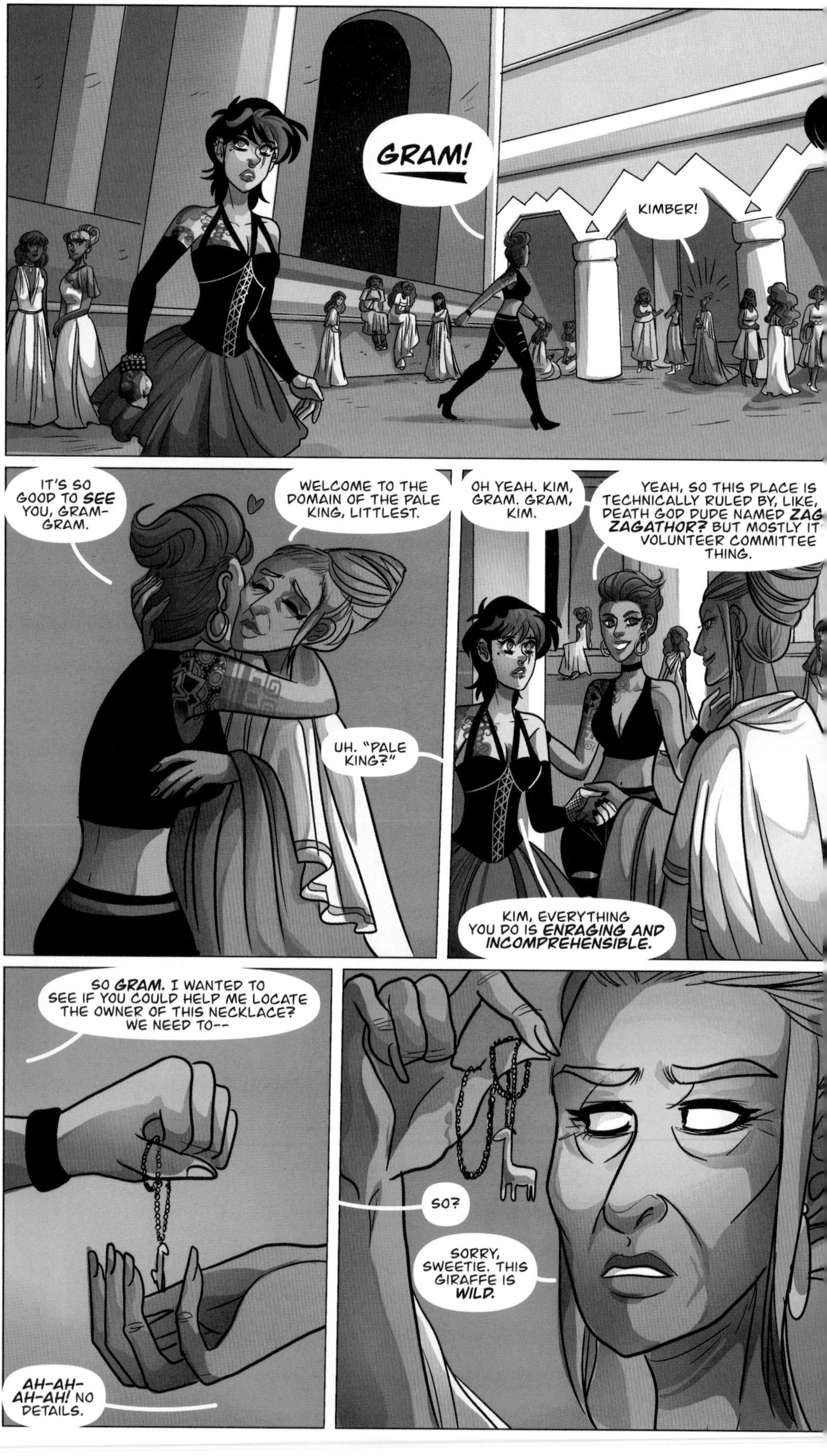
GRAM!
KIMBER!
IT'S SO GOOD TO SEE YOU, GRAM-GRAM.
WELCOME TO THE DOMAIN OF THE PALE KING, LITTLEST.
UH. "PALE KING?"
OH YEAH. KIM, GRAM. GRAM, KIM.
YEAH, SO THIS PLACE IS TECHNICALLY RULED BY, LIKE, DEATH GOD DUDE NAMED ZAG ZAGATHOR? BUT MOSTLY IT VOLUNTEER COMMITTEE THING.
KIM, EVERYTHING YOU DO IS ENRAGING AND INCOMPREHENSIBLE.
SO GRAM. I WANTED TO SEE IF YOU COULD HELP ME LOCATE THE OWNER OF THIS NECKLACE? WE NEED TO--
AH-AH-AH-AH! NO DETAILS.
SO?
SORRY, SWEETIE. THIS GIRAFFE IS WILD.

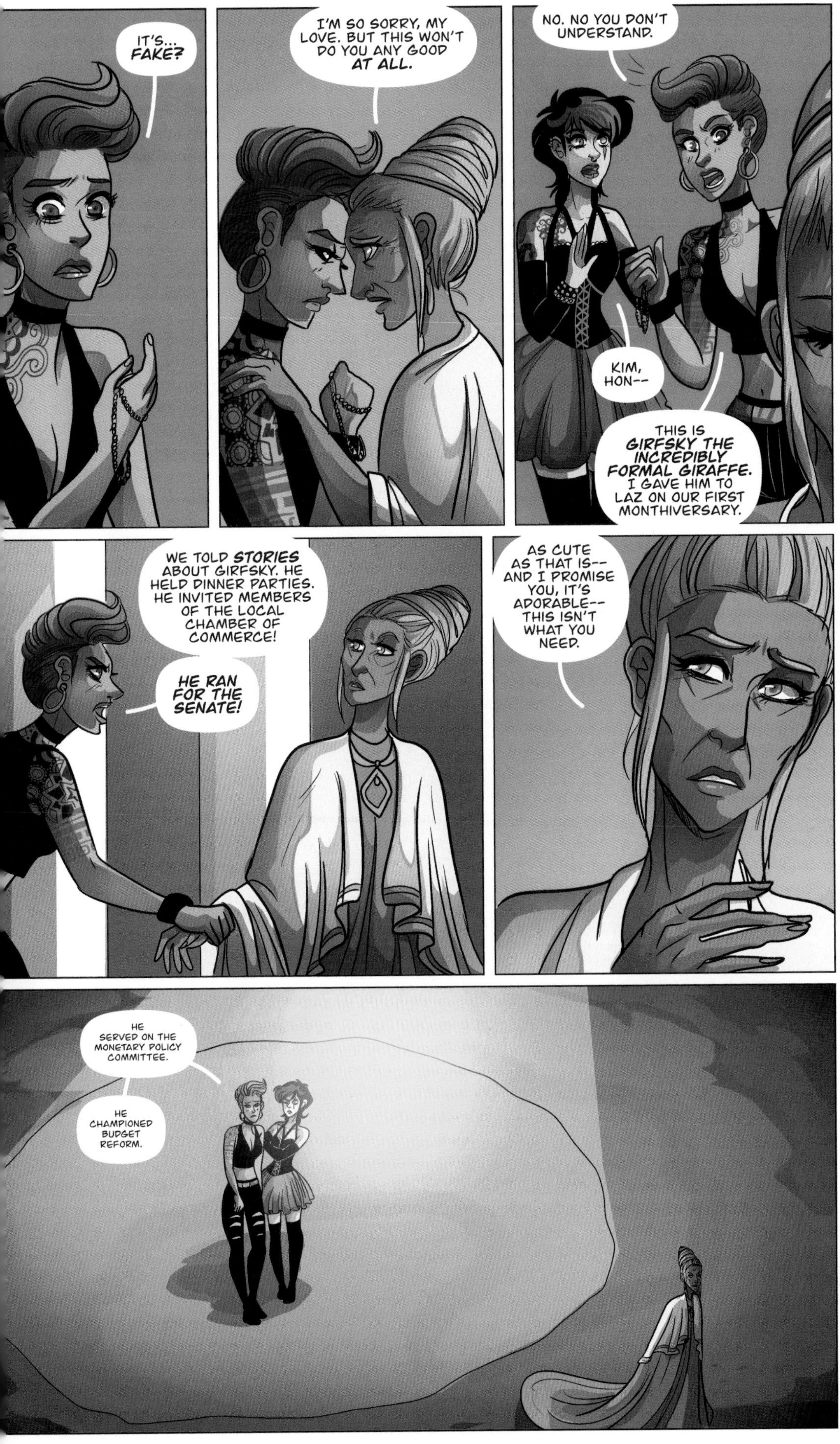
IT'S... FAKE?
I'M SO SORRY, MY LOVE. BUT THIS WON'T DO YOU ANY GOOD AT ALL.
NO. NO YOU DON'T UNDERSTAND.
KIM, HON--
THIS IS GIRFSKY THE INCREDIBLY FORMAL GIRAFFE. I GAVE HIM TO LAZ ON OUR FIRST MONTHIVERSARY.
WE TOLD STORIES ABOUT GIRFSKY. HE HELD DINNER PARTIES. HE INVITED MEMBERS OF THE LOCAL CHAMBER OF COMMERCE!
HE RAN FOR THE SENATE!
AS CUTE AS THAT IS-- AND I PROMISE YOU, IT'S ADORABLE-- THIS ISN'T WHAT YOU NEED.
HE SERVED ON THE MONETARY POLICY COMMITTEE.
HE CHAMPIONED BUDGET REFORM.

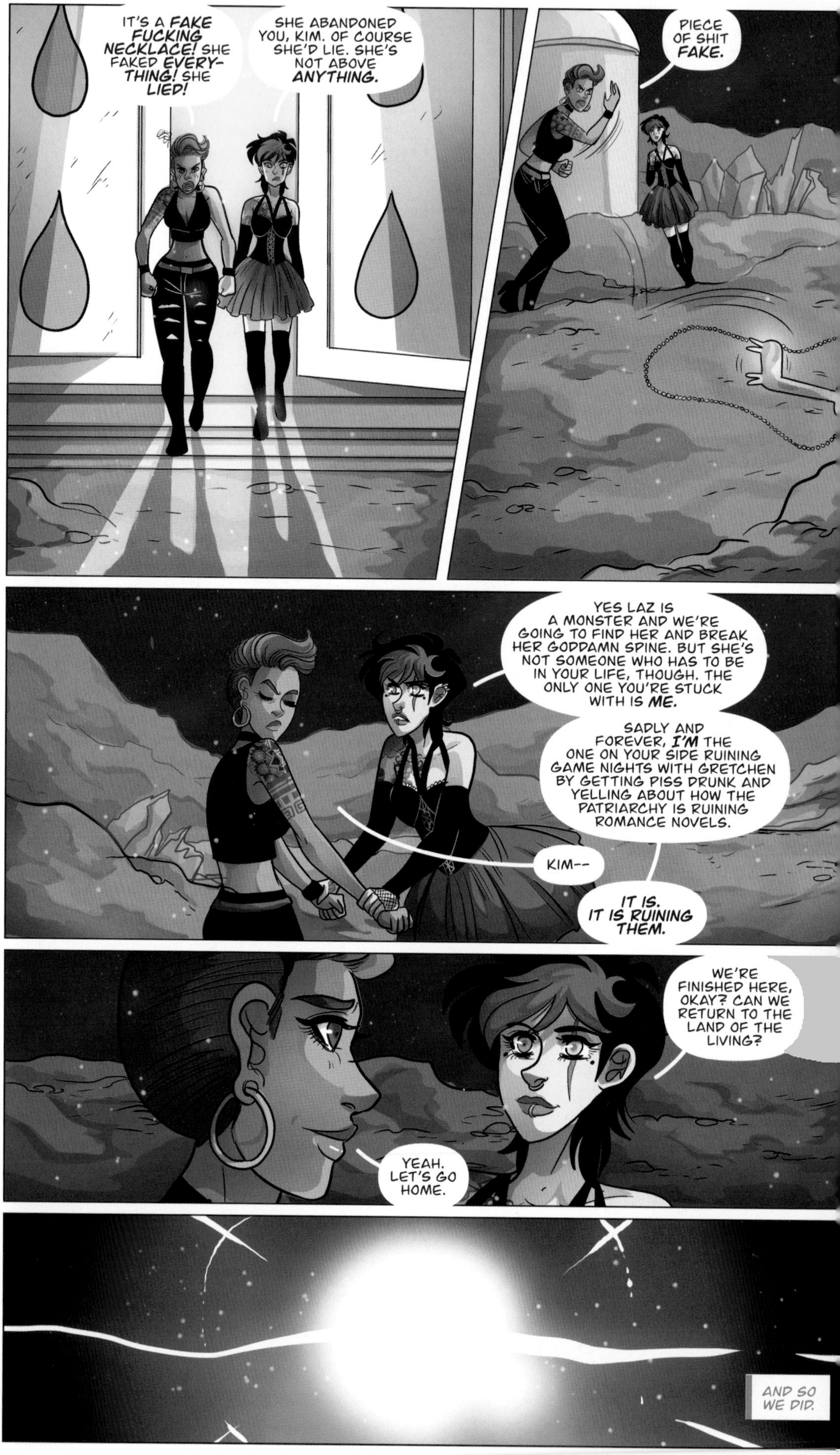
IT'S A FAKE FUCKING NECKLACE! SHE FAKED EVERY-THING! SHE LIED!
SHE ABANDONED YOU, KIM. OF COURSE SHE'D LIE. SHE'S NOT ABOVE ANYTHING.
PIECE OF SHIT FAKE.
YES LAZ IS A MONSTER AND WE'RE GOING TO FIND HER AND BREAK HER GODDAMN SPINE. BUT SHE'S NOT SOMEONE WHO HAS TO BE IN YOUR LIFE, THOUGH. THE ONLY ONE YOU'RE STUCK WITH IS ME.
SADLY AND FOREVER, I'M THE ONE ON YOUR SIDE RUINING GAME NIGHTS WITH GRETCHEN BY GETTING PISS DRUNK AND YELLING ABOUT HOW THE PATRIARCHY IS RUINING ROMANCE NOVELS.
KIM--
IT IS. IT IS RUINING THEM.
WE'RE FINISHED HERE, OKAY? CAN WE RETURN TO THE LAND OF THE LIVING?
YEAH. LET'S GO HOME.
AND SO WE DID.

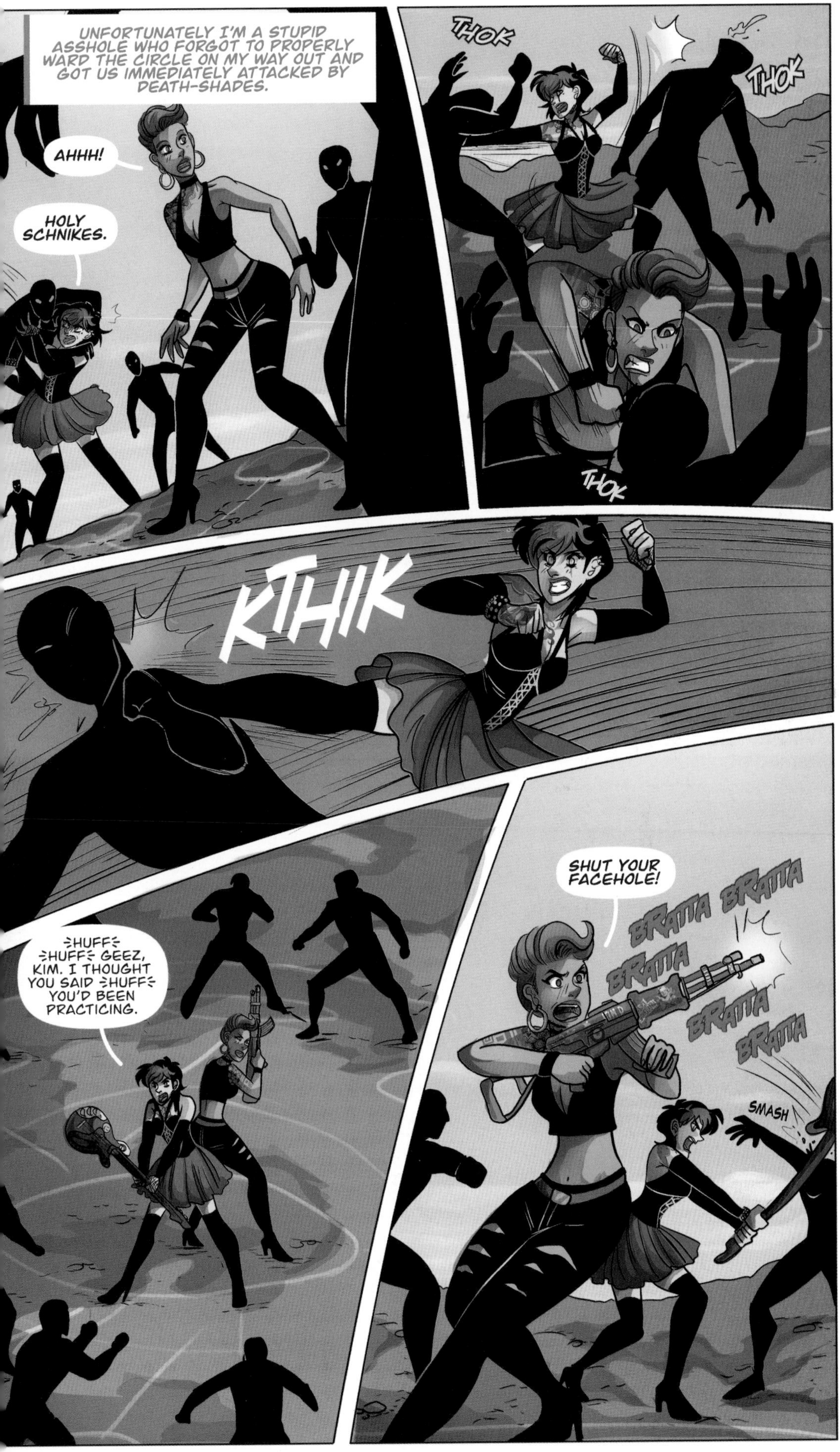
UNFORTUNATELY I'M A STUPID ASSHOLE WHO FORGOT TO PROPERLY WARD THE CIRCLE ON MY WAY OUT AND GOT US IMMEDIATELY ATTACKED BY DEATH-SHADES.
AHHH!
HOLY SCHNIKES.
THOK
THOK
THOK
KTHIK
SHUT YOUR FACEHOLE!
BRATTA BRATTA
BRATTA
BRATTA
BRATTA
SMASH
HUFF HUFF GEEZ, KIM. I THOUGHT YOU SAID HUFF YOU'D BEEN PRACTICING.

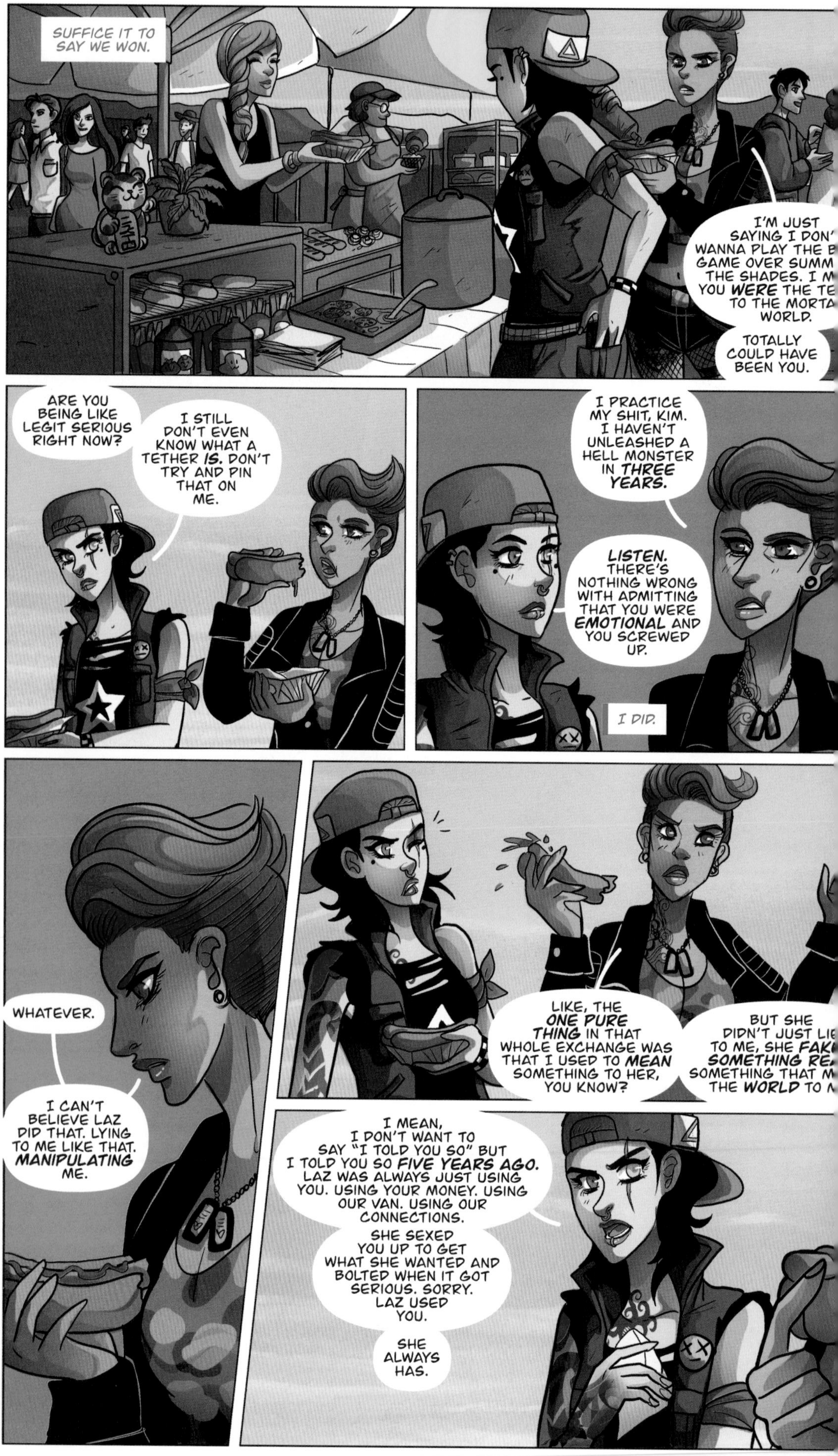

SUFFICE IT TO SAY WE WON.
I'M JUST SAYING I DON' WANNA PLAY THE B GAME OVER SUMM THE SHADES. I M YOU WERE THE TE TO THE MORTA WORLD.
TOTALLY COULD HAVE BEEN YOU.
ARE YOU BEING LIKE LEGIT SERIOUS RIGHT NOW?
I STILL DON'T EVEN KNOW WHAT A TETHER IS. DON'T TRY AND PIN THAT ON ME.
I PRACTICE MY SHIT, KIM. I HAVEN'T UNLEASHED A HELL MONSTER IN THREE YEARS.
LISTEN. THERE'S NOTHING WRONG WITH ADMITTING THAT YOU WERE EMOTIONAL AND YOU SCREWED UP.
I DID.
WHATEVER.
I CAN'T BELIEVE LAZ DID THAT. LYING TO ME LIKE THAT. MANIPULATING ME.
LIKE, THE ONE PURE THING IN THAT WHOLE EXCHANGE WAS THAT I USED TO MEAN SOMETHING TO HER, YOU KNOW?
BUT SHE DIDN'T JUST LI TO ME, SHE FAK SOMETHING RE SOMETHING THAT M THE WORLD TO
I MEAN, I DON'T WANT TO SAY "I TOLD YOU SO" BUT I TOLD YOU SO FIVE YEARS AGO. LAZ WAS ALWAYS JUST USING YOU. USING YOUR MONEY. USING OUR VAN. USING OUR CONNECTIONS.
SHE SEXED YOU UP TO GET WHAT SHE WANTED AND BOLTED WHEN IT GOT SERIOUS. SORRY. LAZ USED YOU.
SHE ALWAYS HAS.

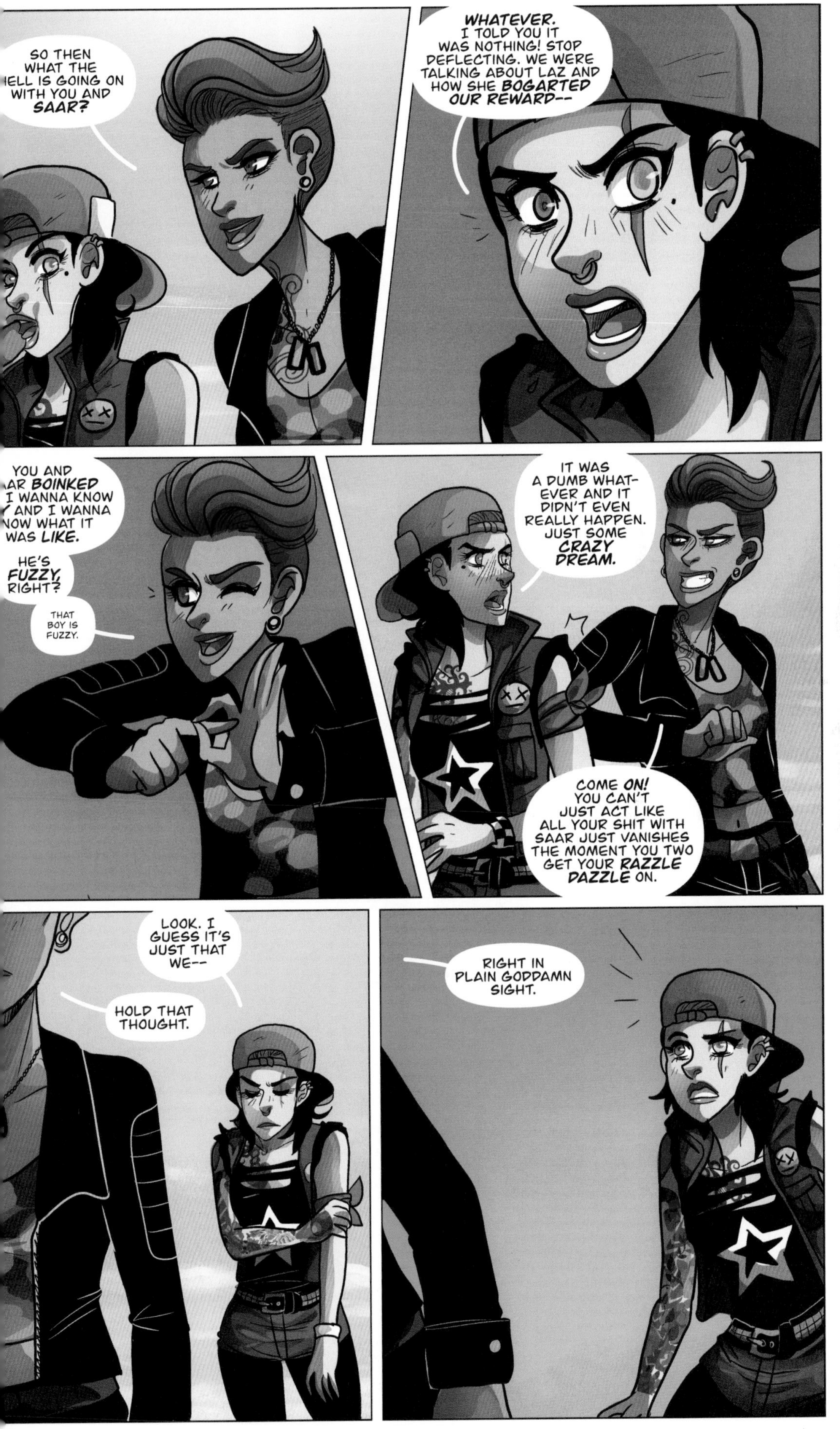

SO THEN WHAT THE HELL IS GOING ON WITH YOU AND SAAR?
WHATEVER. I TOLD YOU IT WAS NOTHING! STOP DEFLECTING. WE WERE TALKING ABOUT LAZ AND HOW SHE BOGARTED OUR REWARD--
YOU AND AR BOINKED I WANNA KNOW AND I WANNA NOW WHAT IT WAS LIKE.
HE'S FUZZY, RIGHT?
THAT BOY IS FUZZY.
IT WAS A DUMB WHAT-EVER AND IT DIDN'T EVEN REALLY HAPPEN. JUST SOME CRAZY DREAM.
COME ON! YOU CAN'T JUST ACT LIKE ALL YOUR SHIT WITH SAAR JUST VANISHES THE MOMENT YOU TWO GET YOUR RAZZLE DAZZLE ON.
LOOK. I GUESS IT'S JUST THAT WE--
HOLD THAT THOUGHT.
RIGHT IN PLAIN GODDAMN SIGHT.

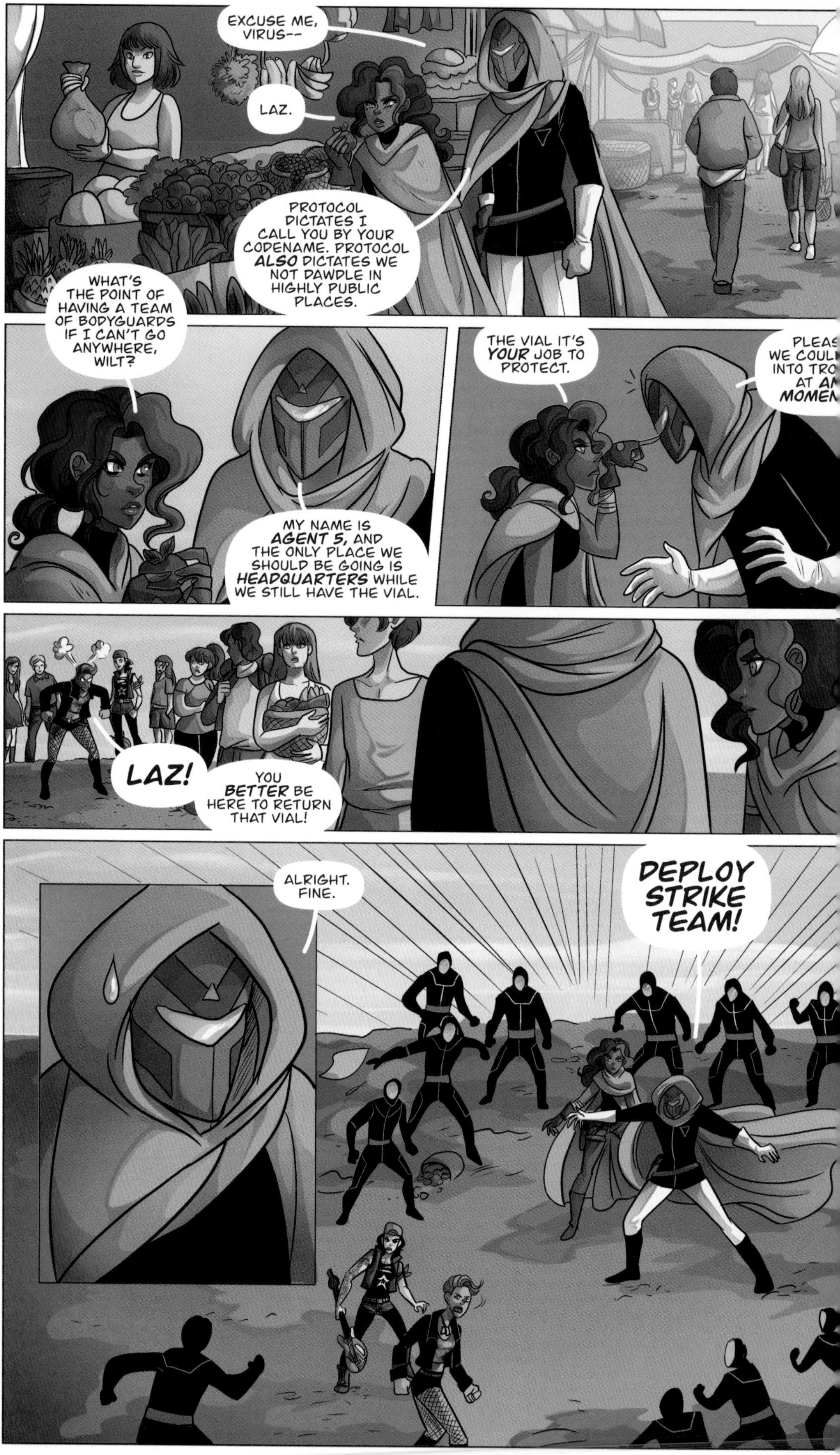

EXCUSE ME, VIRUS--
LAZ.
PROTOCOL DICTATES I CALL YOU BY YOUR CODENAME. PROTOCOL **ALSO** DICTATES WE NOT DAWDLE IN HIGHLY PUBLIC PLACES.
WHAT'S THE POINT OF HAVING A TEAM OF BODYGUARDS IF I CAN'T GO ANYWHERE, WILT?
MY NAME IS **AGENT 5,** AND THE ONLY PLACE WE SHOULD BE GOING IS **HEADQUARTERS** WHILE WE STILL HAVE THE VIAL.
THE VIAL IT'S **YOUR** JOB TO PROTECT.
PLEAS WE COUL INTO TRO AT **AN** **MOMEN**
**LAZ!**
YOU **BETTER** BE HERE TO RETURN THAT VIAL!
ALRIGHT. FINE.
**DEPLOY STRIKE TEAM!**

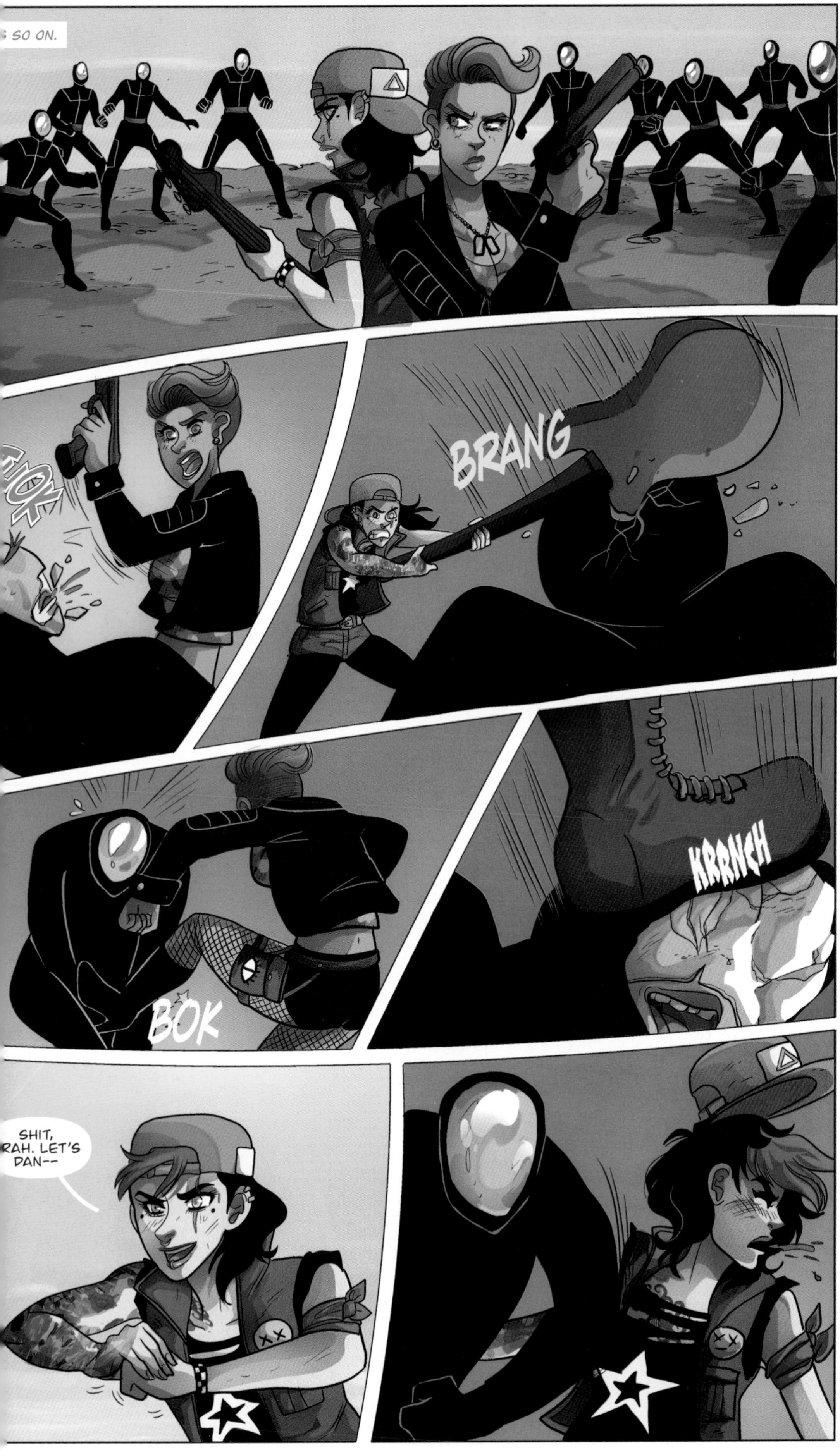
SO ON.
BRANG
BOK
KRRNCH
SHIT,
RAH. LET'S
DAN--

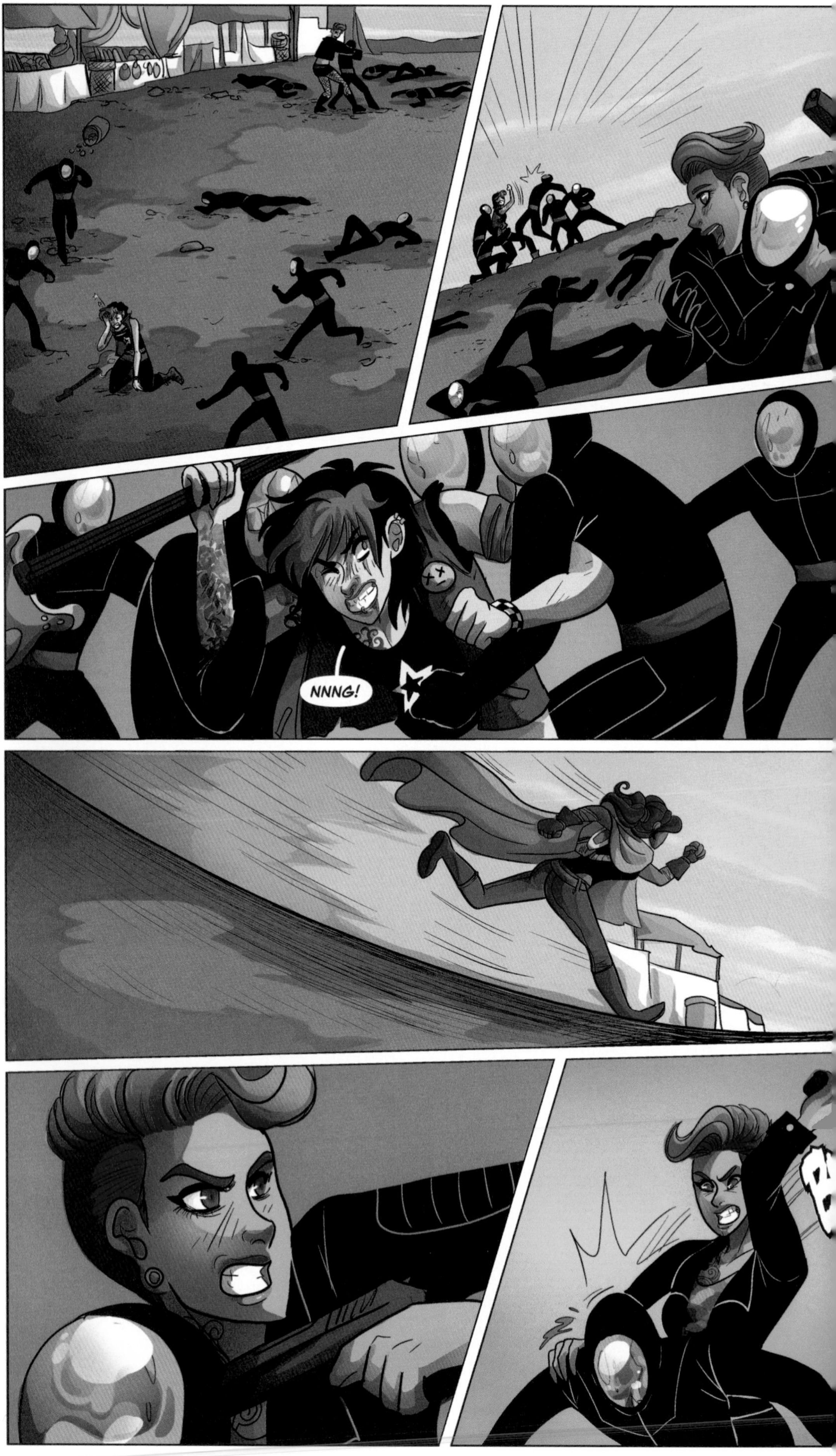
NNNG!

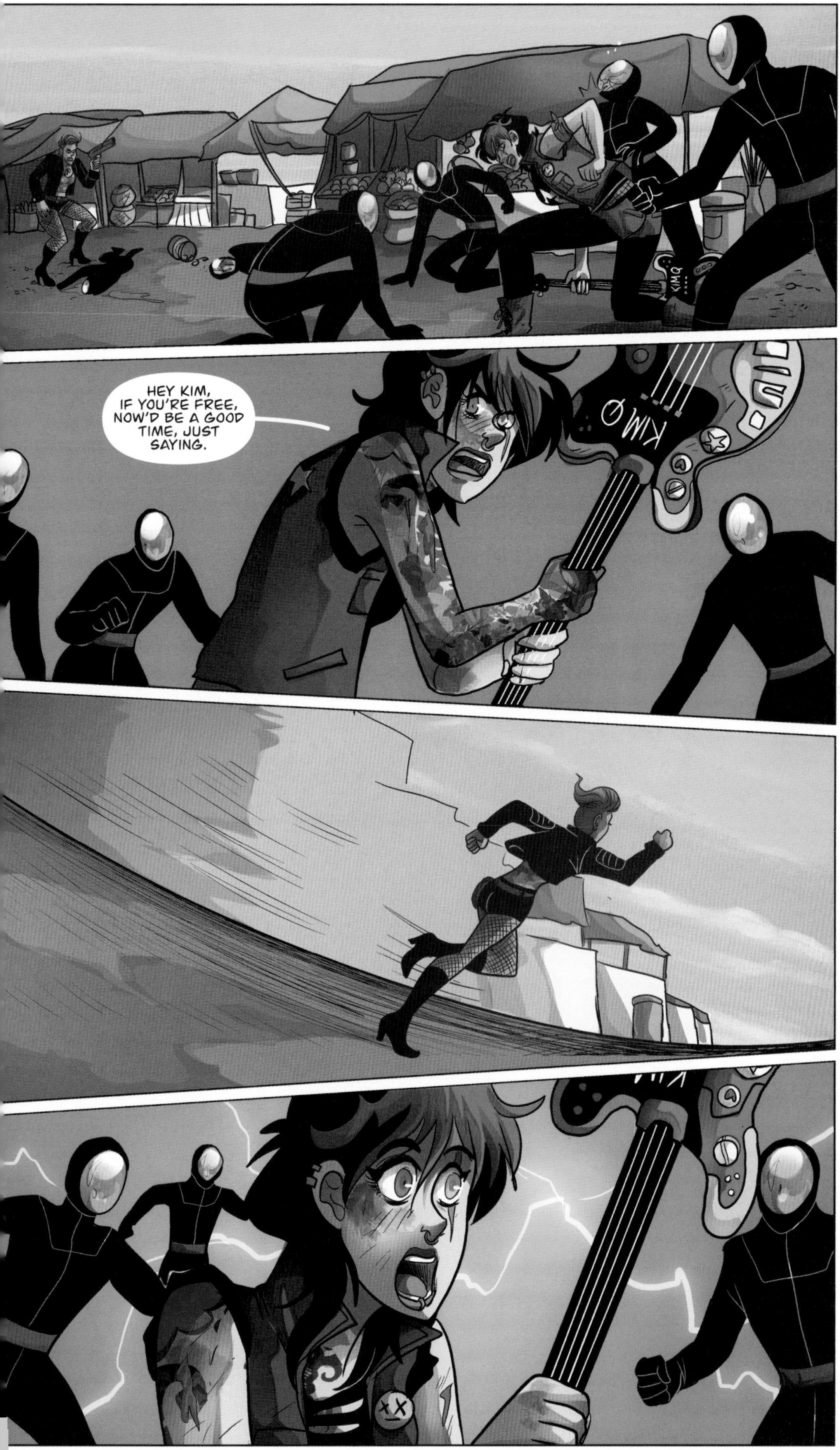
HEY KIM, IF YOU'RE FREE, NOW'D BE A GOOD TIME, JUST SAYING.

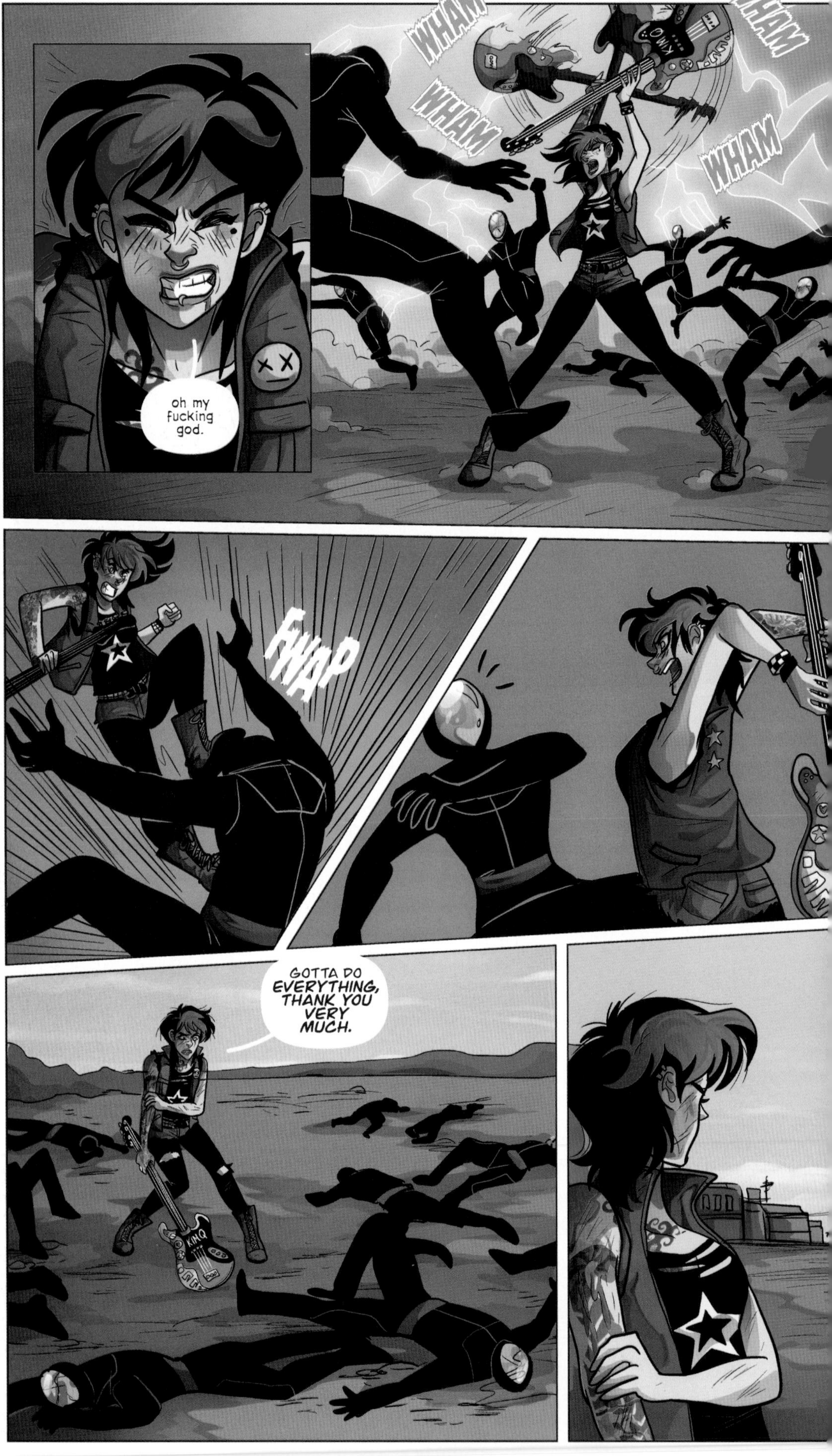
oh my fucking god.
WHAM
WHAM
WHAM
WHAM
FWAP
GOTTA DO EVERYTHING, THANK YOU VERY MUCH.

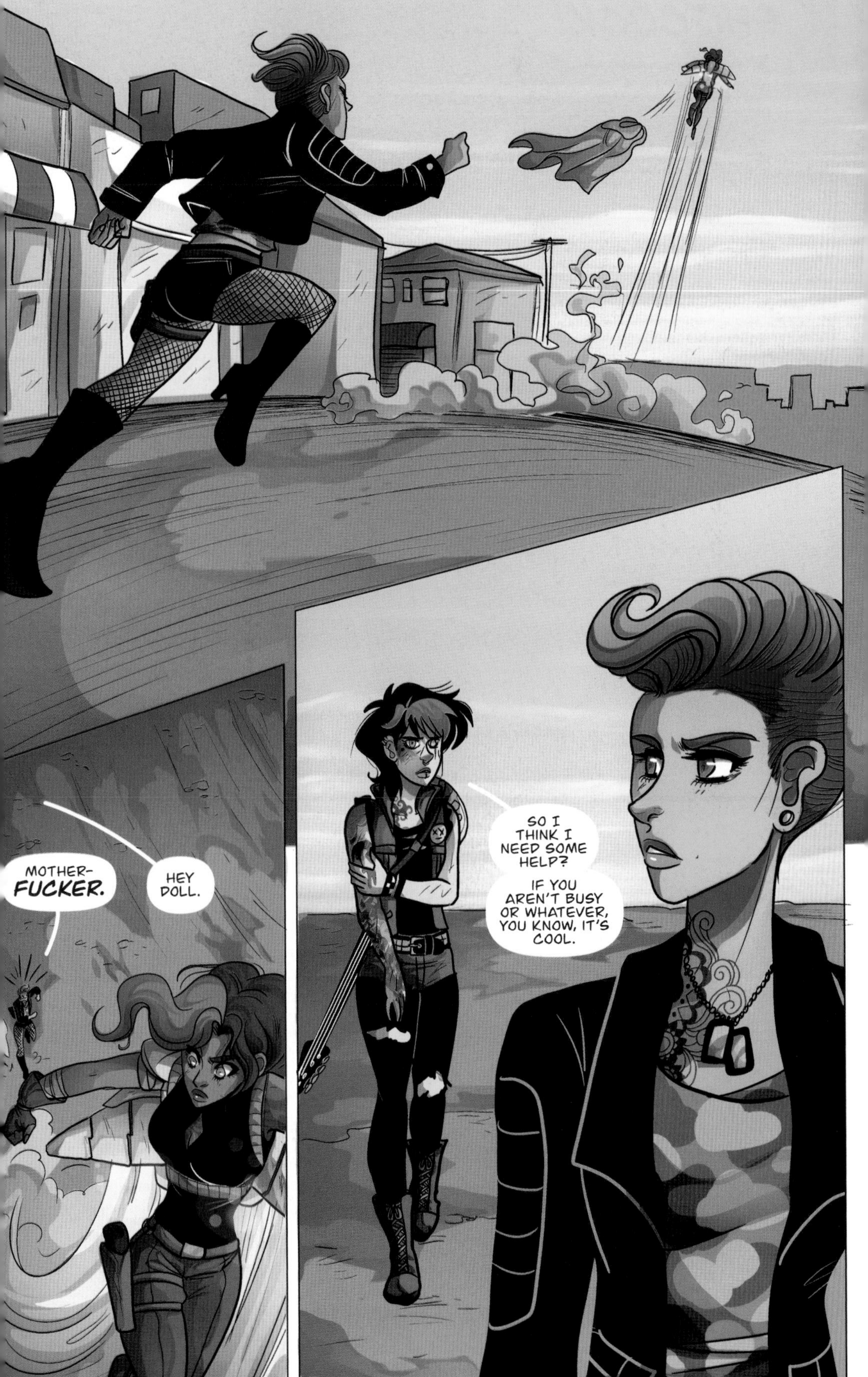
MOTHER-
FUCKER.
HEY
DOLL.
SO I
THINK I
NEED SOME
HELP?
IF YOU
AREN'T BUSY
OR WHATEVER,
YOU KNOW, IT'S
COOL.

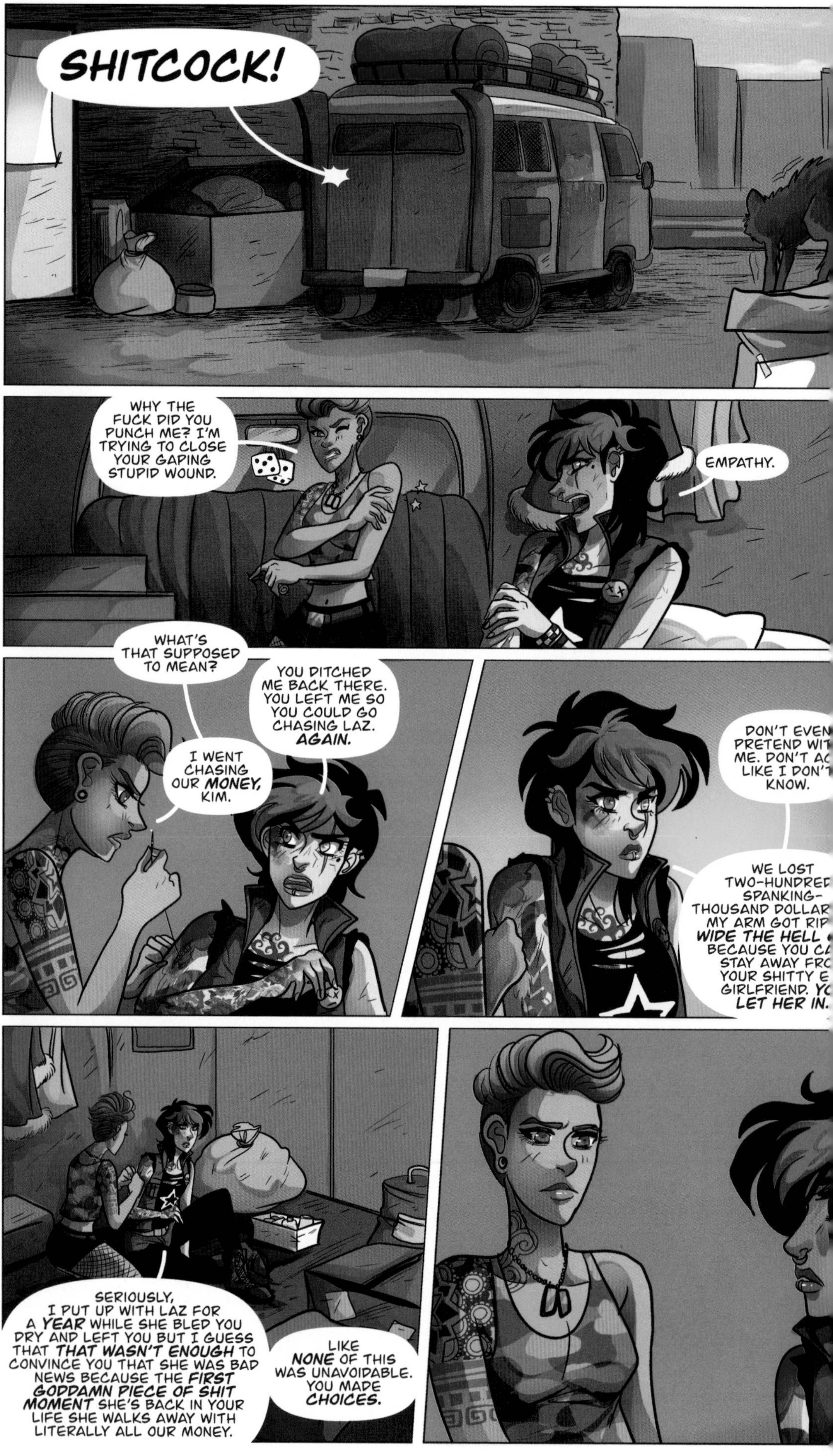
SHITCOCK!
WHY THE FUCK DID YOU PUNCH ME? I'M TRYING TO CLOSE YOUR GAPING STUPID WOUND.
EMPATHY.
WHAT'S THAT SUPPOSED TO MEAN?
YOU DITCHED ME BACK THERE. YOU LEFT ME SO YOU COULD GO CHASING LAZ. **AGAIN.**
I WENT CHASING OUR **MONEY,** KIM.
DON'T EVEN PRETEND WIT ME. DON'T AC LIKE I DON'T KNOW.
WE LOST TWO-HUNDRED SPANKING-THOUSAND DOLLAR MY ARM GOT RIP **WIDE THE HELL** BECAUSE YOU CA STAY AWAY FRO YOUR SHITTY E GIRLFRIEND. **YO LET HER IN.**
SERIOUSLY, I PUT UP WITH LAZ FOR A **YEAR** WHILE SHE BLED YOU DRY AND LEFT YOU BUT I GUESS THAT **THAT WASN'T ENOUGH** TO CONVINCE YOU THAT SHE WAS BAD NEWS BECAUSE THE **FIRST GODDAMN PIECE OF SHIT MOMENT** SHE'S BACK IN YOUR LIFE SHE WALKS AWAY WITH LITERALLY ALL OUR MONEY.
LIKE **NONE** OF THIS WAS UNAVOIDABLE. YOU MADE **CHOICES.**

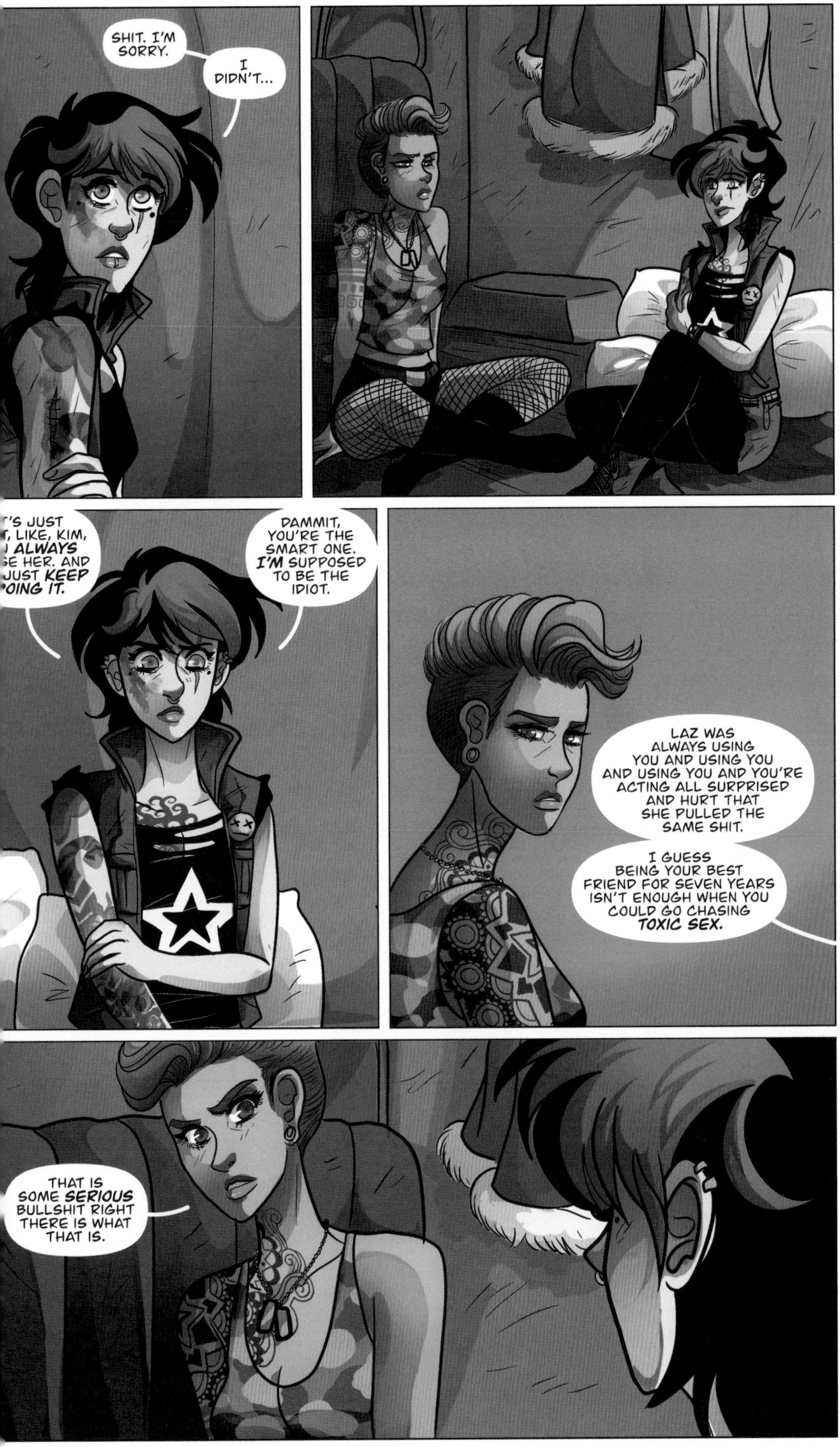
SHIT. I'M SORRY.
I DIDN'T...
'S JUST , LIKE, KIM, ALWAYS E HER. AND JUST KEEP OING IT.
DAMMIT, YOU'RE THE SMART ONE. I'M SUPPOSED TO BE THE IDIOT.
LAZ WAS ALWAYS USING YOU AND USING YOU AND USING YOU AND YOU'RE ACTING ALL SURPRISED AND HURT THAT SHE PULLED THE SAME SHIT.
I GUESS BEING YOUR BEST FRIEND FOR SEVEN YEARS ISN'T ENOUGH WHEN YOU COULD GO CHASING TOXIC SEX.
THAT IS SOME SERIOUS BULLSHIT RIGHT THERE IS WHAT THAT IS.

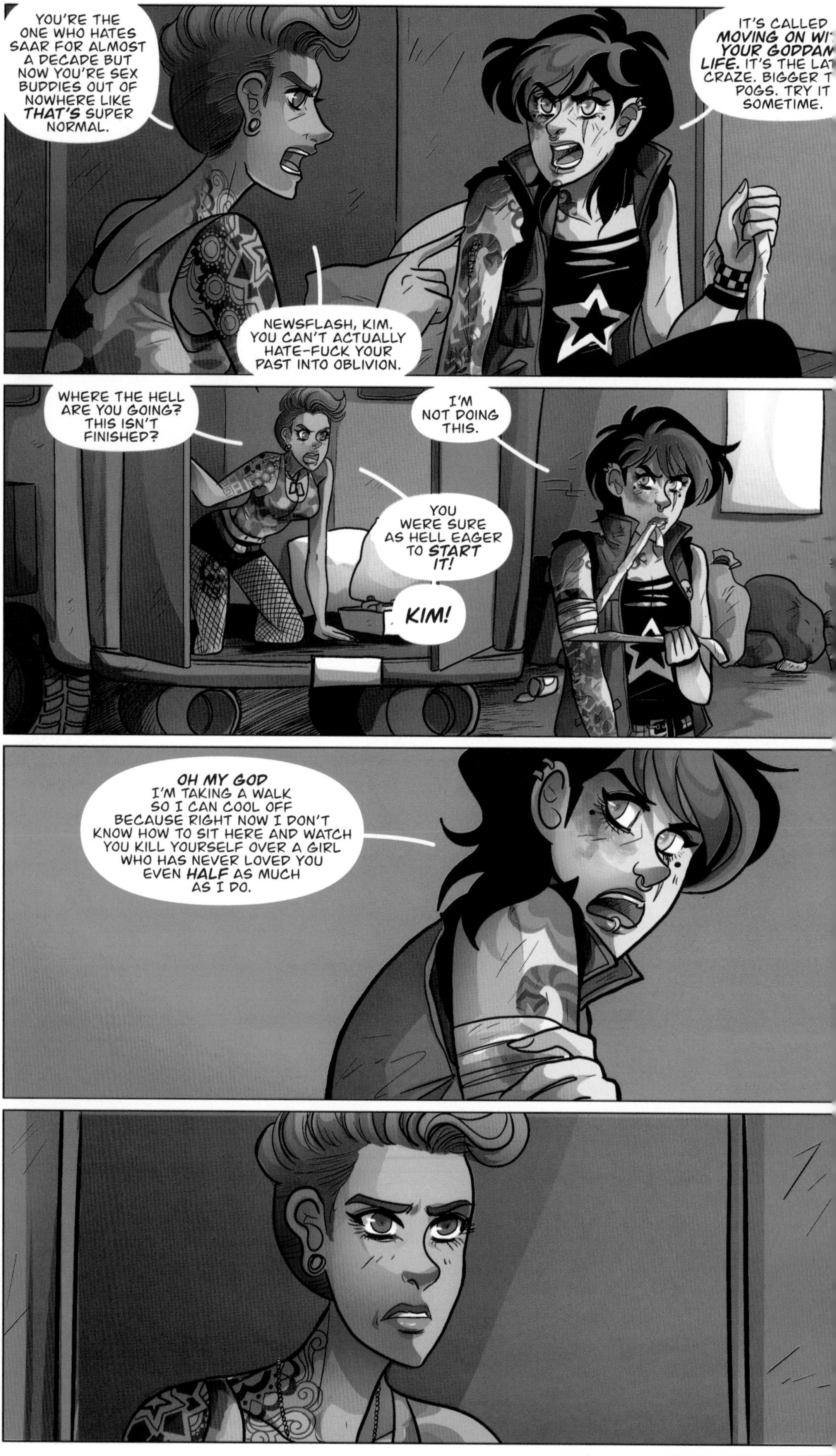
YOU'RE THE ONE WHO HATES SAAR FOR ALMOST A DECADE BUT NOW YOU'RE SEX BUDDIES OUT OF NOWHERE LIKE **THAT'S** SUPER NORMAL.
IT'S CALLED **MOVING ON WI** **YOUR GODDAM** **LIFE.** IT'S THE LA CRAZE. BIGGER T POGS. TRY IT SOMETIME.
NEWSFLASH, KIM. YOU CAN'T ACTUALLY HATE-FUCK YOUR PAST INTO OBLIVION.
WHERE THE HELL ARE YOU GOING? THIS ISN'T FINISHED?
I'M NOT DOING THIS.
YOU WERE SURE AS HELL EAGER TO **START** IT!
**KIM!**
**OH MY GOD** I'M TAKING A WALK SO I CAN COOL OFF BECAUSE RIGHT NOW I DON'T KNOW HOW TO SIT HERE AND WATCH YOU KILL YOURSELF OVER A GIRL WHO HAS NEVER LOVED YOU EVEN **HALF** AS MUCH AS I DO.

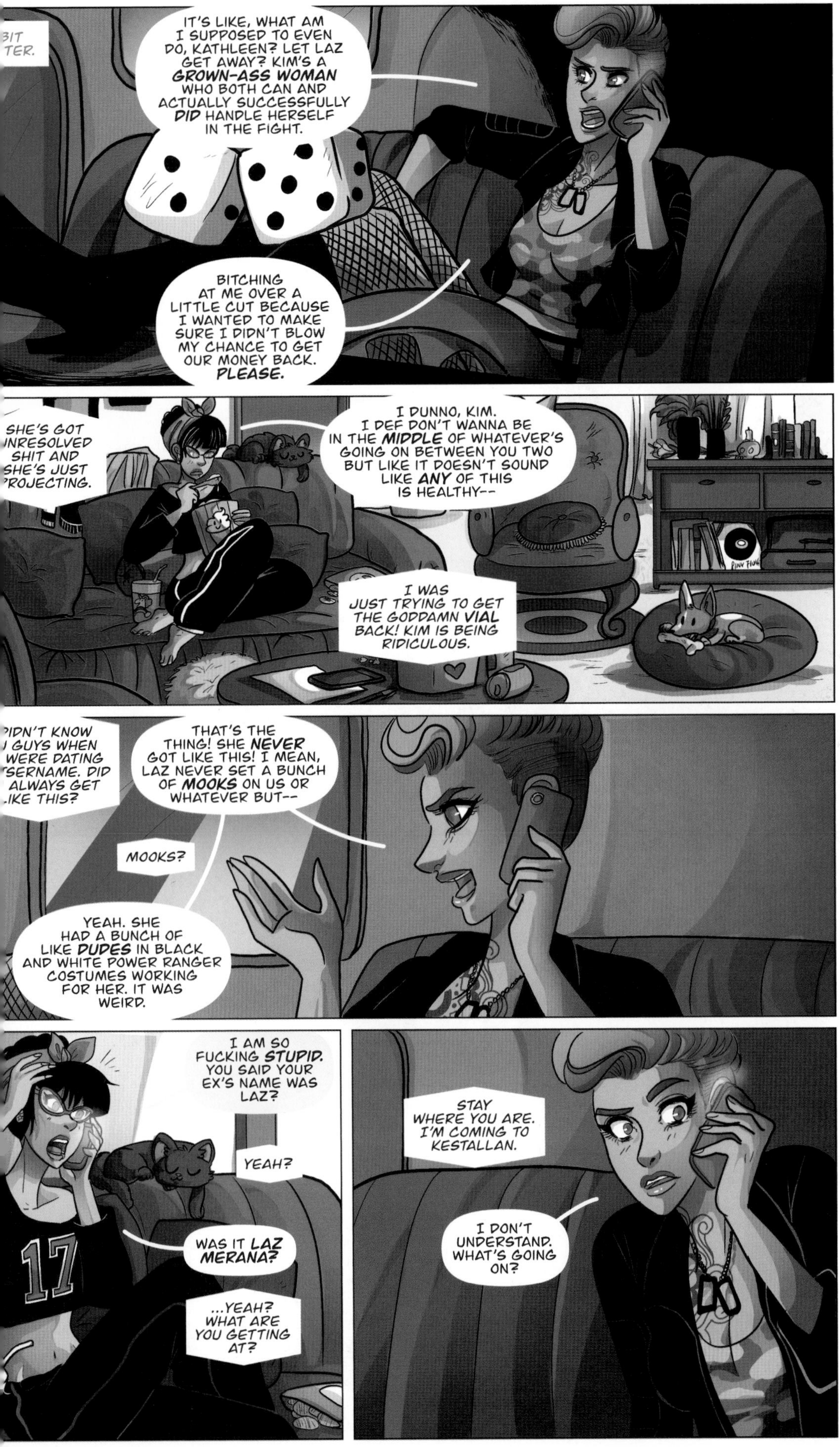
BIT
TER.
IT'S LIKE, WHAT AM I SUPPOSED TO EVEN DO, KATHLEEN? LET LAZ GET AWAY? KIM'S A GROWN-ASS WOMAN WHO BOTH CAN AND ACTUALLY SUCCESSFULLY DID HANDLE HERSELF IN THE FIGHT.
BITCHING AT ME OVER A LITTLE CUT BECAUSE I WANTED TO MAKE SURE I DIDN'T BLOW MY CHANCE TO GET OUR MONEY BACK. PLEASE.
SHE'S GOT UNRESOLVED SHIT AND SHE'S JUST PROJECTING.
I DUNNO, KIM. I DEF DON'T WANNA BE IN THE MIDDLE OF WHATEVER'S GOING ON BETWEEN YOU TWO BUT LIKE IT DOESN'T SOUND LIKE ANY OF THIS IS HEALTHY--
I WAS JUST TRYING TO GET THE GODDAMN VIAL BACK! KIM IS BEING RIDICULOUS.
DIDN'T KNOW GUYS WHEN WERE DATING SERNAME. DID ALWAYS GET LIKE THIS?
THAT'S THE THING! SHE NEVER GOT LIKE THIS! I MEAN, LAZ NEVER SET A BUNCH OF MOOKS ON US OR WHATEVER BUT--
MOOKS?
YEAH. SHE HAD A BUNCH OF LIKE DUDES IN BLACK AND WHITE POWER RANGER COSTUMES WORKING FOR HER. IT WAS WEIRD.
I AM SO FUCKING STUPID. YOU SAID YOUR EX'S NAME WAS LAZ?
YEAH?
WAS IT LAZ MERANA?
...YEAH? WHAT ARE YOU GETTING AT?
STAY WHERE YOU ARE. I'M COMING TO KESTALLAN.
I DON'T UNDERSTAND. WHAT'S GOING ON?

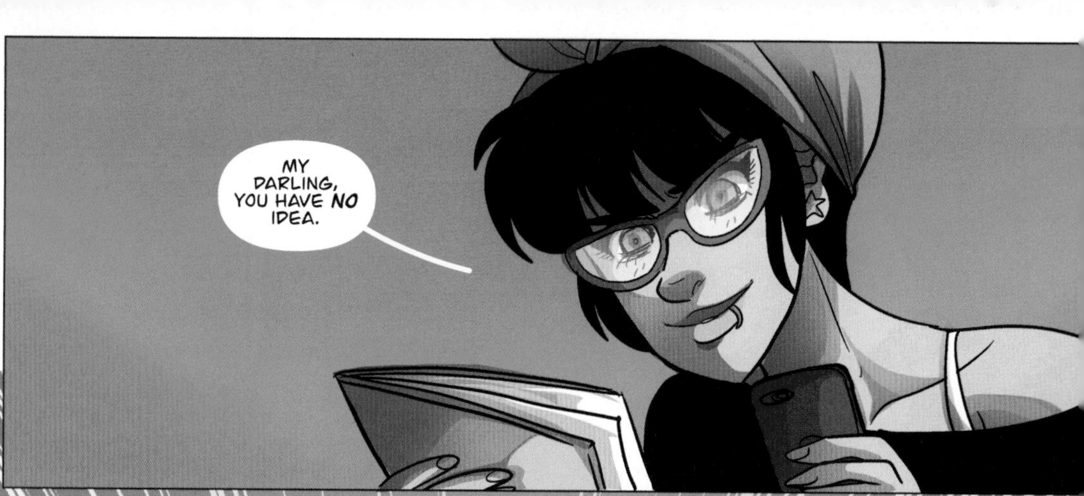
MY DARLING, YOU HAVE NO IDEA.

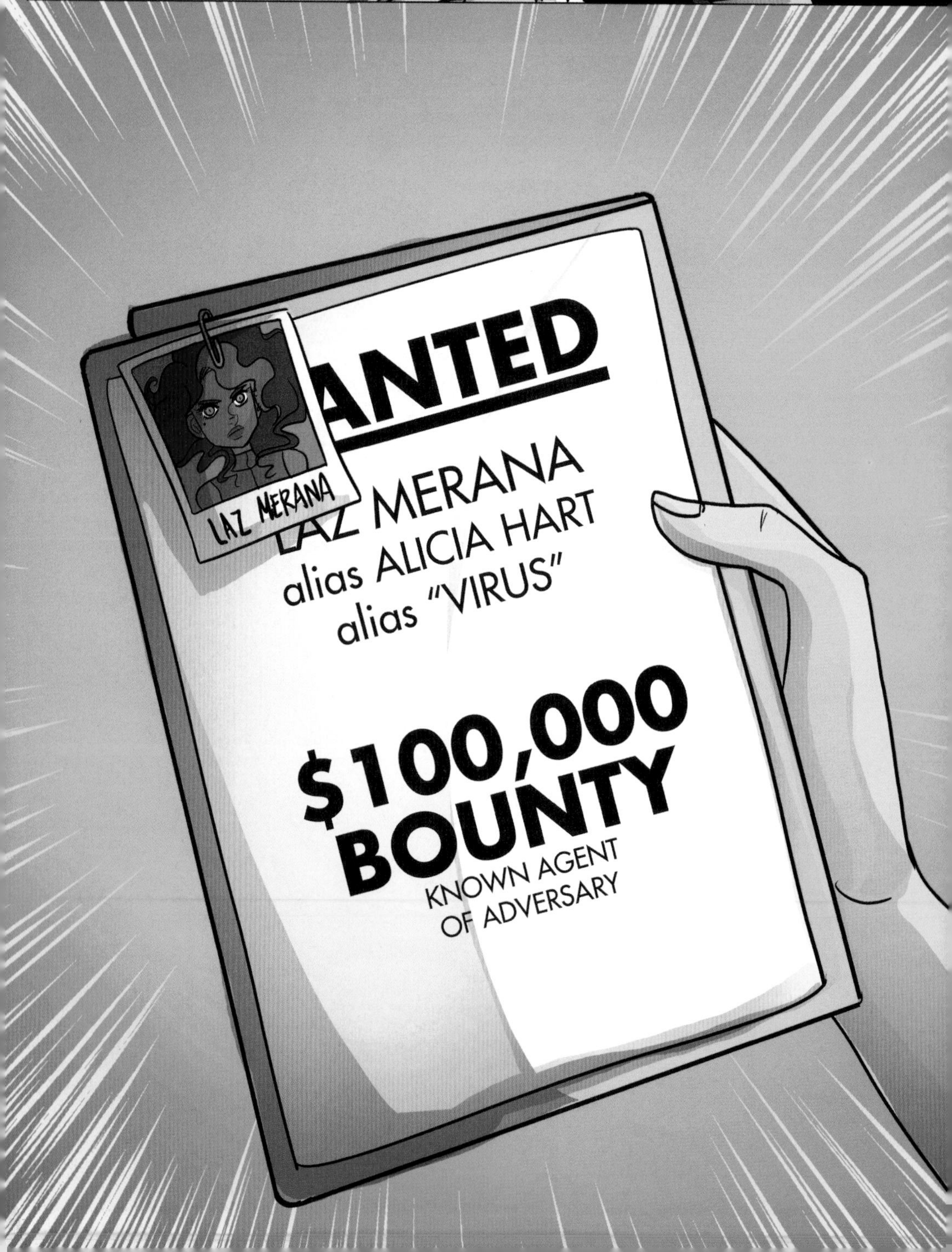
ANTED
LAZ MERANA
LAZ MERANA
alias ALICIA HART
alias "VIRUS"
$100,000
BOUNTY
KNOWN AGENT
OF ADVERSARY

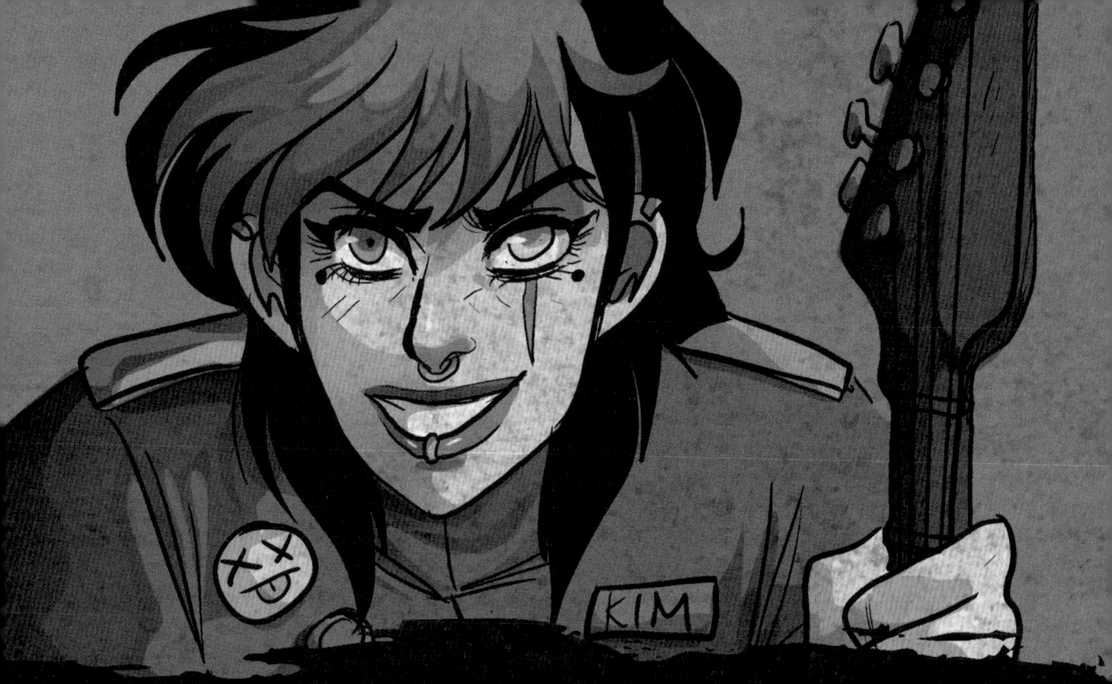
KIM

# 3

## "DON'T MOCK THE PROCESS"

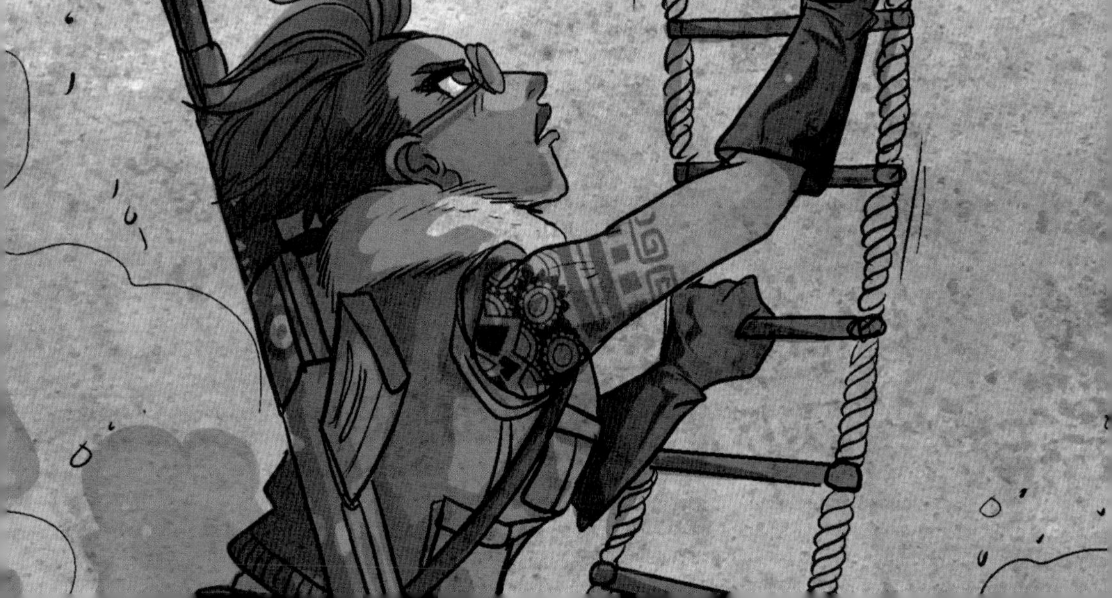

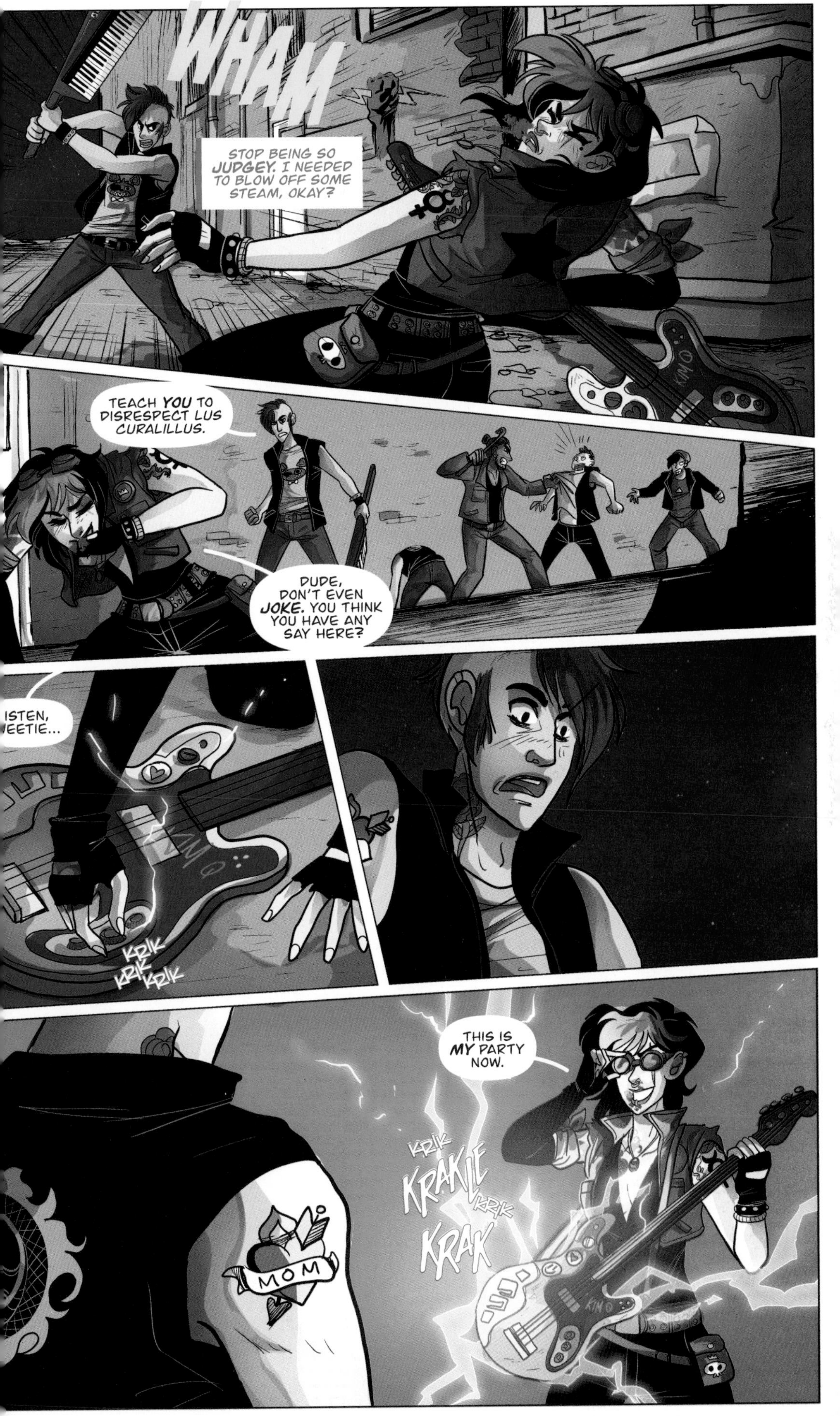
WHAM
STOP BEING SO JUDGEY. I NEEDED TO BLOW OFF SOME STEAM, OKAY?
TEACH YOU TO DISRESPECT LUS CURALILLUS.
DUDE, DON'T EVEN JOKE. YOU THINK YOU HAVE ANY SAY HERE?
ISTEN, EETIE...
KRIK KRIK KRIK KRIK
THIS IS MY PARTY NOW.
KRIK KRAKLE KRIK KRAK
MOM

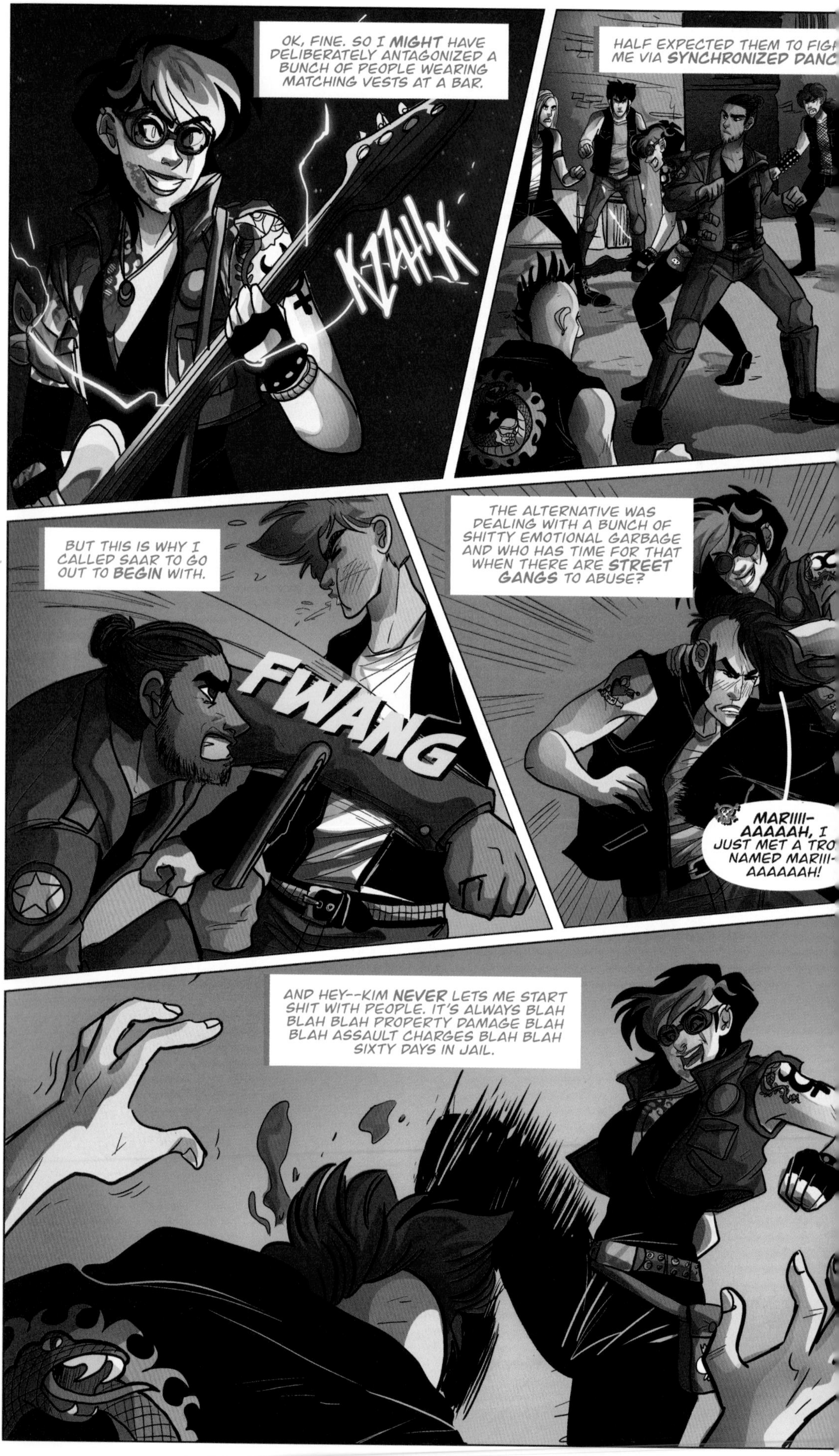
OK, FINE. SO I **MIGHT** HAVE DELIBERATELY ANTAGONIZED A BUNCH OF PEOPLE WEARING MATCHING VESTS AT A BAR.
KZZHK
HALF EXPECTED THEM TO FIGH
ME VIA **SYNCHRONIZED DANC**
BUT THIS IS WHY I CALLED SAAR TO GO OUT TO **BEGIN** WITH.
FWANG
THE ALTERNATIVE WAS DEALING WITH A BUNCH OF SHITTY EMOTIONAL GARBAGE AND WHO HAS TIME FOR THAT WHEN THERE ARE **STREET GANGS** TO ABUSE?
**MARIIII-AAAAAH,** I JUST MET A TRO NAMED MARIII-AAAAAAH!
AND HEY--KIM **NEVER** LETS ME START SHIT WITH PEOPLE. IT'S ALWAYS BLAH BLAH BLAH PROPERTY DAMAGE BLAH BLAH ASSAULT CHARGES BLAH BLAH SIXTY DAYS IN JAIL.

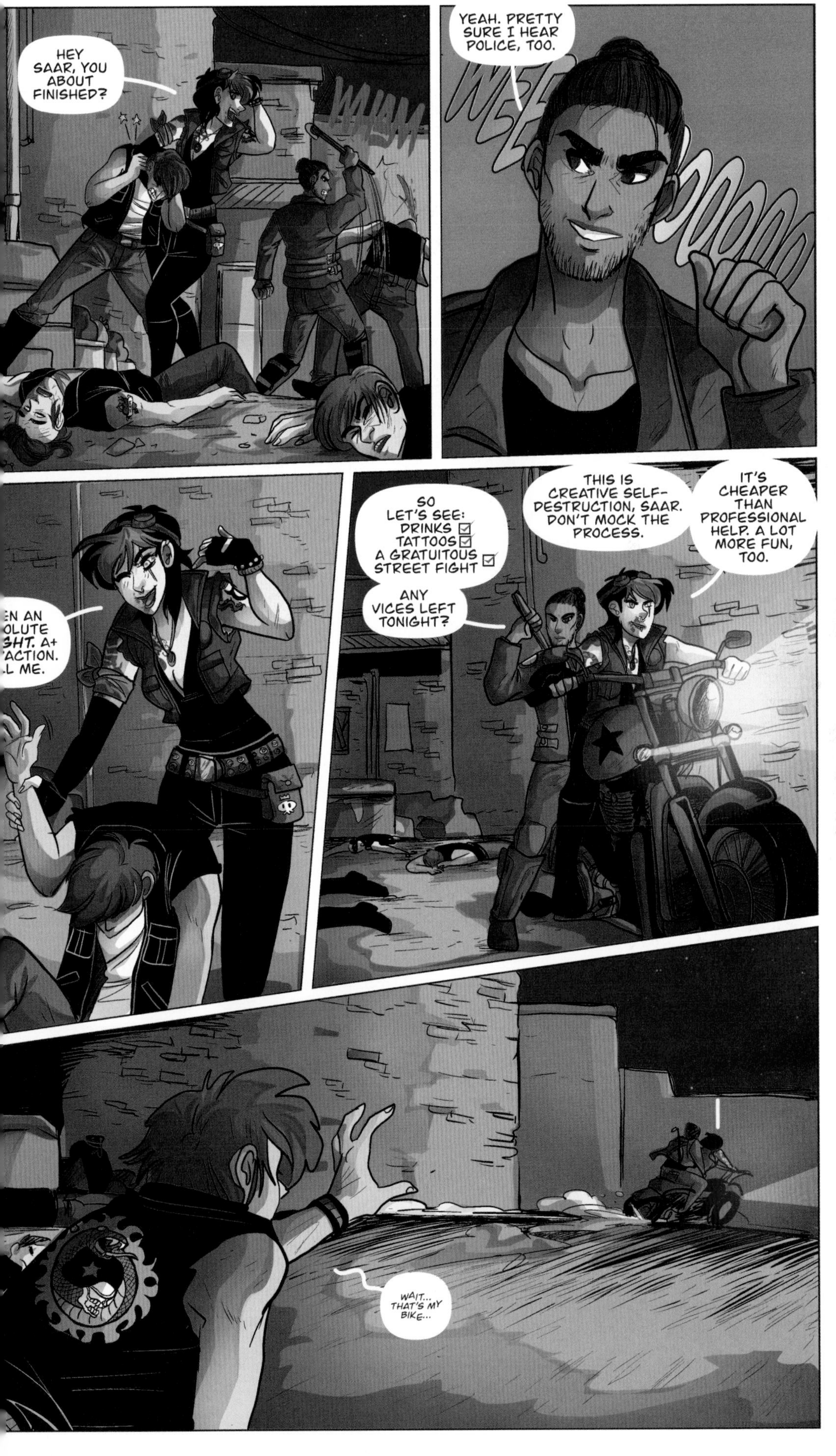
HEY SAAR, YOU ABOUT FINISHED?
WHAM
YEAH. PRETTY SURE I HEAR POLICE, TOO.
WEEOOOOOO
EN AN
OLUTE
GHT. A+
ACTION.
L ME.
SO LET'S SEE: DRINKS ☑ TATTOOS ☑ A GRATUITOUS STREET FIGHT ☑
ANY VICES LEFT TONIGHT?
THIS IS CREATIVE SELF-DESTRUCTION, SAAR. DON'T MOCK THE PROCESS.
IT'S CHEAPER THAN PROFESSIONAL HELP. A LOT MORE FUN, TOO.
WAIT... THAT'S MY BIKE...

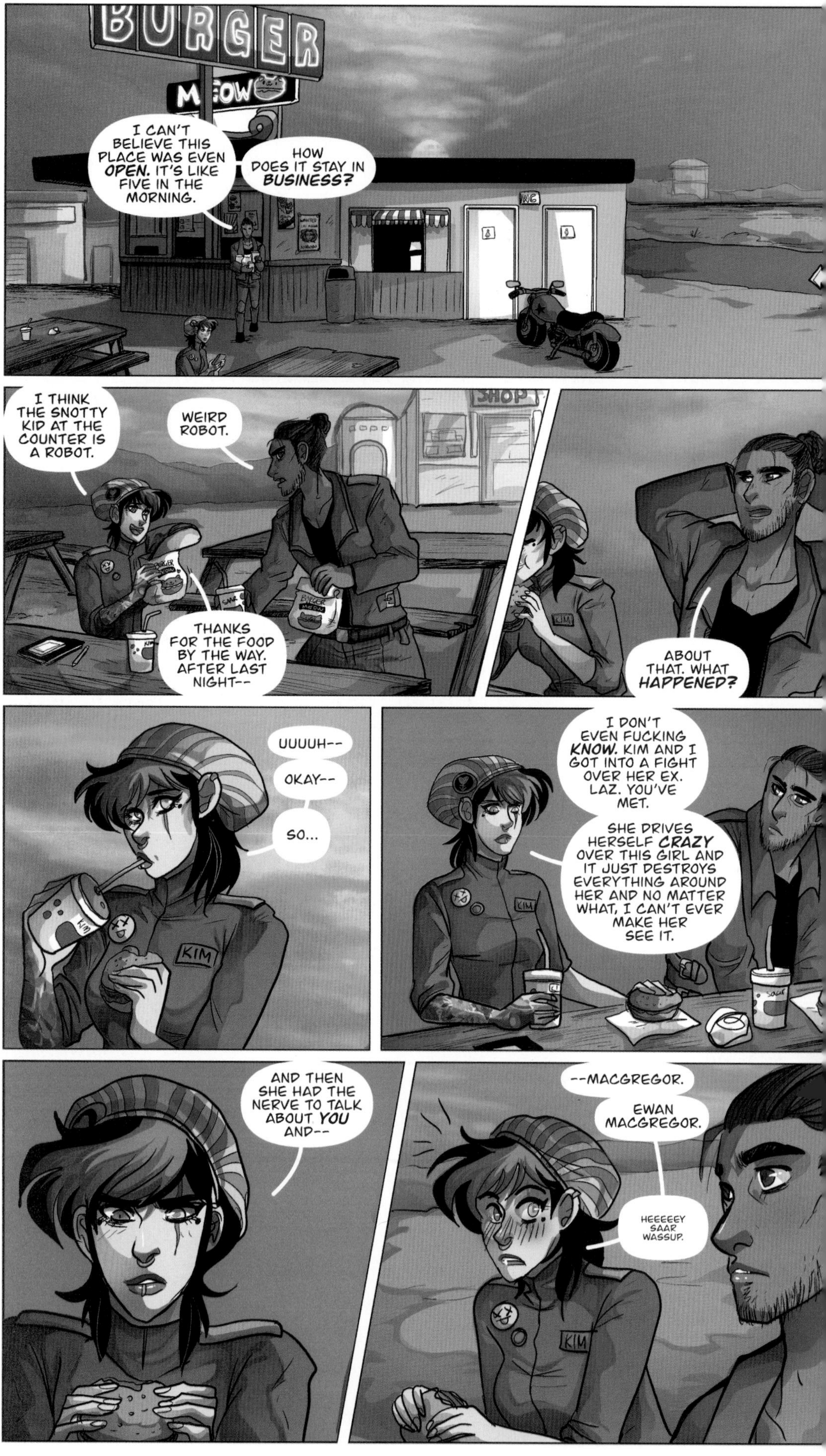
BURGER
MEOW
I CAN'T BELIEVE THIS PLACE WAS EVEN OPEN. IT'S LIKE FIVE IN THE MORNING.
HOW DOES IT STAY IN BUSINESS?
I THINK THE SNOTTY KID AT THE COUNTER IS A ROBOT.
WEIRD ROBOT.
SHOP
THANKS FOR THE FOOD BY THE WAY. AFTER LAST NIGHT--
ABOUT THAT. WHAT HAPPENED?
UUUUH--
OKAY--
SO...
I DON'T EVEN FUCKING KNOW. KIM AND I GOT INTO A FIGHT OVER HER EX. LAZ. YOU'VE MET.
SHE DRIVES HERSELF CRAZY OVER THIS GIRL AND IT JUST DESTROYS EVERYTHING AROUND HER AND NO MATTER WHAT, I CAN'T EVER MAKE HER SEE IT.
AND THEN SHE HAD THE NERVE TO TALK ABOUT YOU AND--
--MACGREGOR.
EWAN MACGREGOR.
HEEEEEY SAAR WASSUP.
KIM

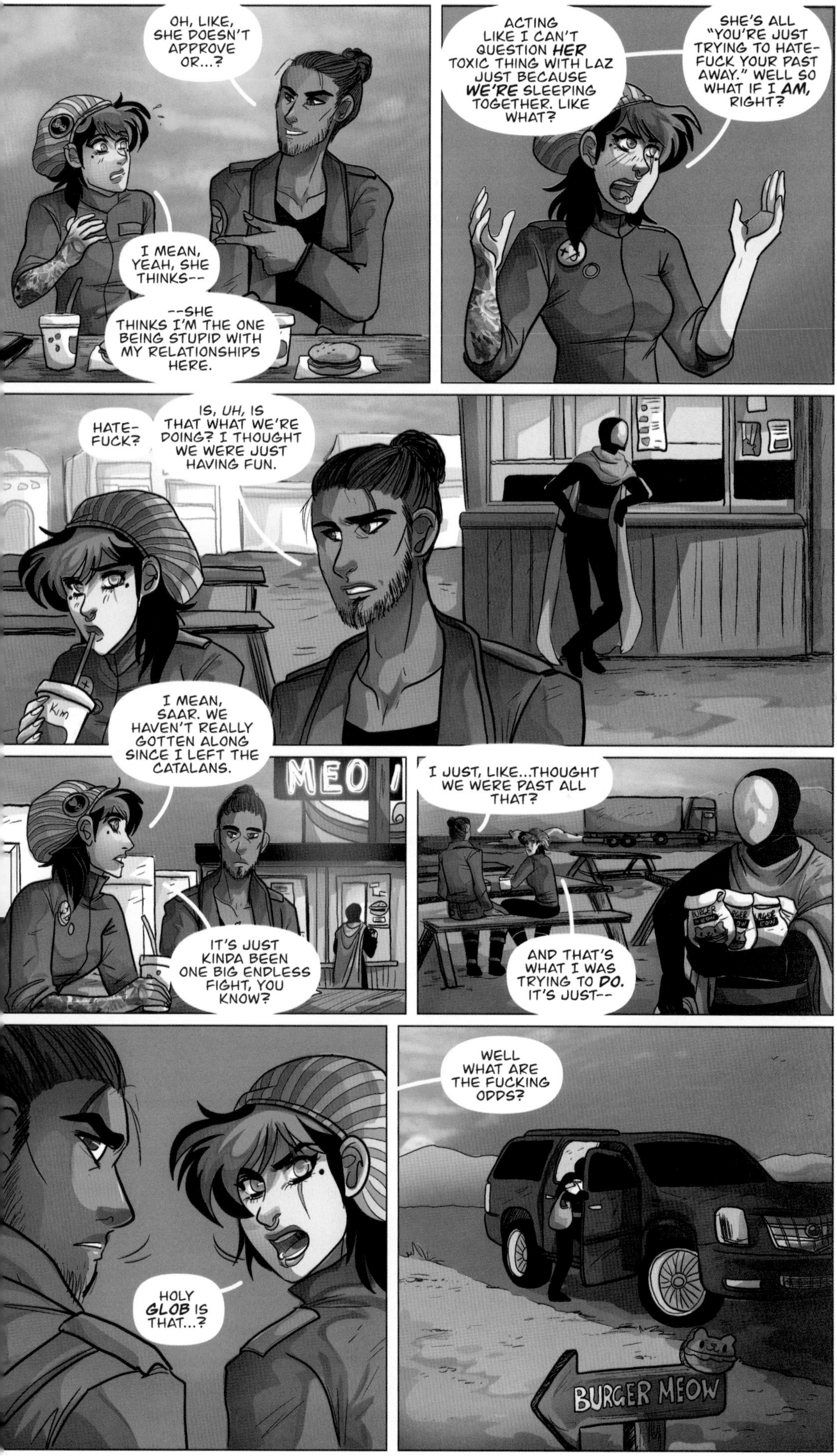

OH, LIKE, SHE DOESN'T APPROVE OR...?
I MEAN, YEAH, SHE THINKS--
--SHE THINKS I'M THE ONE BEING STUPID WITH MY RELATIONSHIPS HERE.
ACTING LIKE I CAN'T QUESTION HER TOXIC THING WITH LAZ JUST BECAUSE WE'RE SLEEPING TOGETHER. LIKE WHAT?
SHE'S ALL "YOU'RE JUST TRYING TO HATE-FUCK YOUR PAST AWAY." WELL SO WHAT IF I AM, RIGHT?
HATE-FUCK?
IS, UH, IS THAT WHAT WE'RE DOING? I THOUGHT WE WERE JUST HAVING FUN.
Kim
I MEAN, SAAR. WE HAVEN'T REALLY GOTTEN ALONG SINCE I LEFT THE CATALANS.
MEO
IT'S JUST KINDA BEEN ONE BIG ENDLESS FIGHT, YOU KNOW?
I JUST, LIKE...THOUGHT WE WERE PAST ALL THAT?
AND THAT'S WHAT I WAS TRYING TO DO. IT'S JUST--
HOLY GLOB IS THAT...?
WELL WHAT ARE THE FUCKING ODDS?
BURGER MEOW

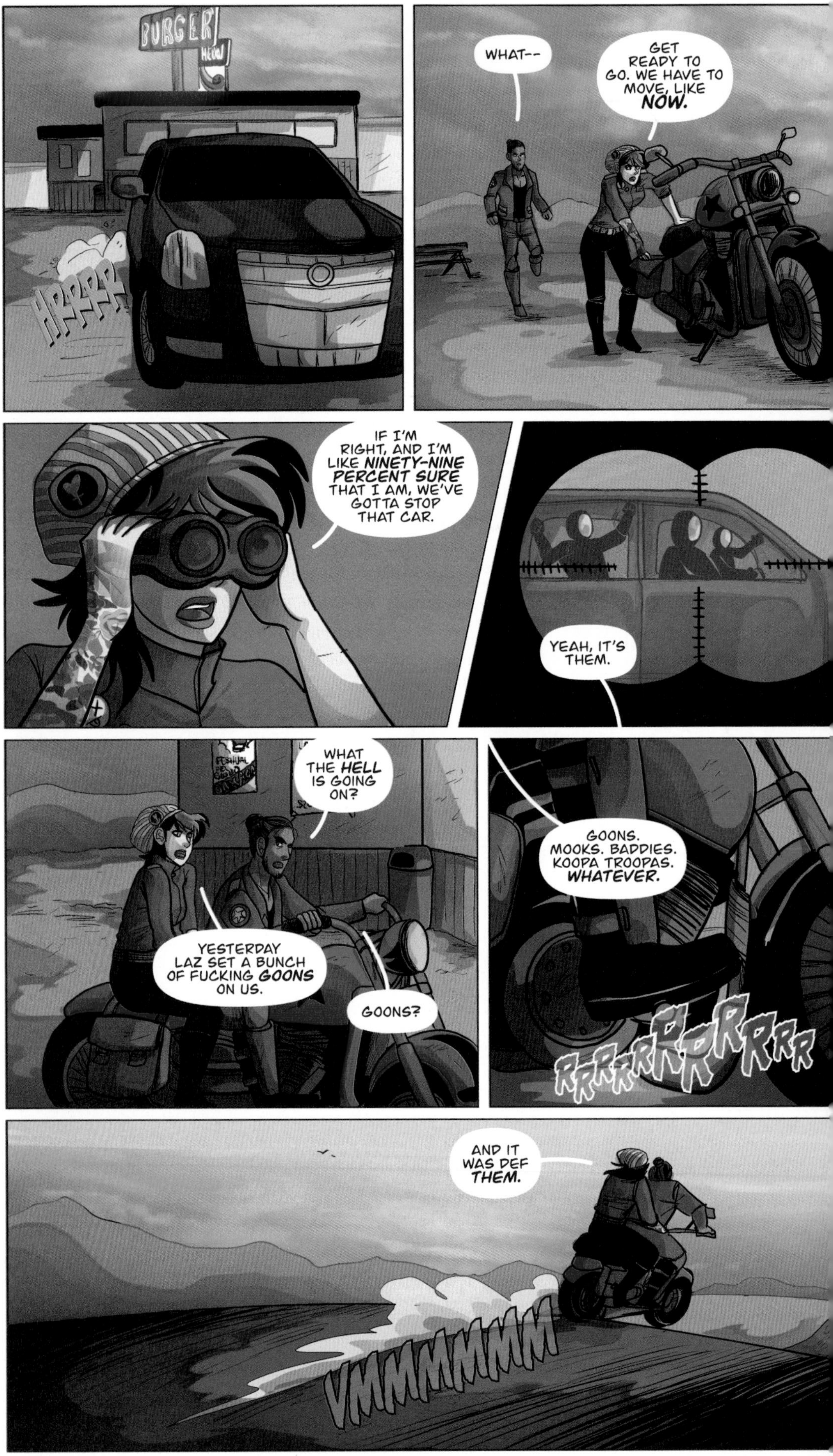
BURGER
HRRRR
WHAT--
GET READY TO GO. WE HAVE TO MOVE, LIKE NOW.
IF I'M RIGHT, AND I'M LIKE NINETY-NINE PERCENT SURE THAT I AM, WE'VE GOTTA STOP THAT CAR.
YEAH, IT'S THEM.
WHAT THE HELL IS GOING ON?
YESTERDAY LAZ SET A BUNCH OF FUCKING GOONS ON US.
GOONS?
GOONS. MOOKS. BADDIES. KOOPA TROOPAS. WHATEVER.
RRRRRRRRRRRR
AND IT WAS DEF THEM.
VMMMMMMM

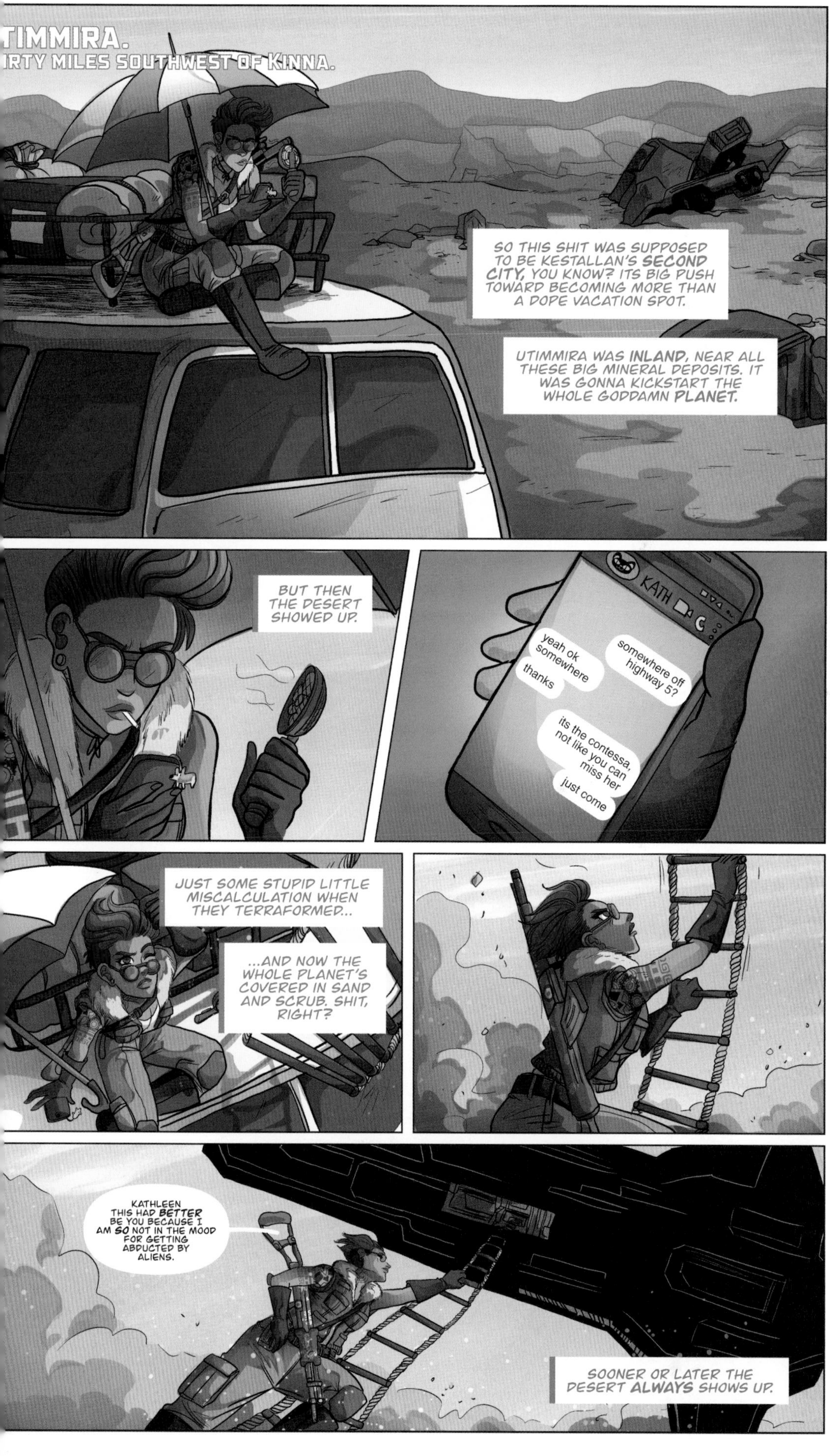
TIMMIRA.
IRTY MILES SOUTHWEST OF KINNA.
SO THIS SHIT WAS SUPPOSED TO BE KESTALLAN'S SECOND CITY, YOU KNOW? ITS BIG PUSH TOWARD BECOMING MORE THAN A DOPE VACATION SPOT.
UTIMMIRA WAS INLAND, NEAR ALL THESE BIG MINERAL DEPOSITS. IT WAS GONNA KICKSTART THE WHOLE GODDAMN PLANET.
BUT THEN THE DESERT SHOWED UP.
KATH
somewhere off highway 5?
yeah ok somewhere
thanks
its the contessa, not like you can miss her
just come
JUST SOME STUPID LITTLE MISCALCULATION WHEN THEY TERRAFORMED...
...AND NOW THE WHOLE PLANET'S COVERED IN SAND AND SCRUB. SHIT, RIGHT?
KATHLEEN THIS HAD BETTER BE YOU BECAUSE I AM SO NOT IN THE MOOD FOR GETTING ABDUCTED BY ALIENS.
SOONER OR LATER THE DESERT ALWAYS SHOWS UP.

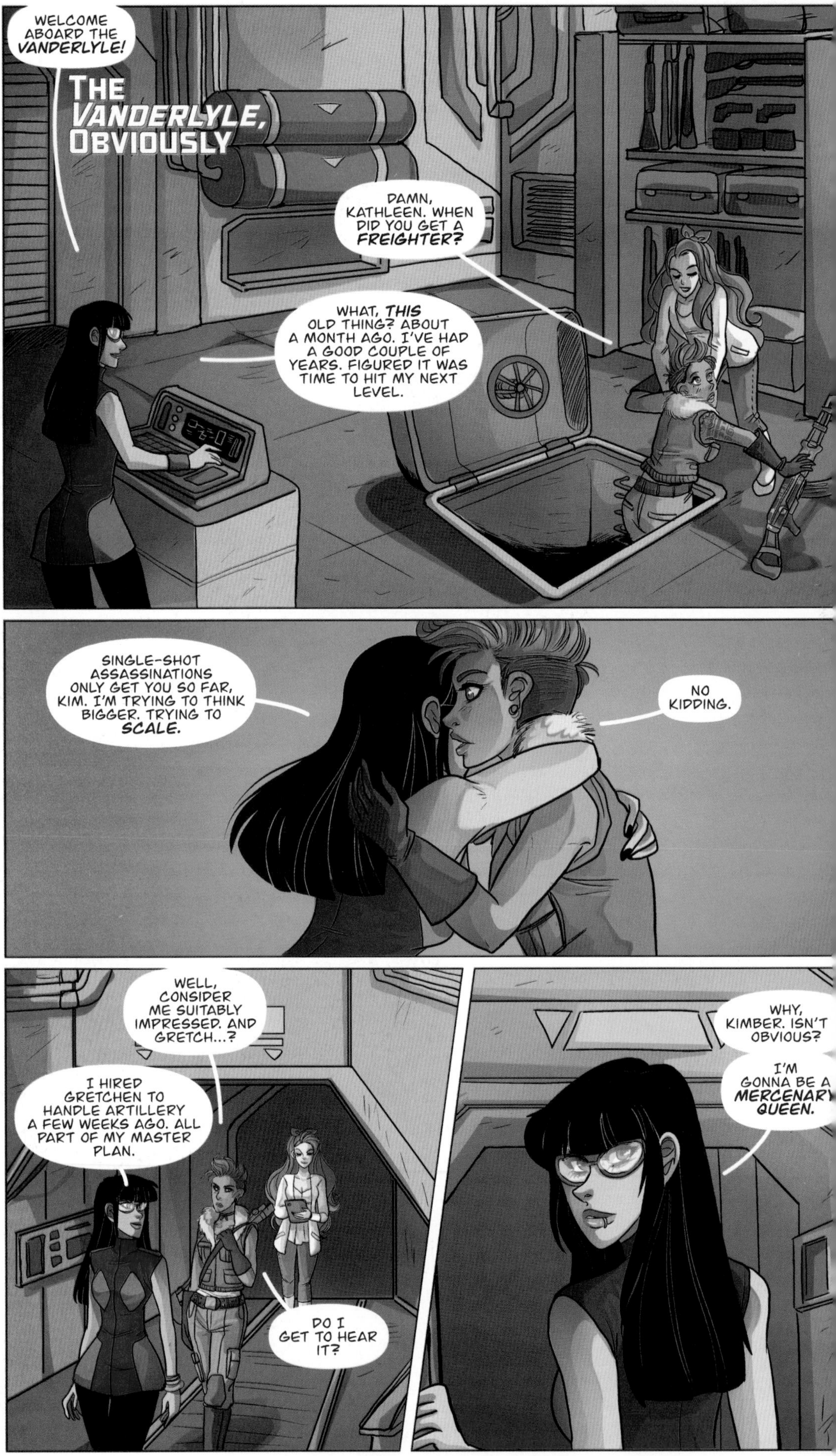

WELCOME ABOARD THE *VANDERLYLE!*
THE *VANDERLYLE*, OBVIOUSLY
DAMN, KATHLEEN. WHEN DID YOU GET A **FREIGHTER?**
WHAT, **THIS** OLD THING? ABOUT A MONTH AGO. I'VE HAD A GOOD COUPLE OF YEARS. FIGURED IT WAS TIME TO HIT MY NEXT LEVEL.
SINGLE-SHOT ASSASSINATIONS ONLY GET YOU SO FAR, KIM. I'M TRYING TO THINK BIGGER. TRYING TO **SCALE.**
NO KIDDING.
WELL, CONSIDER ME SUITABLY IMPRESSED. AND GRETCH...?
I HIRED GRETCHEN TO HANDLE ARTILLERY A FEW WEEKS AGO. ALL PART OF MY MASTER PLAN.
DO I GET TO HEAR IT?
WHY, KIMBER. ISN'T OBVIOUS?
I'M GONNA BE A ***MERCENARY QUEEN.***

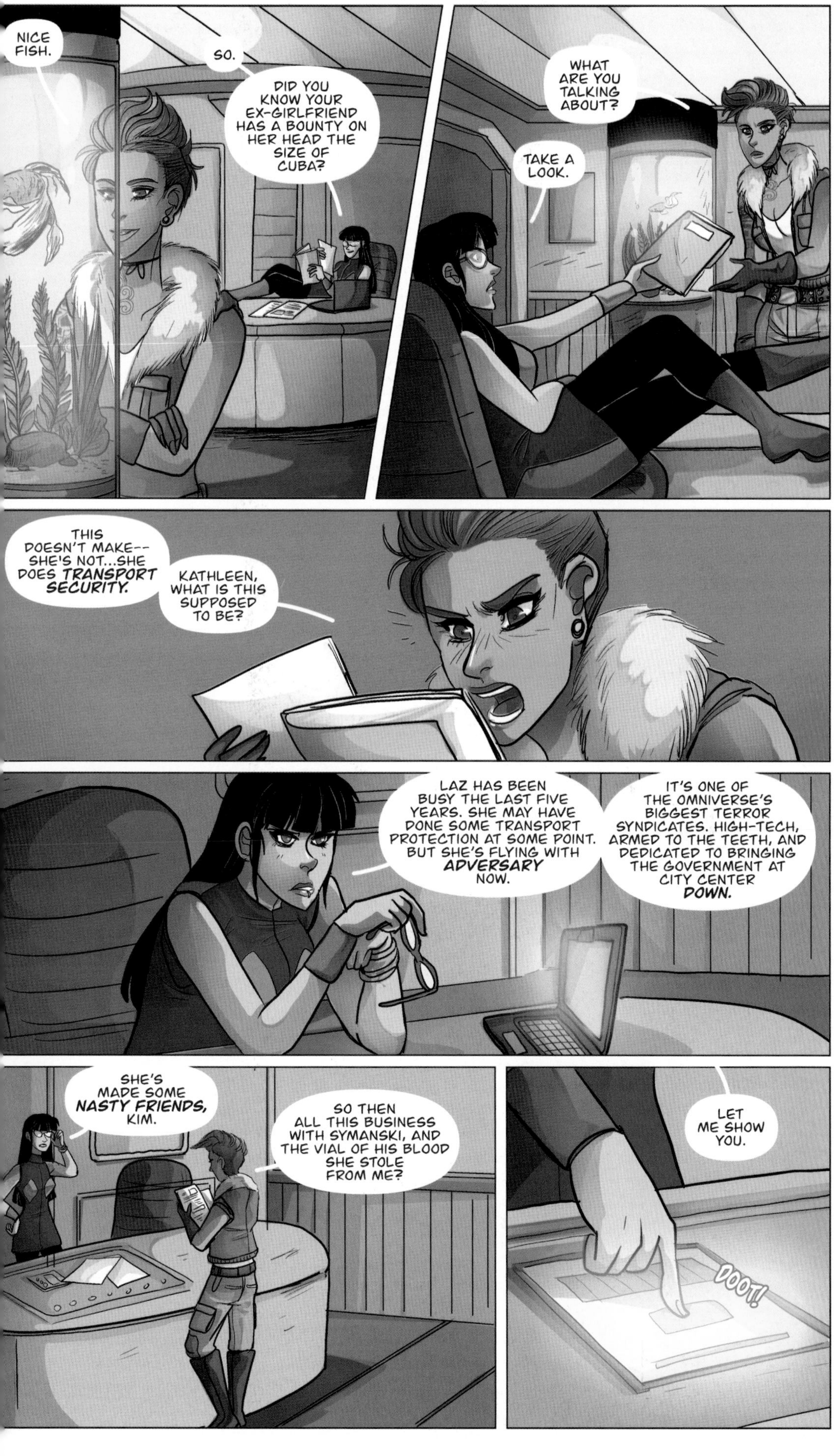
NICE FISH.
SO.
DID YOU KNOW YOUR EX-GIRLFRIEND HAS A BOUNTY ON HER HEAD THE SIZE OF CUBA?
WHAT ARE YOU TALKING ABOUT?
TAKE A LOOK.
THIS DOESN'T MAKE-- SHE'S NOT...SHE DOES **TRANSPORT SECURITY.**
KATHLEEN, WHAT IS THIS SUPPOSED TO BE?
LAZ HAS BEEN BUSY THE LAST FIVE YEARS. SHE MAY HAVE DONE SOME TRANSPORT PROTECTION AT SOME POINT. BUT SHE'S FLYING WITH **ADVERSARY** NOW.
IT'S ONE OF THE OMNIVERSE'S BIGGEST TERROR SYNDICATES. HIGH-TECH, ARMED TO THE TEETH, AND DEDICATED TO BRINGING THE GOVERNMENT AT CITY CENTER **DOWN.**
SHE'S MADE SOME **NASTY FRIENDS,** KIM.
SO THEN ALL THIS BUSINESS WITH SYMANSKI, AND THE VIAL OF HIS BLOOD SHE STOLE FROM ME?
LET ME SHOW YOU.
DOOT!

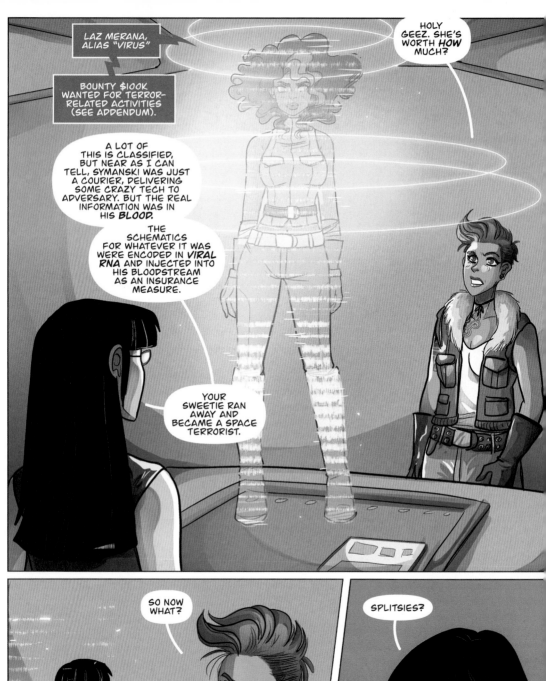

LAZ MERANA, ALIAS "VIRUS"

BOUNTY $100K WANTED FOR TERROR-RELATED ACTIVITIES (SEE ADDENDUM).

HOLY GEEZ. SHE'S WORTH *HOW* MUCH?

A LOT OF THIS IS CLASSIFIED, BUT NEAR AS I CAN TELL, SYMANSKI WAS JUST A COURIER, DELIVERING SOME CRAZY TECH TO ADVERSARY. BUT THE REAL INFORMATION WAS IN HIS *BLOOD.*

THE SCHEMATICS FOR WHATEVER IT WAS WERE ENCODED IN *VIRAL RNA* AND INJECTED INTO HIS BLOODSTREAM AS AN INSURANCE MEASURE.

YOUR SWEETIE RAN AWAY AND BECAME A SPACE TERRORIST.

SO NOW WHAT?

I WANT TO HELP YOU BRING HER IN. WHAT DO YOU SAY?

SPLITSIES?

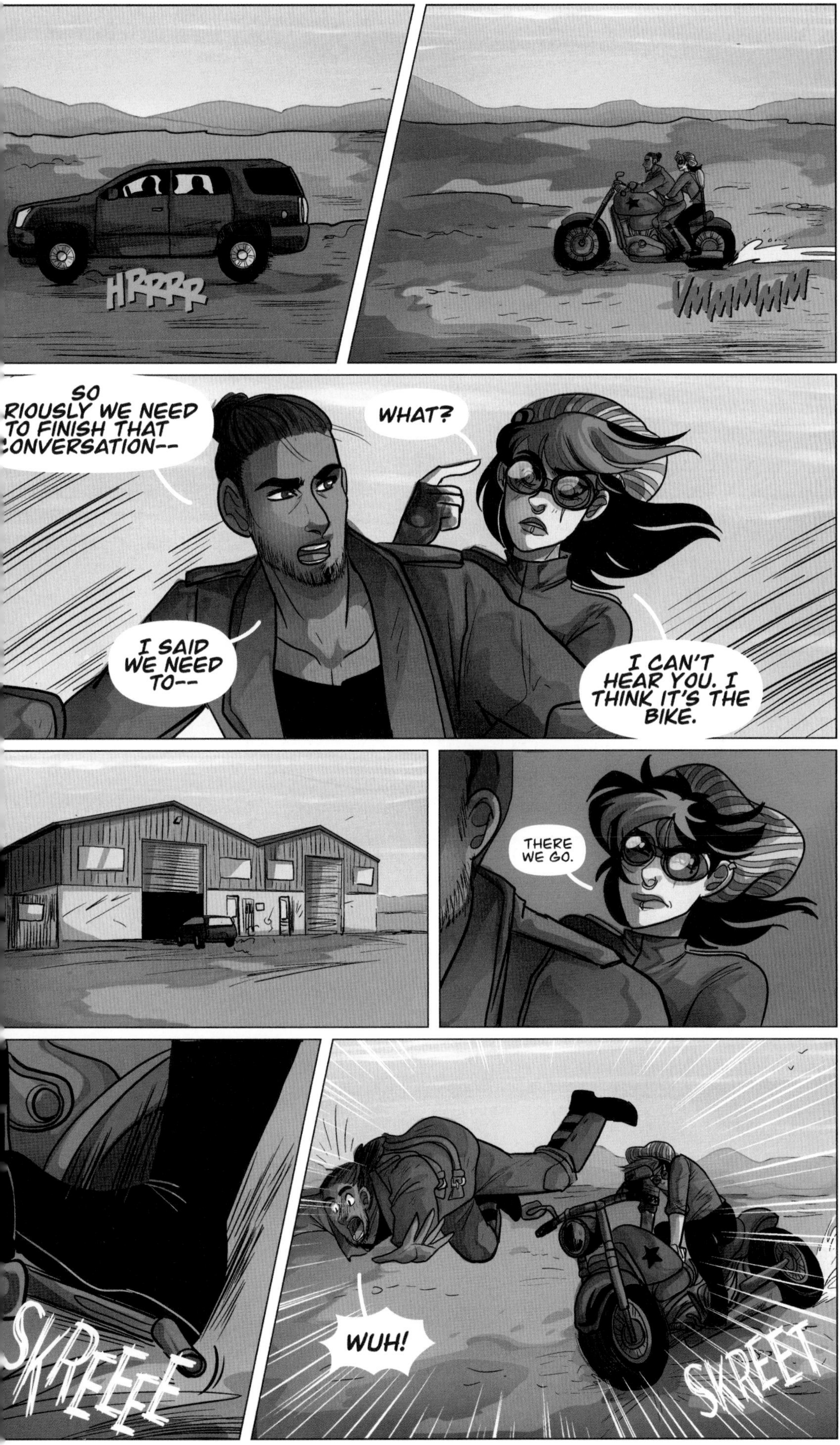
HRRRR
VMMMMM
SO
RIOUSLY WE NEED
TO FINISH THAT
CONVERSATION--
WHAT?
I SAID WE NEED TO--
I CAN'T HEAR YOU. I THINK IT'S THE BIKE.
THERE WE GO.
SKREEEE
WUH!
SKREET

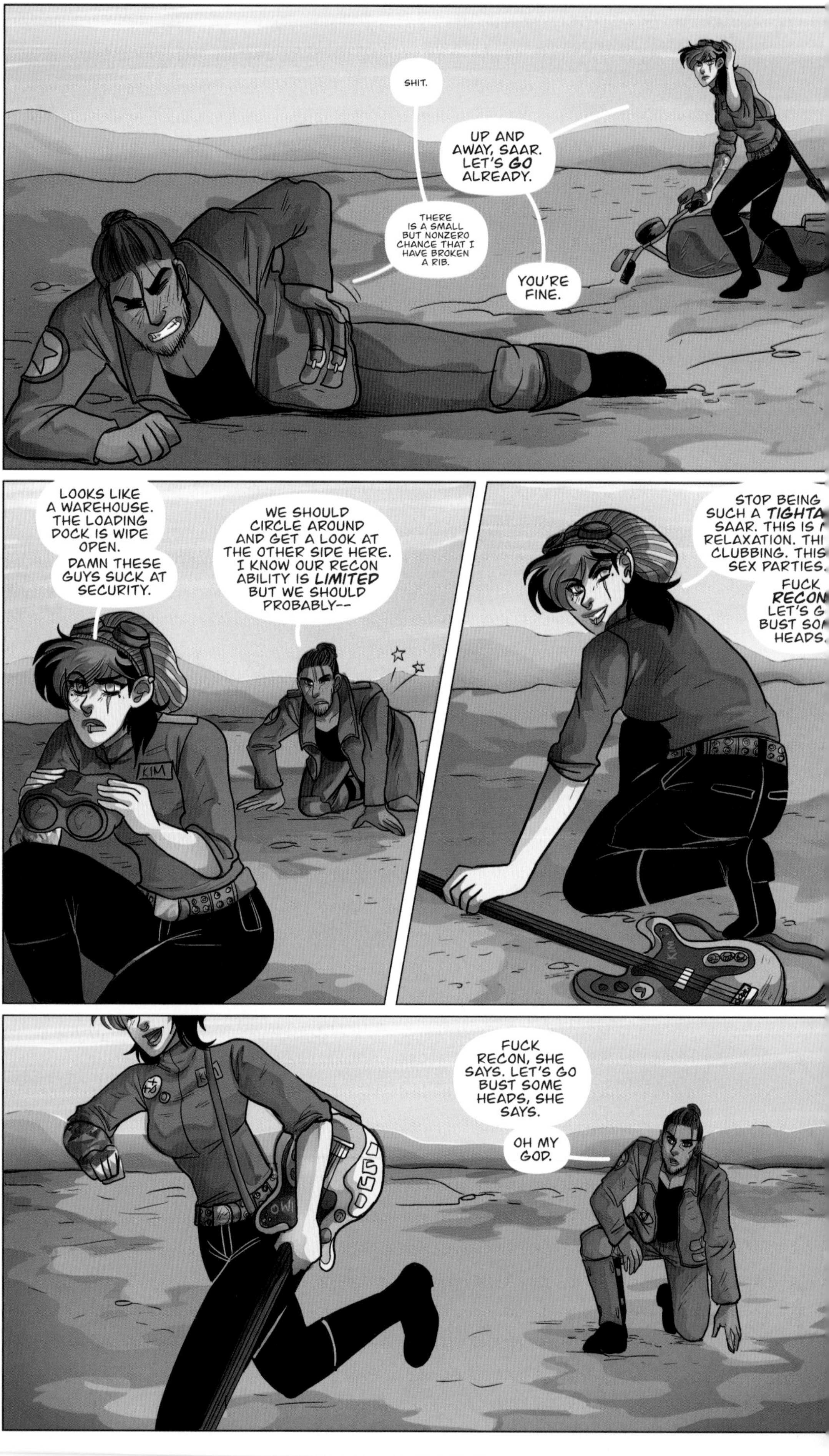
SHIT.
UP AND AWAY, SAAR. LET'S **GO** ALREADY.
THERE IS A SMALL BUT NONZERO CHANCE THAT I HAVE BROKEN A RIB.
YOU'RE FINE.
LOOKS LIKE A WAREHOUSE. THE LOADING DOCK IS WIDE OPEN.
DAMN THESE GUYS SUCK AT SECURITY.
WE SHOULD CIRCLE AROUND AND GET A LOOK AT THE OTHER SIDE HERE. I KNOW OUR RECON ABILITY IS **LIMITED** BUT WE SHOULD PROBABLY--
STOP BEING SUCH A **TIGHTA** SAAR. THIS IS RELAXATION. THI CLUBBING. THIS SEX PARTIES.
FUCK **RECON** LET'S G BUST SO HEADS.
FUCK RECON, SHE SAYS. LET'S GO BUST SOME HEADS, SHE SAYS.
OH MY GOD.

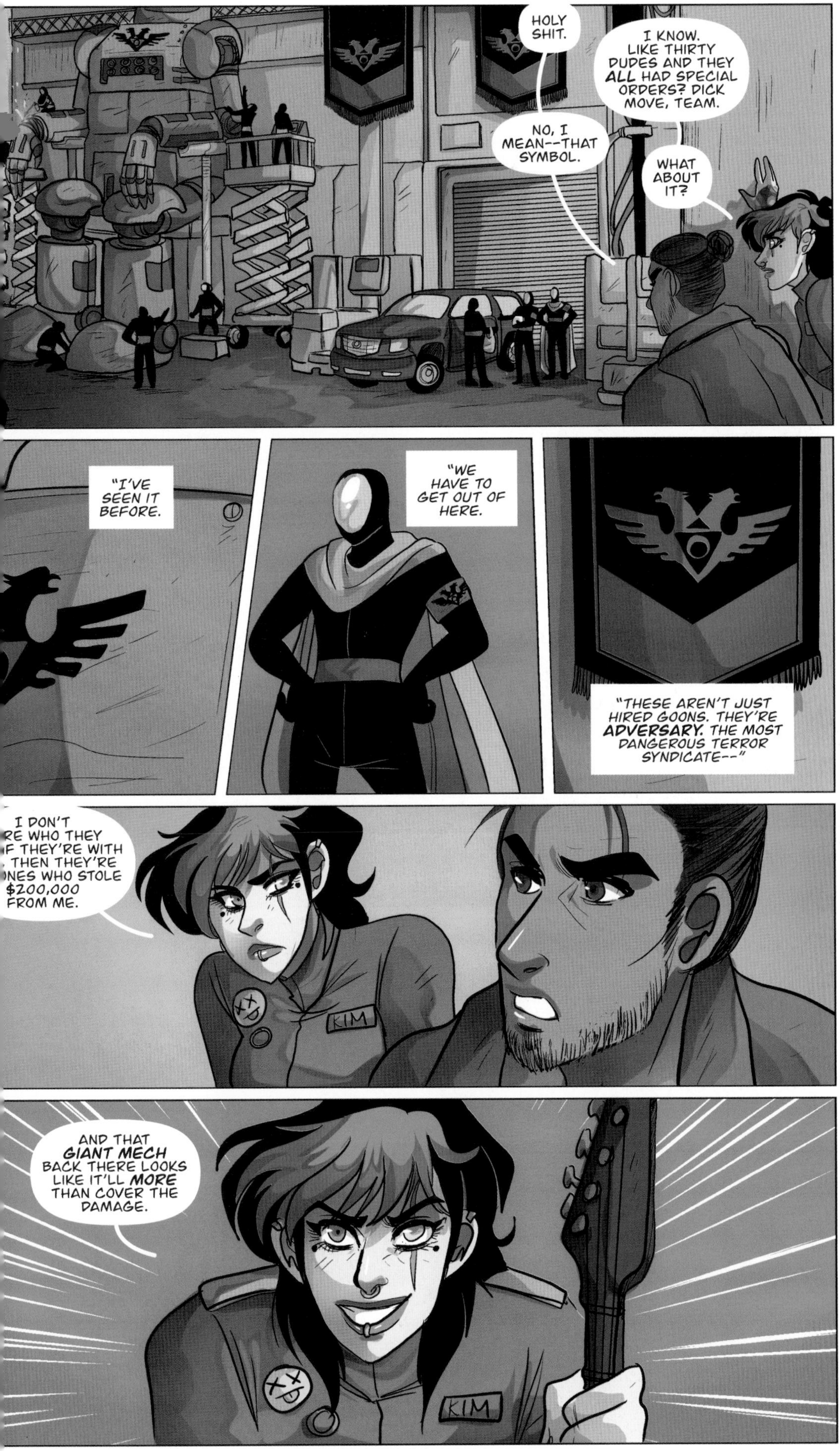
HOLY SHIT.
I KNOW. LIKE THIRTY DUDES AND THEY ALL HAD SPECIAL ORDERS? DICK MOVE, TEAM.
NO, I MEAN--THAT SYMBOL.
WHAT ABOUT IT?
"I'VE SEEN IT BEFORE.
"WE HAVE TO GET OUT OF HERE.
"THESE AREN'T JUST HIRED GOONS. THEY'RE ADVERSARY. THE MOST DANGEROUS TERROR SYNDICATE--"
I DON'T
RE WHO THEY
F THEY'RE WITH
THEN THEY'RE
NES WHO STOLE
$200,000
FROM ME.
KIM
AND THAT GIANT MECH BACK THERE LOOKS LIKE IT'LL MORE THAN COVER THE DAMAGE.
KIM

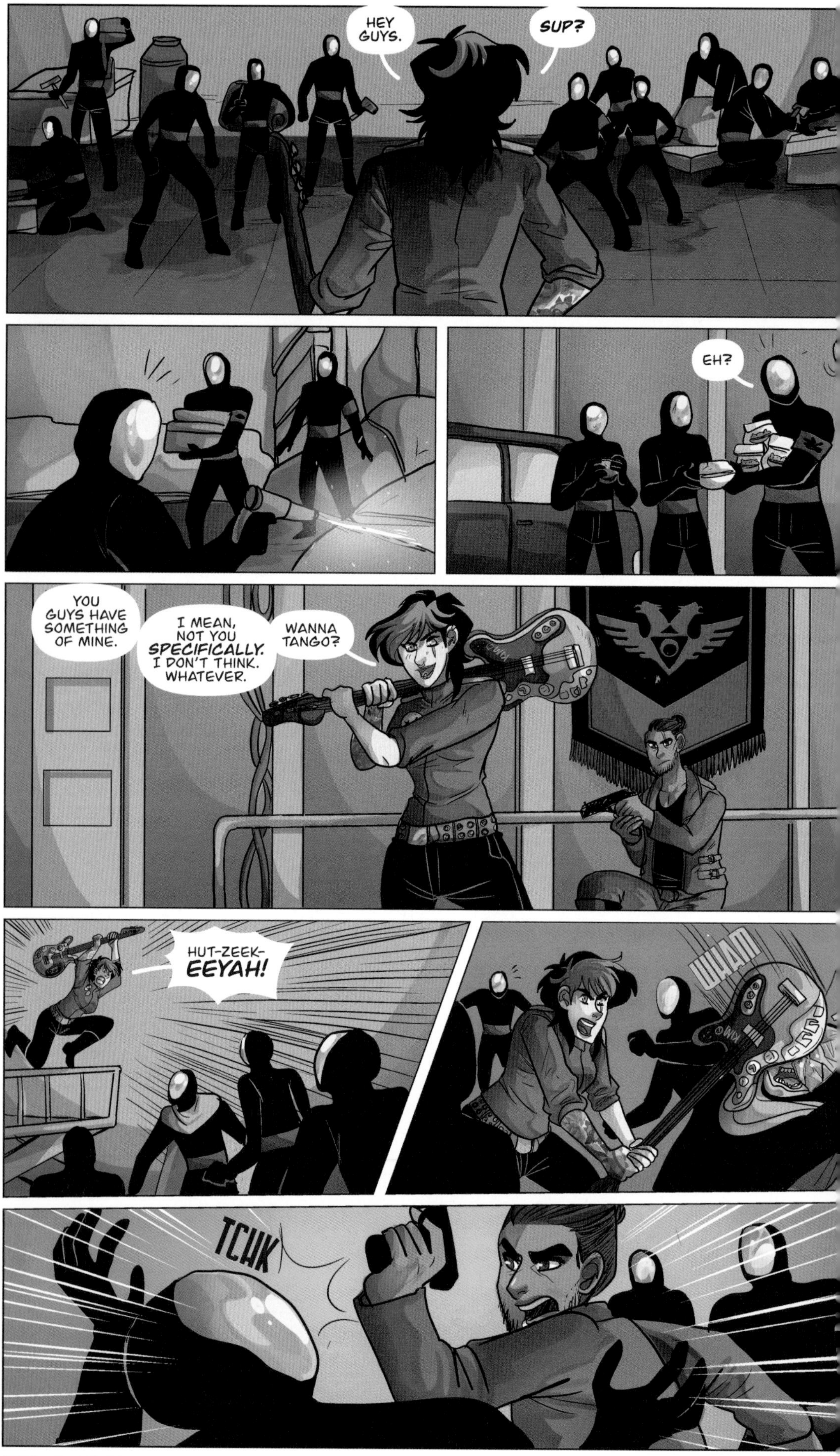
HEY GUYS.
SUP?
EH?
YOU GUYS HAVE SOMETHING OF MINE.
I MEAN, NOT YOU SPECIFICALLY. I DON'T THINK. WHATEVER.
WANNA TANGO?
HUT-ZEEK-EEYAH!
WHAM
TCHK

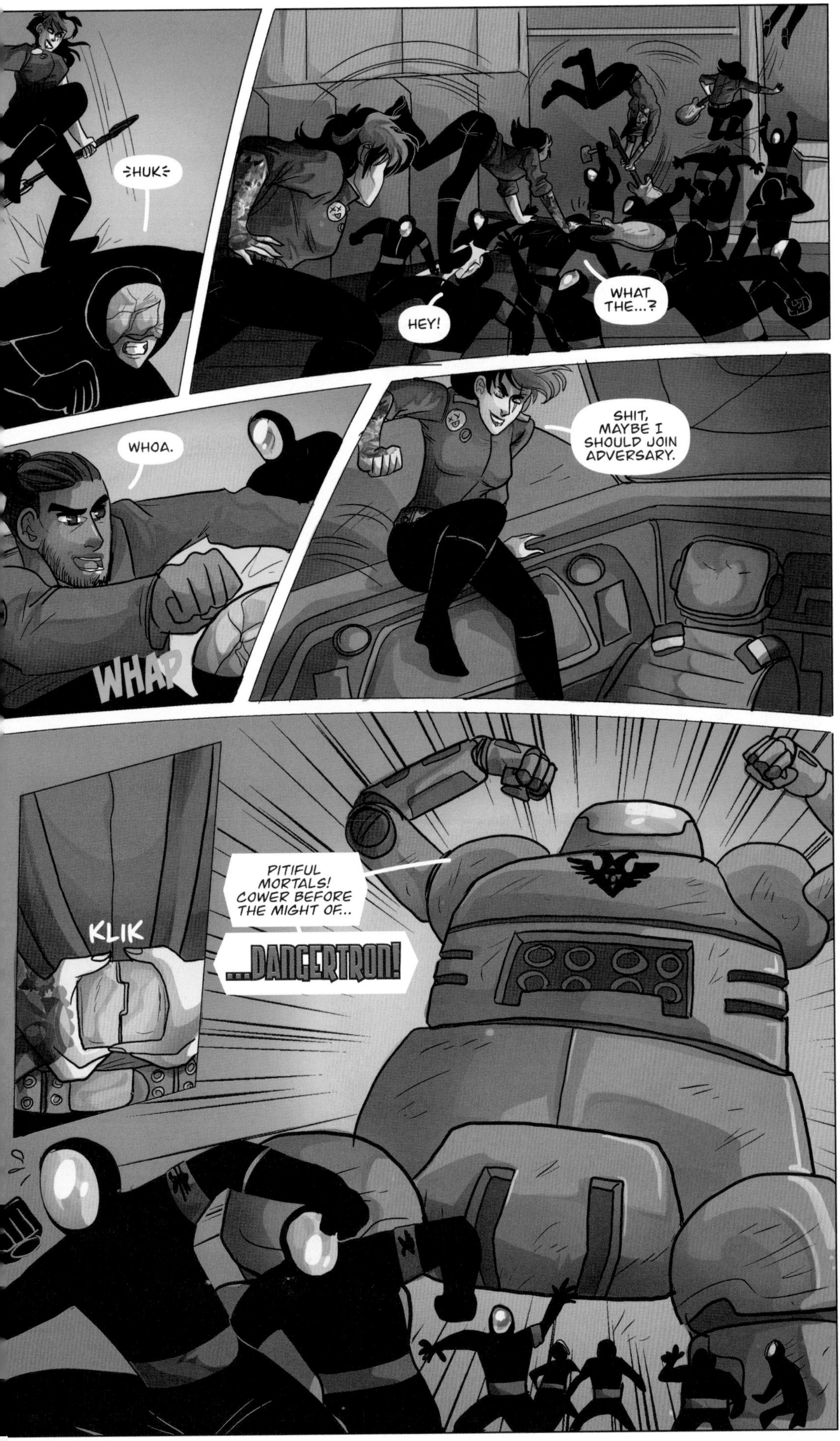
HUK
HEY!
WHAT THE...?
WHOA.
WHAP
SHIT, MAYBE I SHOULD JOIN ADVERSARY.
KLIK
PITIFUL MORTALS! COWER BEFORE THE MIGHT OF...
...DANGERTRON!

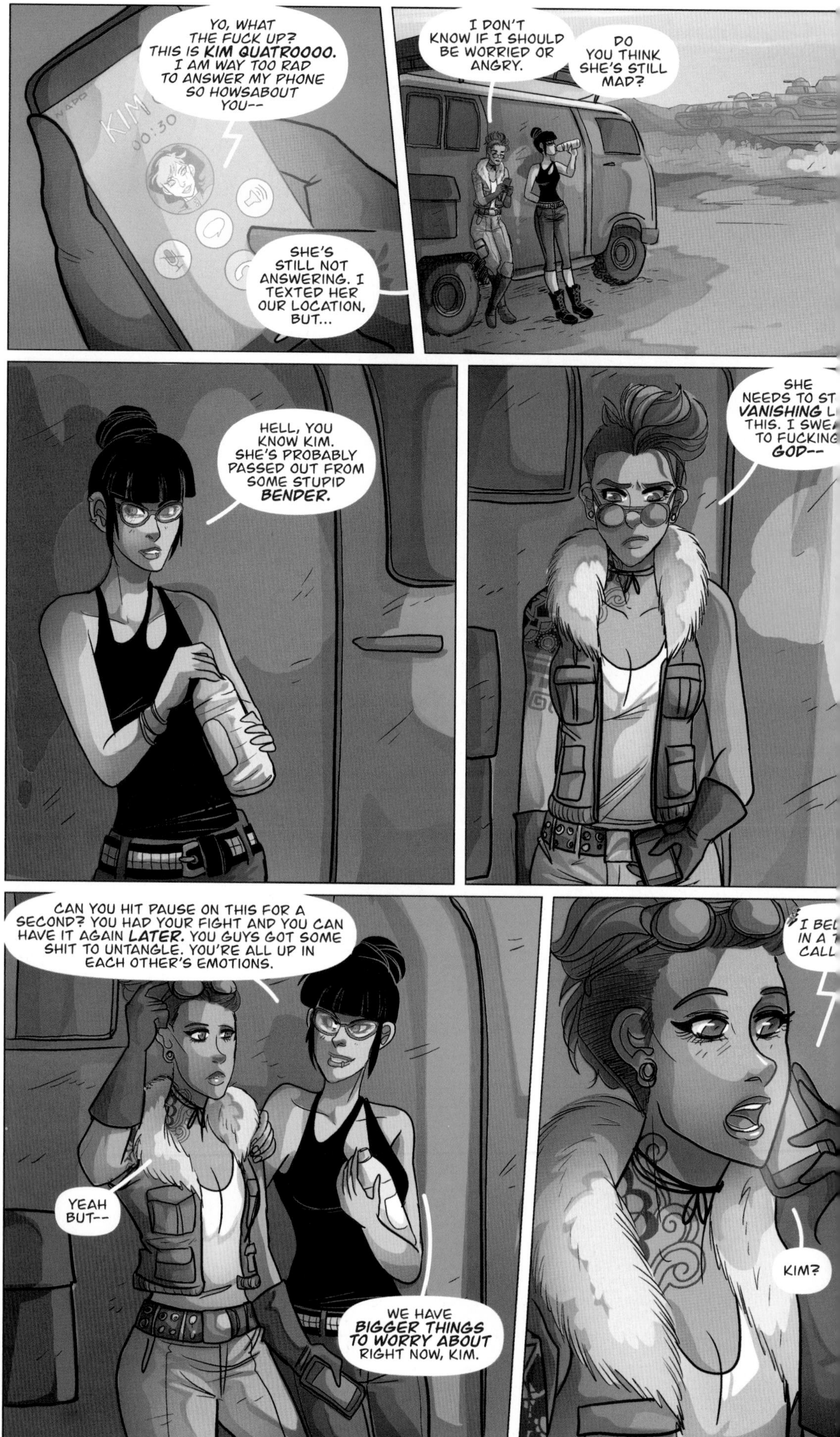
YO, WHAT THE FUCK UP? THIS IS KIM QUATROOOO. I AM WAY TOO RAD TO ANSWER MY PHONE SO HOWSABOUT YOU--
SHE'S STILL NOT ANSWERING. I TEXTED HER OUR LOCATION, BUT...
I DON'T KNOW IF I SHOULD BE WORRIED OR ANGRY.
DO YOU THINK SHE'S STILL MAD?
HELL, YOU KNOW KIM. SHE'S PROBABLY PASSED OUT FROM SOME STUPID BENDER.
SHE NEEDS TO ST VANISHING L THIS. I SWEA TO FUCKING GOD--
CAN YOU HIT PAUSE ON THIS FOR A SECOND? YOU HAD YOUR FIGHT AND YOU CAN HAVE IT AGAIN LATER. YOU GUYS GOT SOME SHIT TO UNTANGLE. YOU'RE ALL UP IN EACH OTHER'S EMOTIONS.
YEAH BUT--
WE HAVE BIGGER THINGS TO WORRY ABOUT RIGHT NOW, KIM.
KIM?

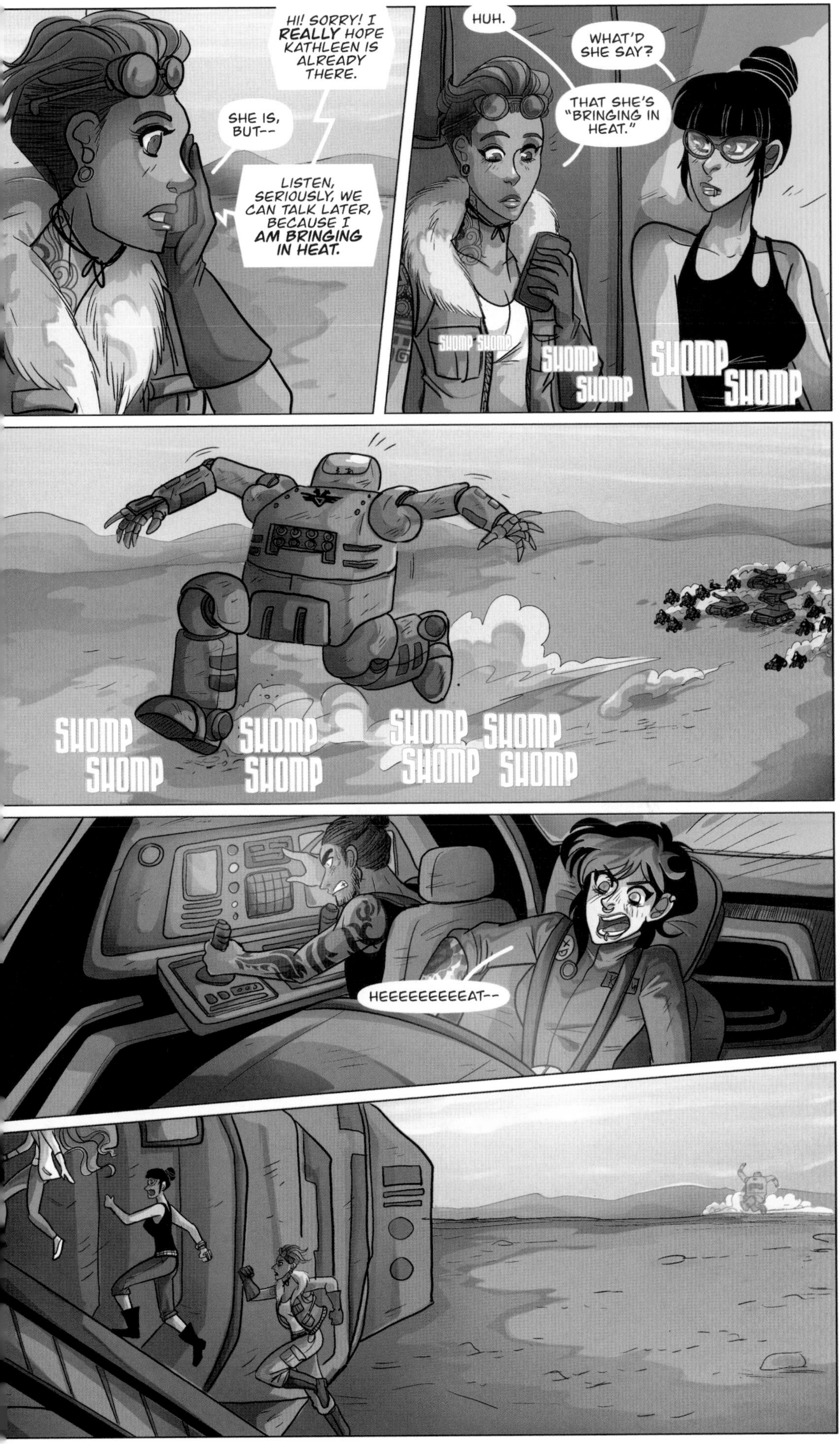
HI! SORRY! I REALLY HOPE KATHLEEN IS ALREADY THERE.
SHE IS, BUT--
LISTEN, SERIOUSLY, WE CAN TALK LATER, BECAUSE I AM BRINGING IN HEAT.
HUH.
WHAT'D SHE SAY?
THAT SHE'S "BRINGING IN HEAT."
SHOMP SHOMP
SHOMP SHOMP
SHOMP SHOMP
SHOMP SHOMP
SHOMP SHOMP
SHOMP SHOMP
SHOMP SHOMP
HEEEEEEEEEAT--

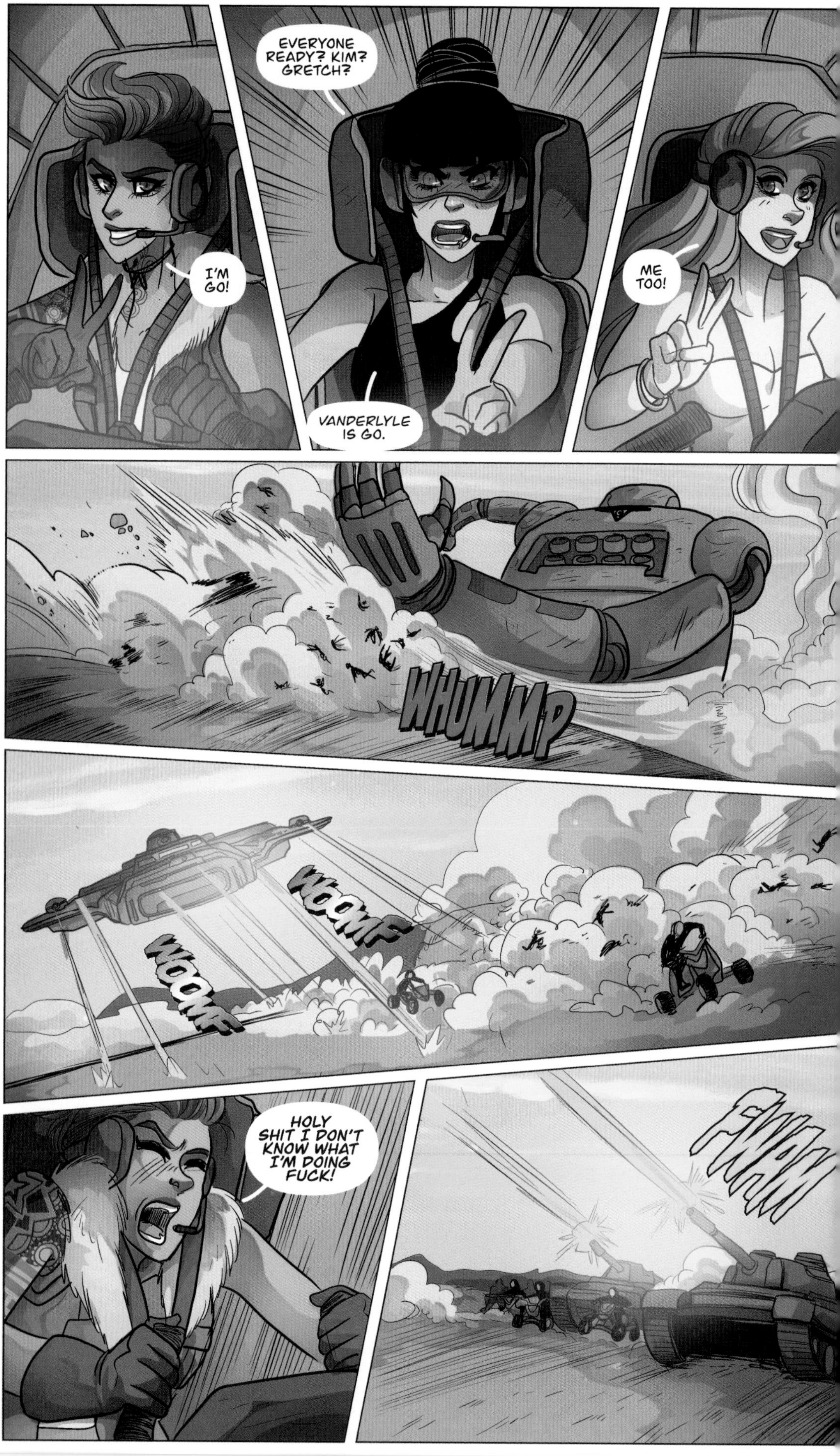
EVERYONE READY? KIM? GRETCH?
VANDERLYLE IS GO.
I'M GO!
ME TOO!
WHUMMP
WOOMF
WOOMF
HOLY SHIT I DON'T KNOW WHAT I'M DOING FUCK!
FWAM

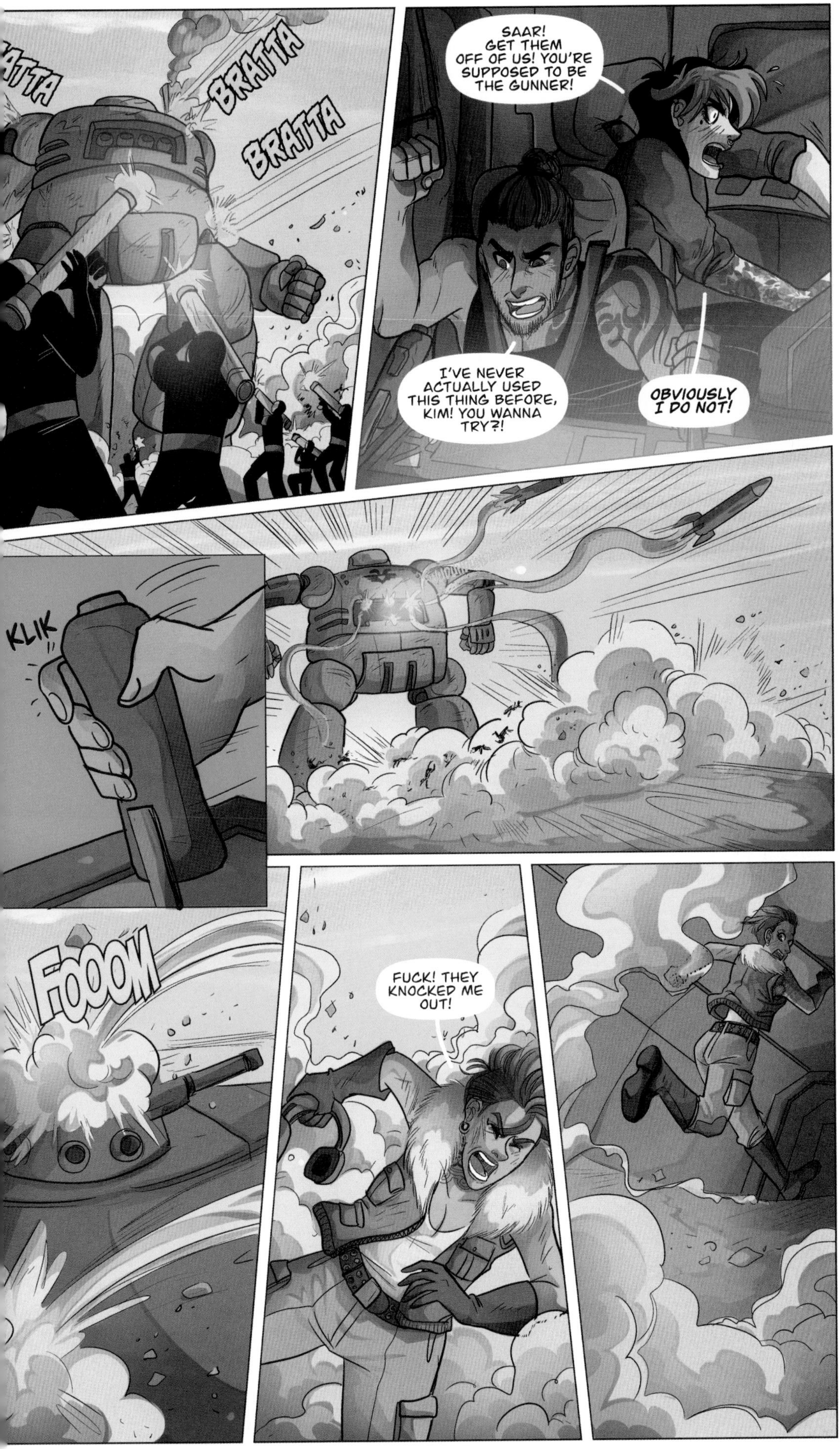
ATTA
BRATTA
BRATTA
SAAR! GET THEM OFF OF US! YOU'RE SUPPOSED TO BE THE GUNNER!
I'VE NEVER ACTUALLY USED THIS THING BEFORE, KIM! YOU WANNA TRY?!
OBVIOUSLY I DO NOT!
KLIK
FOOOM
FUCK! THEY KNOCKED ME OUT!

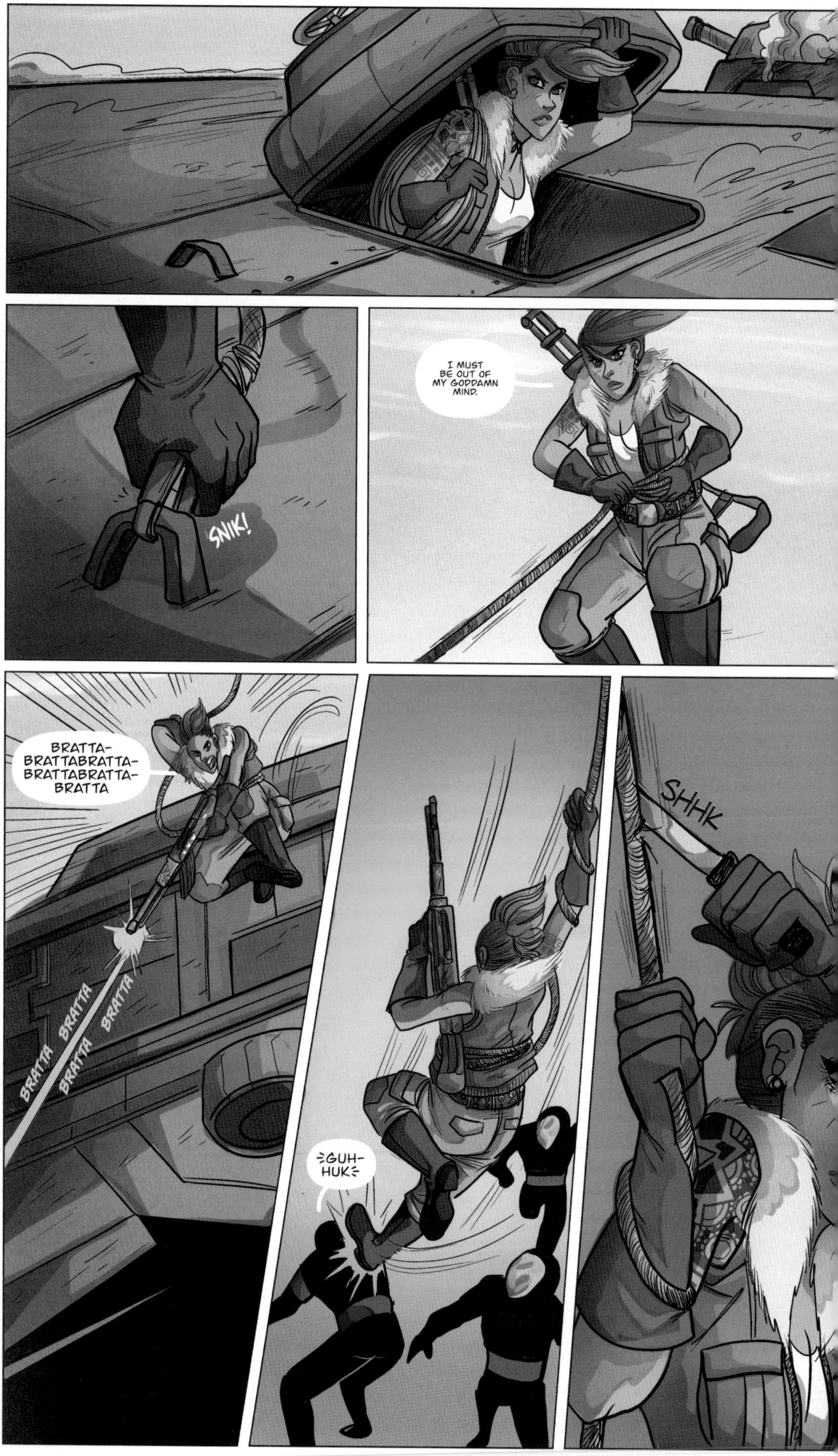
SNIK!
I MUST BE OUT OF MY GODDAMN MIND.
BRATTA-BRATTABRATTA-BRATTABRATTA-BRATTA
BRATTA BRATTA BRATTA BRATTA
GUH-HUK
SHHK

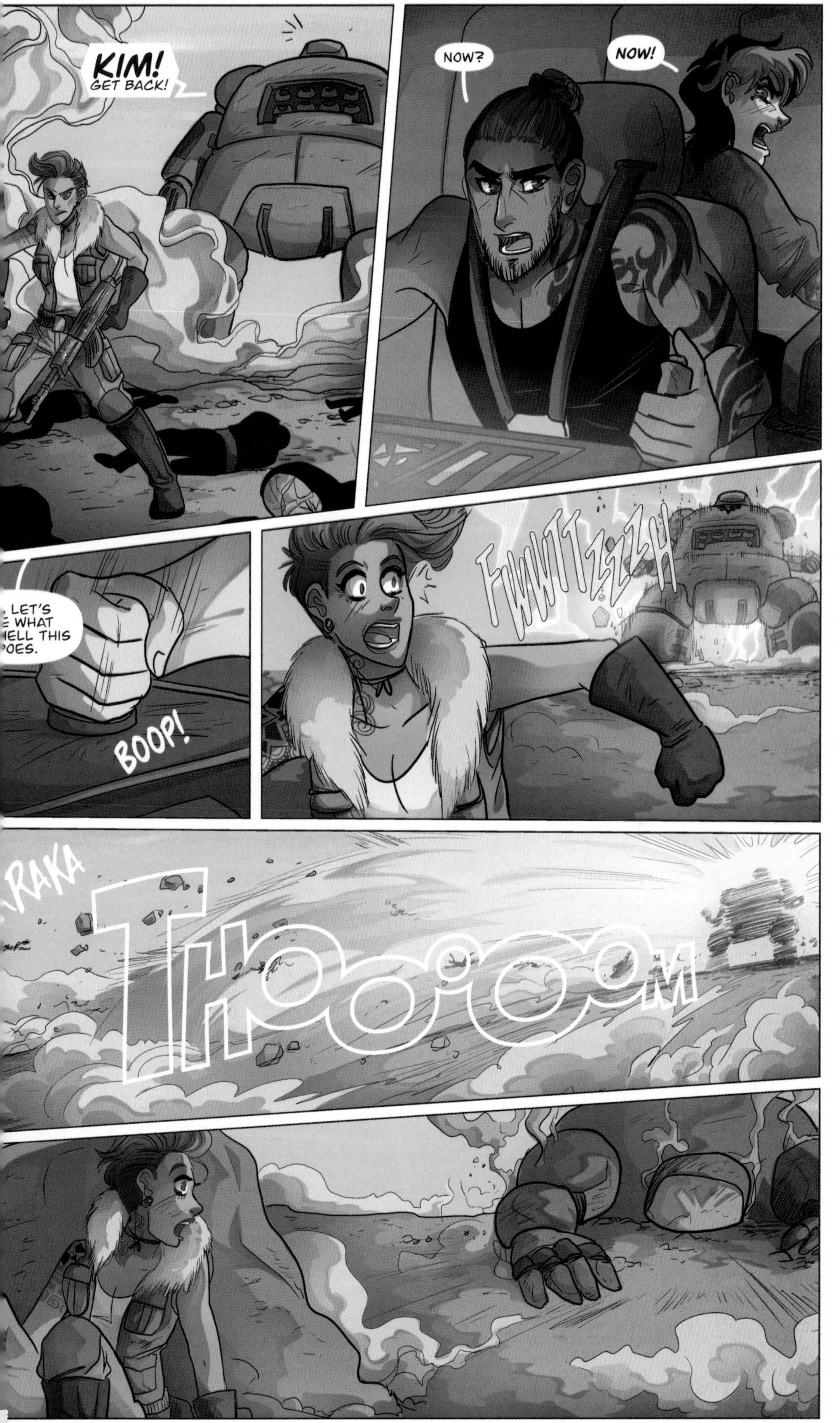
KIM! GET BACK!
NOW?
NOW!
LET'S E WHAT HELL THIS OES.
BOOP!
FWWTTZZZZH
RAKA
THOOOOM

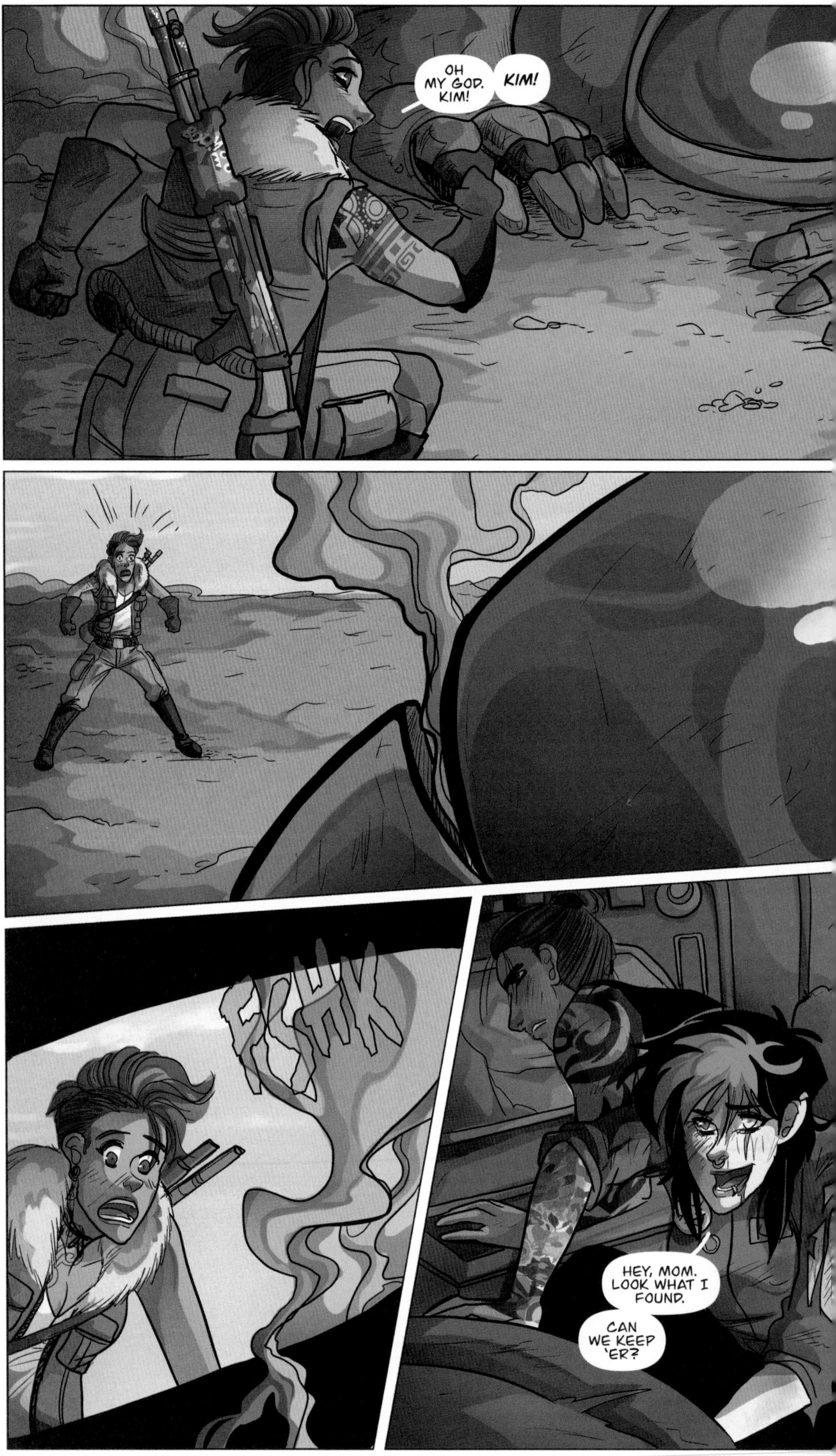
OH MY GOD. KIM!
KIM!
FSSHK
HEY, MOM. LOOK WHAT I FOUND.
CAN WE KEEP 'ER?

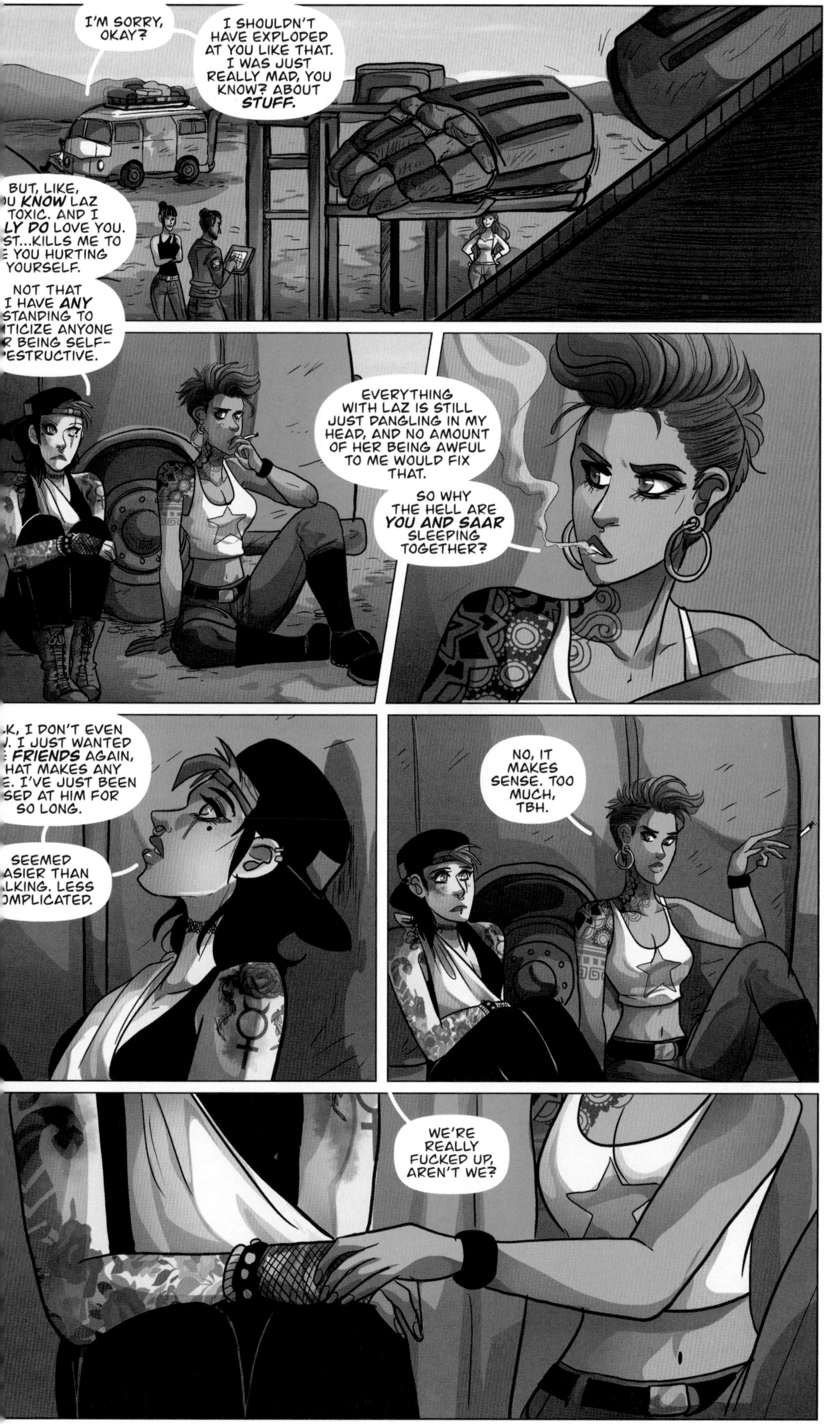

I'M SORRY, OKAY?
I SHOULDN'T HAVE EXPLODED AT YOU LIKE THAT. I WAS JUST REALLY MAD, YOU KNOW? ABOUT STUFF.
BUT, LIKE, U KNOW LAZ TOXIC. AND I LY DO LOVE YOU. ST...KILLS ME TO E YOU HURTING YOURSELF.
NOT THAT I HAVE ANY STANDING TO ITICIZE ANYONE R BEING SELF-ESTRUCTIVE.
EVERYTHING WITH LAZ IS STILL JUST DANGLING IN MY HEAD, AND NO AMOUNT OF HER BEING AWFUL TO ME WOULD FIX THAT.
SO WHY THE HELL ARE YOU AND SAAR SLEEPING TOGETHER?
K, I DON'T EVEN V. I JUST WANTED E FRIENDS AGAIN, HAT MAKES ANY E. I'VE JUST BEEN SED AT HIM FOR SO LONG.
SEEMED ASIER THAN LKING. LESS OMPLICATED.
NO, IT MAKES SENSE. TOO MUCH, TBH.
WE'RE REALLY FUCKED UP, AREN'T WE?

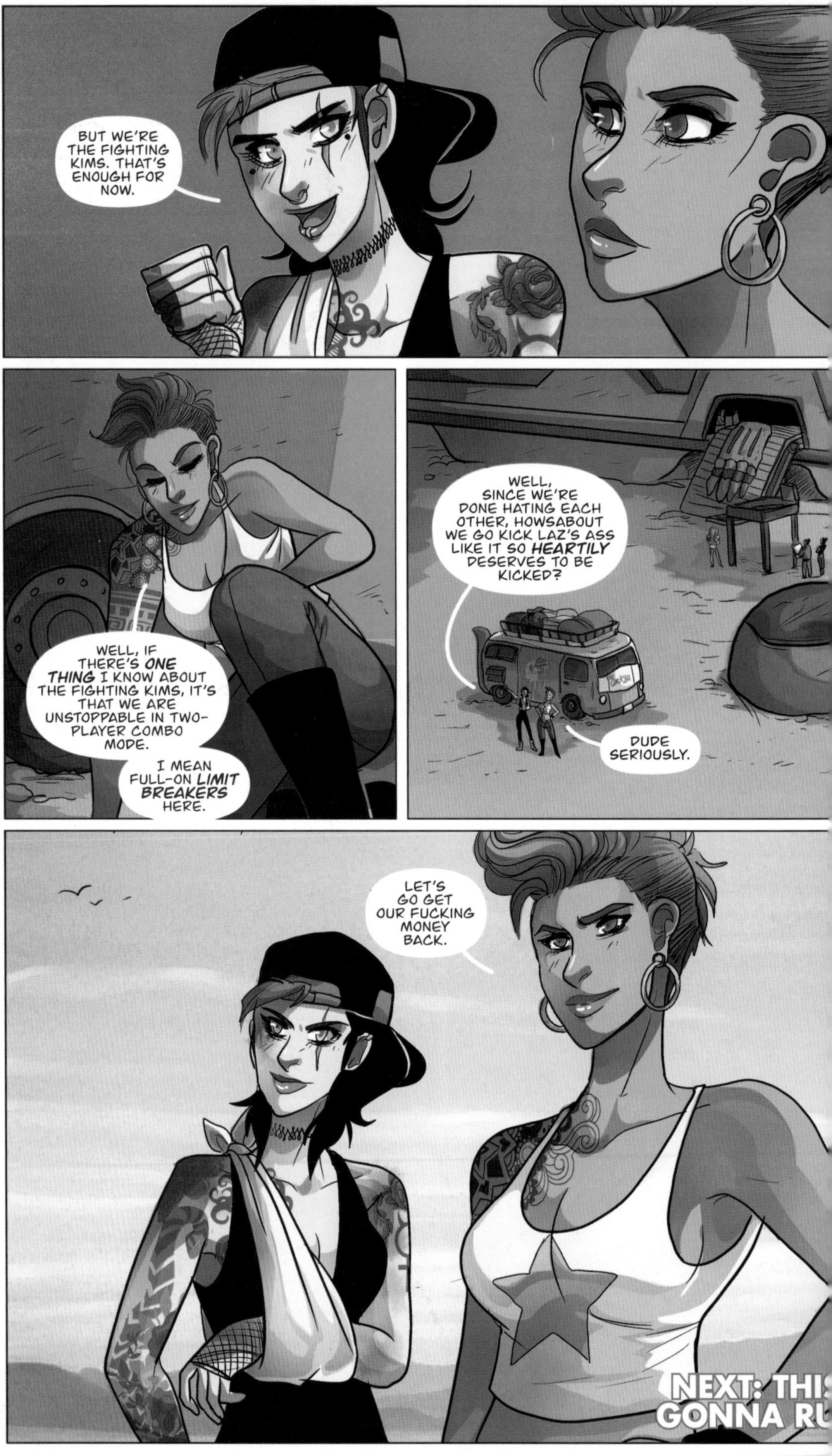
BUT WE'RE THE FIGHTING KIMS. THAT'S ENOUGH FOR NOW.
WELL, IF THERE'S ONE THING I KNOW ABOUT THE FIGHTING KIMS, IT'S THAT WE ARE UNSTOPPABLE IN TWO-PLAYER COMBO MODE.
I MEAN FULL-ON LIMIT BREAKERS HERE.
WELL, SINCE WE'RE DONE HATING EACH OTHER, HOWSABOUT WE GO KICK LAZ'S ASS LIKE IT SO HEARTILY DESERVES TO BE KICKED?
DUDE SERIOUSLY.
LET'S GO GET OUR FUCKING MONEY BACK.
NEXT: THI
GONNA RU

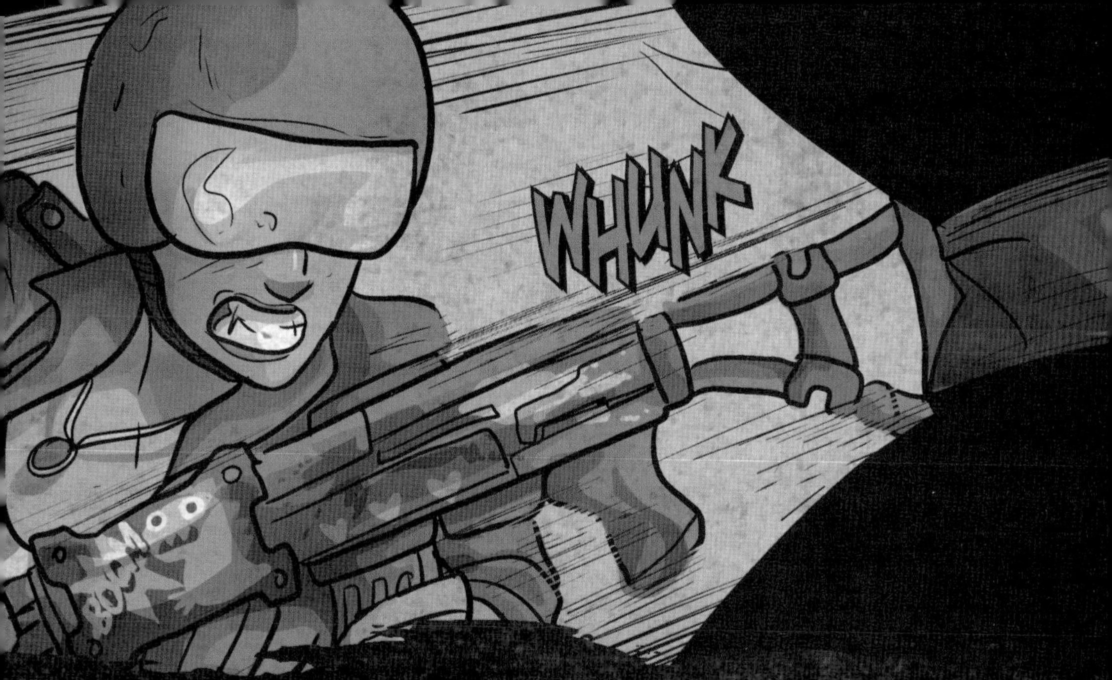
WHUNK

# 4

## “THE BREAKUP FIGHT”

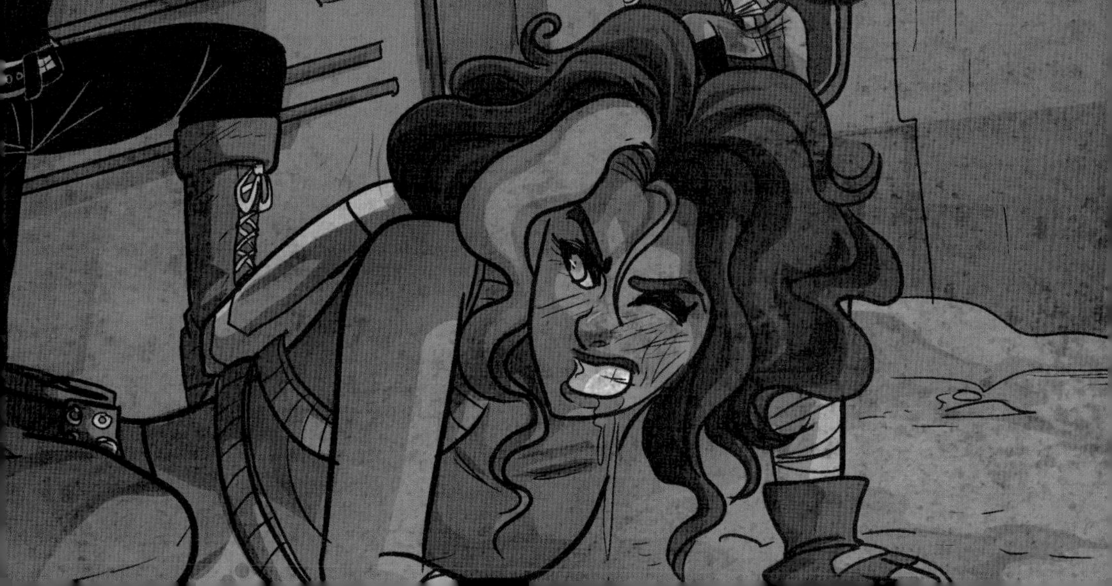

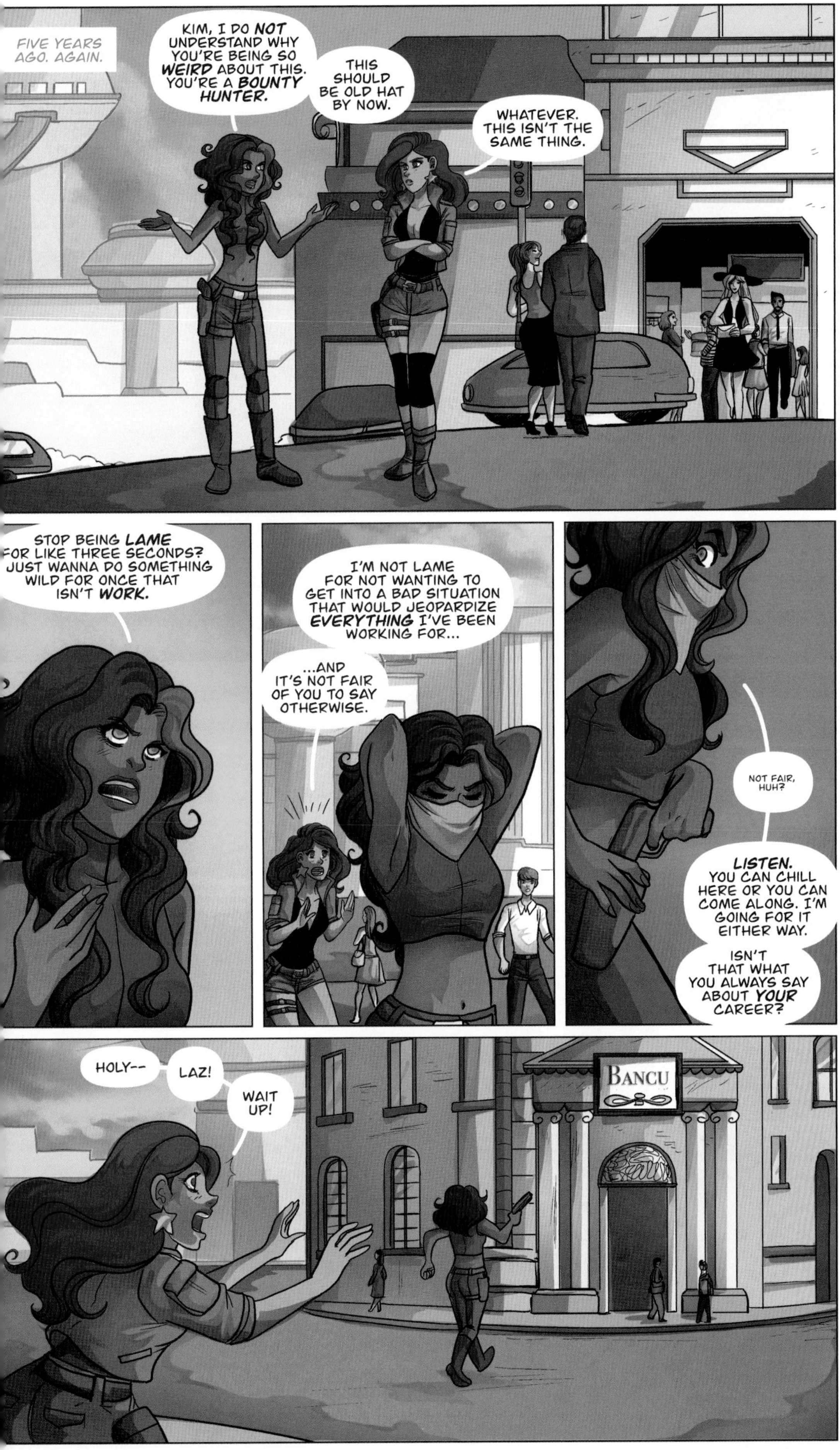
FIVE YEARS AGO. AGAIN.
KIM, I DO NOT UNDERSTAND WHY YOU'RE BEING SO WEIRD ABOUT THIS. YOU'RE A BOUNTY HUNTER.
THIS SHOULD BE OLD HAT BY NOW.
WHATEVER. THIS ISN'T THE SAME THING.
STOP BEING LAME FOR LIKE THREE SECONDS? JUST WANNA DO SOMETHING WILD FOR ONCE THAT ISN'T WORK.
I'M NOT LAME FOR NOT WANTING TO GET INTO A BAD SITUATION THAT WOULD JEOPARDIZE EVERYTHING I'VE BEEN WORKING FOR...
...AND IT'S NOT FAIR OF YOU TO SAY OTHERWISE.
NOT FAIR, HUH?
LISTEN. YOU CAN CHILL HERE OR YOU CAN COME ALONG. I'M GOING FOR IT EITHER WAY.
ISN'T THAT WHAT YOU ALWAYS SAY ABOUT YOUR CAREER?
HOLY--
LAZ!
WAIT UP!
BANCU

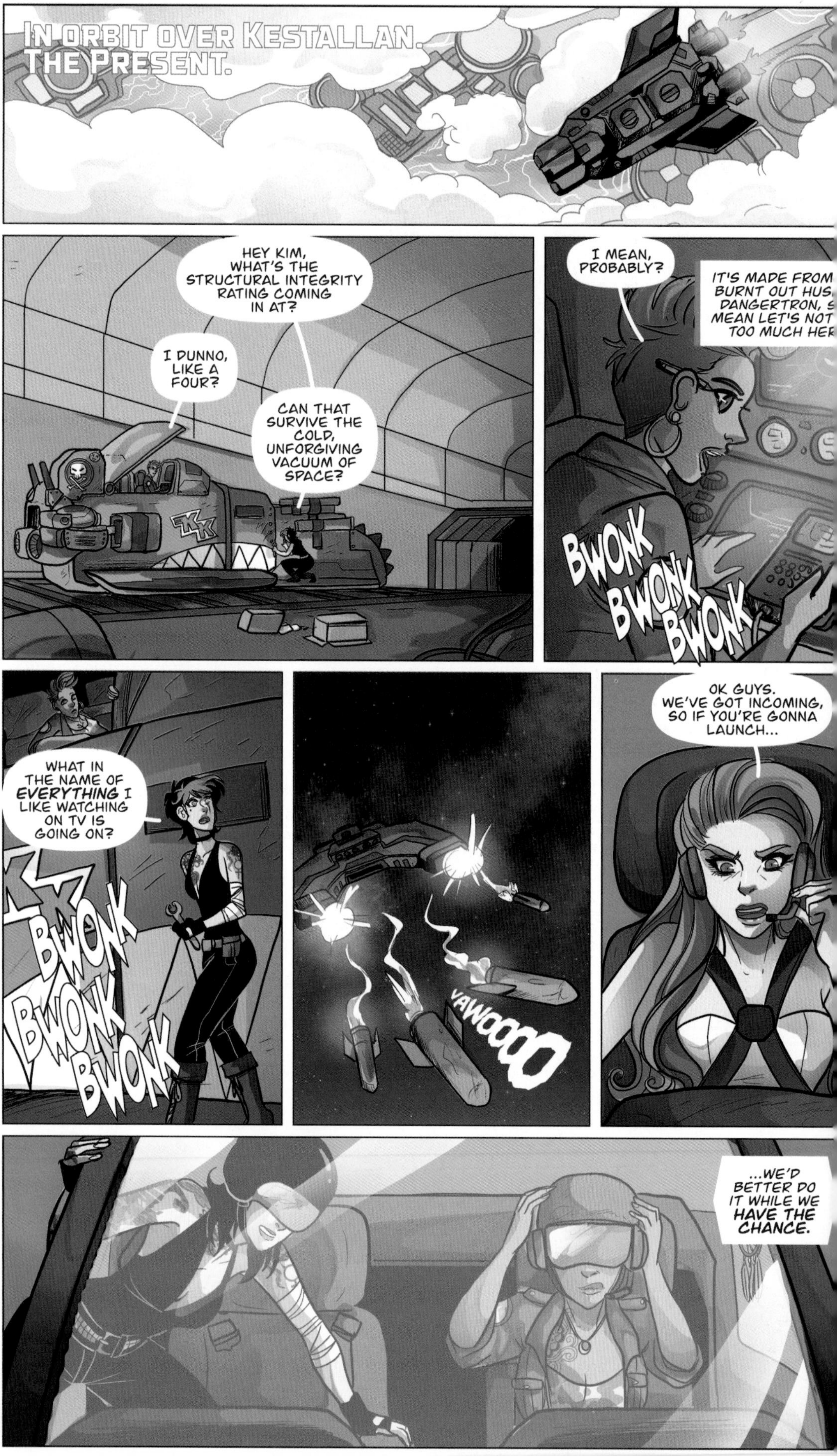
IN ORBIT OVER KESTALLAN. THE PRESENT.
HEY KIM, WHAT'S THE STRUCTURAL INTEGRITY RATING COMING IN AT?
I DUNNO, LIKE A FOUR?
CAN THAT SURVIVE THE COLD, UNFORGIVING VACUUM OF SPACE?
I MEAN, PROBABLY?
IT'S MADE FROM BURNT OUT HUS DANGERTRON, S MEAN LET'S NOT TOO MUCH HER
BWONK BWONK BWONK
WHAT IN THE NAME OF EVERYTHING I LIKE WATCHING ON TV IS GOING ON?
BWONK BWONK BWONK
VAWOOOO
OK GUYS. WE'VE GOT INCOMING, SO IF YOU'RE GONNA LAUNCH...
...WE'D BETTER DO IT WHILE WE HAVE THE CHANCE.

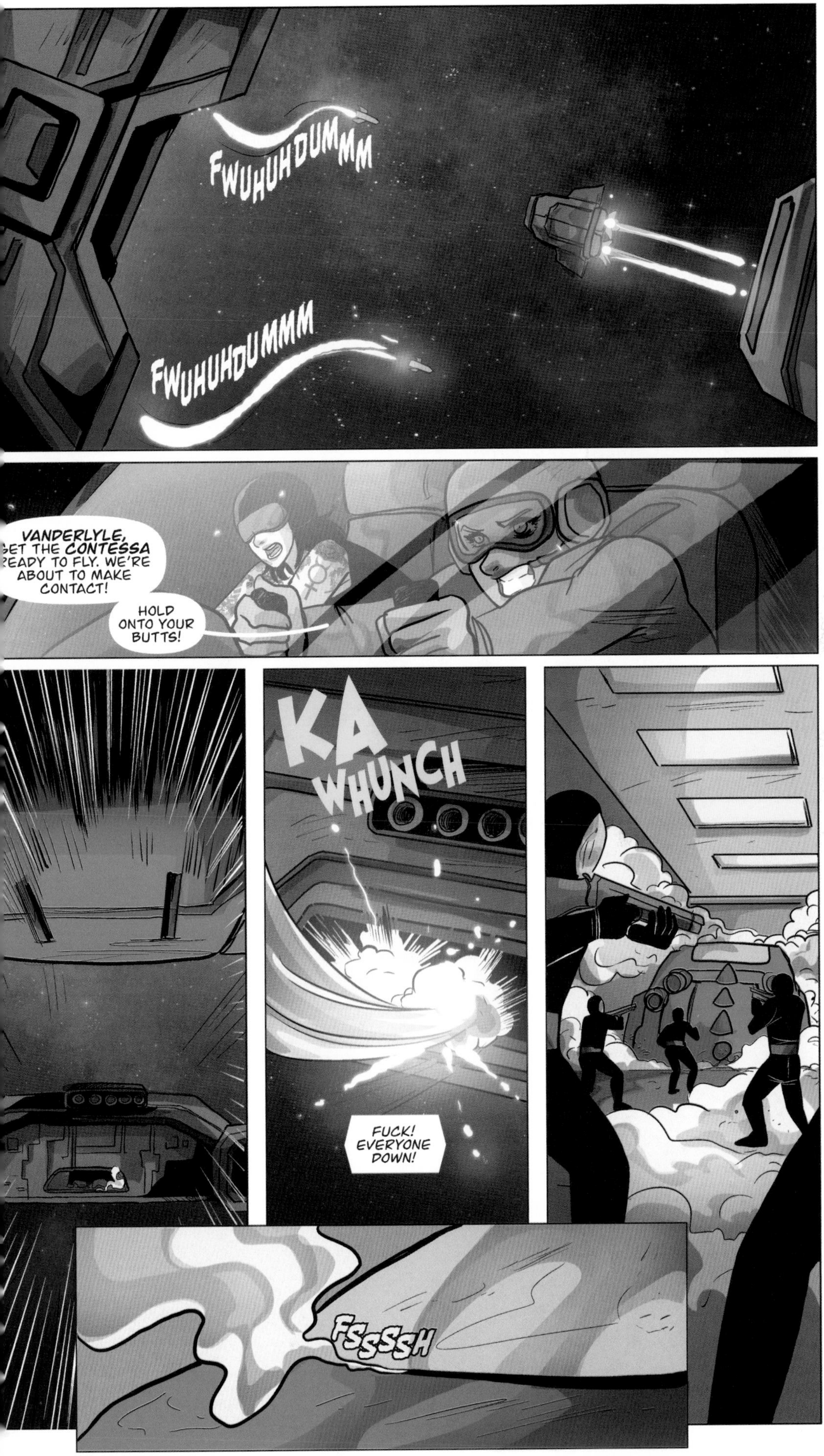
FWUHUHDUMMM
FWUHUHDUMMM
VANDERLYLE, GET THE CONTESSA READY TO FLY. WE'RE ABOUT TO MAKE CONTACT!
HOLD ONTO YOUR BUTTS!
KA WHUNCH
FUCK! EVERYONE DOWN!
FSSSSH

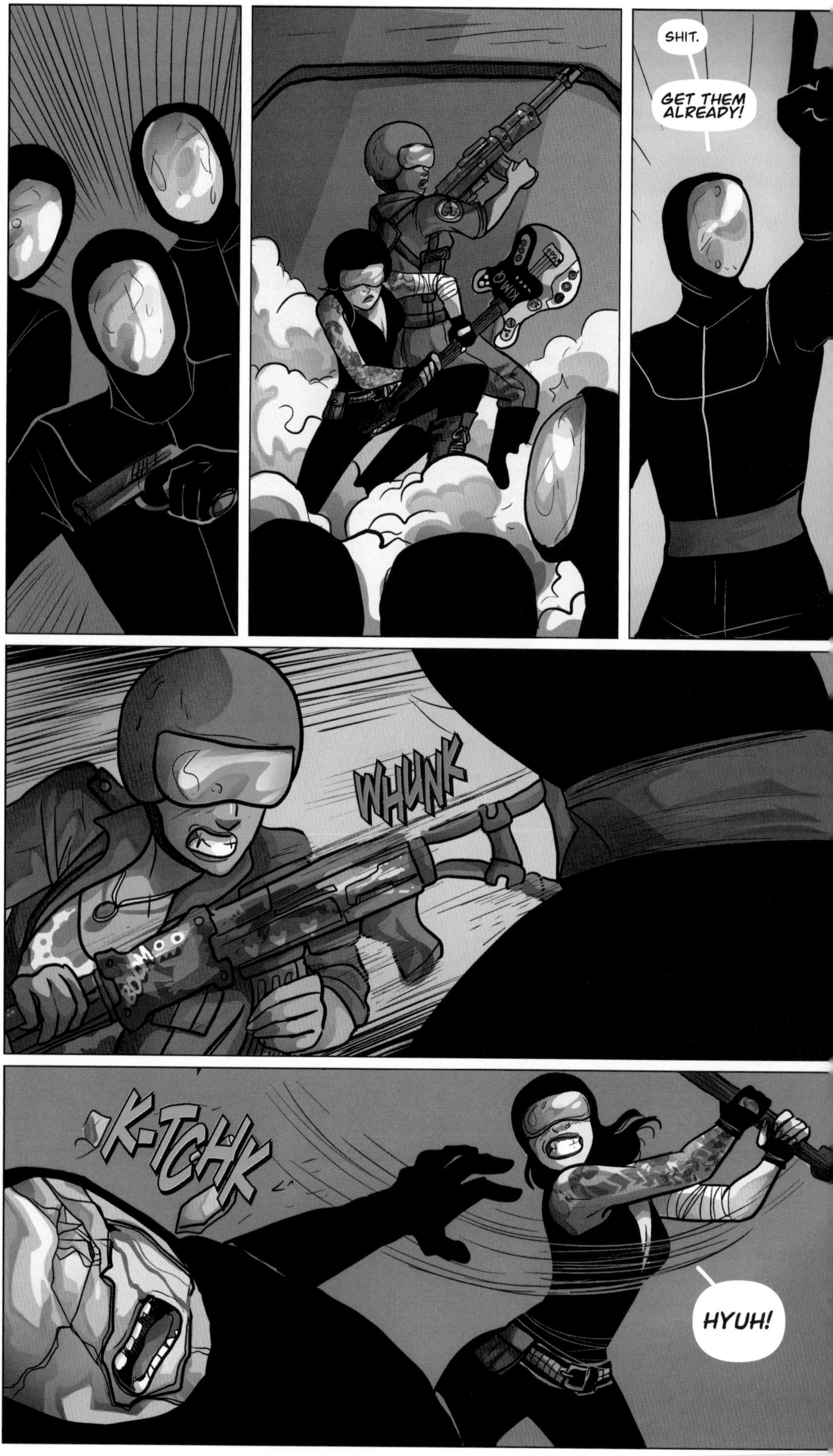
KING
SHIT.
GET THEM ALREADY!
WHUNK
BOOM
K-TCHK
HYUH!

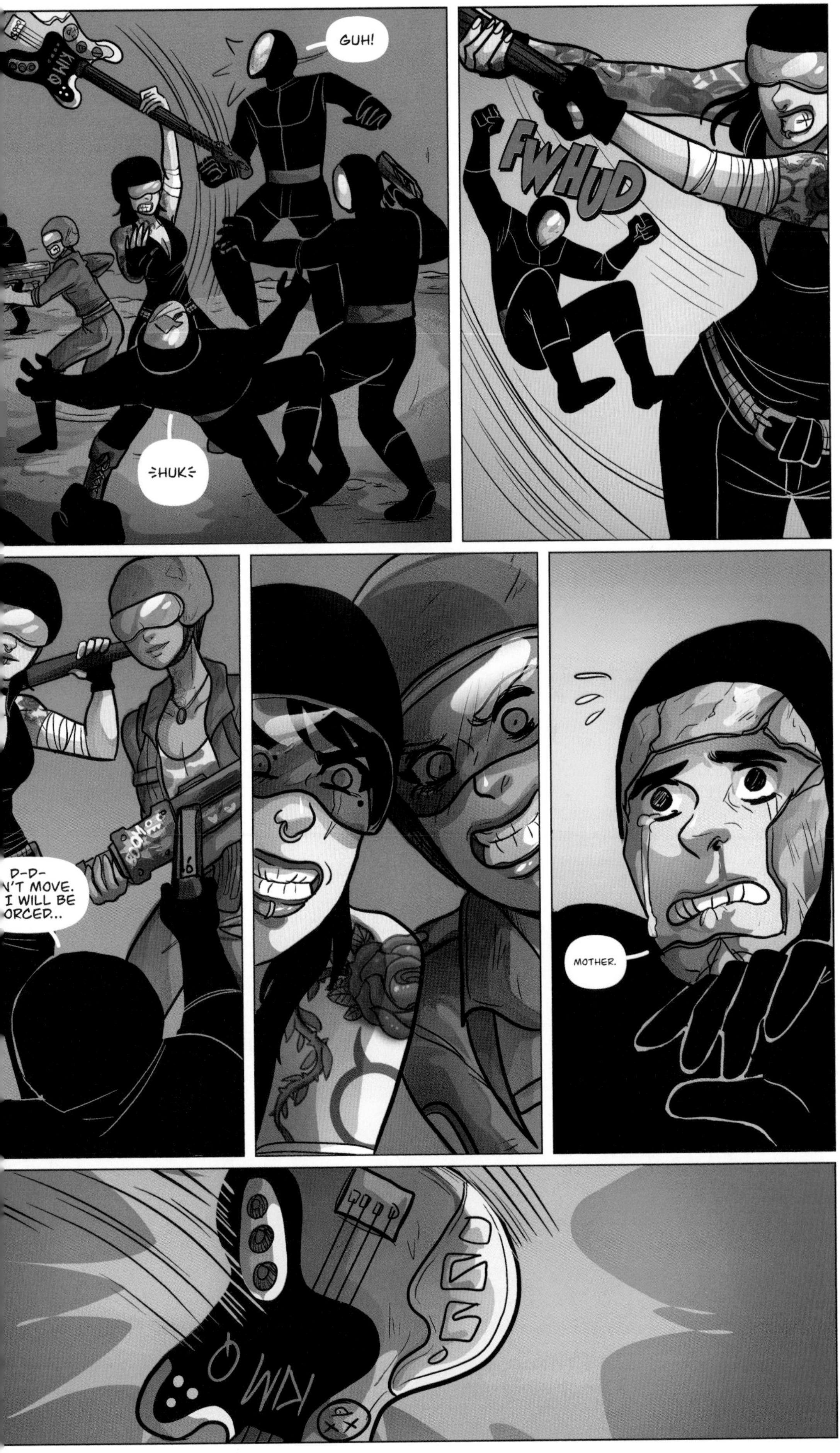
GUH!
HUK
FWHUD
D-D-
N'T MOVE.
I WILL BE
ORCED...
MOTHER.
KIM O
BOOM

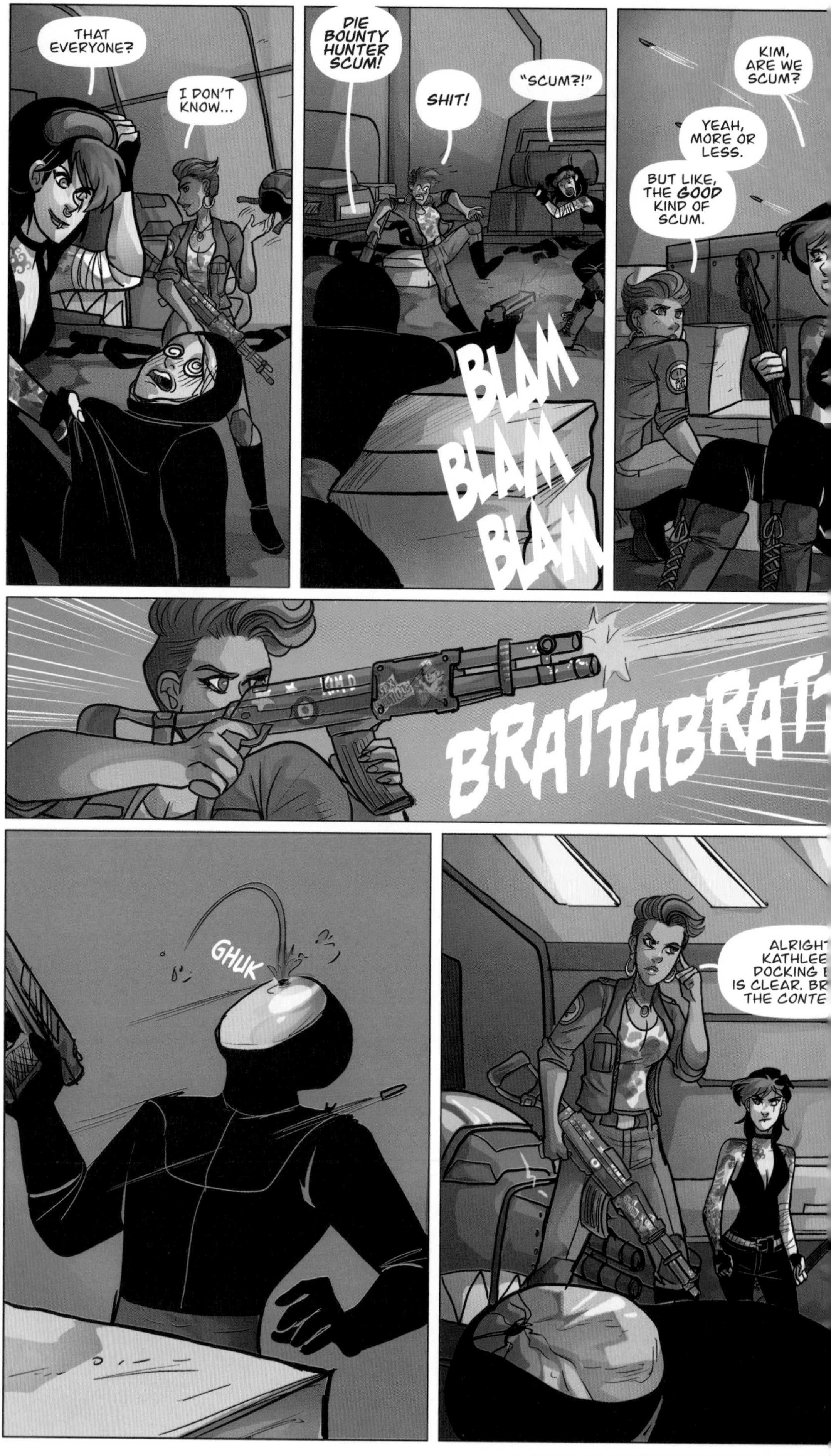
THAT EVERYONE?
I DON'T KNOW...
DIE BOUNTY HUNTER SCUM!
SHIT!
"SCUM?!"
BLAM BLAM BLAM
KIM, ARE WE SCUM?
YEAH, MORE OR LESS.
BUT LIKE, THE GOOD KIND OF SCUM.
BRATTABRAT
GHUK
ALRIGHT
KATHLEE
DOCKING
IS CLEAR. BR
THE CONTE

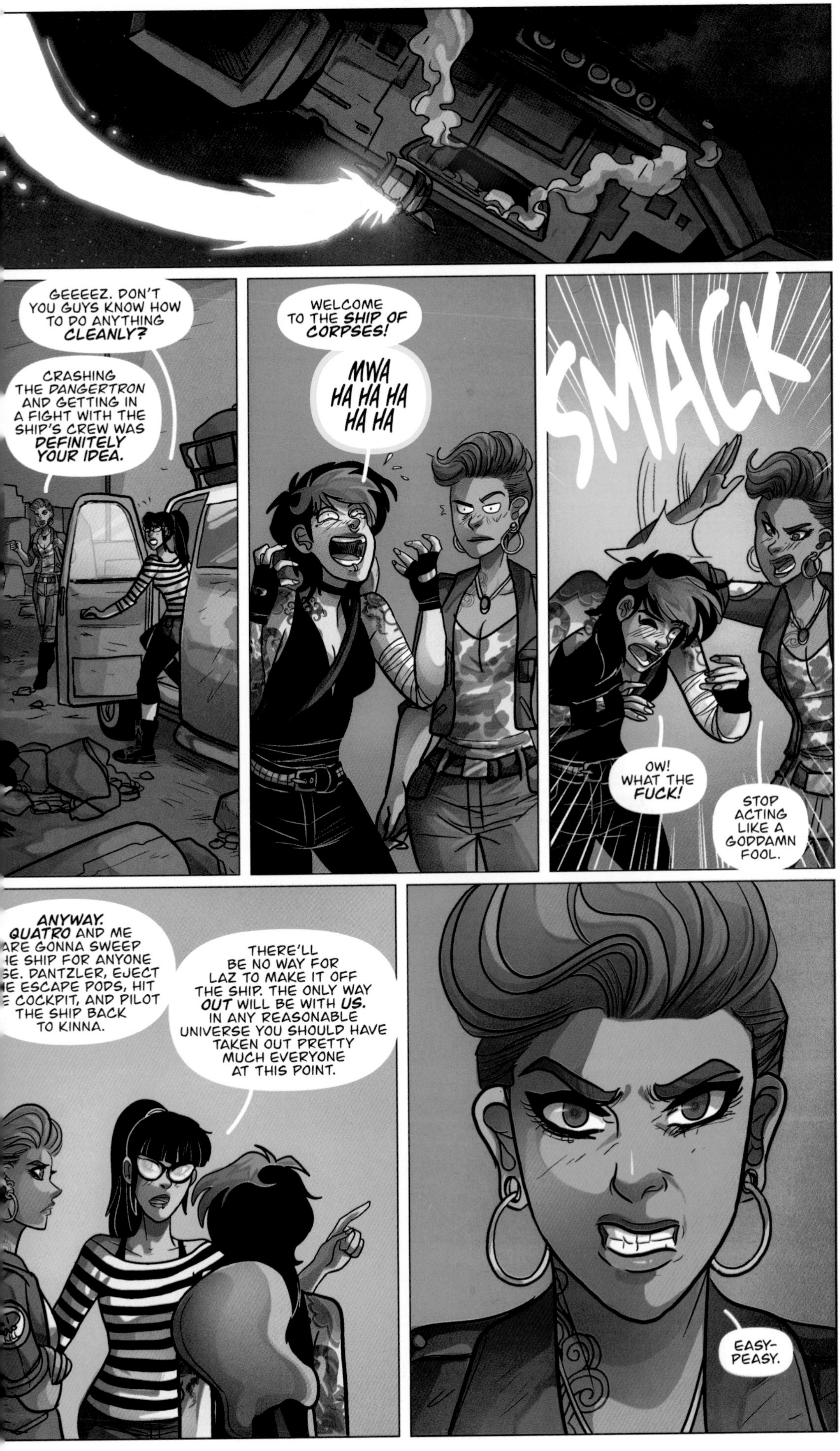

GEEEEZ. DON'T YOU GUYS KNOW HOW TO DO ANYTHING CLEANLY?
CRASHING THE DANGERTRON AND GETTING IN A FIGHT WITH THE SHIP'S CREW WAS DEFINITELY YOUR IDEA.
WELCOME TO THE SHIP OF CORPSES!
MWA HA HA HA HA HA
SMACK
OW! WHAT THE FUCK!
STOP ACTING LIKE A GODDAMN FOOL.
ANYWAY. QUATRO AND ME ARE GONNA SWEEP HE SHIP FOR ANYONE SE. DANTZLER, EJECT E ESCAPE PODS, HIT E COCKPIT, AND PILOT THE SHIP BACK TO KINNA.
THERE'LL BE NO WAY FOR LAZ TO MAKE IT OFF THE SHIP. THE ONLY WAY OUT WILL BE WITH US. IN ANY REASONABLE UNIVERSE YOU SHOULD HAVE TAKEN OUT PRETTY MUCH EVERYONE AT THIS POINT.
EASY-PEASY.

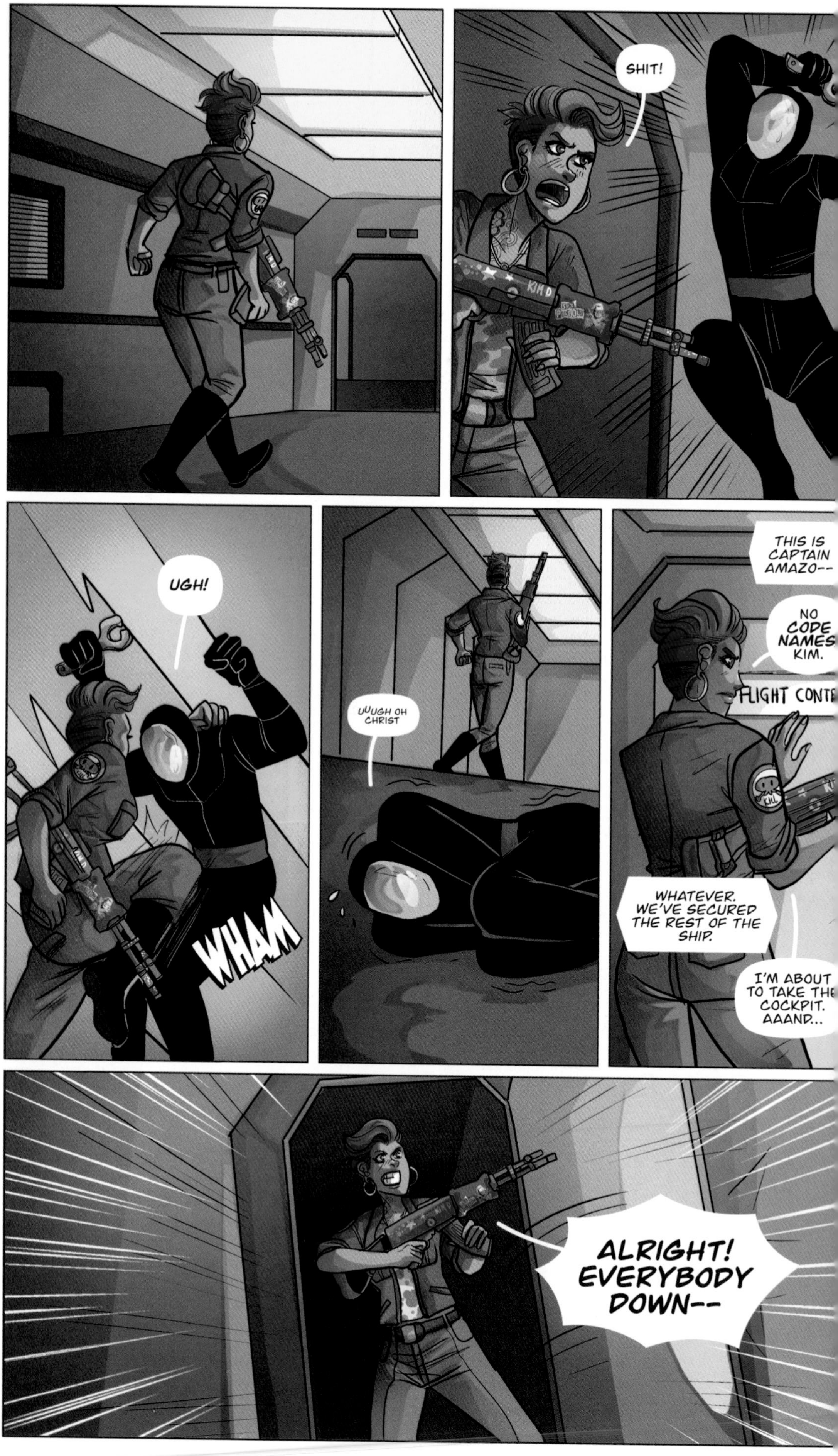

SHIT!
UGH!
WHAM
UUUGH OH CHRIST
THIS IS CAPTAIN AMAZO--
NO CODE NAMES KIM.
FLIGHT CONT
WHATEVER. WE'VE SECURED THE REST OF THE SHIP.
I'M ABOUT TO TAKE TH COCKPIT. AAAND...
ALRIGHT! EVERYBODY DOWN--

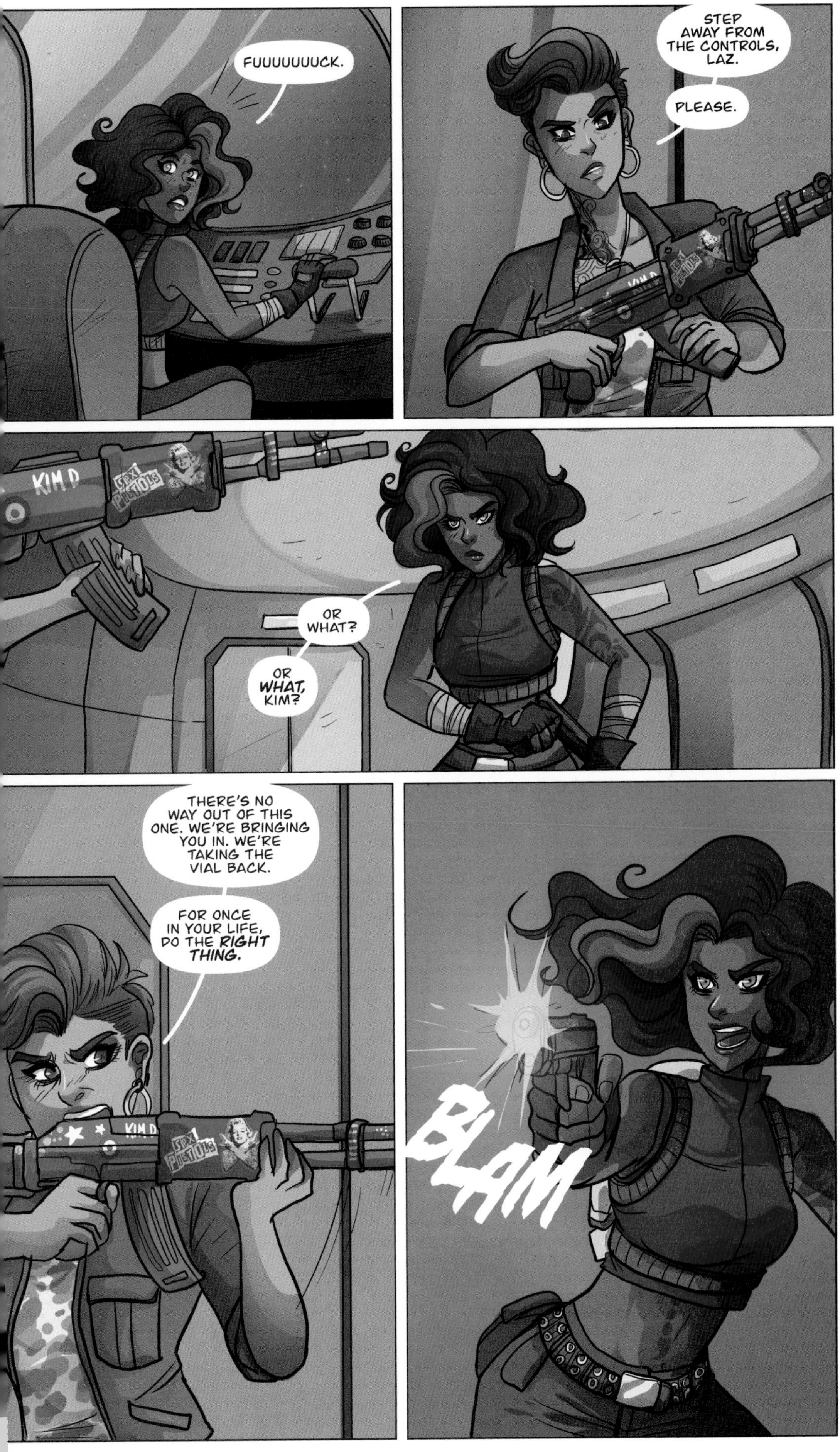
FUUUUUUUCK.
STEP AWAY FROM THE CONTROLS, LAZ.
PLEASE.
OR WHAT?
OR WHAT, KIM?
THERE'S NO WAY OUT OF THIS ONE. WE'RE BRINGING YOU IN. WE'RE TAKING THE VIAL BACK.
FOR ONCE IN YOUR LIFE, DO THE RIGHT THING.
BLAM

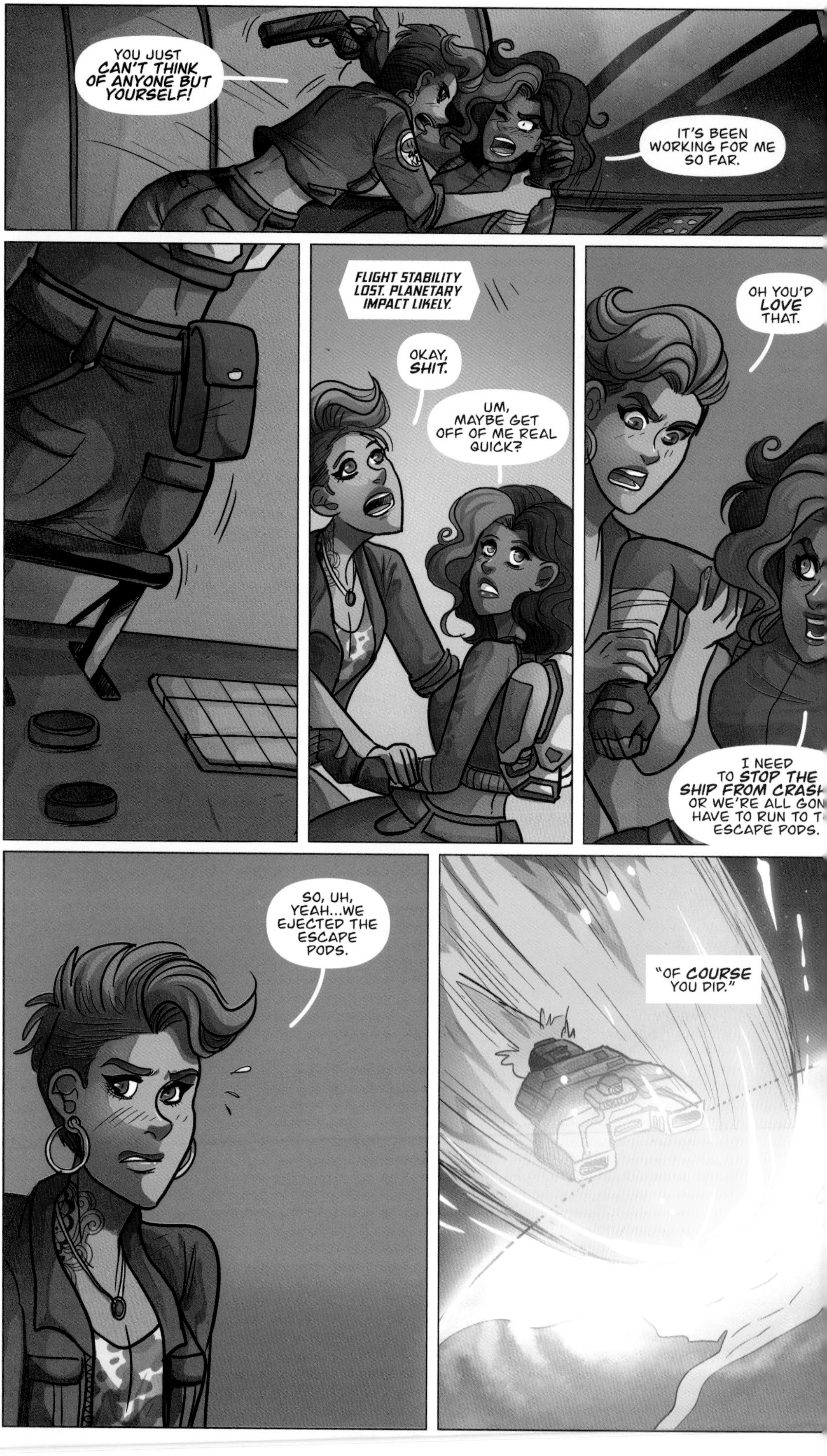
YOU JUST CAN'T THINK OF ANYONE BUT YOURSELF!
IT'S BEEN WORKING FOR ME SO FAR.
FLIGHT STABILITY LOST. PLANETARY IMPACT LIKELY.
OKAY, SHIT.
UM, MAYBE GET OFF OF ME REAL QUICK?
OH YOU'D LOVE THAT.
I NEED TO STOP THE SHIP FROM CRAS OR WE'RE ALL GON HAVE TO RUN TO T ESCAPE PODS.
SO, UH, YEAH...WE EJECTED THE ESCAPE PODS.
"OF COURSE YOU DID."

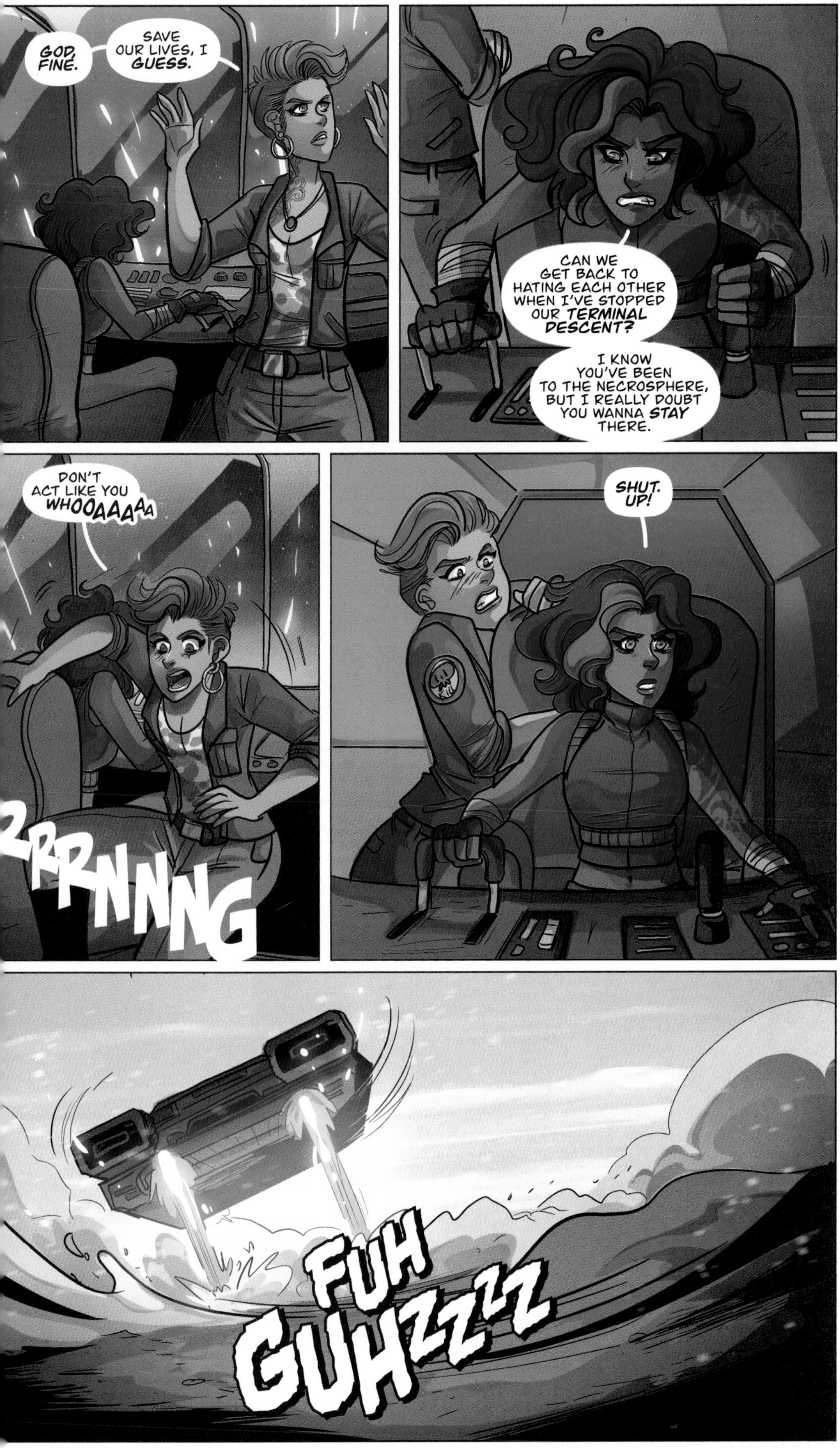
GOD, FINE.
SAVE OUR LIVES, I GUESS.
CAN WE GET BACK TO HATING EACH OTHER WHEN I'VE STOPPED OUR TERMINAL DESCENT?
I KNOW YOU'VE BEEN TO THE NECROSPHERE, BUT I REALLY DOUBT YOU WANNA STAY THERE.
DON'T ACT LIKE YOU WHOOAAAAa
ZRRNNNG
SHUT. UP!
FUH GUHZzzz

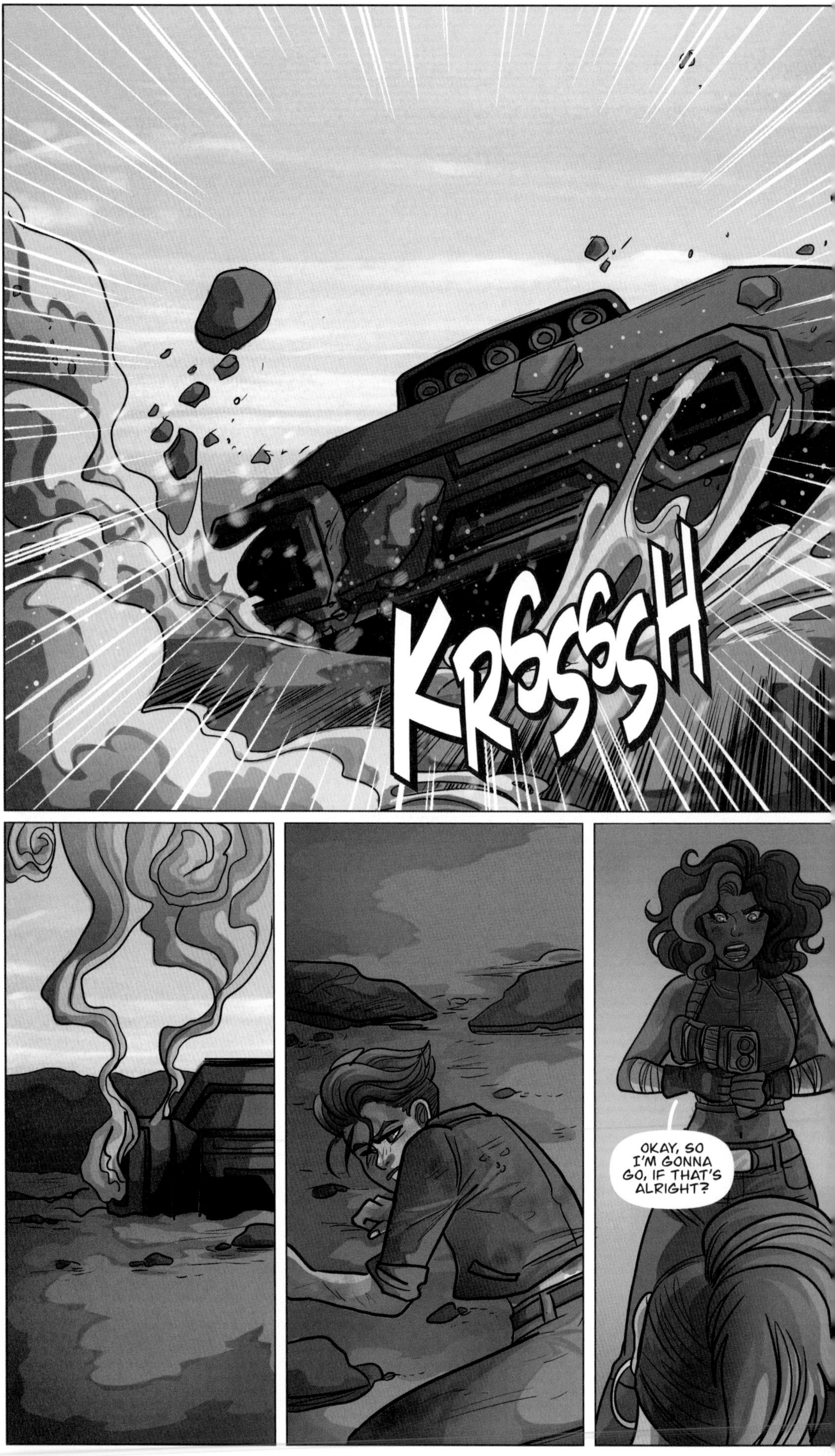
KRSSSSH
OKAY, SO I'M GONNA GO, IF THAT'S ALRIGHT?

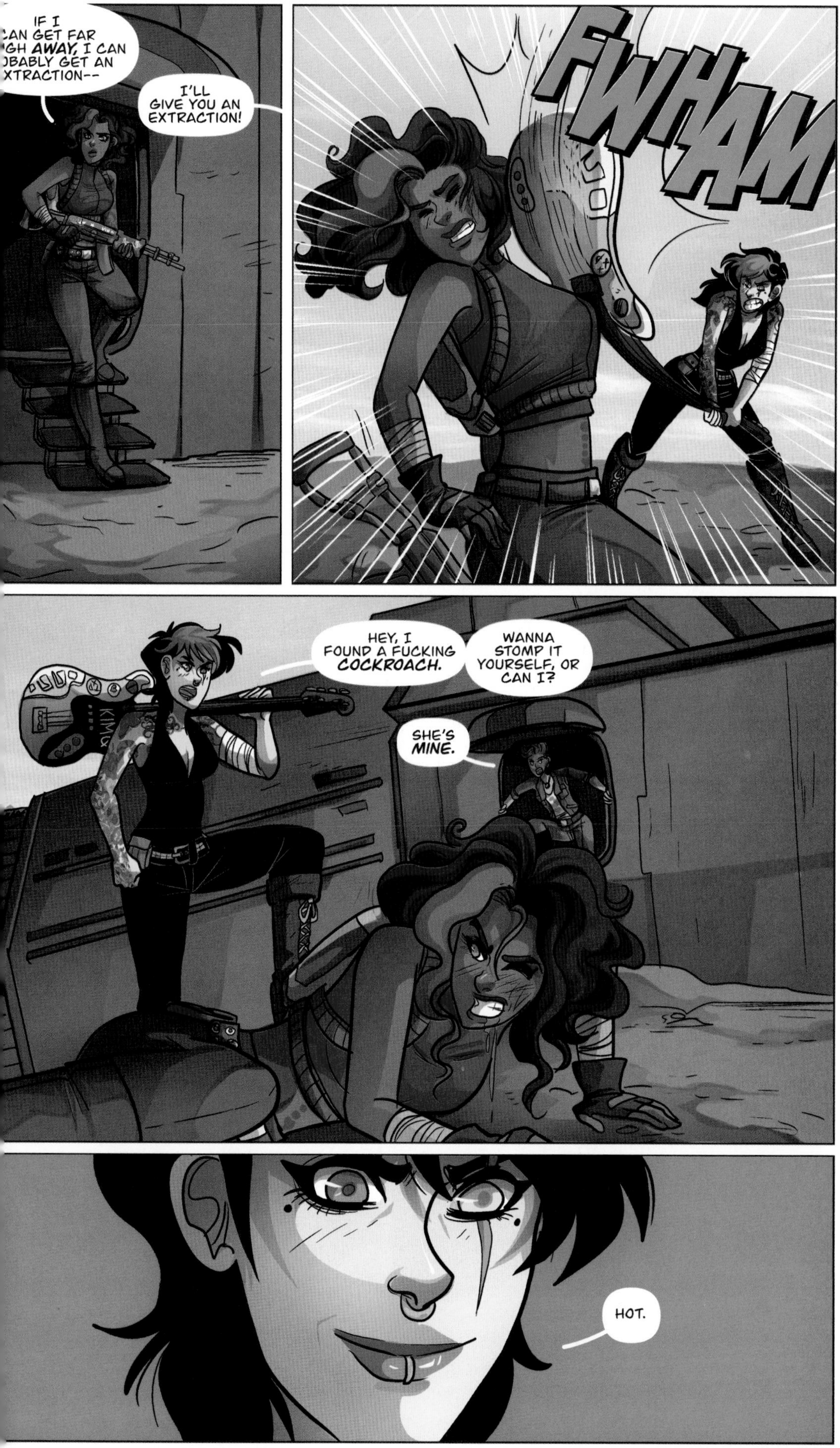
IF I CAN GET FAR GH AWAY, I CAN OBABLY GET AN XTRACTION--
I'LL GIVE YOU AN EXTRACTION!
FWHAM
HEY, I FOUND A FUCKING COCKROACH.
WANNA STOMP IT YOURSELF, OR CAN I?
SHE'S MINE.
HOT.

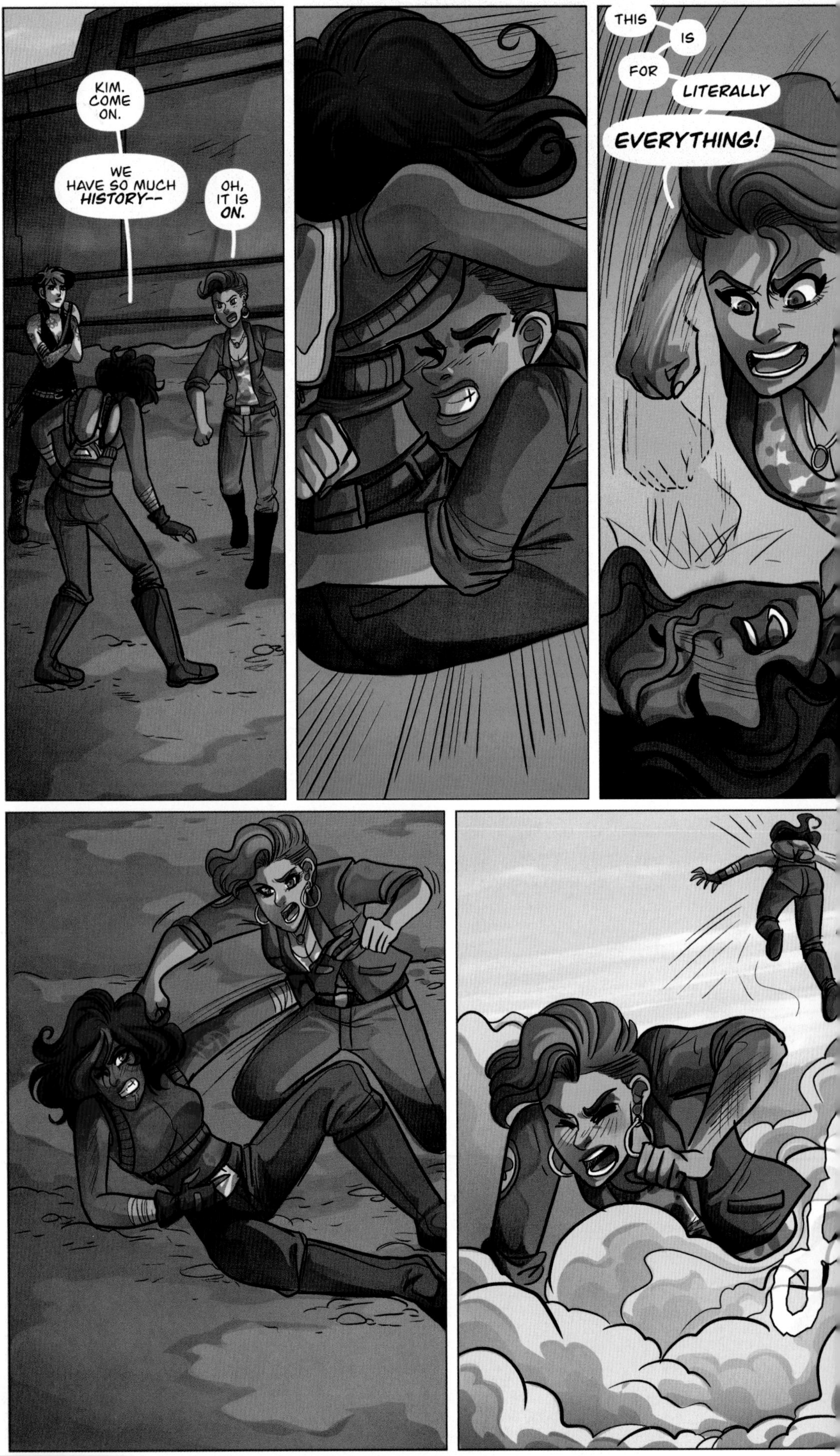
KIM. COME ON.
WE HAVE SO MUCH HISTORY--
OH, IT IS ON.
THIS
IS
FOR
LITERALLY
EVERYTHING!

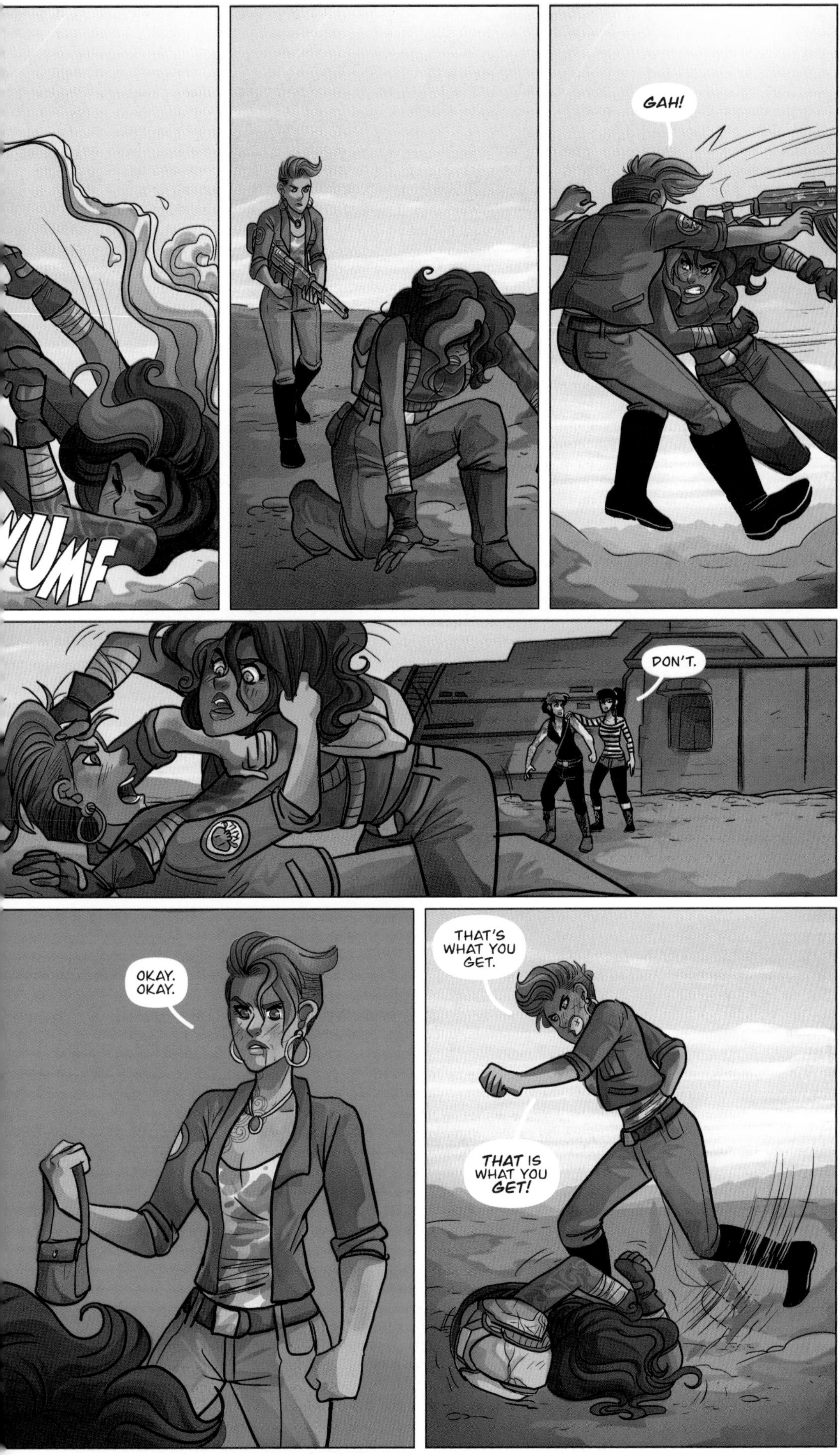
WUMF
GAH!
DON'T.
OKAY.
OKAY.
THAT'S
WHAT YOU
GET.
THAT IS
WHAT YOU
GET!

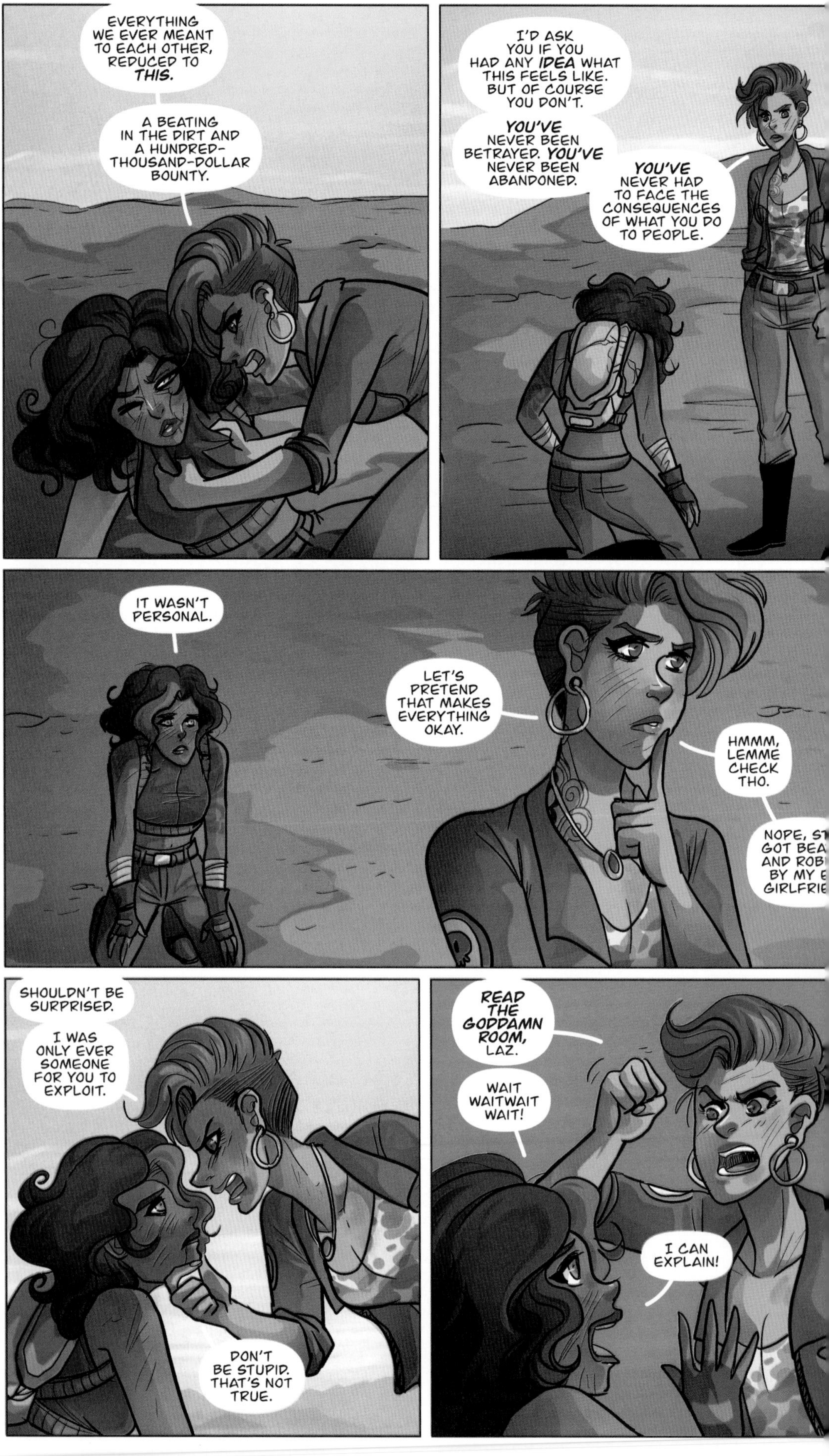

EVERYTHING WE EVER MEANT TO EACH OTHER, REDUCED TO THIS.
A BEATING IN THE DIRT AND A HUNDRED-THOUSAND-DOLLAR BOUNTY.
I'D ASK YOU IF YOU HAD ANY IDEA WHAT THIS FEELS LIKE. BUT OF COURSE YOU DON'T.
YOU'VE NEVER BEEN BETRAYED. YOU'VE NEVER BEEN ABANDONED.
YOU'VE NEVER HAD TO FACE THE CONSEQUENCES OF WHAT YOU DO TO PEOPLE.
IT WASN'T PERSONAL.
LET'S PRETEND THAT MAKES EVERYTHING OKAY.
HMMM, LEMME CHECK THO.
NOPE, ST GOT BEA AND ROB BY MY E GIRLFRIE
SHOULDN'T BE SURPRISED.
I WAS ONLY EVER SOMEONE FOR YOU TO EXPLOIT.
DON'T BE STUPID. THAT'S NOT TRUE.
READ THE GODDAMN ROOM, LAZ.
WAIT WAITWAIT WAIT!
I CAN EXPLAIN!

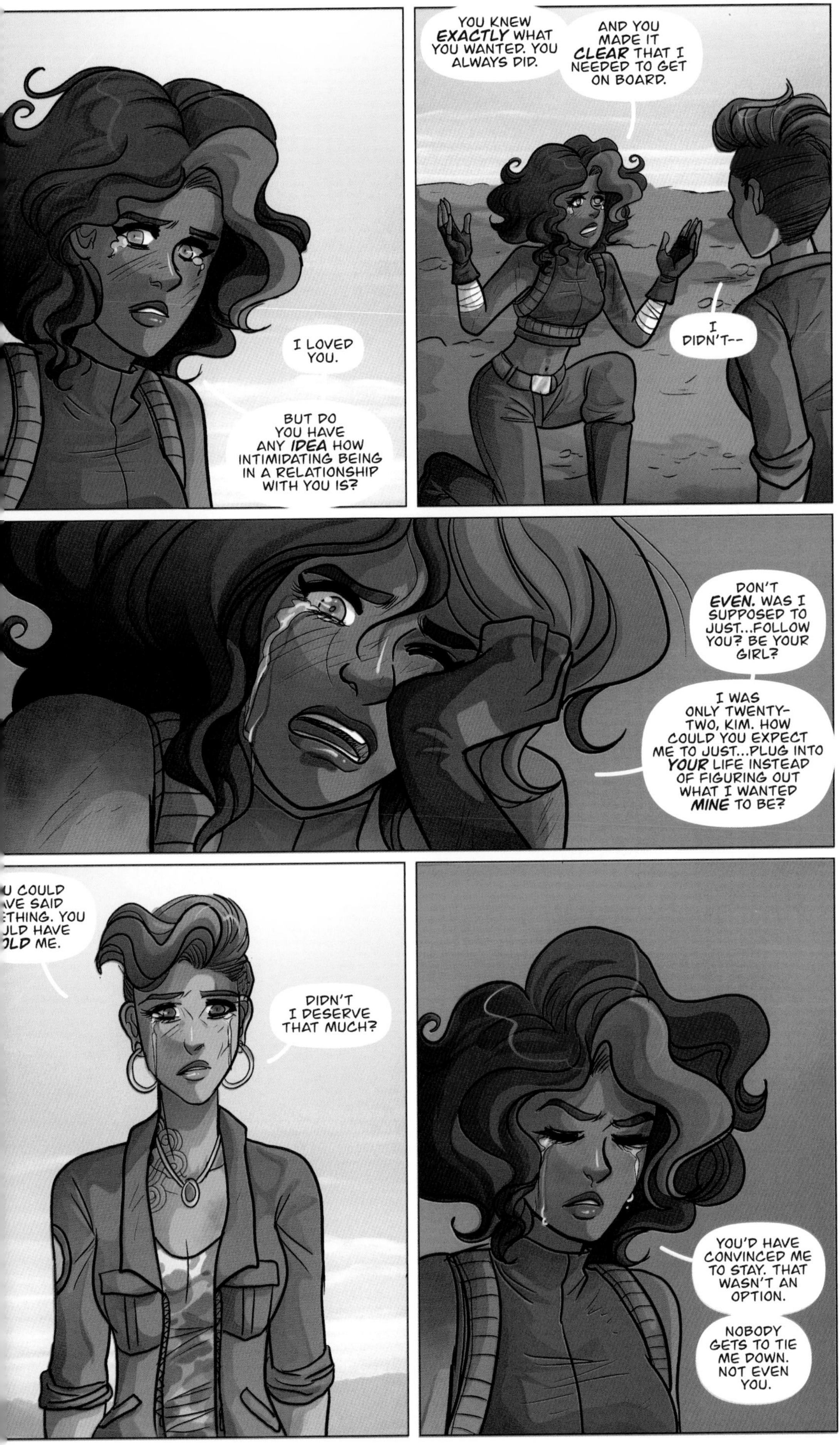
I LOVED YOU.
BUT DO YOU HAVE ANY IDEA HOW INTIMIDATING BEING IN A RELATIONSHIP WITH YOU IS?
YOU KNEW EXACTLY WHAT YOU WANTED. YOU ALWAYS DID.
AND YOU MADE IT CLEAR THAT I NEEDED TO GET ON BOARD.
I DIDN'T--
DON'T EVEN. WAS I SUPPOSED TO JUST...FOLLOW YOU? BE YOUR GIRL?
I WAS ONLY TWENTY-TWO, KIM. HOW COULD YOU EXPECT ME TO JUST...PLUG INTO YOUR LIFE INSTEAD OF FIGURING OUT WHAT I WANTED MINE TO BE?
U COULD AVE SAID ETHING. YOU ULD HAVE OLD ME.
DIDN'T I DESERVE THAT MUCH?
YOU'D HAVE CONVINCED ME TO STAY. THAT WASN'T AN OPTION.
NOBODY GETS TO TIE ME DOWN. NOT EVEN YOU.

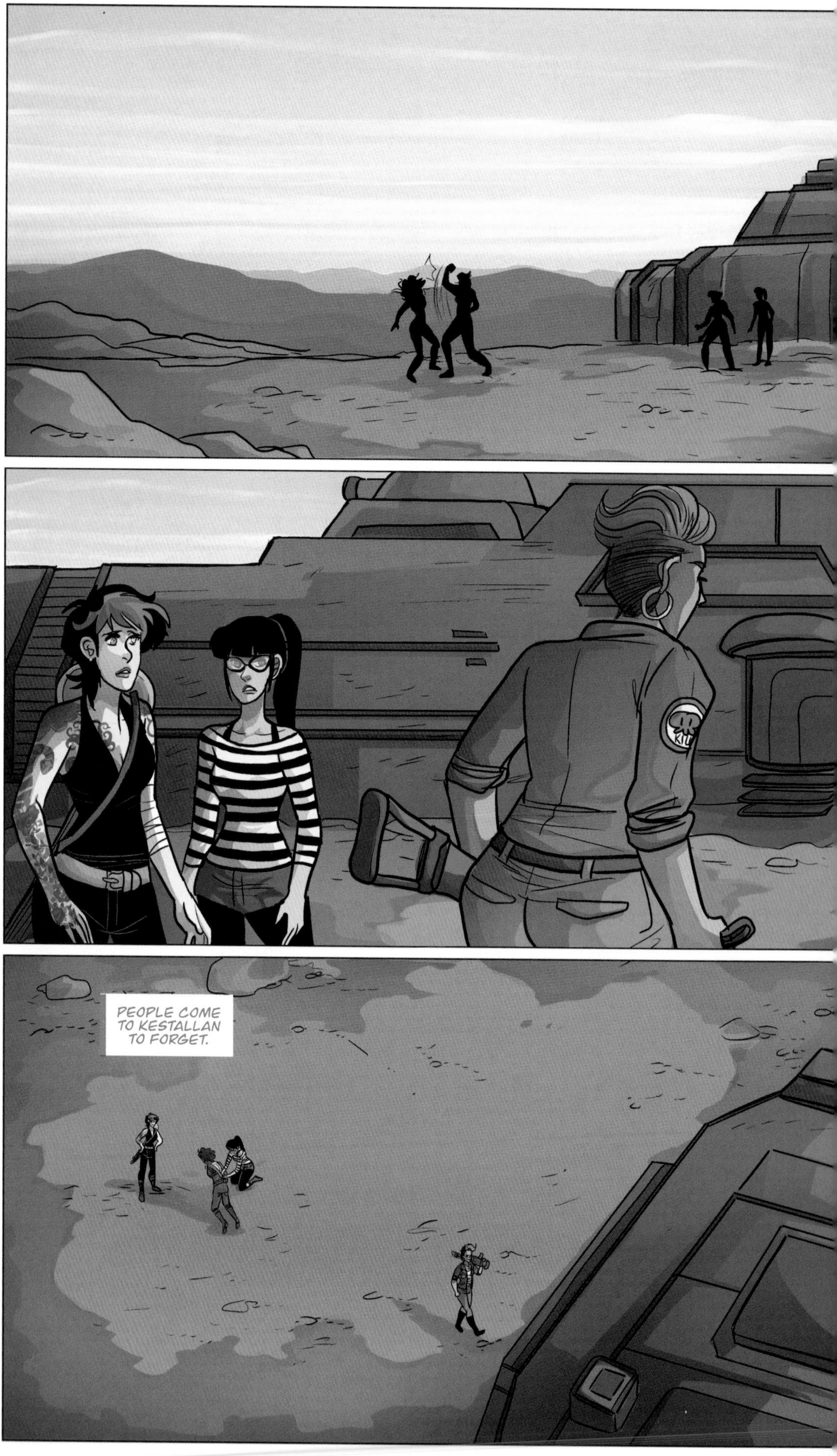
PEOPLE COME TO KESTALLAN TO FORGET.

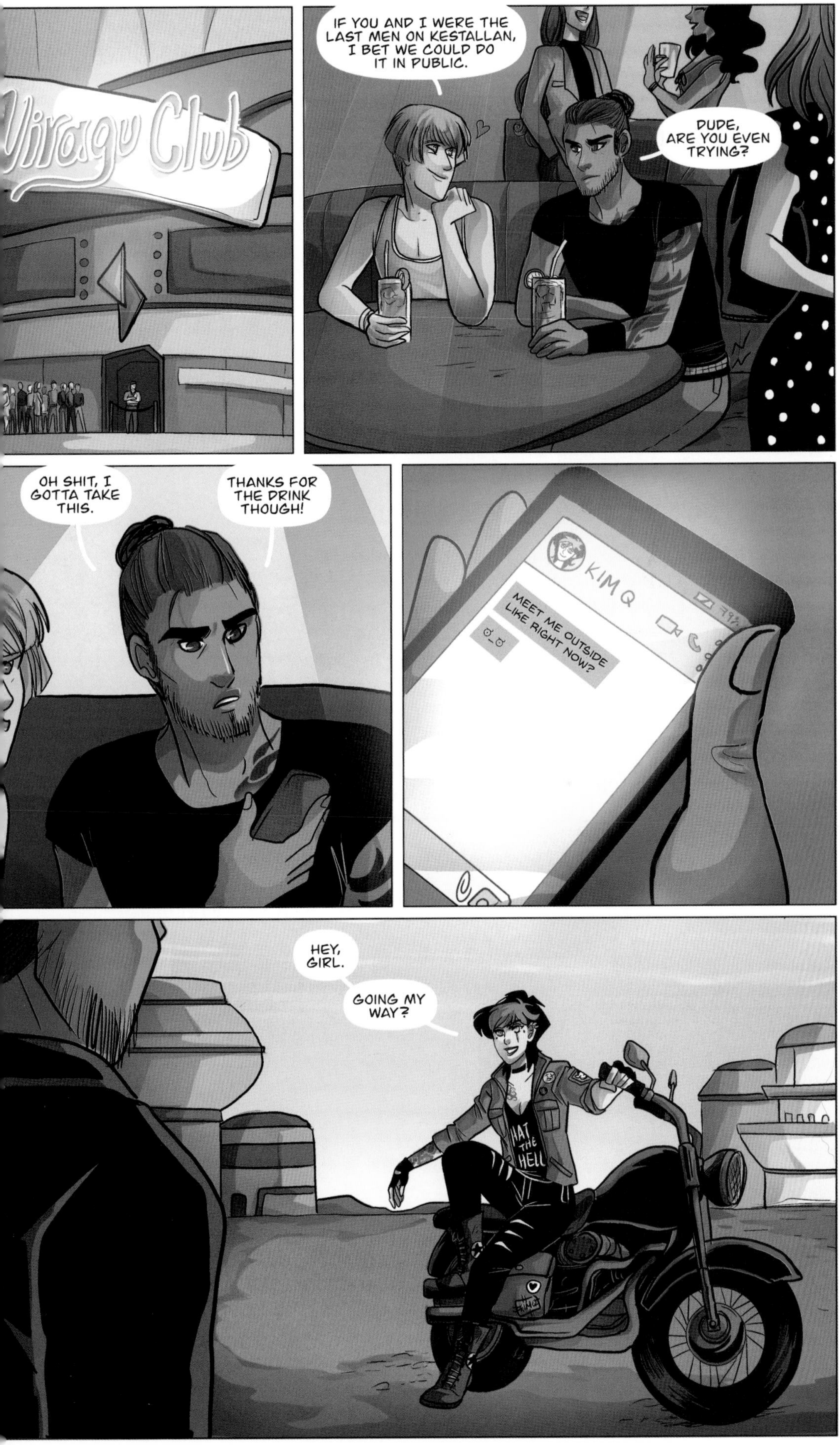
Virago Club
IF YOU AND I WERE THE LAST MEN ON KESTALLAN, I BET WE COULD DO IT IN PUBLIC.
DUDE, ARE YOU EVEN TRYING?
OH SHIT, I GOTTA TAKE THIS.
THANKS FOR THE DRINK THOUGH!
KIM Q
MEET ME OUTSIDE LIKE RIGHT NOW?
ಠ_ಠ
HEY, GIRL.
GOING MY WAY?

WANNA DANCE FOR A WHILE?

CAN'T. KIM WANTS TO BOUNCE ASAP AND, YOU KNOW, SHE'S LIKE MY ENTIRE LIFE, SO...

HA, I GET IT.

LISTEN. I WANTED TO SEE YOU BEFORE I LEFT. I MEAN, ABOUT US AND EVERYTHING.

I JUST... I DON'T KNOW THAT WE SHOULD KEEP DOING WHAT WE'RE DOING.

I MEAN, IT'S BEEN REALLY FUN. OH MAN. SO THANKS FOR THAT. TOP GRADE WORK.

BUT I GUESS...I GUESS I WAN LEARN HOW TO FRIENDS AGA IF THAT MAK SENSE.

NO, TOTALLY. SO, WHAT? YOU WANNA START BACK AT SQUARE ONE?

I MEAN, I DON'T KNOW? BUT WE SHOULD FIGURE IT OUT WHEN WE'RE ALL BACK HOME.

CALL ME?

FUCK SAAR WHAT THE FUCK DID I JUST SAY

WHAT? I FELT THE HEAT!

CALL ME, OKAY? AS FRIENDS.

WE CAN DO THAT, RIGHT?

VRMMMMM

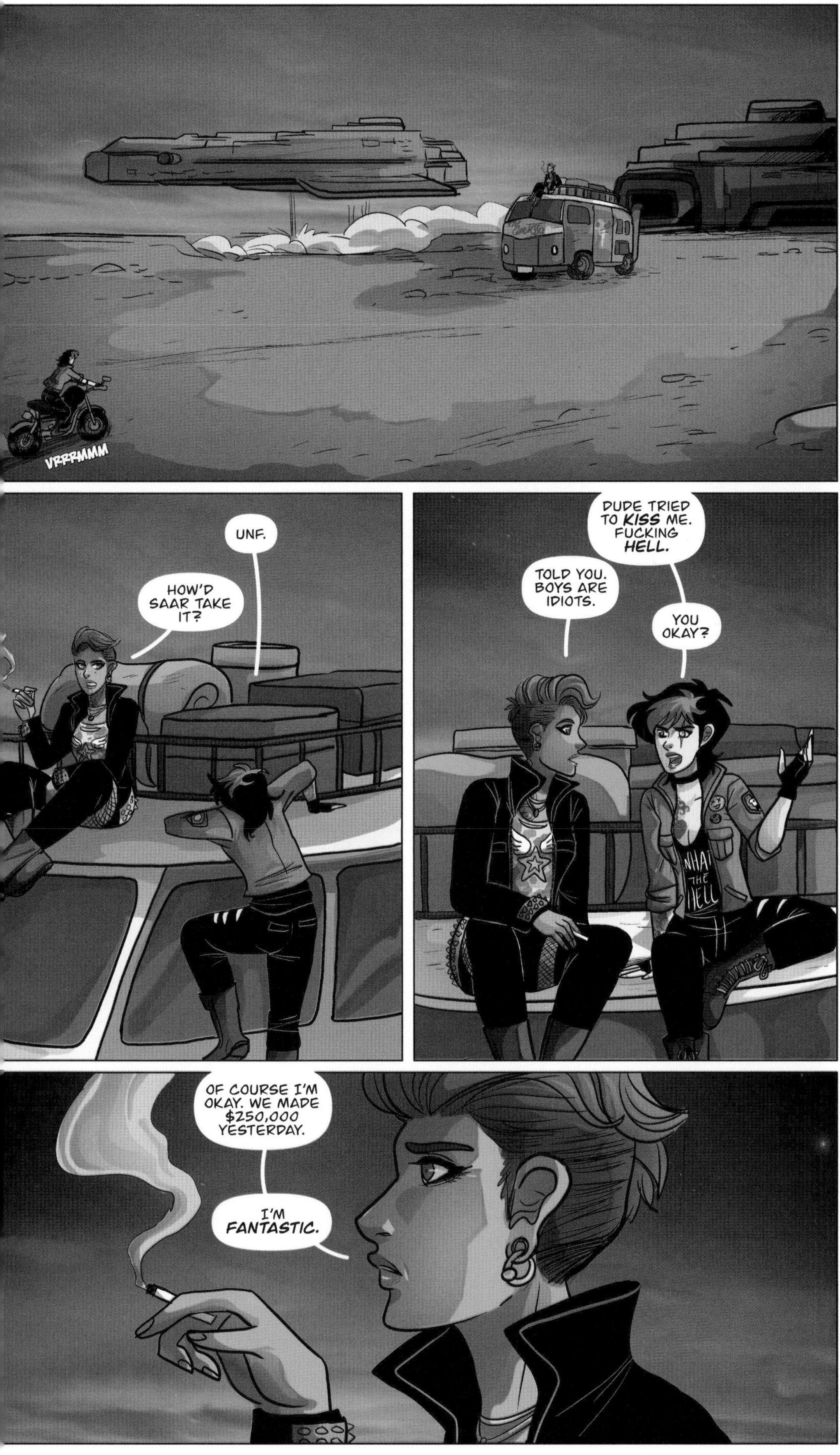
VRRRMMM
HOW'D SAAR TAKE IT?
UNF.
DUDE TRIED TO KISS ME. FUCKING HELL.
TOLD YOU. BOYS ARE IDIOTS.
YOU OKAY?
WHAT THE HELL
OF COURSE I'M OKAY. WE MADE $250,000 YESTERDAY.
I'M FANTASTIC.

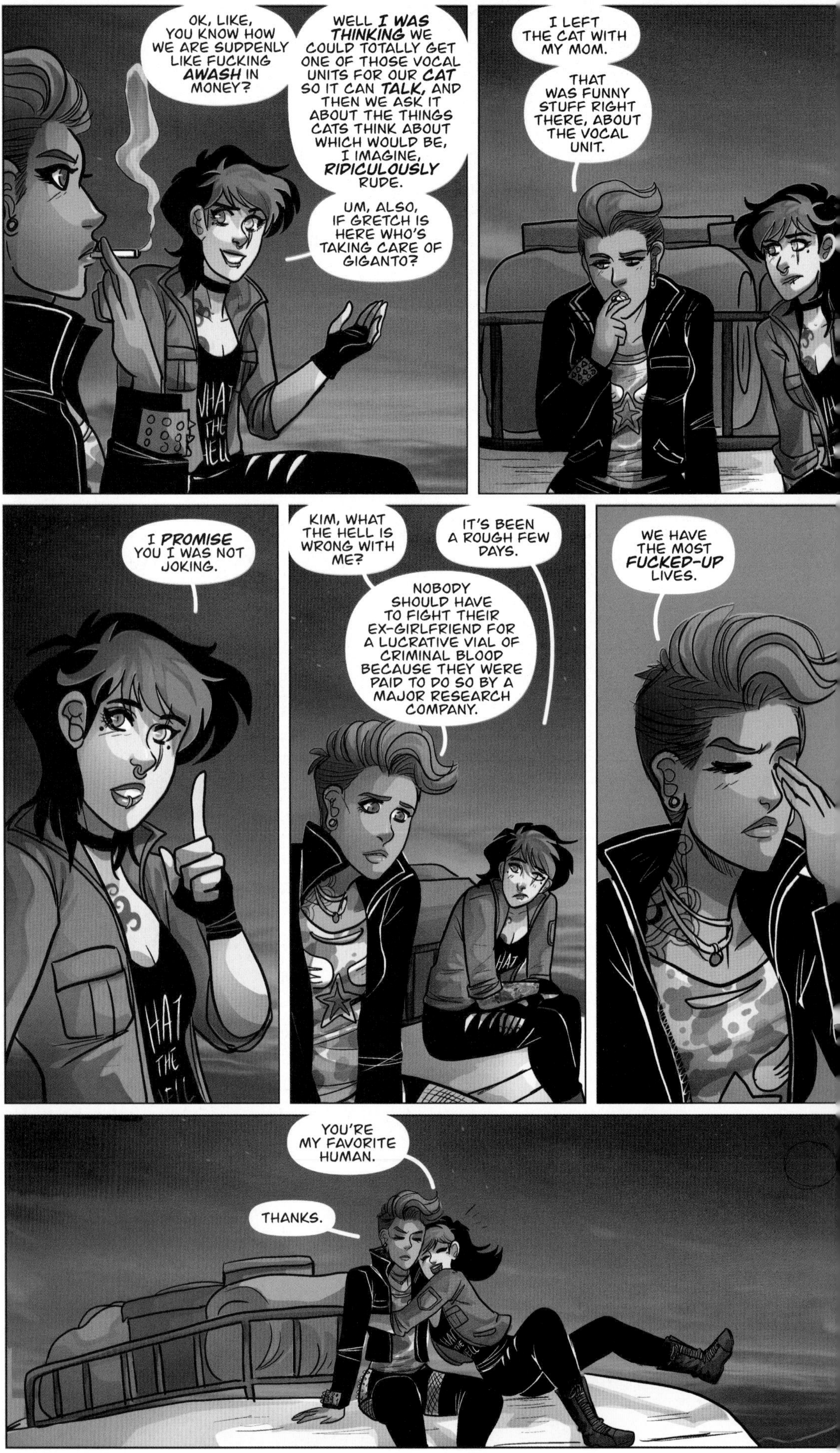
OK, LIKE, YOU KNOW HOW WE ARE SUDDENLY LIKE FUCKING AWASH IN MONEY?
WELL I WAS THINKING WE COULD TOTALLY GET ONE OF THOSE VOCAL UNITS FOR OUR CAT SO IT CAN TALK, AND THEN WE ASK IT ABOUT THE THINGS CATS THINK ABOUT WHICH WOULD BE, I IMAGINE, RIDICULOUSLY RUDE.
UM, ALSO, IF GRETCH IS HERE WHO'S TAKING CARE OF GIGANTO?
I LEFT THE CAT WITH MY MOM.
THAT WAS FUNNY STUFF RIGHT THERE, ABOUT THE VOCAL UNIT.
I PROMISE YOU I WAS NOT JOKING.
KIM, WHAT THE HELL IS WRONG WITH ME?
IT'S BEEN A ROUGH FEW DAYS.
NOBODY SHOULD HAVE TO FIGHT THEIR EX-GIRLFRIEND FOR A LUCRATIVE VIAL OF CRIMINAL BLOOD BECAUSE THEY WERE PAID TO DO SO BY A MAJOR RESEARCH COMPANY.
WE HAVE THE MOST FUCKED-UP LIVES.
YOU'RE MY FAVORITE HUMAN.
THANKS.

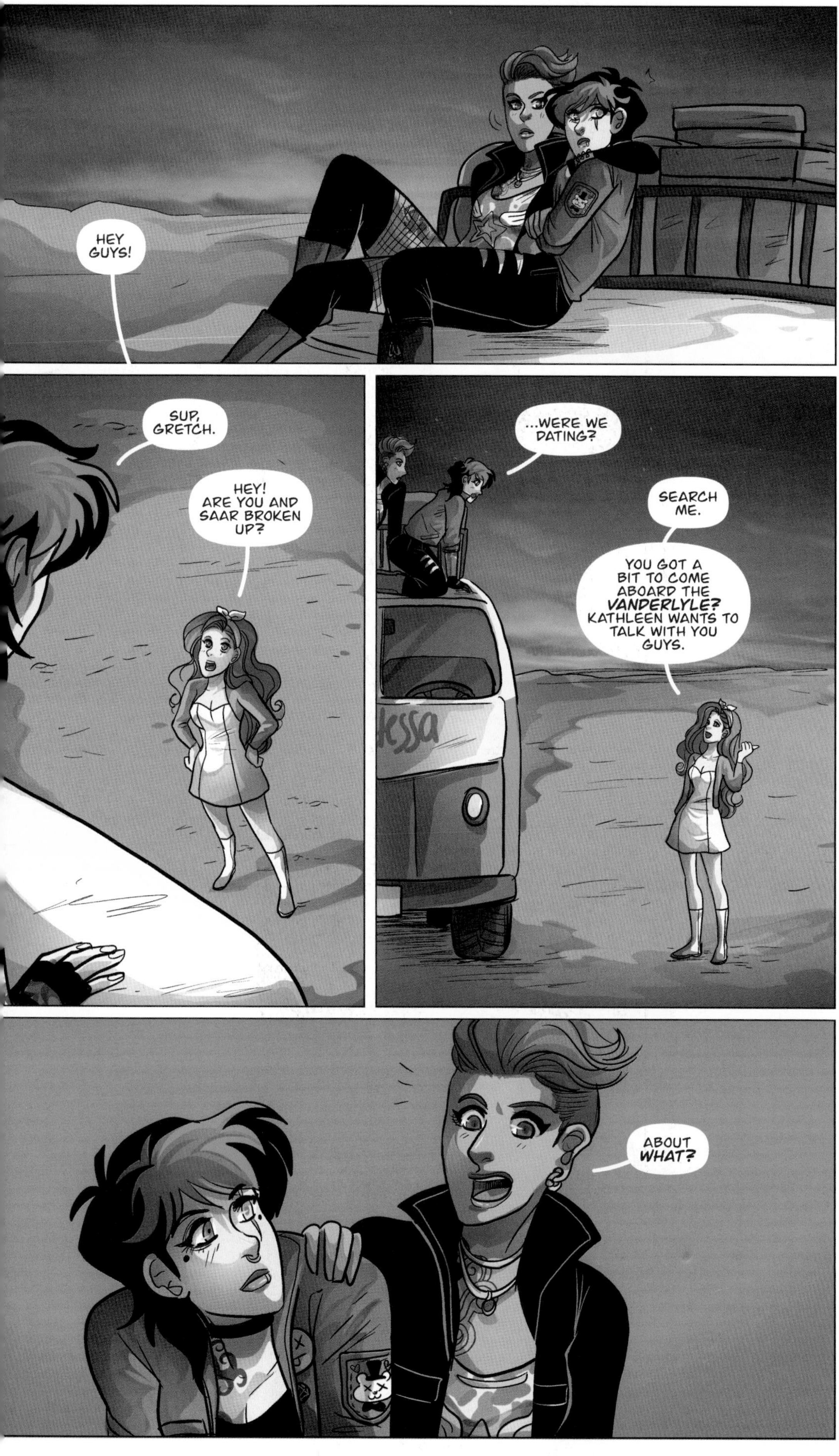
HEY GUYS!
SUP, GRETCH.
HEY! ARE YOU AND SAAR BROKEN UP?
...WERE WE DATING?
SEARCH ME.
YOU GOT A BIT TO COME ABOARD THE *VANDERLYLE?* KATHLEEN WANTS TO TALK WITH YOU GUYS.
ABOUT *WHAT?*

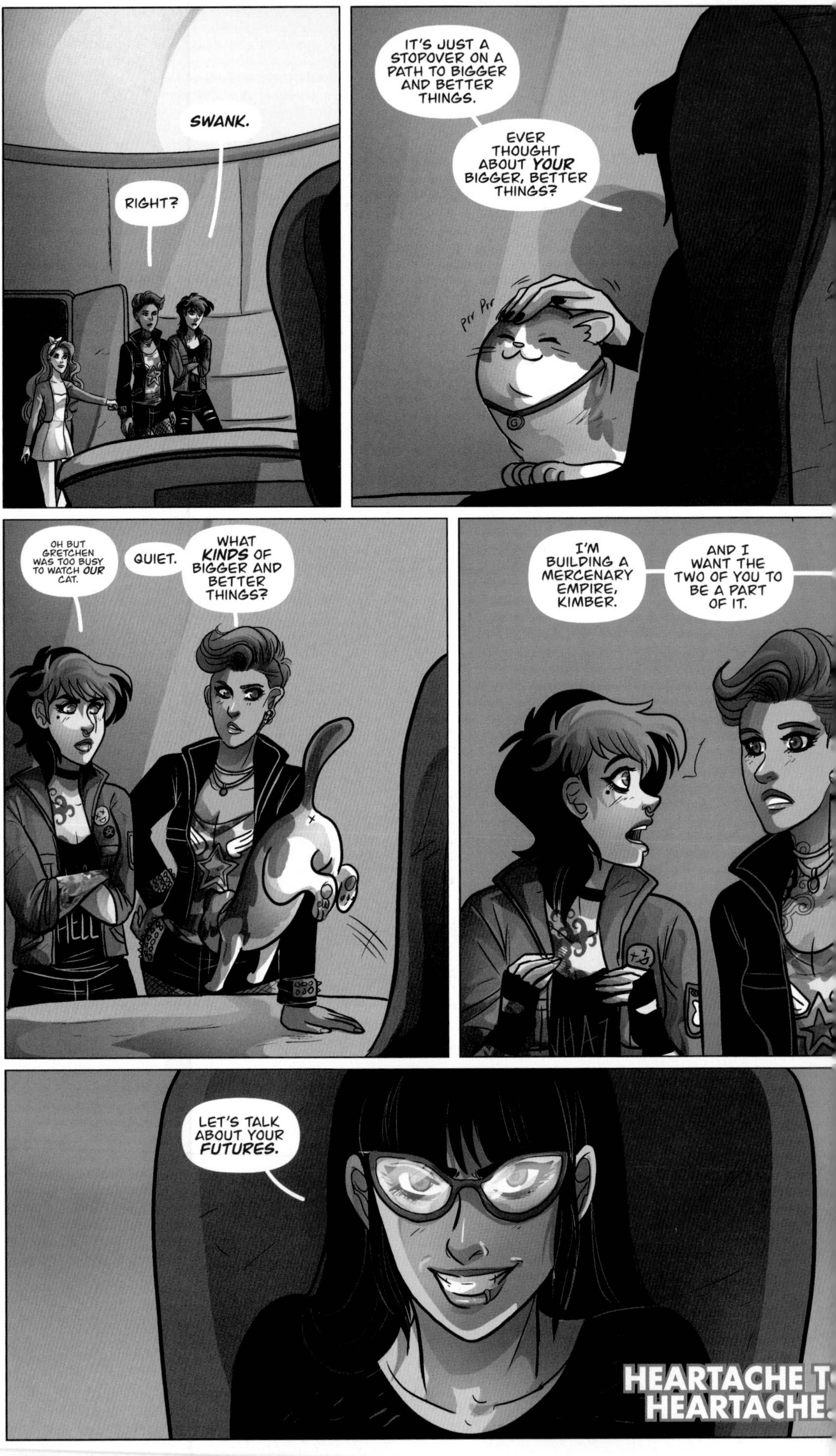
SWANK.
RIGHT?
IT'S JUST A STOPOVER ON A PATH TO BIGGER AND BETTER THINGS.
EVER THOUGHT ABOUT YOUR BIGGER, BETTER THINGS?
Prr Prr
OH BUT GRETCHEN WAS TOO BUSY TO WATCH OUR CAT.
QUIET.
WHAT KINDS OF BIGGER AND BETTER THINGS?
I'M BUILDING A MERCENARY EMPIRE, KIMBER.
AND I WANT THE TWO OF YOU TO BE A PART OF IT.
LET'S TALK ABOUT YOUR FUTURES.
HEARTACHE T
HEARTACHE.

# KIM & KIM

## LOVE IS A BATTLEFIELD

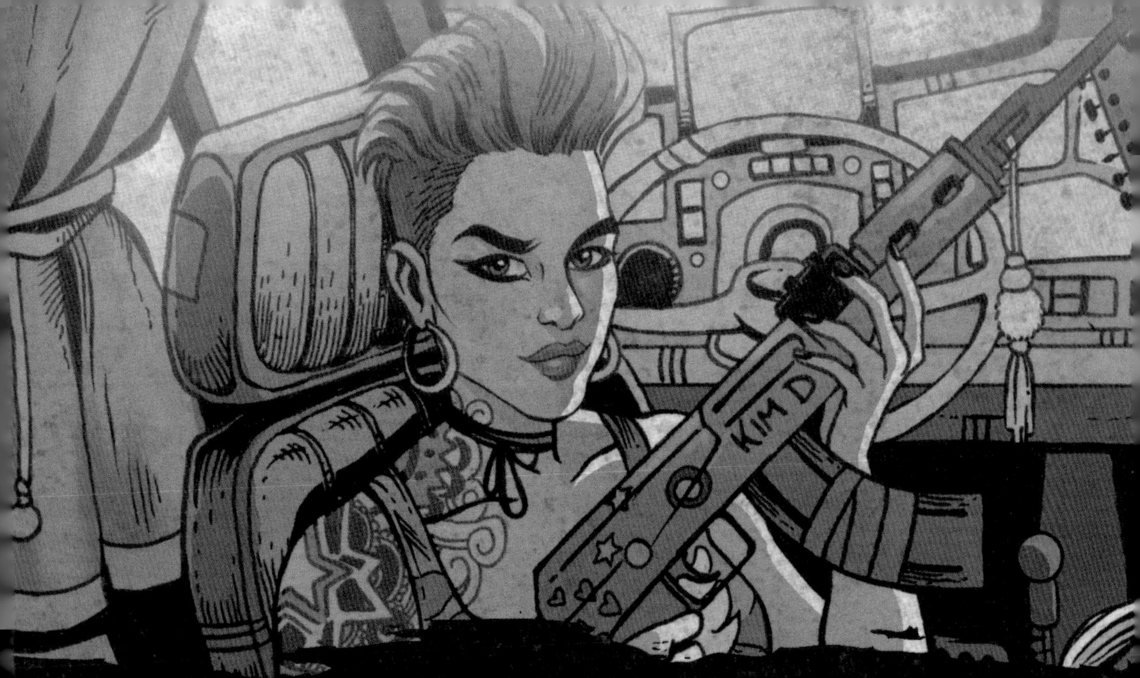
KIM D

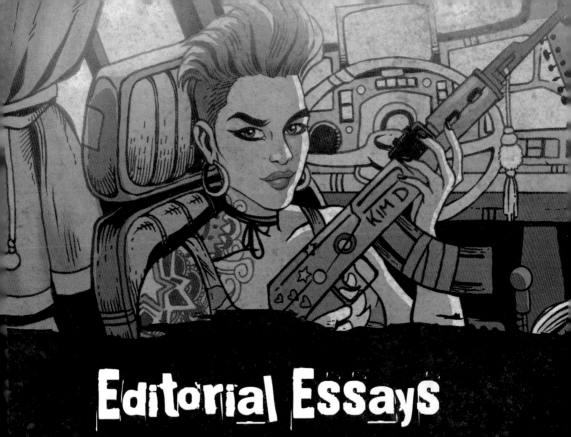

# Editorial Essays

by

**Elle Collins**

**Natalie Reed**

**Nyri A. Bakkalian**

and **Sam Riedel**

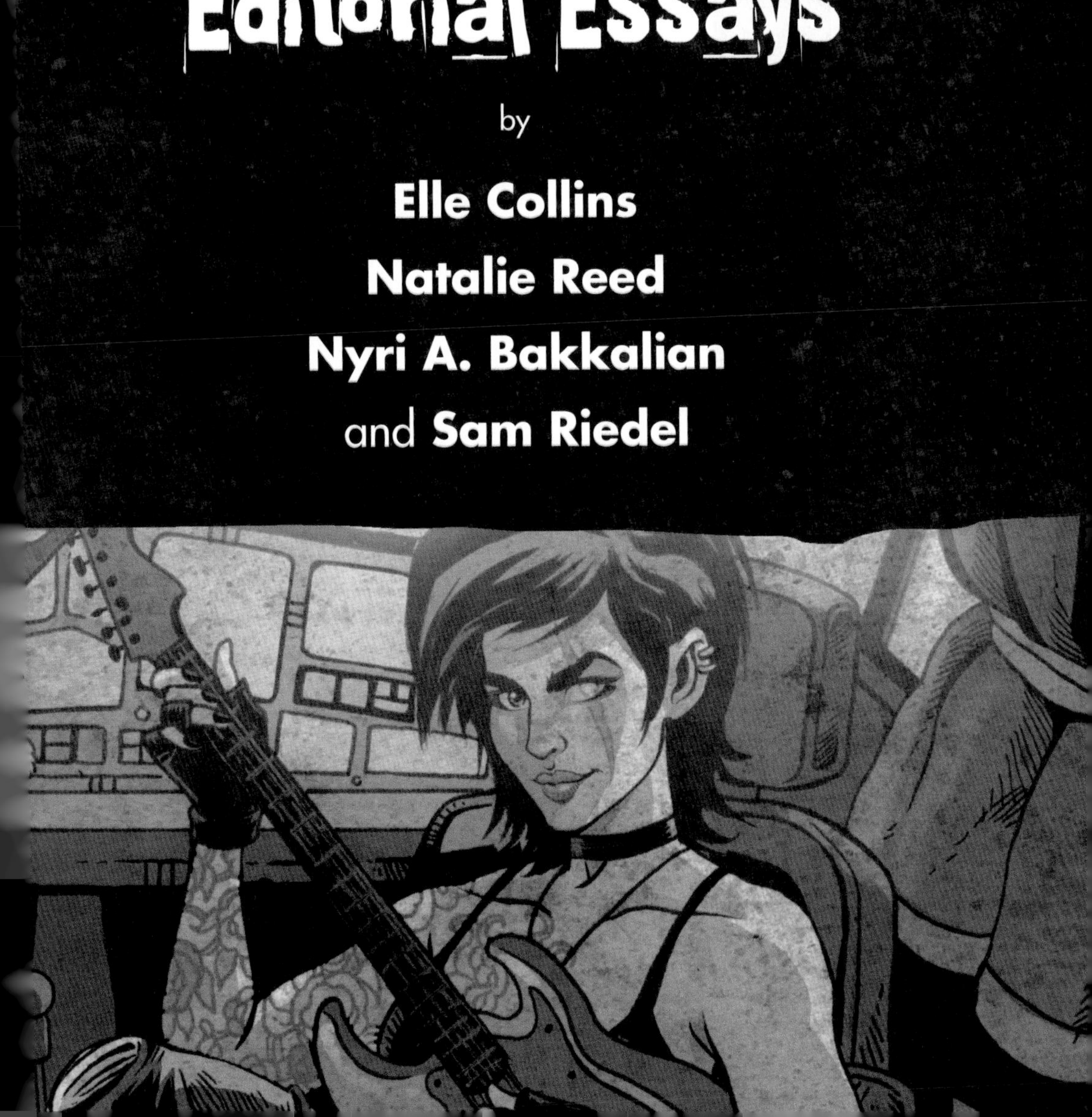

# The Queer Universe

**Elle Collins**

There's this problem I have with depictions of queer people in fiction. Well, let's be honest, there are more than a few problems, but I'm not going to try to cover all of them here today. First of all, don't get me wrong, I'm glad we've reached a point where queer characters in comics and movies and TV shows aren't as unheard of as they once were. There was a time when each individual one felt like a hard-fought achievement. Now they just happen. Sometimes. Less often than they really ought to.

What's changed, really, is that a great many straight and cisgender creators have come around to the idea that they really ought to be putting queer people in their stories. And thank the gods for that. Genre fiction and comics are so dominated by straight voices that if only queer people were creating queer characters, there'd still hardly be any. Any step forward is a step forward, and this is a big one.

Still though, when straight writers include queer characters, they tend to confine what's queer in those stories to the bodies and minds of those specific characters. They may be identified as queer, but they live in solidly cis-hetero universes. And right now I'm going to tell you something, even though it may be something that you, the person who bought this book, already know: No queer person has ever lived this way.

No actual queer person lives in such a heterosexual world as the one occupied by queer supporting characters in hetero fiction. When you're queer, the whole world you live in is queer. Even if you're the proverbial Only Gay in the Village, how you experience everything around you is affected by your identity. Also, you should probably download a dating app, because odds are you're not the only gay in the village.

I'm not just talking about who you're attracted to. If you're a queer woman, your world isn't queer just because you're checking out and perhaps flirting with women wherever you go (although you might be, and more power to you). But my main point is that being queer, growing up queer, and eventually engaging in queer culture—it gives a person a somewhat slanted perspective on the world. A different understanding of interpersonal relationships and cultural signifiers. I suspect that's why so many queer people love camp and kitsch and other stuff that the straight world dismisses as fake and tacky—those are the things that reflect the world as we see it.

Even that's oversimplifying, or perhaps I just got ahead of myself. Because odds are if you're queer, your life is probably full of other queer people, unlike those genre-fiction queers who tend to be the only non-straight person in their superhero team, on the crew of their spaceship, or teaching magic at their school for wizardry.

Straight fiction likes to pair off queer characters into units of two. Comics are especially bad about this: Apollo *and* Midnighter. Wiccan *and* Hulkling. Moondragon *and* Phyla-Vell. Once this pairing occurs, the queerness of each character is confined to their relationship with the other. It's very convenient for heteronormative storytelling, because closir that circuit means that none of that queerness will leak ou onto any of the other characters, who are presumably 100% straight.

But whereas queer superheroes tend to be locked into t one partner, real queer people often have multiple partner whether consecutively or at the same time. Queer people h bitter exes, awkward longterm crushes, people they've flirte with for years but it never quite happened. Queer people h friendships with other queer people that are 100% platoni but that friendship is still deeply and profoundly queer. So queer people don't date at all, by preference or by luck, an their worlds are no less queer.

Once queer creators arrive at the table, this breadth of experience starts being reflected. Queerness is no longer a matter of "I love this one other person," or just as likely, "I lo this one other person, but now they're dead," it can actuall a culture, a perspective on the world, dare I say even a lifes In comics like *Midnighter, Batwoman*, and yes, *Kim & Kim*, finally see queer characters who occupy entire queer unive

When I say queer universes, I'm not talking about utopia timelines where the decor is fabulous and nothing hurts (although I'm in favor of those too). I'm talking about fictio universes that reflect that queer sensibility I described abo worlds that are conveyed to the reader the same way they' experienced by a queer protagonist, through a queer lens.

Let me expand on this further and try to explain, as a qu person, how my own queer universe works. Queerness isn' an individual identity. It's not even just a collective designa Queerness is a force that exists in the cosmos. You might call it a field created by all living things. It surrounds us and penetrates us; you might even say it binds the galaxy toget I'm veering into camp here, but I'm not actually kidding.

When I say that queerness surrounds all of us, I don't mean that everybody's queer. The existence of cisgender heterosexuals may be irritating at times, but that's precise because it's undeniable. But have you ever noticed that wh you pay attention to straight people, they're constantly pu queerness away? Deflecting it, screening themselves agair creating elaborate friendship rituals and absurd gender no to guard themselves against its encroachment. It all seem a dreadful lot of work to me, but obviously I'm biased.

Whatever else *Kim & Kim* does, and it does plenty, it certainly creates a queer universe. One of the queerest I've ever encountered in a comic book. I mean technically, sinc these characters travel between dimensions, Kim D. and K Q. occupy a queer multiverse, and the cosmic force that is queerness expands easily to fill this larger space. This isn't comic where you have to wonder which characters are qu what's queer is in front of you on every page.

*Originally published in Kim and Kim: Love is a Battlefield*

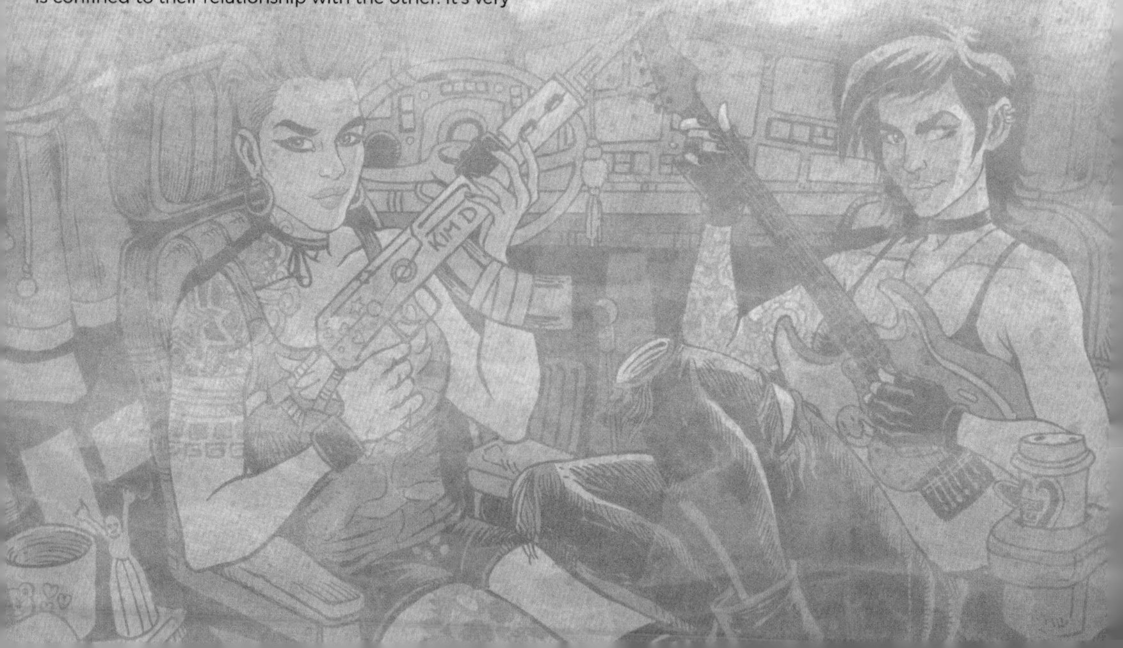
KIM D

# Living in the Gutters: Authentic Queerness in Comics

Natalie Reed

l seems to have lots of gorillas, but comics has changed nt years.

'e found ourselves in a shifting political landscape, d by increasingly hostile tensions over considerations tity, and the power and status linked to it. Things :tured, certainly, but nobody remains in a position oly *ignore* the question of what identities are given entation in our art and media. We are also in a time gender and sexuality can't be locked away in closets to cknowledged as part of these concerns. LGBT themes aracters can no longer be removed from our media t people noticing.

with the advent of the digital age, the tools to create sseminate art - comics included - have ceased to be monopolized. That democratization of media has ed people's expectations about the range of stories to l, even by the traditional administrators of the culture ry. Altogether, the question of Diversity In Comics, less of whether it's regarded as a path forward for e survival and integrity, a means for the industry to ew demographics, an ethical or political obligation tors, an unjust burden on artists inflicted by political tness, or whatever, is simply part of the conversation now, ong with it, the question of Queer Comics. Queer Comics hing that people want, and want to talk about.

y. Cool. But...What are queer comics?

onsiderable portion of the LGBT comics community - if s such a thing- seems satisfied with the answer that comics are comics that have queer people in them. be a byproduct of my truly staggering pretensions ng from my lit-theory education, but this has never e enough for me. I've been a bit preoccupied with it nce a 'Queer Comics' panel I attended at an unnamed ntion, an unspecified time ago. I was struck by the fact e panelists seemed content to spend the majority of me talking about *Steven Universe* and *Sailor Moon* (the , not the manga), which aren't... y'know... *comics*, and presented with the question "what is queer about your s?", each simply listed the queer, trans or non-binary :ters within their work.

uably, this has the queer part. But what about the s part? The medium seems incidental when we talk it like this, like we *might as well* be creating queer tion, queer TV shows or queer prog rock operas. And is esence of a queer, trans or NB character enough to queer ic?

n't really think it is, and think there's a lot of evidence t. Something that I've noticed in several comics recently, t the bizarre stampede of cisgender creators eager to their claim to The Trans Thing and make their very own :haracters to be read and complained about by people e, is a certain kind of character who is ostensibly trans, r whom no trans stories or issues actually take place. gender exists in name, *maybe* even in considerations racter design (though usually not), but they live, talk, e, and are treated exactly like a cisgender character. re accepted utterly by the people around them, and xperience no anxieties or doubts about this acceptance. one to accidentally skip the issue in which the revelation r gender history is dropped (to the delight of comics lists everywhere), one could read the entire comic ut ever noticing this is a trans character. Their gender s and involves no conflict and, as story requires conflict, is no trans story.

so often think of the DC/Vertigo character John antine. Way back in the 80s, when I was but a small *ndoubtedly* delightful babe, *Hellblazer* had a filler issue, n by a guest writer, appearing between arcs, and set in a romat, in which Constantine's internal monologue had waway line about his past sexual history including "the onal boyfriend".

e decades of *Hellblazer* and Constantine appearing s of LGBT comics and characters, even as the comic ined absolutely no actual bisexuality.

an Azzarello's run featured John in a same-sex onship with an irreverent Batman pastiche, but this was art of a long-con... John's actual feelings and sexuality rrelevant to the (unseen) sex. It wasn't until James Tynion cent run, which followed *Hellblazer's* cancellation and antine's de-aged reintroduction to DC proper, that sexuality was finally treated as an actual facet of his cter. But that didn't prevent approximately *thirty years-worth* of comics discourse citing him as a Queer Character in a Queer Comic.

Queer comics without any of the messy queerness to get in the way. Sounds convenient.

The comic you are holding in your hands -or viewing on a device you are holding in your hands, or looking at while it is being held in someone else's hands, or looking at on a device held in some...whatever... is *not* such a comic.

*Kim and Kim* is not a "trans comic" or a "lesbian comic", not in the sense of placing the genders and sexualities of its characters front and center in the narrative. It is not a *Blue Is The Warmest Colour* or a *Wandering Son*. From a superficial narrative standpoint, the primary characters being LGBT is completely incidental. But those *are* genuine aspects of who they are, and they inform their characterization, their relationships, and their (frequently and wonderfully bad) decisions. Kim Q's gender has an impact on all of her major relationships - with her ex, with her father, and with Kim D too - and those relationships have all had an impact on her gender in turn. Or at least on how she feels about it, and contextualizes herself and her history in terms of it.

But this is still just limiting the question to queer characters, and how that does or doesn't effect narrative. Even "queer narratives" isn't everything we can ask of queer comics. What about the medium? What about *comics itself* could be queer, or queered, or do some queer queering?

Comics is certainly fucking *weird*, what with the gorillas and costumes and planet-eating monsters with funny hats (seriously, so many gorillas). And the medium is also saturated with liminality. It's young, but also calls back to the ancient, early development of language. It's full of potential, but keeps getting stuck in a select few genres. Those dominant genres tend to be loud and action-packed, but comics is a silent, still medium. It's frozen images, but all about the perception of time, and the shifts of meaning achieved through the context of other frozen images.

That liminal quality, I think, is perhaps the most queer thing about comics as a medium. These days we often feel compelled to think of LGBT identities as categories of human being, and we seem a bit obsessed with creating and pursuing new taxonomies and infographics (which are arguably comics themselves; Genderbread Man as LGBT superhero of the decade?). Like we're trying to finally, at last, once and for all, pin down All The Sexualities And Genders. But to be queer, or trans, is at its heart about *not* quite fitting into the existing categories and ideas. To be caught in a liminal, contested space between what you feel and desire and how you see yourself, and what the world thinks you ought to feel and desire, and thinks you are. Living in the gutter between one panel of gender/sexuality and another.

And it's in these qualities that comics can convey things about queer or trans experience that aren't necessarily available to other media.

A favorite moment of mine in the first volume of *Kim and Kim* is a single panel that appears while Kim Q and her father are playing phone tag. Her dad keeps her caller ID listed as her deadname, Joaquin, and the image displayed is a photo of her as a child, prior to her transition. This communicates an *enormous* amount about her father's feelings towards her in a single image. Which also happens to be a funny one.

The thing is, the reader can feel the depth of what's communicated here because they can *linger* on that image. Were this a film or animation, giving the audience time with the image would necessitate also letting the *character* linger on it, which would distort the meaning. He's not having a big emotional moment here, looking back on his lost son and choking back tears. This is simply *how he still thinks of her.* He refuses to accept the reality. To him, it's nothing, it's casual. To him, there's no meaning to that image whatsoever beyond just "my son's calling and probably wants some money or whatever". To *us*, that image represents a lifetime of pain.

*That's* queer comics. Or, at least, the closest thing to a satisfying answer my aforementioned pretensions will allow.

All I can hope is for us all to keep poking and prodding at the question, keep finding new ways for comics to express, in all its weirdness, all the wonderfully not-quite-fit-able beauties and tragedies and triumphs of queer lives, ideas and perspectives.

And that it continues to provide plenty of gorillas.

*Originally published in Kim and Kim: Love is a Battlefield #2*

# Nyri A. Bakkalian

For the past eight long years of my grad school education in history, I've often heard the phrase "publish or perish." I've gotten my share of publications, and despite some rather tense courses and exams, I thankfully haven't perished. But I could've scarcely imagined at the beginning that just after graduation I'd get to write something that'd run with one of my favorite comics. So take *that*, ivory tower expectations: here I am in *Kim & Kim!*

So: grab a seat and if you'll excuse the ramblings of a recovering academic, let's talk stories for a moment.

The great Japanese author and novelist Tanizaki Jun'ichiro once wrote an essay called *In Praise of Shadows*. With that title as my inspiration, I want to take a moment (*dear reader*), to talk to you here beside the pages of *Kim & Kim*, and say a few words in the paragraphs that follow, "in praise of messy." Why breaking boundaries, and why queer stories in general, matter.

Aside from the infamous "publish or perish" adage, something else I often heard about in grad school was the importance of putting together stories (or in my case, histories) that aren't simple or neat. After all, human beings, and their actions, are complicated. Sometimes, they make no sense at all. So, my professors used to tell me, we have to remember to allow for this. But although this is a constant in human history, it seems to me that our tendency is toward wanting these stories to be simple and neat in how they unfold, and in general, to make a sort of cut-and-dried sense.

Now, as I find myself reading (and re-reading) *Kim & Kim*, and I think about the queer and trans-focused stories in fiction that I've seen, or would like to see, I find myself thinking about "messy" all over again.

I guess at this point I should back up for a moment, and clarify just what kind of "mess" I mean. After all, there's a very long tradition of queer-as-victim in modern popular media (look up "Bury your Gays" on *TvTropes* if you're unfamiliar with this, though I make that recommendation with a stern warning that it's both depressing and gruesome reading). Those sorts of stories are plenty messy, but that's not quite what I'm getting at here.

The "messy" I mean is the gloriously kickass narratives that defy simplicity and easy categorization. In a sense, we queer and trans folks have an advantage there. We challenge and break binaries, we upend expectations and assumptions, we actively pioneer new vocabulary, and in general, our stories tend to turn and twist and meander around society's (imagined) straight lines. We are extraordinarily resistant at being pigeonholed. And against all odds, I'd say we do pretty damn well there!

This isn't easy in real life. Hell, it's no hyperbole to say that it's a matter of life and death. The people, and societal forces, that drive that pigeonholing, have a lot invested in it, and don't look kindly on those who break those boundaries. But that risk is worth it.

There's authenticity to be found in breaking those boundaries. There's unexpected ties—friendships, chosen family, even the unlikeliest of reconciliations—that can grow there. One's path may not quite progress how one expects at times it can get hairy and even awful, but there's also a l room for collecting stories that are the stuff of years upon y of wide-eyed disbelief: *shit, do you remember that time wh*

The same goes for fictionalized depictions of that experience. We are far from the victims some would believe to be. Hell, for surviving and flourishing the way we do, we' kind of badass. Telling these kinds of stories not only serves expose non-queer and non-trans audiences to our own sto told in our own words, but is also inspiring to the coming generations of us out there. I guarantee you that in some comic shop or bookstore out there is some kid furtively lea through these pages, dreaming futures for themselves tha they never thought possible, and in general, quietly going *shit, this is kickass.*

I should know. Seventeen years ago, with a totally differe generation of queer stories in my hands (or via much poore images over a slower internet connection on a shittier, earl internet), I *was* that kid.

Oh, one more thing, especially in times like these that se to grow darker by the day. Not only is telling ass-kickingly gloriously messy and boundary-breaking stories important but we also need more stories that end happily. Not neatly but happily, or at least, happily enough. Call me sentiment but the happily-ever-afters, or at least the "happy enough i the midst of the mess"es matter. They show us that better outcomes and destinations are possible, even if we meand and drove offroad to get there.

*Ahem.*

At any rate: these words, dear reader, are my way of encouraging you. Embrace the complicated, the not-easily pigeonholed, the "crashing-through-the-wall-to-kick-ass-a look good" queer stories. (like this one!) Do what you can to support the people who write, draw, and otherwise create these stories. And hey, don't just consume them, if you car After all, the world needs your story, too. If the pages you h in your hand are any indicator, you'll certainly be in good company. And take it from a girl whose journey to this bra spankin' new PhD started with *Rurouni Kenshin* fanart: do let anyone give you crap if your jam is fanwork.

That's the long and the short of it. So, are you in?

* * *

*Nyri A. Bakkalian, Ph.D. is a queer Armenian-American by birth, an adoptive Pittsburgher by choice, and a militar historian by training. She has written for Gutsy Broads, Metropolis Japan, QueerPGH, Con-course, and other venue Come say hi to her on Twitter at @riversidewings What's h secret, you ask? Garlic and Turkish coffee. But really, mostl Turkish coffee.*

*Originally published in Kim and Kim: Love is a Battlefield #*

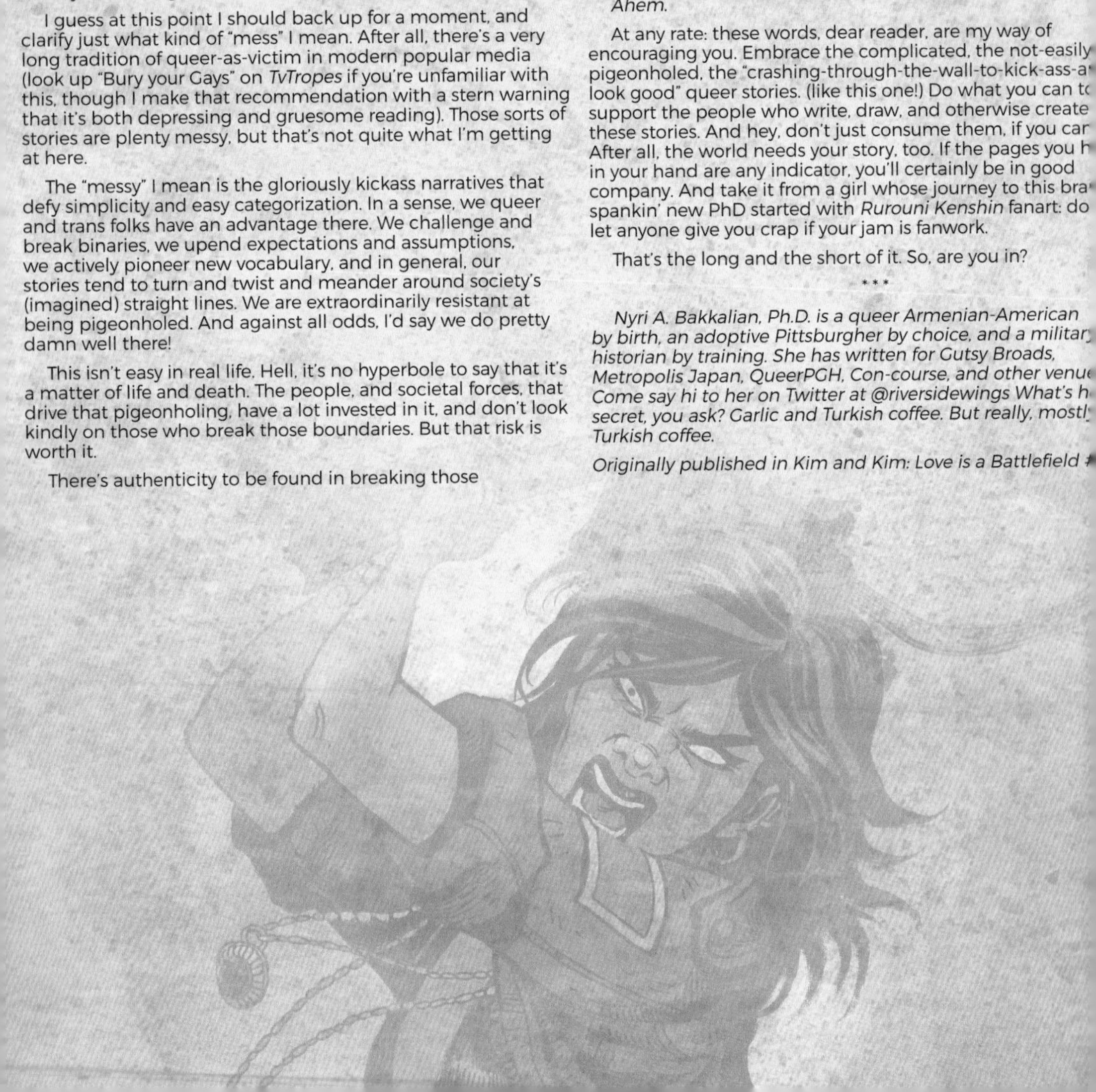

# How to See the Future

**Sam Riedel**

ı not quite enough of a fangirl to make a Kim & Kim ape (though I'm close), but if I were, I'd save the first track L.O.S.S., the dearly departed transfeminist quintet from pia, Washington. Introducing the band on their demo EP, "Switchblade" Smith howls "We're fucking future girls/ ɡ outside society's shit." Then the guitars and drums kick in everything fucking *explodes*.

und like anyone you know?

far back as I can remember, I've been fascinated by the tainty of what's to come. Maybe it's because of my father, irst thrust comic books into my hands and read "Have esuit, Will Travel" to me for a long-running bedtime story. v up to devour *Star Trek* and *Foundation* and *The Legion oer-Heroes*, always chasing visions of weird and wonderful bilities. If I had H.G. Wells' time machine, I don't think I'd d much time dwelling on how to change the past. Living future has always been more my style.

u could argue that this is just an offshoot of escapist sy, and in part, you'd be right. Daydreaming about the e pokes many of the same buttons as when I play D&D or rk on my yearly *Lord of the Rings* marathon. It's soothing merse oneself in worlds that are recognizably not our But there's always the possibility that my favorite science n plots might come to pass for real, and I'll see their sis in my lifetime. In the past, it's been enough to keep me d for what's ahead.

it kind of excitement is in short supply these days. As I this, record-shattering storms batter the United States, and China; North Korea rattles its nuclear sabre more ully than ever; and unhinged white supremacists, aided betted by morally bankrupt billionaires, threaten millions s in America alone. Each passing day is more frightening the next, and I hold little hope that things will have ved by the time you read this book.

asten to add that for many of us, this anxiety for what the will hold is nothing new. Impoverished communities or in particular have borne this burden for centuries-- ng under daily socioeconomic uncertainty, forced to walk ghtrope of colonialism without a net. My queer elders ately know this feeling as well: the background radiation nakes us wonder how the end will come, and when.

ore I understood my transfeminine identity, I drifted gh life with the security of a lower-middle class white aybe I was wracked with dysphoria in ways I didn't stand, and God knows I hated my jobs, but I was nably certain that everything would work out in the end. It wasn't until I began transitioning that I realized how many holes there were in my worldview, and how rosily I'd tinted my idea of the future.

Suddenly, I was more vulnerable than I'd ever been. I was threatened in subways and on the street; I began carrying mace on my keychain. It was a curious feeling: although I was developing more of a will to live with every passing day, I was freshly aware of how many others wanted to take that away from me. I was grabbing massive handfuls of sand on a stormy beach, clinging to each grain as the wind whipped them from my grasp.

The anxiety of the future, I now understood, is terrifying. It's the fear of death, failure, and oblivion all rolled into one. I had been idly consuming futurism in the way afforded only to those who have little terror for the present. But as I immersed myself in my new community and hungrily gobbled down its knowledge, a new outlook on the world to come presented itself. My future thus became not something to abstractly anticipate, but a tangible form to be seized and sculpted.

A recent trip to visit friends in Brooklyn brought this all home for me. I was tagging along with my partner to a trans-oriented sex party which, in addition to being all kinds of hot, was also witchy as hell. I don't mean that in the Kim D "accidentally followed by death-shades" sense; this was far more positive and involved fewer automatic weapons. Through a series of rituals (of varying sexiness), we invoked our own futures, pulling them into our present lives to shape them with our passion and joy. Through force of will and exuberant nudity, we would make a better world--for ourselves, our families, and all our communities.

I don't have a progress report for you on that front. That reality still needs some more time in the oven. But I'm reminded of it when I flip through the luminous pages you've just finished reading, filled with the joy of freedom and thrill of uncertainty that can only be captured by the Fighting Kims, LLC. As my beloved irresponsible badass Kim Q is wont to say, "Fuck the haters." We're gathering momentum, and soon we'll be unstoppable.

Not everything will be perfect in the future. The Kims know it, and even on my most optimistic days, I know it too. We've got so much work left to do. But we're going to build those rapturous futures together, and stories--like the one you just read--will pave the way.

So I ask you, reader: what's the story of your future?

*Originally published in Kim and Kim: Love is a Battlefield #4*

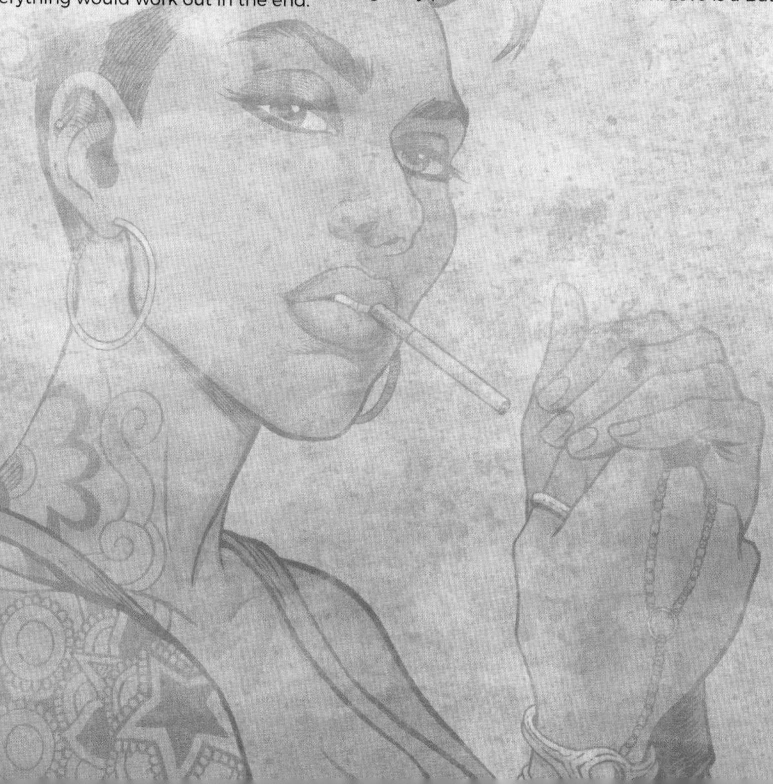

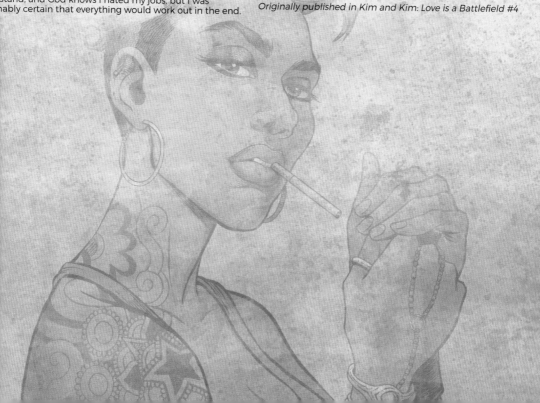

# Cover Gallery

line art by **Tess Fowler**

cover colors issue #1, 3 and 4 by **Matt Wilson**

cover colors issue #2 by **Tamra Bonvillain**

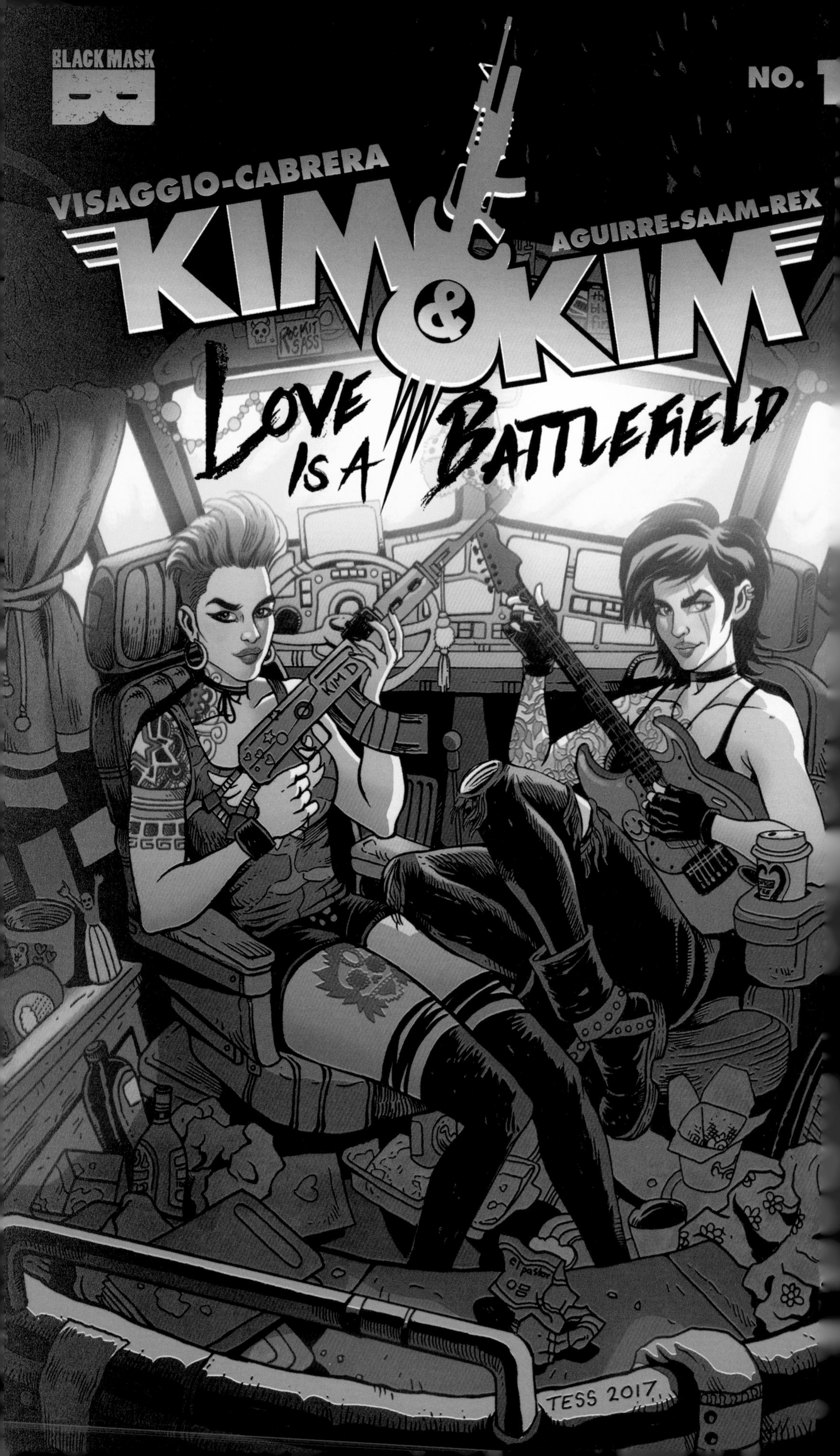
BLACK MASK
NO. 1
VISAGGIO-CABRERA
AGUIRRE-SAAM-REX
KIM & KIM
LOVE IS A BATTLEFIELD
KIM D
TESS 2017

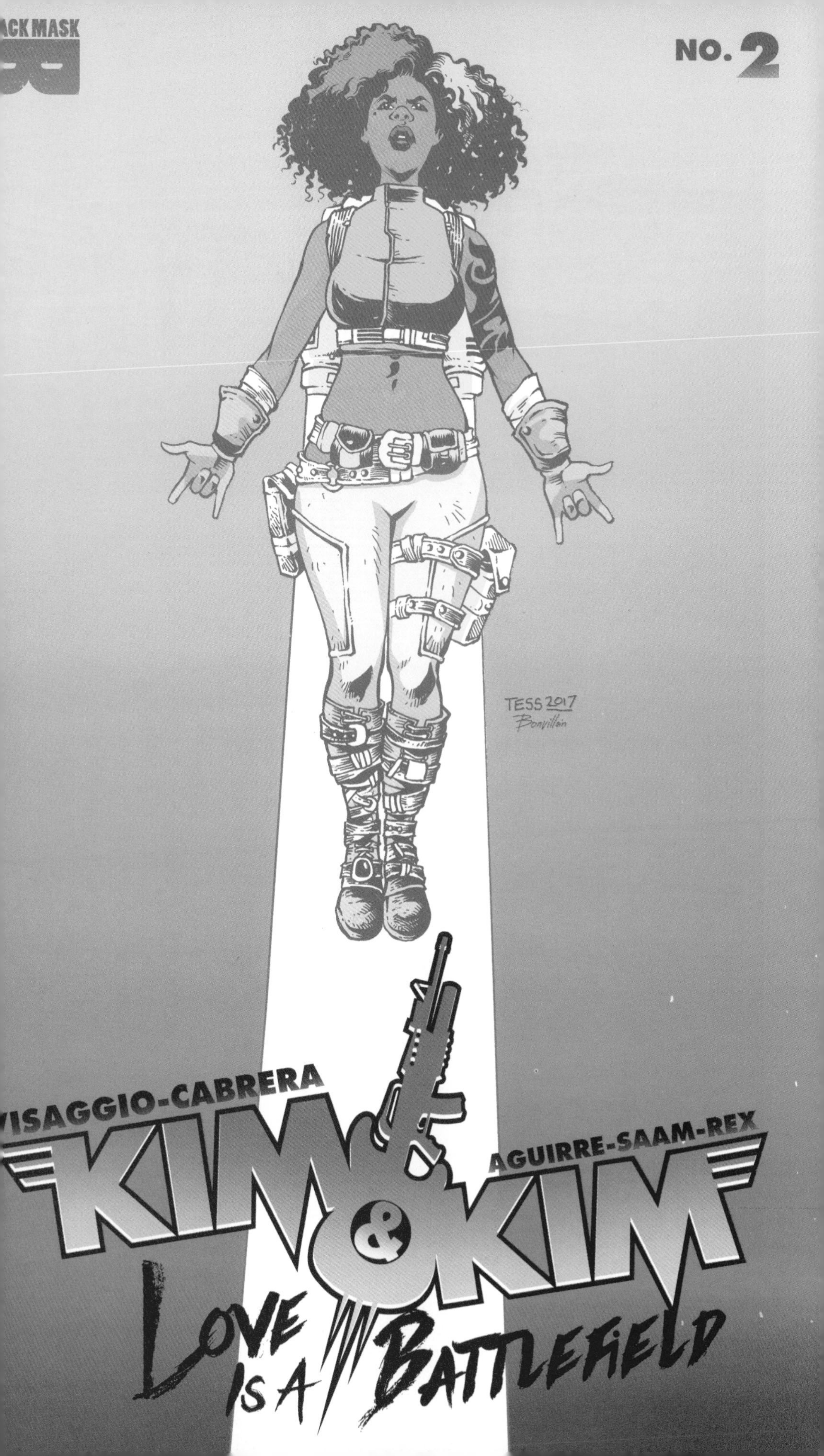

BLACK MASK
NO. 2
TESS 2017 Bonvillain
VISAGGIO-CABRERA
AGUIRRE-SAAM-REX
KIM & KIM
LOVE IS A BATTLEFIELD

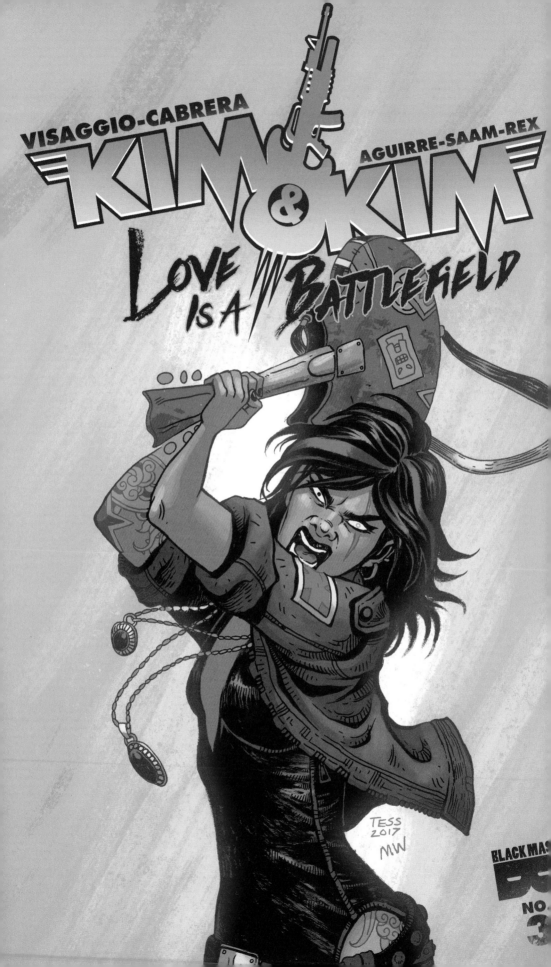

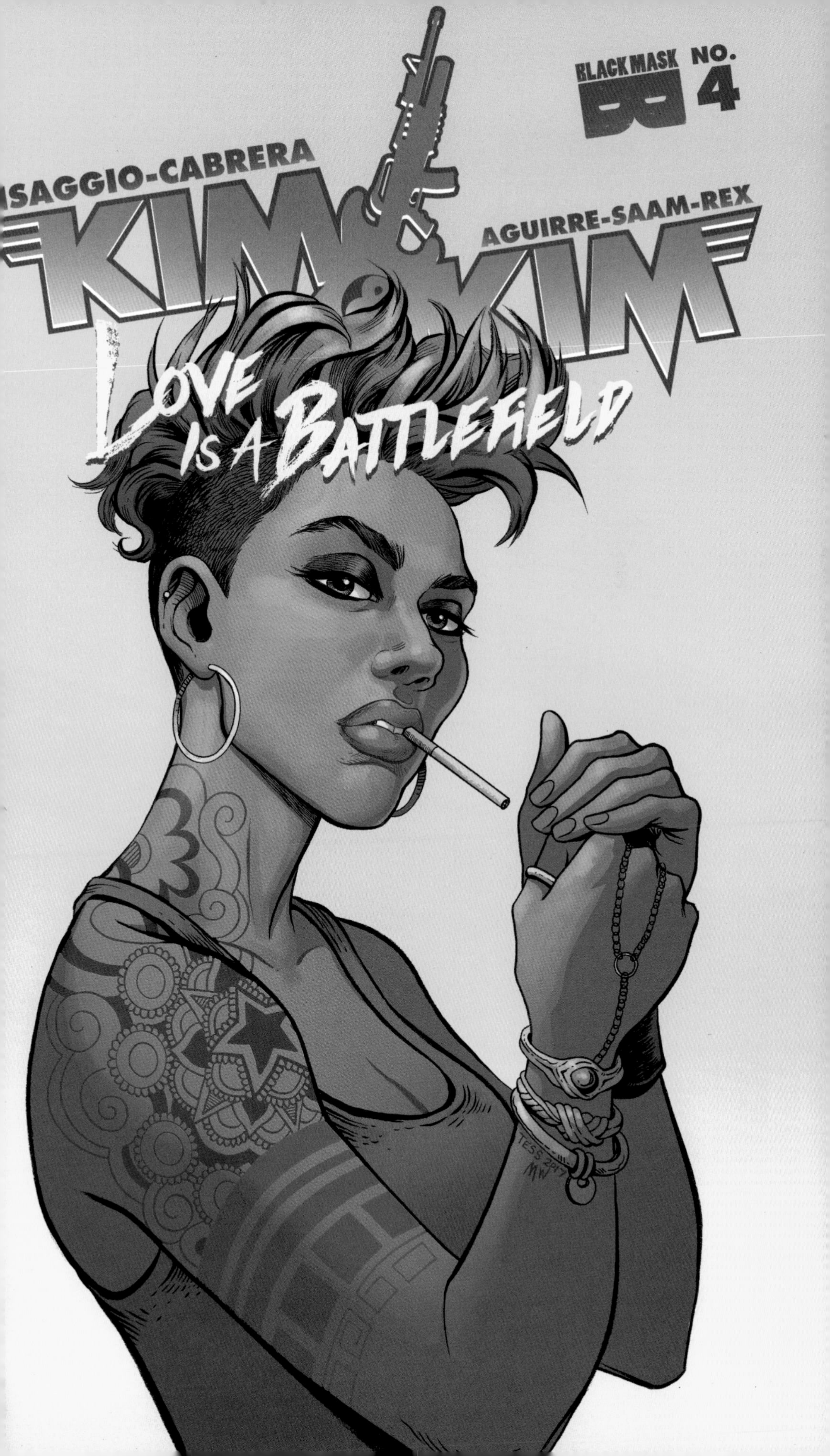
BLACK MASK
NO. 4
ISAGGIO-CABRERA
KIM & KIM
AGUIRRE-SAAM-REX
LOVE IS A BATTLEFIELD
TESS 2017
MW